The Golf Widows

A novel by

Ian C Jones

thegolfwidows@yahoo.co.uk

Chapter 1 Jill

Jill arched her body backwards with her arms outstretched towards the pastel blue bedroom ceiling, she had now been packing her and David's, her husband, suitcases for the past hour and a half and her back was complaining from constantly bending over their king size bed which currently housed the two large black Samsonite cases they had used for their holidays for the past five years. The last items packed for David were his five vulgar ultra-bright Hawaiian shirts he had bought on their family holiday to the Hawaiian islands six years ago which he now insisted on taking on their twice yearly week long golfing holidays they had been taking for the last four years with his two golfing friends Tony and Steve and their wives Michelle and Julie respectively.

Noticing the electronic alarm clock by the bed as it approached 5.00pm she could almost taste the wine she had promised herself as soon as the bags were packed and labelled, David could drag them downstairs into their front entrance hallway when he returned from work which could be anytime between 6 and 9pm but he had promised to be early this bright and warm September Friday evening. Jill knew David's promises and it showed on her frowning face as she thought about what time he might deem to show.

On her third stretch she glanced out of the bedroom window which housed the beds cream silk lined headboard to witness Mr George Armstrong walking his jet black ratty attitude Jack Russell named Custer. George's sense of humour no doubt; the little black rat had a nasty disposition to everybody but George. George noticed her in the window as he was looking around whilst waiting for Custer to stop peeing on the concrete lamppost outside of number 37, the Davis', he took off his glasses and waved up towards Jill, Jill waved back smiling as she noticed him taking his glasses off.

Jill and David had lived on their street for nearly seven years but only last summer had the opportunity to meet George socially at a barbeque held by Pete and Mildred Best at number 52; it was a fairly typical English summer barbeque at a middle class neighbourhood with approximately twenty street dwellers attending and half a dozen friends of the Bests. It began at 2.00pm on a reasonably warm June Sunday afternoon, arriving shortly after 2.15pm Jill and David handed Mildred the bottle of Chardonnay , a relatively good one bought at Marks and Spencer's anyway, they had brought with them and couldn't help noticing that Mildred had already been over indulging herself with red wine, umm they thought, it could be one of those afternoons!

Mildred showed them through their immaculately clean house and out into the back garden which was a similar size to their own with flagged area from the house for about 15 yards and which contained a brick built quite large barbeque which was fully loaded with sausages, burgers and chicken wings, in charge of the cooking was Pete who on seeing Jill and David came over to welcome them and show them "the dipsomaniacs table" upon which was every conceivable drink in large measure. Returning to his self-imposed cooking duties Pete left Jill and David to help themselves to a Chardonnay each.

They noticed George sitting at one of the garden tables waving them over, they introduced themselves to each other, having seen each other before but not having spoken together until now. Jill took an instant liking to the 70 year old George who was the complete opposite to Custer, with a warm smile and demeanour, they began chatting immediately sending David off to refresh drinks as and when necessary, he could certainly tuck away the whiskey which didn't seem to have any effect on him at all despite his age, it showed a little with his bright red nose, Jill couldn't help herself from wondering whether a nip or two would help Custer's aggression.

Food was a constant stream from the barbeque to a large dining table which had been brought outside from the main dining room and was displayed with various relishes, bread rolls, baps, French bread, butter, new potatoes, salad, coleslaw, dips, cakes; much more food than would be needed by the number of guests that had shown up so far.

George jumped to his feet at a speed which denied his age announcing his intentions to partake of the bounties on offer clearly expecting Jill to join him and looking a little jilted when she didn't. George's temporary departure allowed Jill and David to discuss when they thought it would be safe for them exit without causing any dismay to their expansive hosts, they concluded at least another hour depending on some of the other guests as they did not wish to appear ungrateful by being the first to leave.

George returned with a plate full of chicken wings, bread, sausages and cake; he reached deep into his right trouser pocket and pulled out a bright red handkerchief which Jill thought he was going to tuck into the top of his shirt like a bib, he didn't, instead he opened it out and raised it to his mouth proceeding to take both sets of teeth out of his mouth, wrapping them in the hanky and returning the hanky to his pocket, he now picked up the first of his chicken wings and sucked the meat from the bone and sort of chewing the meat if you can call it that it was more like gumming the meat with an open mouth. Jill could not watch, grabbing David's arm and pulling him up with her she said to George they have just seen someone they need to talk to and that she hoped he enjoyed his food. When they were out of Georges' earshot Jill cracked up laughing to David's surprise, she explained that she had never seen anyone take their teeth out to eat before, David said " well don't look around now then because he has started reading a newspaper he has brought with him and he has taken his glasses off to read!"

Time was closing in to where they would be able to leave, one couple had already left, it was 5.00pm and Mildred was clearly intoxicated not able to walk straight as she headed towards the house with her baggy Peach coloured summer dress flowing in the light summer breeze, Jill and David both noticed her bounce off the door architrave on her first attempt at entry into her house and looked at each other both shaking their heads. Some ten minutes later she resurfaced from the house seemingly a little steadier on her feet and for the first time all afternoon minus a wine glass in her hand but when she passed in front of them where she had been became all to evident. On the rear of her Peach dress just below her bottom was a 6 inch circular wet patch! She must have sat down for a pee forgetting to lift her dress. Time to leave.

Jill decided that it was now time for the long promised glass of wine so she proceeded out of the bedroom along the landing and turned right to descend the stairs, halfway down she noticed a piece of carpet to the left was frayed and she made a mental note to cut the frayed end when she returned from holiday, she could not wait any longer for her wine after all it had been in the fridge cooling all day. Two steps down she glanced at the full length mirror on the wall and giggled out loud at the image reflecting back at her, turning to return to the bedroom she thought it would be an idea to put some clothes on. She further giggled when she realised why George Armstrong had taken his glasses off a few minutes ago when he had seen her at the window, he would have had a wonderful view of her plump naked breasts from where he stood across the street, ah well lucky him she thought.

She grabbed her short white tennis skirt, not that she played tennis anymore but she liked how it felt and she knew she had great legs along with the skirt she put on a short white blouse just doing up a couple of buttons as it felt so much better loose. Making it this time to the bottom of the stairs she walked a couple of steps straight ahead and made sure the front door was locked then turned to her left and opened the door into the lounge room. It was a long room, they had knocked down the central wall some years ago turning two rooms into one, at the far end they had built a conservatory which to the left led into the kitchen, she was delighted with the addition of the conservatory it made the living room feel enormous; she had persuaded David to add the conservatory rather than move as David had wanted. The concession she had to make was the bar David had built halfway down the living room on the left as you looked through the door from the stairs. It was to this bar she now found herself taking out a chilled bottle of Chardonnay from the wine fridge; the wine fridge was her insistence if David was having a bar. The glasses were her choice as well, large. She took her glass of wine and turned on the radio low with some easy listening music which seemed to be mainly from the 1980's,easing herself onto their large and oh so comfortable sofa.

The first glass of wine disappeared no sooner than she had sat down, returning to the bar to replenish her drink she stood for a few minutes thinking about the packing she had completed, had she forgotten anything, she did not think so, although she wished she could forget the bloody awful Hawaiian shirts, just not worth the heartache it would cause though. Her glass was nearly empty again so she refilled it before returning to the sofa. She began thinking about David and the fact he had not touched her sexually for nearly two years, where had she gone wrong, she was still the same size she was when they married could it be he had found himself a lover? She dismissed the idea as she did not believe he was the type, when they were first married they could not keep from making love, anywhere and everywhere, it was divine.

The wine was starting to go to her head she thought of those early days, her right hand moved towards her stomach massaging herself, moving further down as she remembered the early days of lovemaking, she began to move her fingers slowly between her legs, she felt wet as she moved her fingers inside herself rubbing her clitoris as David used to, she heard herself moan with delight and then she seemed to just drift. The front door banged shut; she woke with a start her empty wine glass still in her left hand her right hand moved from between her legs still wet as she wiped the drool from her chin with the back of it. She turned in time to see David and her 15 year old pregnant daughter Bianca enter the room.

"Good evening" they both said at the same time.

"Evening" Jill replied

"I'm just going upstairs to change, can you make me a drink, may as well start the holiday now"

"Whiskey and coke?" Jill asked

"Great, perfect"

Jill was now up wide awake and making her way to the bar, with an ever so slight grin on her face which Bianca picked up on.

"Mum?"

"What"

"What are you up to mum?"

"Nothing darling, don't you want to change?"

"I'm just going, I'll be down in a minute" said Bianca

At which Bianca turned and followed her father out of the room and up the stairs. Jill's grin now became more pronounced as she took a large tumbler from the glass rack for David's drink. She began to run the rim of the tumbler around her lips wetting the edge of the glass, when she thought it was suitably moist she brought the glass from between her legs placing it on the bar opening the fridge and retrieving 3 large ice cubes, then she filled the glass covering the ice cubes with Bells whiskey before topping it off with Pepsi. She also made Bianca a drink of fresh orange, she did not drink alcohol just had underage sex!

Bianca had broken her mother's heart when she announced her pregnancy, that was five months ago, the boyfriend had made himself scarce not wanting to know and had indeed moved onto another girlfriend now.

Jill heard her husband's heavy feet descending the stairs, she tried to compose herself allowing one final giggle before he re- entered the room, Bianca followed shortly behind. Jill handed the tumbler of whiskey and Pepsi to David who immediately took a huge gulp.

"Ah, that's better, how's your day been?" asked David.

"Oh full of ironing and packing" Jill could not help a giggle at the end of her statement which she tried to swallow.

David did not notice but Bianca did and she gave her Mum a knowledgeable disapproving look as she picked up her drink turning to face her father she nearly died at what she saw; there was clearly a pubic hair hanging out of the side of her father's mouth. Turning to her mother she began to open her mouth to say something but stopped as she saw the horror on her mother's face. They both now turned to face David who was taking another gulp of his drink, Jill was now praying that the gulp would wash away the offending pubic hair but it became apparent it was stuck in David's tooth. Bianca now rushed to the kitchen leaving her mother alone with her husband and the offending pubic hair, Jill wore a half smile half frown and fear on her face.

Bianca returned from the kitchen with a bowl of cheese and onion crisps, her father's favourite, and a bowl of ready salted nuts which she immediately thrust under David's nose. Thankfully he took a handful of crisps which he greedily devoured; Jill and Bianca looked at each other before turning to see if David had eaten the pubic hair down with the crisps. It appeared to have gone! Jill moved behind the bar and refilled her glass and slurped down a couple of gulps of Chardonnay before taking David's tumbler from him and refreshing his drink giving the glass the once over for hair before returning it to David. Bianca looked daggers at her mother half shaking her head stating she was going to her room as she needed to check her emails.

Jill could not help thinking it was the closest she had come to oral sex in two years, in fact the closest she had come to any kind of sex in two years.

After the hair incident the rest of the evening passed relatively quietly, the three of them enjoyed an evening meal of roast chicken, salad and French bread. Jill and David watched some television, Two and a

Half Men followed by an episode of CSI Miami before retiring to bed at 10.00pm as they needed to be at Manchester Airport at 10.15am ready for their flight to Malaga Airport leaving at 12.15pm.Bianca had returned to her bedroom and computer once she had finished dinner.

Jill was dreading leaving Bianca for the week but the damage had now been done, well five months ago, and anyway her mother June would be calling by regularly to ensure there were no unexpected guests or indeed parties.

In bed Jill was struggling to sleep as she hated these golfing holidays, the men disappeared around 8am each day and did not return until gone 7pm in the evening leaving Jill, Michelle and Julie to their own devices which may sound alright three women together but so far they had not really found common ground which made spending time together difficult. Jill decided things needed to change she was determined to enjoy herself for a change and so to this end she would arrange for the women to have a drink together at the airport to outline her intentions for this and any future holidays together. If they could not become good friends and begin to enjoy each other's company then the men may as well holiday by themselves in future. With these thoughts Jill drifted off into a deep sleep only waking to the alarm at 7am.

David was already up showered and dressed as Jill reached over David's side of the bed to kill the alarm.

Jill's head was a little groggy from the wine she had consumed the previous evening and what she could not take right away was David's over the top cheeriness. He did not ever have hangovers, and the constant questions, have you packed my Hawaiian shirts…yes…all of them…yes…my pastel coloured golfing trousers…yes…all of them…yes and so on and on until she escaped into their ensuite bathroom and locked the door.

After an extra-long hot shower Jill emerged back into the bedroom to find herself alone and the suitcases had disappeared so she sat at her dressing table and plugged in her hair dryer and dried her hair then realising she had not packed the hairdryer, never mind it would fit in her hand luggage. With her hair now dried and styled she moved onto her makeup, a light touch of eye shadow and mascara, not ever needing much mascara as she was blessed with naturally long lashes, a little blusher on her cheeks would finish the effect. Now for the clothes, a short pleated peach pastel coloured skirt and a slightly baggy yellow blouse, she had bought some delightfully fussy yellow knickers and was still debating as to whether to wear a bra. Beginning to dress starting with the knickers a bra naturally went on and so her outfit was complete, shoes were a cheap but comfortable flat canvass in yellow.

Her husband was now calling her as he wanted to leave for the airport even though it was still early but he had little patience for travelling. Jill was halfway down the stairs when she heard the taxi pull up outside and give a short blast of its horn.

David had the front door open and was heading towards the taxi with one suitcase in his hand passing it to the taxi driver he returned to collect the second suitcase and his beloved golf clubs. On returning to the house David found his wife in the living room checking through items in their carry-on bag, Jill was removing their passports and Euro's handing them over to David for safe keeping who placed them in his jacket pocket alongside their tickets.

"It would have been nice to have had a cup of coffee before we left" Jill protested

"I'll buy you one at the airport, c'mon" David said impatiently, turning to leave.

"Do you think I could say goodbye to my daughter before we leave?"

"Where the hell is she, the taxi's waiting" David countered irritably.

"I don't think she is up yet, I'll just check her bedroom, won't be a minute"

Jill ran up the stairs to Bianca's bedroom, and found her daughter sitting cross legged on her bed still in her pyjama's with her laptop open in front of her, she gave her a kiss saying they were leaving now and thrusting £100 in twenties into her hand. Bianca opened her hand letting the money fall on the bed and calling after her Mum saying she hoped they have a great time; she just caught her Mum calling back, "That will be a first!"

They enjoyed an uneventful journey to Manchester Ringway Airport that took just under half an hour; David managed to find a trolley and loaded the bags and golf clubs onto it before they proceeded into the Airport to find their point of departure.

Chapter 2   Michelle

Michelle sat at her desk in the classroom which had just been vacated by 38 fifteen year old boys and girls who had left in an overly exuberant mood as the weekend beckoned and Michelle had forgotten to set them any homework.

Caroline Hurst, one of her colleagues some 10 years younger than Michelle at 32 was very pretty and petite with long flowing blonde hair, asked if she had time for a quick drink at The Commercial, an old style pub close to the school with many regulars both male and female but none from the school.

"I have packing to do, we are leaving first thing in the morning," Michelle said half-heartedly as she could murder a drink right now.

"Oh come on, it's just turned 4 o'clock, it won't take long," famous last words she thought.

"Ok but it will need to be quick, I just need to finish up here, give me 15 minutes, ok?" Michelle succumbed without much pushing.

"15 minutes, great I'll meet you here then," Caroline said grinning as she trotted out of the classroom.

As Michelle returned to her paperwork she was interrupted again this time by David, Jill's husband.

"Time for a quick drink?" David enquired.

"No, I've told you it's over, what part of over do you not understand?" Michelle was furious.

"But I just thought we could talk, clear the air before the holiday, we could meet up as we did on the last holiday" pleaded David with a little too much sweat showing on his forehead.

"I told you never again and I meant it now fuck off!" Michelle now shouted at him just as Caroline re-entered the classroom who had clearly heard the argument as she asked,

"Everything ok Michelle?"

"Yes, this is Mr Jones, Bianca's father; he was just leaving, weren't you?" Michelle was clearly flustered.

"Yes well I suppose I better had then" David said almost under his breath as he turned to leave wiping the sweat on his forehead away with the back of his hand.

Caroline sauntered up to Michelle putting her hands onto Michelle's shoulders and looking into her eyes she moved her head ever so slightly nearer to Michelle's, not being rebuffed she tried what she had been longing to do for so long, she kissed Michelle ever so gently on the lips, it felt so good so she pressed a little harder wanting so much to explore Michelle's mouth with her tongue but daren't. Caroline pulled back to reveal her smile, she was exited but also scared as to what Michelle's reaction would be.

"Well that was nicer than I thought it would be to kiss another woman," gasped Michelle in total shock and surprise.

"Shall we go for that drink now" asked Caroline, surprised by Michelle's reaction and so pleased by it she dared to believe sex was now on the agenda.

"Oh boy do I need a drink now!" exclaimed Michelle as she had just gone from being extremely mad at David for not accepting the end of their relationship to having her first sexual encounter with another woman which she would not have believed possible but she had to admit to herself that she had been aroused a little by the kiss.

Michelle followed Caroline out of the side entrance of the school which only teachers used as it led to the school car park, which had recently been tarmacked and could now accommodate 40 vehicles at a push. Michelle was in her car first, a Peugeot 206 convertible in bright red, as she always arrived early in the morning and so parked near the exit. She waited for Caroline to pull up behind her in her battered blue Ford Ka before moving forward onto the road heading for The Commercial which was a little over a mile away.

On arrival they both parked in the gravelled car park which was almost empty but come 5.30pm you would not be able to find a space. They walked swiftly to the pubs entrance which was on the main road, Michelle thought at one point she saw Caroline's hand coming to meet hers but it did not transpire, Caroline must have thought better than to try and hold her hand.

Entering the pub first through the large wooden double outer doors and then slightly smaller inner doors which led into the large bar area which had been created by knocking three rooms into one, it had a high ceiling and was carpeted in patterned red which was discoloured in areas showing its age. The bar was semi-circular on the left against the wall, tables and chairs surrounded the room except in the far left corner where a pool table could be found. There were three men and two women barflies sat on stools together around the bar, there were five men in the pool area, two of which were playing pool whilst the others waited their turn for a game, pound coins on the side of the table marked their turn. There were a further ten or so people scattered about the room in groups of two's and three's.

Michelle strode confidently up to the bar and ordered a large vodka and coke with ice, turning to Caroline she noticed several of the men's eyes upon her, asking Caroline what she would like to drink she replied, "Pernod and water in a tall glass please, no ice,"

Collecting and paying for their drinks from the bar they made their way to a table at the back of the room which was the furthest away from anyone else they could find. Sitting next to each other Caroline could not wait to ask, "So what is the storey with Mr Jones?"

Michelle took a couple of sips of her drink before answering.

"It was a huge mistake really which I cannot believe I have let continue off and on for nearly two years now. We have been having sex that's all, it's not love or anything like that just sex, well for me anyway, and not that bloody good sex either, Jesus why did I let it go on for so long?"

"But isn't Mr and Mrs Jones one of the couples you go on holiday with twice a year?"

"Yes and I've been craping myself in case Jill found out, I think she's been going short."

"Shit, you've not been fucking him on holiday as well have you?" Caroline asked slightly incredulously.

"Well yes, when we could….well quite a lot actually"

"And your husband doesn't suspect anything?" Caroline now enjoying what she was hearing and probing further.

"Why would he? He has it whenever and wherever he wants he never goes short, I make sure of that."

"Mr Jones wasn't expecting it this afternoon in the classroom was he?" Caroline digged deeper as her eyes circled the room.

"Probably, we have done it before in the classroom, he has bent me over my desk several times, we were nearly caught two weeks ago by Ken Docherty the Headmaster, it was only the steel caps he wears in his shoes that warned us, I am still not sure whether he saw my knickers on the floor under my desk and David only just had time to pull his trousers up, they weren't fastened, he held them up with his wrists pressed against his belly."

"Holy shit! And I was worried about kissing you!"

"Yes about that kiss, I've not experienced that before you know" Michelle half whispered.

"How was it for you?" Caroline asked eagerly and with trepidation.

"Different and soft and surprisingly enjoyable," admitted Michelle.

Caroline could hardly believe her ears, she began to tremble ever so slightly and she realised she was aroused and moist. A couple had sat down at the next table to them so Caroline leaned close to Michelle, close enough to feel the warmth of her body, she turned her head to Michelle and whispered, "enjoyable enough to take it further?"

"I really need to think about that and anyway I go away tomorrow for a week, give me that week"

"Well it will be a long week but hopefully worth the wait."

Caroline left it at that as she did not want to push it and therefore lose any hope, changing the subject she asked,

"Do you think Mr Docherty has sex with his eye in or out, I've seen him take it out and clean it in the staff room when he thought no one was looking."

"But you being the nosey sod that you are!" Michelle remarked, amused at what Caroline's response would be, she is nosey by her own admission and prides herself on knowing everyone's business, she now knows slightly more of Michelle's business than she did before.

"It's good to be informed, anyway back to the subject of sex and Mr Docherty, can you imagine him on top of some poor woman pumping away naked and ever so hairy, winking at her with his glass eye, strange stigmatism he has it must irritate him, he would look like a rampant wolf on heat!" said Caroline.

"That's not very nice of you Caroline, you know he lost his wife to cancer three years ago, he took it really poorly to start with taking it out on everyone at work with his tirades and temper tantrums. Thankfully he has calmed down now, people take the piss out of him because of his glass eye and because he keeps himself to himself, no one really knows him, he could be a really nice bloke," retorted Michelle.

"Yes he could be I'll give you that but I couldn't do anything with a guy that hairy, I know I couldn't do anything with a guy anyway. Back to Mr Jones, what would you have done if he had made you pregnant?" asked Caroline.

"Thanked God for a miracle! Others at work know so I may as well tell you, I cannot conceive, medically. It's a long storey but the crux of it is when I was six years old my father ran over me with his Land Rover Discovery, it was an accident of course, I was playing in our driveway when my father jumped in his Land Rover to go to work and without seeing me reversed down the driveway, my Mum could see what was about to happen and cried out which saved my life as my father heard her but he didn't stop soon enough, one of the rear wheels trapped me around my stomach and hip. I couldn't move, Mum called for an ambulance, it arrived along with the fire brigade who managed to free me from under the car. On arrival at hospital the ambulance paramedics took me straight to an operating theatre, I woke up three days later and spent six weeks recuperating on a children's ward. Mum and Dad did not tell me I could not have children until I was 13 years old and that was that as they say," explained Michelle.

"My God, how sad, I'm sorry, I didn't mean to pry, your poor Dad, did he ever forgive himself?" asked Caroline.

"No, he still hasn't, I forgave him years ago after all it was an accident and anyway it has given me certain freedoms for which I have taken full advantage off," Michelle spoke softly as she wiped a tear from her cheek.

"Freedoms?" asked Christine.

"Jesus! Christine! You don't have to keep proving how bloody nosey you are!"

"Sex, Sex, OK!"

"Oh! Yes I see yes of course yes, what exactly do you mean?" Christine pushed.

"Fuck me Christine! Really! I put it about a bit ok, understand?" Michelle explained in finality.

"Yes, yes understand, ok, so put it about a bit with me will you!" Christine applauded trying not to sound desperate but failing.

"I told you give me a week and I meant it!" Michelle asserted. "Now I really should be leaving, I have two sets of packing to complete as Tony won't return home from the car dealership until gone 7pm"

With that the two of them finished their drinks and sauntered outside to the car park where Christine leaned over to Michelle to give her a kiss before heading to her car, Michelle reciprocated, well she had enjoyed the first one and anyway she wanted to leave Christine wanting more.

Michelle's car pulled onto the driveway and parked in her normal space of the large detached Georgian house, as she rose from her seat grabbing her handbag from the rear of the car she could vaguely see a shadow of someone through the two slits of stained glass of the large heavy original front door of the almost mansion like house.

She was three yards from the door as it opened slightly and the shadow of a figure moved out of sight into the rear drawing room, Michelle entered closing the door behind her and dropping her handbag on the floor as she slowly walked through the darkened corridor of what appeared a gloomy house which clearly had not been decorated for some twenty years; she began unbuttoning her navy blue blouse allowing it to drop to the floor, now undoing her navy blue bra also allowing it to fall to the floor, she now entered the darkness of the rear drawing room her skirt falling to the ground leaving her naked except for her high heeled Jimmy Choo black patent leather shoes and her bright red frilly French knickers.

She could feel the man's nakedness in the darkness, a sliver of light shone through a small opening in the closed   dark dirty curtains, she could see dust circulating in the lights shaft, the man stood and moved slightly towards her, Michelle could just make out the schoolmaster's cane in his right hand and mortar board placed squarely on his head, the only other thing Michelle could make out was the thick black and in places grey hair that pervaded his entire body except for a triangular shaved area around his groin which looked bloody ridiculous but Michelle had insisted.

"For fuck's sake Ken put your fuckin eye in, you know I hate looking at your empty socket!" said Michelle.

This was Michelle doing her bit for the sanity of the school, once a month she gave Ken Docherty the headmaster a blowjob, it stopped Ken's inane blowouts at staff and sometimes the children. He had become very insular and irritable since his wife's death, this monthly meeting had made school life palatable again and it was only once a month although Ken had asked for more Michelle had flatly refused suggesting Ken should make an effort with his private life and go out more and socialise to try and make new friends, who knows he may even meet another woman.

To be fair to Ken he had tried, joining a sports club he had played squash and swam regularly, Michelle knew this because Ken had recounted to her his first visit to the club where they had arranged a game of squash for him with a 72 year old man, he had at first been furious with them for pitting him against someone so much older than him but he had been thrashed 3-0, that was some six months ago but what had angered him more was when he had entered the showers after that first game, the curious looks from other members, not of his monstrous body hair but of his triangular shaved area for which he was sure he had heard muffled sniggers.

Michelle's monthly duty accomplished it was time to rush home as she had not started packing yet and it was now gone 6 pm, Tony was due home at hopefully just gone 7pm he had promised not to be late but he never knew if they would have any late arriving customers at the car dealership.

Arriving home at nearly 6.15pm Michelle rushed upstairs taking them two at a time she threw off all her clothes placing them into the washing basket placed near the door to their ensuite bathroom.

Starting with Tony's suitcase first she threw in golfing trousers and shirts first then suitable trousers and shirts for the evening and finally threw in underwear and socks, completed in under 10 minutes. Michelle's suitcase was next with which she took much more care but did not have the complication of underwear as she never wore any on holiday. Once the packing was complete she jumped in the shower.

The shower had revived her; she pulled an old stretched T-shirt over her head which was baggy and comfortable which just covered her knees. Quickly brushing her hair she trotted joyfully downstairs into their plush white lounge, the walls were white the carpets were white, the sofas were white, an absolute nightmare to keep clean but she loved the room that way.

Making her way to the drinks cabinet she took out the ice bucket and filled it with fresh ice from the large American style fridge in the kitchen before making herself a large vodka and Pepsi in a tumbler with 4 ice cubes, she sat on the largest of the two sofas and turned on the TV with the remote to be greeted with the opening music for Emmerdale, all done and drink in hand it was 7pm.

The front door slammed shut at just gone 7.20pm as Tony rushed upstairs shouting down to Michelle, "Beer, in a pint glass, best make it a Stella, please, be down in a mo.!"

Arriving in their bedroom Tony stripped off and rushed into the bathroom and into the shower, he had showered in two minutes flat, back in the bedroom still slightly wet he threw his hair back with his hands, pulled on a pair of football shorts and walking out of the bedroom put on a T-shirt as he threw himself down the stairs into the lounge taking the pint glass from Michelle's outstretched arm and gulping down half the liquid whilst continuing to the kitchen and opening the fridge and retrieving another can of Stella Artois downing the remainder of beer from the glass so that he could immediately refresh it from his newly acquired can.

"Jesus Tony! It's only 7.30pm slow down for Christ's sake!" suggested Michelle.

"Only catching up with you dear, shit, what a fuckin day!" said Tony.

"Why? What happened?" asked Michelle, as if she was interested.

"Seven deals for the day, brilliant, and with good money in them, on a Friday!" Tony cried out.

"Good, I'm so pleased for you, what do you want for dinner, I really can't be bothered cooking, do you fancy a carry out?" pleaded Michelle.

"Sure, what do you fancy, Chinese or Indian?" asked Tony.

"I'm easy" said Michelle.

"I know that honey but what do you want to eat?" grinned Tony who was clearly in a good mood.

"Cheeky sod, just for that I will have Chinese from the Yangzi Palace," Michelle was grinning too now.

"Fuck me, that's just cost me hasn't it, what do you want, the usual, ribs and all?" asked Tony checking his wallet for cash.

"Ring it through as quickly as you can, it'll be an hour as it is." Michelle instructed as she rose from the sofa to refresh her drink from the cabinet, as she was putting the ice in her tumbler Tony thrust his glass into her hand for refreshment as he started to order their food from the restaurant on his mobile phone.

"They said it would be about an hour, time for a few more drinks, I take it you have packed?" Tony enquired; he took it for granted Michelle had packed as he never in all the years they have been married packed a single bag.

"Of course and as usual it took hours, you owe me" lied Michelle but Tony was not to know.

They watched some television whilst waiting for their food to arrive, Coronation Street and a rerun of You've Been Framed, after demolishing the Chinese, they were both ravenous, they briefly thought about having sex but decided against it as they were both done in with their eating exertions, Tony really shouldn't have ordered so much and they both shouldn't have eaten so much and as the time was now 10pm they were both feeling slightly the worse for wear with the amount of alcohol they had consumed in a relatively short space of time so they decided to go to bed as they were up early in the morning.

Michelle turned to Tony and said," While I take all this rubbish from the Chinese outside to the bin you ring the taxi firm and make sure the taxi is ordered for 9.15am, ok?"

Michele returned inside and locked the kitchen door turning the lights out as she walked through the lounge she saw Tony had left their glasses so she picked them up returning to the kitchen putting the light back on she rinsed them under the sink leaving them on the draining board before yet again switching the light out and walking through the lounge switching lights out as she went and checking the front door was locked before retiring to the bedroom where she found Tony already in bed and asleep, Michelle took off her t-shirt and joined her husband in bed.

Michelle woke to find Tony on top of her, "Christ Tony you could have waited for me!"

"But you looked so adorable sleeping so soundly," pleaded Tony.

"What and I don't when I'm awake...hurry up then, I'm not going to catch you up now am I!"

As Tony continued his rhythmic pumping action Michelle checked her watch, 6am, then checked to see her dress hanging on the door to the bathroom, just as she was looking to see if her yellow high heeled shoes were within sight Tony cried out coming inside of her.

"I never bore making love to you, Shell, you feel so good, you smell of garlic though,"

"You want to try letting me join in!" protested Michelle.

"I'm sorry but you did look adorable," said Tony as he threw the duvet off the bed and jumped up making his way into the bathroom.

"Thanks, have you noticed the time, what are we supposed to do until 9.15am?" Michelle enquired as she raised herself up on her elbows.

"Thought we could go to The Pantry for breakfast, we have time," Tony called back as he ran the shower.

"Great, hurry up in the shower as I need to do my makeup, I am not going to The Pantry naked!"

Michelle may as well have been talking to herself as Tony was now in the shower and could not hear her. Lying on the bed waiting for Tony to finish his ablutions thoughts drifted to the holiday and spending the week in the company of Jill and Julie as it was always so awkward as they were all different personalities and they only spent time together on these golfing holidays, it was not as if they were friends.

It would be so much easier if they were friends perhaps she should make an effort bringing them all closer together as it was clear these golfing holidays were now established and were going to continue, it would be nice for once to enjoy the holiday. With that thought in her head Tony appeared through the doorway naked and wet except for a towel he was rubbing and twisting about his head drying his hair, on seeing him Michelle jumped off the bed rushing into the bathroom slapping his cock as she rushed by him sniggering loudly, clearly in holiday mood.

They arrived at The Pantry, which was part of the Robinson Crusoe Hotel, just on 7am which also happened to be its opening time. The Pantry had its own entrance just off the carpark to the side of the Hotel as they walked through the entrance they were welcomed by the warm scintillating smell of freshly percolated coffee. Quite a number of the tables were already taken by Hotel guests as they walked towards the centre of the room they were greeted by Ken Livermore one of the restaurant managers who showed them to a table near the rear window which overlooked the Hotels large mature garden.

The Pantry was renowned for its full English breakfast which was large and included; bacon, eggs, sausages, black pudding, kidneys, beans, tomatoes, fried bread, mushrooms, toast and the usual tea or coffee; it was expensive but oh God was it good.

It had taken them longer than they had thought to eat the monster of a breakfast but they had both thoroughly enjoyed it and as it was now 8.20am it was time to leave and return home. Michelle left Tony to pay their bill and headed to the carpark jumping into Tony's light blue metallic Ford Mondeo Estate; she started the engine and waited for Tony to appear which he did within a couple of minutes inching the car forward while Tony jumped in she sped off the carpark onto the A635 heading for home.

Once home Michelle left Tony to check the passports and Euros and travellers cheques whilst she checked all the windows were locked first upstairs then downstairs, after a few more minutes waiting they heard the horn blast from the arriving taxi they both turned to each other and smiled, Tony grabbed a suitcase and his golf clubs whilst Michelle grabbed the remaining suitcase and a carryon bag along with her handbag, Tony was putting his clubs in the back of the taxi as Michelle locked their front door as she bent to pick up the suitcase the taxi driver beat her to it smiled and strode down the path to the taxi, leaving Michelle to ponder if she knew the driver.

They had an uneventful ride to the airport Michelle grabbed a luggage trolley whilst Tony paid the taxi driver. They entered the airport together managed to check in straight away and whilst they walked through towards the departure lounge to find the bar they both turned to each other at exactly the same time and giggling to each other as they realised they were almost skipping through towards the departure area but were holding hands as they had always done.

Chapter 3   Julie

Julie bought a glass of lime flavoured mineral water from the bar of McGinties, one of four bars within The Cloisters Hotel, a four star establishment which bordered Westminster in London; and turned to choose where to sit.

The bar could comfortably house a hundred people but at this moment only entertained around sixteen who were sat around various tables in groups of 3 and 4 which were closest to the walls leaving the centre of the room vacant. Julie chose a table just off the very centre of the room 3 tables from the bar which she believed would be discreet enough for her guest once he arrived. Sipping her drink delicately she could not help but notice a tall gent in a light blue quality suit enter the bar almost nervously, it was a look she recognised as that of one who was unaccustomed of staying in a hotel, making his way to the bar he ordered a whiskey and coke and turned to find a table at which to sit, his eyes crossed over Julie and as he decided on his table walked slowly towards it his eyes moved back to Julie, he smiled at her as he would anyone in a strange place.

The minutes passed as Julie's guest was now late but to no avail as she had been paid substantially in advance except for any particular extras that may be required. Julie looked up for a second only to notice the tall gent who was now reading a James Patterson paperback book, his eyes looked away quickly as hers fell upon his, she smiled at his shyness as she checked her watch. Her guest was now some 30 minutes late as she nursed her drink carefully, again the tall gent looked nervously at her, she felt a little overdressed for the bar as her guest was to have taken her first to a restaurant in Covent Garden and then they were to proceed to one of the more opulent casinos of London's West End. Julie wore a very elegant dress, a Christian Dior copy but a very good and expensive one, in deep purple which just reached beyond her knees, she also wore matching underwear, silk purple knickers with suspenders and very delicate silk black stockings, her bra straps were slightly uncomfortable and digging into her skin as it was new and a little too small for her 34C breasts.

Julie's guest was now more than an hour late and unlikely to show, she took a sip of her mineral water as she decided to leave, she had not noticed the tall gent put his book down on the table in front of him and walk behind her.

Caught unawares as he asked her, "I hope you don't think me impertinent but if you are waiting for someone I think they are terribly ungracious to have left you alone for so long, perhaps I may buy you a drink and keep you company until they arrive?"

Julie turned and smiled at the tall gent replying "I don't believe my friend will be coming now so I was about to leave but thankyou anyway"

The tall gent persisted, "My name is Steve, you have clearly spent a considerable time and effort readying yourself, what a pity it would be to waste such effort, just one drink and if I bore you how could I blame you for leaving?"

"I'm Julie and I would be happy to have one drink with you, perhaps I may have a Bacardi and coke"

"You may, excuse me whilst I go to the bar" turning towards the bar Steve showed the barman the broadest smile as he ordered their drinks, the barman just shrugged his shoulders as he had of course seen this same scenario some many times before.

After several drinks with mostly idle chatter it occurred to Steve that Julie may be hungry especially if she had been expecting a meal from her missing companion. "You must excuse my manners Julie, you must be hungry we could find a restaurant, I'm sure there is one close by"

Julie glanced at her watch to find it was now 11.10pm,"I think I've gone past eating now, I hadn't realised how late it is I really should be going"

"I really don't want to let you go just yet, we could go to my room and order a snack from room service," Steve was desperate not to let Julie go as there was something captivating he found in her.

Here it is thought Julie perhaps he is not quite so naïve as he makes out but she had to find out so she accepted his invitation. Once ensconced in Steve's room he indeed asked her what she would like from room service the menu being relatively simple but sufficient, they both agreed on coffee and so Steve rang through to room service and a pot of steaming hot coffee arrived ten minutes later. The coffee soon evaporated as they again talked late into the night, they talked mainly of Steve's wife and the cancer which took her life some six years earlier at the tender age of thirty and his two sons who were now 11 and 12 years old who acted as twins rather than just brothers, they were inseparable especially since their mothers' death. Steve talked of his garden centre business that he had taken over from his father who was now in a residential care home for the elderly in Stalybridge. Julie quickly turned any conversation of her past around by asking Steve about his children or business, the less he knew of her past the better as she was warming to Steve's easy charm and manner, she was actually hoping she might see him again however implausible that may be. A meeting in a hotel in the centre of London between a northern businessman and a prostitute was not a sound foundation for any relationship and she knew it.

With that thought clearly in her mind she noticed from the electronic clock at the side of the bed it had just crept past 1.30am, now thoughts of seeing Steve again dissipated, she rose to leave so suddenly it took Steve by surprise, "can I have your phone number, I am leaving for home tomorrow but will be back in two weeks, I would love to see you again, perhaps we could go for that meal."

Julie was now at the door with her hand on the doorknob her wrist turning, "I don't think it would be a good idea, you live so far away, and I.....well I just don't think it would be a good idea."

Julie had the door open and was on her way through it when Steve thrust his business card into her hand pleading, "please ring me, anytime, I really want to see you again."

"I don't think so, goodbye Steve, it really was nice meeting you."

With that Julie was out of the door making sure she closed it behind her to avoid Steve trying to follow her, it closed with a loud bang which she had not intended, she ran to the lift and pressed the button several times in frustration to summon it. Thankfully it arrived with a clunk within a few seconds so she jumped in and allowed a tear to form as the doors closed and transported her to the ground floor.

People like her did not meet people like Steve and if by chance they ever should nothing could ever come of it so best not to start anything. Julie was in a taxi halfway home before she realised she had left her newly acquired coat in Steve's room, well that was £300 she would not see again she thought as the black

London taxi pulled up outside the 1960's built high rise block of flats where she currently resided.

Julie's eyes opened ever so slowly as the pain hit her senses immediately, she took a cursory glance around to find she was in a sterile hospital ward with about 20 beds all of which appeared to be occupied by people with varying degrees of sickness. Trying to raise herself up to more familiarise herself with the surroundings she was stopped by the sudden pain in her left arm which she then saw was encased in plaster up to her elbow.

Slowly the images surfaced of a man, a Middle Eastern man she thought, well built for his age which she put at about 50, of average height and not much hair on his head but clean shaven, and a hotel room, she was lying prostrate on a bed in her underwear, she felt decidedly groggy she knew she had drunk Champagne earlier in the night but this grogginess was more than Champagne, she felt weak and helpless, she had been drugged but why, she had been paid as usual before she left home. The man was finishing his drink as he turned to move towards her removing his navy blue sports jacket allowing it to fall to the floor, he moved quickly now and before Julie could move out of the way she felt the full force of the punch that pounded into her jaw, she became instantly dizzy but still felt the second blow hit the other side of her face, this time it was her right eye which took the full brunt of the blow. Losing consciousness rapidly she tried in vain to move as further blows rained down on her face and body, hardly conscious she felt her knickers being ripped from her as her legs were spread apart she could not move and knew she had been entered as darkness finally surrounded her.

A young female nurse arrived at her bedside to explain she had been brought in the previous evening at just gone midnight by an ambulance with police in attendance, the nurse then asked if she knew what had happened to her. At this point Julie lost consciousness again.

When Julie next awoke the drab beige privacy curtains were drawn around her hospital bed and a student nurse of no more than 19 years old sat beside her on a solitary plain blue plastic seated chair, the nurse smiled brightly at Julie as she rose explaining she was going to summon a senior nurse, nurse Shirley Symonds arrived taking Julie's right wrist to check her pulse at the same time introducing herself and again asking if she remembered what had happened to her the previous evening. Julie was in pain, groggy and tired but still managed to acknowledge the nurses question whilst shaking her head slowly. The nurse offered Julie some water which she gratefully accepted as she sipped at the water Shirley explained that the Doctor would be coming to see her in about an hour and that she should rest until then and also that a solitary police Constable was waiting to talk to her.

It was approximately 2pm in the afternoon as consciousness struck Julie again, the front of her gown was open and an Indian middle aged man with a thick beard had his hands around her waist prodding and poking, she spontaneously jerked away from him with an audible gasp of shock at which point she then saw and recognised nurse Shirley Symonds, she relaxed back slightly onto her pillows as she caught sight of the stethoscope around Doctor Jimi Mistry's neck. Julie cried out in pain as the Doctors' hands explored her bruised and discoloured ribcage, there was quite severe pain from the right side which she later found that three fractured ribs were the cause of her pain. The Doctor spoke quietly and with respect as he began explaining the extent of her varied injuries. The main injury which caused the Doctor most concern were the blows to her head she had suffered which had given her concussion, therefore the Doctor explained they would keep her in hospital for 48 hours under observation. The other injuries were, apparently, superficial, they did not feel superficial! Julie had suffered injuries to her head, her face remained swollen on both sides from her eyes which were now black and virtually closed, to her jaw which she was told how lucky she was that it was not broken, " oh I certainly feel lucky!" thought Julie. Julie's left arm was broken just above the wrist, lucky it was not the wrist, "God look how lucky I am" thought Julie again. Next the Doctor explained she had three broken ribs which they would strap up for her and of all things she had a sprained left ankle which had been bound tight. All Julie knew at this point was the considerable pain she was feeling acutely all over her body and the pain between her legs and thighs. The Doctor was preparing to leave and said something to Julie which she missed totally her thoughts being elsewhere, as the Doctor pulled back the curtain that surrounded Julie's bed she saw the constable make his move to introduce himself.

The Constable stood to Julie's right; she could just make out his face which was almost pale, clean shaven, a nose which may have been broken at some point, short blonde hair and a scar to the side of his right eye approximately half an inch long which pointed towards his mouth that showed thin pale lips. He was tall maybe 6 foot 2 inches and young only 22 or 23 years old; he introduced himself as Constable Ron Evans. He did not look like a Ron; Julie could not imagine someone calling this very attractive young man Ronald. The Constable's nervousness became apparent as he began asking Julie what had happened in that hotel room and that unless she wanted to pursue the matter then there would be very little the police could do. What he did not divulge was his Sargent's comments targeted at him before he left the police station earlier that day. The Constable who had attended the scene in the room at the hotel shortly after the paramedics had arrived had reported back to his Sargent that hotel security had observed Julie and a male in the bar before they had retired to the man's room and that the security staff were under no illusions about Julie's profession, the Constable had been firm with them that even if her profession was confirmed she certainly did not ask or deserve the treatment exacted on her by the well dressed and clearly affluent man on the security tape. The hotel clearly did not want any adverse publicity this incident could and no doubt would provide should it go to court and the staff the Constable had been in contact with had been carefully instructed by senior management of the hotel to try in some way to make out Julie was at fault.

Constable Ron Evans found he was talking to himself as he glanced down at Julie who was now sound asleep.

Julie was dreaming of Steve Anderson the tall gent she had met in McGinties bar, Julie was naked in his hotel room bed as Steve walked into the bedroom from the bathroom with just a towel around his waist his hair still damp from the piping hot shower he had just taken, his body glistened as steam rose from his broad shoulders in the half light from a single imitation Art Deco lamp which stood alone in the far corner of the room. Steve walked slowly around the bed to where Julie lay, she felt her pulse rising she was breathing heavier, he took her head in his hands as he raised her lips towards his as he bent forward Julie slid her legs out of bed just in time to feel his damp towel fall onto her feet, she shook with delight as his tongue searched her mouth she wanted to look down at his nakedness her hands were caressing his legs just below his bottom, Julie was so aroused and wet as their lips parted she pulled him closer and licked around his belly button, his hardness dug into her throat her hands now moved down and caressed his testicles as she opened her mouth and consumed him whole.

"Keep it still in your mouth no need to move it in and out, the thermometer won't take a proper reading unless you keep it still" said Shirley Symonds.

Julie realised she had been dreaming, "must have been a good one she thought, I'm so wet and feel a little giddy".

Shirley addressed Julie by saying, "it's a little high but not so high as to worry about".

"So can I go back to sleep now?" asked Julie as there was but one thing on her mind.

"Sure when you have taken your medication, here," Shirley gave Julie the small paper cup with the medication, two white pills, and a glass of water to help it down.

Try as she did sleep eluded her, thoughts turned to her client and why he had attacked her so violently, Caroline, her Madam, a word Julie detested and never used would have known the client as he had made payment in advance; had he been violent to any other of Caroline's girls surely if he had there would be no way Caroline would have accepted him as a guest. Did Caroline know what had happened to her? There had been no sign of her at the hospital and no calls from anyone enquiring as to her health." Let's face it," thought Julie "who gave a damn what happens to a prostitute."

Reasoning why she had made the decision originally to seek out such a profession, it was the only way she had been told that she could pay off her gambling addicted husband's debts in a reasonable time. The man suggesting, suggesting really! The man insisting she take up the profession was none other than Charlie "head butt" Butterfield a low life small time crook but extremely violent loan shark.

Unbeknownst to her Kevin, her husband had borrowed fifty thousand pounds from Charlie and had not paid back a penny and had not been seen again. It had taken Julie two years to pay back the money with interest to Charlie, two hundred and fifty thousand pounds she had paid back with nothing to show for it for herself.

A few months before she had paid back all the money she had met Caroline, who had asked her to work for her explaining how much she could make and that she would be safe as all her clients were scrutinised before they were allowed to see any of Caroline's girls. It had sounded good to Julie who thought that she had put up with all sorts working for Charlie and only having enough money to live on, now she wanted to make some money for herself so that she could start a small business and never have to sell herself ever again.

The time had come to end working in this goddam awful profession Julie thought as she began working on a plan to leave the hospital and London behind her, hopefully forever.

The 48 hours of observation passed quickly as Julie slept most of the time, the constable had taken her statement and said detectives would be in touch shortly probably when she had left hospital. The swelling on her face had subsided a little but her face was now pretty much all black, she could see much better as her eyes had opened more. It was her ribs which now gave her the most pain with any slight movement excruciating. What she was not sure about was her left ankle which had been bound tightly although she felt pain from it the pain was nothing compared to her ribs but as she had not been allowed out of bed she did not know how it would feel when she tried walking on it.

The Doctor was due on his rounds at 4.00pm today and she was hoping he would allow her to leave the hospital but should he wish to keep her in longer Julie had decided she would be leaving in the morning anyway. The plan was formulating in her head, she would return to her flat but only to collect a few belongings, one suitcase only the rest she would leave as they were "tarts clothes" anyway and she was leaving that profession vowing never to return under any circumstances. The plan then was to find a bed and breakfast establishment in another part of London, one in which she had never been and hopefully would not be recognised; "Jesus" she thought, "just how many men have you had sex with these past three years?"

The Doctor duly arrived for his rounds a little after 4,00pm and arrived at Julie's bedside at 4.15pm, he took Julie's blood pressure and retrieving her notes from the end of her bed began to write with a tacky end bitten Bic ball point pen the reading he had just taken whilst assessing fully what notes had been added since his last rounds, he then proceeded to raise Julie up from her prone position so that he could listen to her lungs from at first her back and then her chest. After raising eyebrows several times he announced, "Another 48 hours I feel is needed, we can review it tomorrow." At which without a by your leave he had moved on to his next patient leaving nurse Shirley Symonds to smile awkwardly in Julie's direction before running to catch up with Doctor Jimi Mistry as he looked around uncertainly for his next patient.

Julie had realised her plan needed a slight change in as much as if she left the hospital in the morning as planned she would stick out like a sore thumb anywhere she ventured during the day as the only clothes she had were the ones the police had brought to her from the hotel room. A bright turquoise low cut silk short blouse and a sky blue pleated short skirt which positioned itself approximately 4 inches above her knees and also left an inch gap between the band of her skirt and the bottom of her blouse revealing skin. The outfit was completed by a pair of Jimmy Choo 4 inch high heels finished in deep blue suede and her accompanying sky blue jacket had not made the journey from the hotel. Clearly the shoes could not be worn with her ankle still bound tight so the plan now was to leave at around 7.00pm, she had checked that her handbag still contained her purse and that nothing was missing. There is normally a Freephone for a taxi firm in a hospital entrance she knew so once in the taxi she could be transported in relative safety home where she would pack what was needed and then summon another taxi for the next part of her journey.

Julie had found a Gideon's bible in her bedside cabinet and within that was a business card for a bed and Breakfast establishment in Epping called the Wetherby Bed and Breakfast. It gave the names of the proprietors as Mr and Mrs Trevor Faversham. Julie decided to make this her next port of call. She mentioned the bible to nurse Symonds saying she had not realised the Gideon's were leaving bibles in hospitals now to be informed it belonged to the previous occupant of the bed who now no longer needed it.

It was two weeks since Julie had left the hospital and ensconced herself in the Wetherby Bed and Breakfast in Epping, it was a very basic room which comprised a bed and a wardrobe with a set of drawers placed in front of the solitary window which overlooked a backyard and the yards of the buildings beyond. In the corner of the room had been built an ensuite bathroom, the furnishings were clearly from the 1970's as was the wallpaper and carpets but it was clean. The proprietor was Mrs Faversham a jovial lady of ample proportions which was exacerbated by her 4 foot 11 inch frame who always wore a woollen brown cardigan with frayed elbows with a flowered pinny which held her hanky in its pocket and dressed her hair in a bun and then there was the moustache which was embarrassing as it drew ones eye to it you just could not help staring at the damn thing, Julie had thought that she had started waxing it. Mrs Faversham was 74 years old and ran the B&B by herself having lost her beloved husband Trevor 50 years ago in a car accident, she never stopped talking whether you were listening to her or not and had collected a number of stray cats and dogs over the years which were all called Alfred, when Julie had asked one day why she called them all Alfred she simply said it was so she would not forget their names.

Mrs Faversham was a kindly old lady who on Julie's arrival had not mentioned her bruised and battered appearance but simply showed Julie to her room on the first floor leaving her with the key and although telling Julie her rates for the room had not asked for any money upfront, she had returned to Julie's room ten minutes later with a tray laden with a teapot with two cups, milk and sugar bowls, a sandwich of fresh smoked salmon and two pieces of homemade fruitcake. Mrs Faversham poured the tea and presented Julie with the sandwich whilst she talked incessantly as Julie ate her sandwich and drank her tea, they both ate their cake as Julie could not help noticing that Mrs Faversham had waited for Julie to finish her sandwich and start on her piece of cake before Mrs Faversham took the second piece of cake. Julie loved her from that moment on despite or maybe because of her eccentricities.

Julie's swelling and bruises to her face had now all but gone her ankle was no longer giving her any trouble and her ribs were now just giving her the occasional twinge so it was time to try and call Steve Anderson. Julie sat on her bed and turned on the pay as you go mobile phone she had bought a couple of days ago on a market stall in the High Street and lifted the card from the bed which contained Steve's phone number, she flicked the hair from her face and began to dial the number looking into the vanity mirror that perched atop the chest of drawers as she did so and stopped what she was doing immediately, "Shit" she thought, "Better put some clothes on first", not that he could see her but she dressed anyway and then not satisfied began putting on some makeup, once her makeup was complete she then decided to brush her hair. Sitting on the bed again she told herself she was just putting off the inevitable, even if he answered the phone he may not remember her and if he did remember her he probably would not want to see her.

"Make the phone call Julie," she told herself. Julie held the phone to her ear as it began to ring, one ring, two rings, three rings, four rings. "Steve Anderson" "My God" Julie thought "what do I say, what do I say."

"Uh, hello, uh, it's… "Julie stammered into the phone.

"Julie! Is that you Julie?" screamed Steve.

"Ur yes ur I ur I wasn't sure you would remember me" Julie said as she tried hard to compose herself, she was decidedly hot and bothered and in need of one of Mrs Faversham's cups of tea.

"Remember you! I have done nothing but think of you, where are you? What are you doing? My God! I sound like a little child, I'm sorry I have so many questions," Steve was now struggling to compose himself.

"You said you may be coming to London again soon, I thought we may go for the meal you promised me," said Julie barely able to control her emotions as she waited for Steve's response.

"Yes I was, I mean I will be in about six months, I've just been in London, in fact I am actually on the train back to Manchester now we are just passing through Birmingham," Steve could not keep the deflation out of his voice.

"Oh," was all Julie could muster.

There was a silence between them and Julie thought about hanging up when Steve piped up, "Come to Manchester! You can stay at my house there is plenty of room, so long as you don't mind sharing with three men, well one man and two boys actually, you must come, say you will come."

The silence returned as thoughts raced through Julie's mind, what if they did not like each other when they saw each other again, you are staying in a B&B from the 1970's and the man you love has just asked you to join him and stay at his house what is there to think about and then she realised, "the man you love", "Yes" Julie thought "I do love him."

"Do I need a passport?" said Julie as she was dancing on the bed and waving her hands about.

"No Julie, just bring yourself."

They discussed the finer points of travelling by train from London to Manchester, "Just jump on the train in London and I will meet you at Piccadilly train station in Manchester," Steve said.

Julie agreed to take the 10am train from London the following day; she could take the underground directly to the station from Epping. Julie skipped out of her room but before taking the stairs down to Mrs Faversham's room she returned to her own room and recovered a pair of small scissors she used for her eyebrows when they needed a slight trim. Mrs Faversham had a large mole on the top of her right cheek with a single Black hair protruding from it about an inch long which, thought Julie, made Mrs Faversham shake her head violently from side to side every few seconds. Julie thought she would use the scissors to cut the offending hair and stop Mrs Faversham's violent twitches, half way down the stairs the thought occurred to Julie, "What if she still twitches when I cut the hair? What if she was born with the twitch?" Julie turned about on the stairs and returned the scissors before going downstairs to inform Mrs Faversham of her plans, she knocked on her door which was opened a few minutes later by a flustered Mrs Faversham who informed Julie she was having problems with Alfred.

"He's not been the same since he has been neutered," she told Julie who looked confused as a Jack Russell stood before her, noticing her confusion Mrs Faversham said, "Not that Alfred.. Alfred," gesturing with her neck towards a cat who was taking a bath in the kitchen sink.

"I thought cats didn't like water!" enquired Julie.

"They don't," said Mrs Faversham "But Alfred thinks he's a dog," with all sincerity.

Julie stifled a laugh and began to explain to Mrs Faversham her plans for leaving the next day who immediately put the kettle on and proceeded to bring a fresh fruit cake from out of her bread bin, they sat drank tea and ate cake and chatted as old friends for two hours before Julie rose and paid Mrs Faversham for her room and said she would leave the key on the hall landing when she left in the morning as she did not want to disturb her.

7am the next morning Julie closed the front door of the Wetherby Bed & Breakfast for the last time to be greeted by a confused looking postman who asked her, "You've not been staying here have you? Mrs Faversham hasn't had a paying guest for 30 years!"

"Well that explains the décor," answered Julie on her way past him making her way to the station.

The Virgin train bound for Manchester Piccadilly left Euston Station bang on the stroke of 10.00am precisely, Julie sat bored and full of trepidation. The train was full of passengers and Julie began to wonder what their stories were for their journey to Manchester today, Julie's thoughts were interrupted by the little old lady who sat beside her offering an old and much read copy of National Geographic which Julie took with a warm smile. The old lady wore a tweed skirt and Jacket with a beige blouse and dark brown stockings and brown shoes, her light brown hair was tied in a pigtail and had been wound up and tied in a circle on the crown of her head and placed a pair of thick horn rimmed glasses on as she took out of her old flowered fabric bag a tatty Harold Robbins paperback which made Julie look at her twice and smile.

The old lady introduced herself as Thelma who was 78 years old and began to explain the tattiness of the book as she had read it several times and was still unsure as to the identity of the murderer, when Julie had asked if the author had not provided the murderers identity Thelma explained she did not know as someone had ripped out the last 25 pages of the book before she had bought it from the Age UK shop. A smell of pungent lavender emanated from the old lady who now reminded Julie of Agatha Christie's Miss Marple, Julie could only hope that she would not vanish from the train.

After an hour or so of looking through the copy of National Geographic Julie had dozed off waking an hour and a half later to find the little old lady had indeed vanished along with the National Geographic and realised they were now passing through the outskirts of Manchester.

Nerves took a hold of Julie now as the train slowed and gradually ground to a holt; people were standing and taking their belonging from the overhead racks making their way to the exits. Julie decided to wait until everyone had left before taking her suitcase from the stand by the exit behind her, the moment had come so Julie rose more nervously than she had anticipated and took her suitcase to the exit first stepping down onto the platform and then dragging the bag after her. Successfully ensconced on the platform Julie looked around for Steve but realised she would need to leave the platform before she could possibly see him therefore began walking towards the back of the cue forming where tickets were being checked.

Her nerves were taking over now as she handed her ticket over to the guard with shaking hand she told herself to take a grip. Walking through the exit she saw Steve immediately and smiled at him instinctively, Steve stepped forward picking Julie up in both arms and squeezed her tight as he swung her around with delight only stopping to kiss her full on the lips. Only when their lips parted did Steve realise that Julie's legs were in the air as he was considerably taller than her, he slowly lowered Julie to the ground allowing her at last to take a breath. Julie was somewhat taken aback by her welcome she was both surprised and delighted as Steve took her hand in his and motioned her towards a down escalator, a voice from behind them was shouting they turned instinctively to find a guard waving his hand in the air whilst his other hand pointed at Julie's suitcase which they had walked off forgetting. Steve hopped back taking the case in one hand and Julie in the other as they exited the station towards a car park to retrieve Steve's car.

In the coming weeks it became clear to the both of them that they were indeed in love and so after 3 short months together they married much to the consternation of Steve's two sons, Trevor and Daniel.

They did not like Julie from the start for no other reason than she was taking, as they thought, their father's love away from them. In the coming months and then years Trevor and Daniel at first begrudgingly began to like and then love Julie.

That was six years ago and the family had spent a wonderful six years in the company of Julie, the two lads had become very protective of Julie the more so when they found Julie had no family of her own. Julie had told them, as she did not want anyone knowing the truth of her past, that she was an orphan having been brought up in an orphanage in London and had had several foster parents before the age of sixteen, then leaving to rent a flat and making a living on her own in various mundane office jobs.

The two boys, Trevor and Daniel, were 19 and 18 years of age respectively and were both studying at Manchester University for Degrees in Accountancy whilst still living at home. Their home was a large 5 bedroom house set in a quarter of an acre of land with a small stream at the bottom of their mature garden which they had purchased shortly after their wedding. Steve had made a sizable amount of money when the land his garden centre was sat on was compulsory purchased by the council to make way for a large out of town shopping and leisure complex on some 50 acres. The council not only purchased his land but then gave him land just off the new complex and paid for the new construction; although Steve's family had owned the land for over sixty years financially it was a superb deal for them.

They were now about to jet off to Malaga with their friends for one of Steve's golfing holidays. Julie hated these holidays as she was left most of the day with Jill and Michelle, the other wives, whom she did not like, the women were there only for their husbands. Julie had decided things needed to change as they were together all day the three of them and these holidays were twice a year, if these holidays were to work they somehow needed to become friends even if it was just for the sake of their husbands.

Trevor drove them to the airport in his father's new Range Rover arriving just after 10.00am; Trevor took the suitcases out of the rear of the car whilst his father retrieved a trolley to transport them inside. After giving Julie a hug and a kiss farewell Trevor jumped back into the Range Rover and drove off leaving his father to say goodbye to the departing car as he shook his head looking at Julie and smiling, "Kids! Who'd have 'em?"

They took their luggage and entered Manchester Ringway Airport.

Chapter 4   Saturday

Arriving at the departure lounge bar the men and women of the party separated, well the men certainly did, arriving at the bar first they bought themselves three pints of larger and found a table to sit at which had only 4 chairs leaving their wives to fend for themselves. Jill, Michelle and Julie arrived at the bar and took a cursory disgusted look at their husbands in turn, as their drinks arrived they turned to look for a table only to find that they were all occupied so they took up their position at the bar, this is what they had in common in that once the holiday started the men went into golf mode and tended to forget their manners as far as their wives were concerned.

David, Tony and Steve had begun laughing and joking whilst the wives were enjoying yet another pregnant pause which was only broken by Jill. Jill had farted but unfortunately had followed through a little, her face paled at the realisation as a gooey wet mass invaded her knickers, "Christ!" was her only words as she looked around for the toilets, she spotted them off to her right and began moving in that direction, exclaiming, "excuse me" as she trotted off she hoped no one had been able to smell her mishap.

Entering the toilets she found it housed six booths and six wash basins the first of which was occupied so she made her way to the farthest away passing two women at the basins as she did so. Once ensconced in the booth she carefully took off her skirt as she needed to inspect the rear which she was dreading, what on earth does she do if it was soiled? The skirt was clean and she gave a huge sigh of relief as she ever so delicately inched off the knickers which initially stuck to her bottom, allowing them to drop to the floor the smell wafted into her nostrils at which point she wished they had not had the chicken last night as it must not have been cooked properly. She took a handful of toilet paper from the roll which kept sticking and would only allow her two very thin pieces at a time, "my God" she thought "this will take forever", as she was wiping her backside for the fourth time her fore fingernail dug into her skin right next to her arsehole and she could not help screaming in pain.

"Are you ok in there," enquired the women in the first booth

"Yes fine thanks, just scratched myself but I'm fine," Jill answered who was far from fine with no spare knickers and blood seeping down here leg now almost to her knee.

She grabbed for more paper and taking the very last toilet paper in the roll she dried up the blood as best she could but it continued to bleed. Needing more paper Jill needed to check the other booths but would need to be quick as she was naked from the waist down. She listened intently but could not hear anyone else in the toilets except her and the women in the first booth who did not sound well at all, all she had been hearing was a constant stream of wet farts and faint groans.

Jill made a dash for the first booth next to hers but that was empty of toilet rolls as was the second and third, arriving at the last booth she managed to drag half a handful of paper before that too ran out, rushing back to the sanctuary of her booth she could not help thinking of the woman in the first booth and whether she had checked to see if there was toilet paper in the booth before she sat down because she would clearly need quite a lot from the sounds of the activity in the booth.

Jill just managed to lock her booth again as the main door opened and she could hear a couple of women enter chatting as they did so, one woman entered a booth whist the other went to a basin still chatting incessantly, Jill could not hear any water and so assumed the women was adding makeup. Jill now attended to the constantly flowing blood, with her moving around the blood had made its way below her left knee and as Jill moped up the blood it stained her skin. There was still the problem of what to do about the soiled knickers as she did not wish to be seen putting them into the bin by the washbasins so she began to lift the top off the cistern where she thought she would dump the knickers and could dampen the remaining toilet paper so she could remove the stain the blood had left. The problem now was the flow of blood was persistent and she needed something that would soak it up until it stopped bleeding, the solution came to her when she realised that when she was out of her booth in search of toilet paper she had noticed there were two dispensing machines on the wall, one which housed sanitary towels which would be perfect and the other tampons which would not be.

Another dash would be necessary so Jill checked her purse for change and took out all the change she thought the dispensing machines may take. A toilet flushed, a booth door opened and the two women left still chatting incessantly.

Jill made her move quickly putting a pound coin in the sanitary towel machine and pulling the handle but nothing happened, she could see towels in the machine through the little window display so she pulled the handle again but nothing happened then she saw the out of order sign and she sighed audibly as her shoulders dropped, she placed another pound in the tampon machine and a packet dropped as the main door began to open so Jill rushed back to her booth closing the door behind her with the tampons still in the drop box of the machine. A booth door closed and locked and Jill thought about making a dash now for her tampons but decided to wait for the woman to leave first. A couple of minutes later there was the sound of swearing as the person realised there was no paper then a toilet flushing and a door unlocking and opening as the woman left without washing her hands, "Ugh!" Jill thought as she rushed the vending machine for her tampons.

Back in the safety of her booth Jill ripped the packet apart to find two tampons, "two tampons for a quid!" she thought, "the robbing bastards!" Jill needed to use one to wipe away the flow of blood again before placing the second between the cheeks of her bum and against the offending cut, now she could put on her skirt again and her shoes and open the door to the booth as if nothing had happened, before leaving Jill bought another packet of tampons and placed them in her bag.

Jill walked out of the toilets throwing back her hair as she did so, her cheeks were red and flushed, she wished she had cooled them at one of the sinks. The tampon felt strange between the cheeks of her bum as she walked and she was self-conscious in case any droplets of blood escaped the tampon, she needed to squeeze the cheeks of her bum together to keep the tampon in place. Jill was so self-conscious as she tried to walk normally, she looked around hoping no one noticed her walking strangely or that anyone thought she was walking as though she had a vibrator stuck up her arse on full vibrate!

No sooner had Jill left the toilets than David came rushing up to her asking, "Where have you been? The plane is boarding! C'mon this way, quick!" he grabbed Jill's hand and rushed her forward beginning to run.

"Don't do that! I can't run....not in these shoes," Jill protested as the shoes were not the problem.

"Don't be silly, your shoes are flat, we'll miss the plane!" David cried out.

"Stop, if we miss the plane then we miss the plane, don't rush me!" Jill protested loudly as she needed to cool down.

At which point they saw Steve Anderson walking slowly towards them, "There's been a slight delay, we board in another 10 minutes" Steve said still walking towards them.

The relief was clearly visible on Jill's face which was flushed and bright red as they now walked slowly to their allotted boarding area where they found Julie with Michelle and Tony. They boarded the plane 10 minutes later and were sat poles apart from each other, Jill and David towards the rear which Jill was glad of as it was near the toilet should she need it and Michelle and Tony about 15 rows in front of them, they could not make out where Julie and Steve were sitting.

Jill had been allocated a window seat as she always tried to have one as she enjoyed looking out of the window especially at take-off and landings. Before sitting Julie took out of the pocket of the seat in front the airlines magazine opening it in half and placing it on the seat and then just before she sat on it she lifted her skirt behind her so she sat on her bare bum and tampon as she did not want to find her skirt stained when they arrived in Spain, crumpled she would accept stained certainly not. David placed their carryon bag in the overhead locker and sat down next to his wife and smiled at her.

"I need a drink!" was all Julie could say.

Chapter 5. The Arrival

The coach transporting them arrived at their hotel, The Hotel Deborah, on the outskirts of Fuengirola, Costa Del Sol, Spain a little after 3.00pm, the hot afternoon sun beat down on them as they waited for their luggage to be unloaded which turned out to be a slow process as their driver was in his early sixties and would not allow anyone to help with the unloading, it did not help that he was nearly six foot 8 inches tall with a bad back which made him groan each time he stooped to grab a bag from the coaches hold. After each bag was deposited on the pavement by the driver he would hold his back and mutter something inaudible in Spanish before moving onto the next bag.

The receptionists at the hotel were all very jovial and helpful to their new arrivals and when eventually they all had their room keys it was very nearly 4.00pm so they made arrangements to meet up at the hotel bar at 5.00pm where they would have a drink whilst they decided on a plan of action for the evening. They were fortunate in as much as their rooms were all on the same floor the 6th.

Jill on entering the room opened her suitcase immediately and took out her washbag which held her toothbrush, soap, shower gel, brush, etc. and rushed into the bathroom. The first item taken off was her skirt so that she could tackle the offending tampon, removing proved slightly painful as the blood had dried fast to it and the offending cut began bleeding again immediately the tampon was removed.

Jill took off her blouse and bra to leave her naked as she reached over the bath and started the shower feeling the flow of water for the right temperature before she immersed herself under it. After a good 10 minutes under the shower Julie dried herself and felt much better now she was clean, wrapping the towel around herself and tying it inside her cleavage she opened the bathroom door releasing clouds of steam as she did so. David was sat on the bed already changed and ready to leave, he checked the time on his watch making sure his wife saw him as Julie walked towards the bed where she had dumped her suitcase.

"You go down to the bar while I change, I have to dry my hair and put some makeup on yet" said Jill as she did not want to ready herself with David checking his watch all the time.

"Ok, the lads may be down at the bar already anyway" agreed David, he did not need asking twice and gave Jill a kiss on her cheek before leaving the room.

Once David had left the room Jill relaxed and took out a small vanity mirror from her suitcase and removed the towel then tried inspecting her damaged backside with the aid of the mirror. It only appeared to be a small cut she had given herself but at least it had stopped bleeding for the time being anyway. Because of her cut backside she decided on wearing a pair of Armani jeans with a yellow T-shirt with a pair of yellow Nike trainers, she had already decided on very little makeup but did add a little yellow eyeshadow to accompany the blusher and red lipstick she had already put on.

Not wanting to be the first of the women in the bar she opened the doors to their balcony and stepped out to take in their surroundings. The hotel was on the front of the resort so the view of the sea was uninterrupted and she could see for miles to the left and right, the beach was still busy with sun worshippers and off to the left about a mile away she could make out the fishing boats in the harbour of Fuengirola, they were just on the outskirts of the town and just to the side of Mijas Costa. Below her was the hotel swimming pool which looked deserted with just a few people still on the sun loungers, this was to be there home for the next 7 days, with that thought Jill picked up her bag and room key and left to find the hotel bar.

Jill was the last of the party to arrive at the bar which was only occupied by the six of them; Steve had asked the barman why it was so quiet at this time of day to be answered that most of the guests where starting their evening meal as they were at an all-inclusive Hotel.

The conversation turned to food as they were all hungry not having bothered with the food offered on the plane, they were incredulous at the early time for the evening meal, they would realise later why it was such a popular time but for now they decided on finishing their drinks and moving on to a bar nearer to the centre of Fuengirola.

Leaving the hotel at just gone 5.30pm they found themselves walking towards the centre of town in bright warm sunshine, such a profound change to the chill they had left behind in Manchester. Julie and Steve took the lead walking close together with Steve's arm around Julie's shoulder, they did not hold hands although they liked to but with Steve's height and Julie's lack of it they could look a little odd. Michelle and Tony followed behind them holding hands as they almost always did with Michelle showing her figure to full advantage as she wore a pastel orange short dress that showed Michelle's cleavage to the full as she was almost hanging out of it and would certainly have to be careful if she needed to bend over and she most certainly would find the occasion to do so whether it warranted it or not, as usual she wore no underwear. Bringing up the rear was Jill and David walking together with no intimacy at all, Jill watched Julie and Steve walking arm in arm, Steve's arm warmly tucked around Julie's shoulder his hand occasionally moving to her breast with a slight squeeze before returning to her shoulder and Jill's head would playfully hit his arm when he did so, her arm firmly fixed around his waist. Jill's eyes then fell upon Michelle and Tony hand in hand as they walked together with a spring in their step.

Jill's blood was boiling as she walked along with her husband with no intimacy between them at all, Jill knew she had done nothing to deserve this and further her blood boiled, at what point she began to wonder would she blow.

Jill's thoughts were cut short as Julie and Steve walked them into a bar, Curley's Manchester Bar.

"Seems a good place to start" Steve stated as he began ordering drinks from the bar, "You find a table, I'll bring the drinks over" Steve instructed as he began talking to the large bald man behind the bar.

"Guess who I've been speaking to?" Steve asked as he began placing the drinks on the table from the tray he had brought from the bar.

"Curley" Michelle and Tony cried out in unison.

"Bang on!" Steve confirmed, a little annoyed they had guessed, "He was telling me he had hair 15 years ago when he opened this bar and he was 5 stone lighter; anyway he was telling me about a fantastic Venta he goes to that does slow cooked lamb that melts in your mouth, it's about 20 minutes away by taxi, what do you think?"

"I think a few more bars and then find somewhere in town to eat, that place will do again when we can go straight from the hotel" Tony argued finishing his drink and rising to leave followed by Michelle leaving the others to follow.

They soon found another bar and then another at which point it had turned 8.30pm and David pointed out they were teeing off at 8.00am and they still had not eaten, Jill could not help thinking what a killjoy, what an arsehole! More fully described what Jill was thinking.

They were now walking in the centre of Fuengirola all quite merry except for Jill who was feeling quite lonely despite her husband being alongside her. Julie spotted an Italian restaurant and swung around to the others asking, "How about pizza? It's quick and easy as it's nearly past the boys' bedtime."

"Hey! Easy with the bedtime will you," protested Tony, as they all piled into the restaurant.

The restaurant was almost full but they managed to find a table at the back of the restaurant near the kitchen, it was an annoying place to sit as the doors to the kitchen were opening and closing incessantly as the serving staff transported food to the various tables. They ordered drinks and settled down to inspect the menu but whilst doing so Steve suggested they just order a few pizzas that they could share then they could take in another bar before the men would need to return to their Hotel and rooms to sleep before their first game of golf in the morning. The waitress arrived at their table to take their order, an American Chinese woman in her 50's, as the men ordered for everyone Julie asked the waiter, "You're not Italian are you?"

"No, I'm American," the waitress answered abruptly turning her back to Julie as she made her way to the kitchen.

Steve turned to Julie saying, "Don't upset the waiting staff; I wanted to order another round of drinks before she left."

"Quick here comes another waiter; well he doesn't look very Italian either!" Julie added.

Steve managed to corner the waiter and order another round of drinks before Julie asked the Indian looking waiter, "You're not Italian are you?"

"Si, I was born in Milan," he answered smiling before turning towards the bar, he had been asked the same question so often, he just asked himself, why do people assume?

A very rotund black woman arrived at their table with their drinks; Steve leaned towards his wife putting a hand on her knee and quietly whispered in her ear, "Please don't ask if she is Italian."

Julie just looked at him with consternation and with that Steve knew he had prevented the question being asked. Julie could be and often was a little stupid not maliciously but just lacked a little thought and tact at times.

The restaurant was now bursting at the seams as people left so more people arrived at the tables before the staff could clean them and put clean utensils out, the bar area was also full of customers waiting for tables and when the food arrived they knew why, it was very good pizza which everyone wolfed down within minutes of its arrival.

Steve asked for and paid the bill which again was very reasonable for the food and the number of drinks they had consumed. They rose to leave and as they did so the American Chinese waitress appeared from the kitchen with a tray of piping hot food rushing past them she pointedly said in the direction of Julie "Arrivederchi!"

They had decided in the restaurant that they would head back towards the Hotel but would walk down the road behind the front as they did not want to pass where they had already walked.

Exiting the restaurant they turned left onto a side street which accommodated a number of bars on both sides which they ignored until they arrived at a main road which ran parallel to the front road, turning left they did not have to walk far before Michelle decided she wanted to try a bar with pink and blue neon lights outside which spelt out the name "Blues".

On entering they found it to be a little dimly lit and it took their eyes a few seconds to adjust, there was a long bar to the right which traversed the entire length of the room and again was illuminated by pink and blue neon. To the far left of the room were a series of booths and in the centre tables and chairs, all the booths were taken they noticed as they made their way to the bar. David ordered their drinks from a very thin attractive young man with very neat short black hair, he wore a shirt opened to his navel and he was wearing a very tight pair of sky blue hot pants. David turned back to Tony passing him a pint of lager whilst winking at him and nodding his head towards the barman making sure Tony had taken in the barman's attire.

The women were busy taking in their surroundings, Michelle being the first to notice some of the occupants of the booths, they were mainly couples, same sex couples, Michelle smiled as she realised they were in a gay bar and were probably in for a good night as there was a stage at the far end of the room which was being prepared for the nights turns whoever they might be. With that thought in her head she heard Julie cry out, "Look there's Lilly savage by the stage!"

A young man standing at the bar next to her retorted, "That's not Lilly Savage, that's my Gran!"

"Oh, sorry" was all Julie could muster as Jill and Michelle fell about laughing and Steve just held his head in his hands whilst Tony managed a giggle.

David took a large gulp of his lager as he continued to take in his surroundings and he was now sure of his findings so beckoned everyone to come closer as he was about to share something very profound, "I don't want to alarm you but I think we are in a gay bar," he whispered to everyone as they leaned in towards him, everyone rolled about laughing.

Tony said, "No shit!"

The bar was beginning to fill up as David suggested they grab a table whilst they still could, "You lot grab a table while I order some more drinks," said Tony as he finished the remaining dregs in his pint of Becks lager.

"Nice drink isn't it Becks? Better be careful as it goes down so quickly, I'll give you a hand with the drinks," Tony asked as he also finished his pint of Becks lager.

David and Tony arrived at their table with a fresh round of drinks just in time to hear the announcer welcome everyone to Blues and that the karaoke would start at 12.00 midnight but they were starting with a special guest and to introduce our guest is our resident DJ and compere Camp Teddie. After allowing the initial applause to die down a little, Camp Teddie jumped onto the stage in bright yellow trousers that were two sizes too small for him and a woman's pink blouse showing the top of a hairy chest which had been dyed purple to match the hair on his head which rose in spikes with the sides shaved an inch above his ears. He jumped up and down on the stage waving his arms in the air as he began to introduce the star act of the evening.

"For those of you who are first timers at Blues, welcome and have a great night with us, we want you to come back with friends and tell everyone what a great time you had here, and if you're straight, well it's not your fault we like you anyway and so let me start by saying at no expense at all we have starting our show tonight Rod "fat boy" Stewart, let's hear it for Rodders!"

At which a sixty year old 20 stone bald man climbed on stage and started singing "It's raining men" by the Weather Girls in the style and voice of Rod Stewart. Despite his appearance he sung his heart out and everyone in the bar rose to their feet singing along and dancing, he followed it by "We are sailing" again to raucous applause.

It was at this point that Julie noticed that two women in one of the booths were kissing passionately and said, "Look! There's two women over there kissing each other!"

"They are lesbians Julie," Michelle informed her.

"They are letting anyone into Europe these days," answered Julie.

"What! Where do you think they're from?" asked Jill.

"That war place," Julie said frowning at not being able to remember.

"Do you mean Lebanon?" asked Jill.

"Yes, yes that's it," confirmed Julie.

"They are Lebanese not lesbians," said Jill finding it difficult keeping a straight face.

"Well where do lesbians come from?" asked Julie now totally confused.

This left Jill and Michelle in a fit of hysterics; Julie joined in the laughter but did not know why. The men by this time were enjoying their own conversation as David constantly checked his watch. It was nearly 11.30pm and the night was just starting in Blues as the Rod Stewart impersonator continued to please the crowd, the men had decided it was time to leave as their thoughts turned to their mornings golf. None of the women were amused by this but rose to leave with their men, as soon as they left their table it was filled by a group of Geordie women who were just starting their evening.

On the walk back to the Hotel the men walked in front together ignoring the women as they talked of their golf plans for the day ahead. The women walking ten paces or so behind the men were bemoaning having to leave what appeared to be the beginning of a great night in Blues. With the distance between them and their men they openly discussed their resentment at having to leave and they decided they would have a drink at the Hotel bar whilst their men tucked themselves up in bed.

On the walk back to the Hotel they passed people on their way into the centre of town for a night out and people going from bar to bar enjoying themselves and here they were, three forty something year old women being escorted back to their Hotel by their husbands because they wanted to go to bed because they needed to be up early for a game of golf.

Also on the walk back to the Hotel David had developed an annoying trait of looking at his watch and then looking back at Jill, not a good idea with the mood Jill was in. On arriving back at the Hotel the men made their way to the lifts expecting their wives would follow but no, the women marched straight into the bar and ordered themselves a drink. When after a couple of minutes the wives had not arrived at the lifts the men looked at each other expecting one of them to make a decision. It was Steve that eventually did saying, "Suppose we better go look for them," at which the three of them went in search of their missing wives only to find them in the bar sat at one of the many empty tables with drinks in hand and chatting amiably between themselves.

Steve was again the one silently appointed to speak on behalf of the husbands, "We are going to bed now," he said lamely.

"Goodnight," the three wives answered in unison.

"Ur, ahem, are you not coming?" Steve muttered.

"No," the three wives said again in unison.

"Oh," was all Steve could muster as he turned and consulted with David and Tony.

"Goodnight then," the three husbands said in unison.

"Goodnight," the three wives answered again in unison.

The husbands turned on their heels looking at one another in some confusion as they made their way back to the lifts with their wives laughter ringing in their ears.

Jill rose from her seat saying, "Same again girls?" a statement not a question as they were still laughing at their husbands confusion and consternation. Jill returned to the table with their drinks and sat down putting her purse back into her handbag which she had placed under the table before saying, "I'm glad we're together as I wanted to have a word at the airport before my accident, which I am not going into by the way."

"Oh go on," insisted Michelle.

"Certainly not, anyway I don't know about you two but I am totally pissed off with these golfing holidays, it's all about the men and sod us we are just along for the ride. Let's face it we haven't exactly found common ground between us which has made things worse."

"So what do you propose?" asked Michelle whilst Julie took another slurp of her drink, clearly quite tipsy by now.

"It's quite simple really, we become friends, we may have to work at it but it will be worth it as these holidays are clearly going to continue and if they are then we should be enjoying ourselves. It shows with tonight, at Blues the night was just starting and the men decide they need to go to bed so they will be ready in the morning for their bloody golf so they expect us to follow them to bed, well no thanks, the night is young!"

"I don't see a problem with trying to be friends, it makes sense, especially if we have a good time, what do you think Julie?" said Michelle.

"Absolutely, whose round is it?" Julie slurred, she was pretty tipsy by now as she was not used to drinking.

"Mine I think," Michelle said bending to grab her purse from her bag which was also under the table.

"Shit Michelle, put that one back in, I thought they would've fallen out before now," Jill said playfully giggling at the freed breast.

Michelle returned her freed breast to within the confines of her dress smiling herself as she did so and gave Jill a hug before going to the bar. Returning with the drinks a couple of minutes later Michelle asked as she placed the drinks on the table, "Have you noticed we are drawing company?"

At which Jill and Julie looked around and both burst out laughing, they had indeed drawn company which made Michelle careful as she returned her purse to her bag, with her other arm she held her boobs in place so they would not fall out again. The company Michelle had been talking about were gentlemen of varying ages around seventy and eighty who had on seeing three attractive women enter the bar been drawn to them. What they had left was the Hotels evening entertainment which consisted of a lone female singer who was in her mid 60's and was over enthusiastically singing Dame Vera Lynn's "They'll be blue birds over the white cliffs of Dover," and terribly out of tune and so was the piano accompanying her.

"I don't think much of yours," said Jill to Michelle as Julie was now plastered and appeared to be in a world of her own.

"You'd be surprised! Give him half a lager and a packet of Viagra leave him for two hours to ferment then watch what happens when you show him a picture of Angela Rippon!" Michelle retorted.

Jill and Michelle chatted for another 15 minutes or so until they were interrupted by one of the men who had fallen asleep and had begun to snore, "We had best take Julie up to her room, shall we meet by the pool at 9.30am tomorrow?"

"Sounds good," said Michelle as she began lifting Julie out of her seat whilst Jill grabbed her handbag.

"I'll knock on for Julie as I don't think she'll remember a thing tomorrow," Jill added as the three of them made their way to the lift under the intense glare of old eyes upon them.

Jill arrived back in her room at just gone 1.00am and found David in bed supposedly asleep. Kicking off her trainers as she entered the room she began undoing her jeans before sitting on her side of the bed to pull them off, with her jeans on the floor she removed her t-shirt allowing that to drop beside her jeans and then throwing her bra on top of her t-shirt before making her way to the bathroom in just her knickers. Going for a pee as noisily as possible as she did not mind waking David before inspecting her damaged bottom, all well with her bottom she was halfway back to her bed when she realised she had not flushed the toilet, she turned and could not control the grin on her face as she pushed the button on top of the cistern, "Ooh, that's quite noisy for a toilet," she thought as her grin grew larger, returning to the bedroom she threw back the covers and fell into bed.

She did not hear the "Tut" that came from David.

Chapter 6 Sunday

Jill woke suddenly the next morning from the loud bang as their door closed shut, David clearly banging the door in reprisal for the toilet flushing incident the previous night from Jill. Rolling to her right and raising herself up on one elbow she stretched to grab her watch off the bedside cabinet, moving the watch toward her eyes then away again to focus clearly on the dials she saw it was 6.30am, "Bollocks" was all she could muster as she crashed down on the bed again and rolled over on her left side pulling the covers over herself. She had 3 hours until she was to meet Michelle and Julie; the sun had begun to shine through the windows as David had opened the curtains before leaving the room, "Tosser" she said as she realised what he had done and pulled the sheets over her face to block out the suns glare.

The sun's glare was stronger now and much warmer as Jill stretched out an arm to where she thought she had placed her watch on the bedside cabinet, moving her hand about she found her watch and brought it under the sheets to check the time, "Shit!" she screamed as she threw the covers off and jumped out of bed pulling her knickers off at the same time she almost fell over as she made her way to the bathroom, it was 9.00am.

Jill showered in rapid time and brushed her teeth as she did so she could not help noticing her eyes were a little bloodshot, she took hold of her vanity mirror and began moving it around under her bum again inspecting the damage which was now healing nicely although still had a scab. Throwing the mirror into the sink she ran into the bedroom and rummaged through her suitcase until she found the new tangerine bikini she had bought especially for this trip, she ripped off the price tags and put it on returning to the bathroom to check that it looked alright on in the mirror, not bad at all, it certainly showed off her breasts nicely as it pushed them up slightly making them look a little larger than they were, not that she needed that with her breasts. She now looked in her suitcase for her pleated white short tennis skirt and she found a short orange t-shirt which she also put on, she grabbed her handbag from last night and emptied the contents onto her bed whilst she found a small multi coloured fabric bag which she normally used on holiday for sunbathing or just during the day, she couldn't be bothered with shoes so she just put on some flip flops grabbed her room key and abandoned the room.

Jill had just pressed the button to summon the lift when she realised that she had told Michelle she would knock on for Julie before they met up at 9.30am by the pool. Knocking on Julie and Steve's door proved fruitless and so she decided to go down to the pool and see if Julie had somehow remembered to meet up.

Walking through the large empty entertainment area where last night the singer was murdering Vera Lynn's songs Jill could make out Michelle and Julie putting their towels on a couple of sun loungers, Michelle waved as she noticed Jill approach, "Not many people out here yet" she said, "Take your pick, if we don't like it here we can move anywhere."

"Christ, do think it's going to be like this all day?" Jill responded.

"Dunno, hope not, it's a bit boring like this isn't it?" Julie cut in.

"Well let's give it an hour and see what it's like then," Michelle decided.

They began to make themselves comfortable; the sun was beaming down on them as Michelle took off her baggy beach dress to reveal bare breasts and the skimpiest bikini bottoms that could just about not be classed as a G-string, as she took out of her bag a bottle of Ambre Soliel Julie began removing her blouse to reveal a multi coloured flowered pattern bikini she then unzipped her skirt allowing it to fall to the concrete ground.

The three of them sat on their sun loungers, Michelle being the first to apply sun tan lotion to her shoulders and arms before squirting a large amount into both palms to tackle her voluminous breasts. Jill and Julie now began to apply suntan lotion to their fronts as

Michelle said, "Looks like there's going to be a charge for the sun lounges," as she flicked her head in the direction of the Hotel entrance they had just come from. There were about thirty people coming towards them mainly men only about six elderly women, they were about to be engulfed by male pensioners one actually had a Zimmer frame and two were riding mobility scooters. They were approaching the girls like a hoard of zombies, albeit very old and slow zombies.

"Oh fuck this!" Michelle cried out as she grabbed her beach dress and began to pull it over her head, as it passed over her breasts you could almost visibly see the zombies stop in their stride and slowly start up again. Jill and Julie began to dress as well.

"Suppose we can try the beach," suggested Julie.

"Don't want to go to the beach, bloody sand finds its way into every orifice, it's like masturbating with sandpaper!" protested Michelle remembering a time some years prior on the sand dunes of St. Anne's near Blackpool.

"Hadn't planned on masturbating," Julie said almost to herself.

They collected their things together, towels, sun tan lotion etc, and placed them in their bags as they began to walk out of the pool area by the exit which leads directly onto the front road. They turned right out of the Hotel complex as they said they had been left the night before having decided to find a café where they could have a coffee and something to eat as none of them had breakfast.

Once ensconced in a café they could discuss their next course of action as the Hotel appeared to be a dead loss to them. They came upon a Spanish venta with numerous tables outside that were occupied by mainly Spanish people which occurred to them to be a good sign so they made their way inside and ordered coffee which they were told would be brought outside for them if they would like to find a table. They began discussing their options which early on they discounted the Hotel as it was clearly focused on an elderly clientele. They then decided they needed to find a base but where, it went silent as they drank their coffee and thought individually about their predicament. Jill had decided she was hungry so suggested they order some tapas and more coffee while they further considered their best options. They authorised Jill to go to the tapas bar and order for all of them, she was not sure what the individual tapas were but the waiter was young and his English was very good and he could not have been more helpful or patient as Jill ordered far too much for the three of them or so he thought.

While they waited for their tapas to arrive the conversation dried up and so Jill looked around her at the people in the café which were mainly Spanish, a table which seemed to be occupied by Germans, a table with 3 women but Jill could not make out what language they were talking, another table with two English couples in their late twenties, an old Spanish man occupied a table by the entrance door, he had placed his walking stick on the table and had a jet black Jack Russell dog lying across his feet, his waiter arrived with his coffee and a bowl of water for his dog. Inside the café there were two tables of Spanish men playing drafts whilst others standing watched the games progress.

Jill found it relaxing in the café as there was no rush, the waiters went about their business at a leisurely pace and one was heading towards them with his tray held high laden full of tapas for the women, he placed them on the table one by one with a larger plate of fresh cut French bread, before turning to leave he said he would return in a minute with fresh coffee for them and smiled at each one of them in turn, Jill was sure he left Michelle with the larger smile no doubt to match her breasts which once again were nearly hanging out.

From where Jill sat she could see all the way into Fuengirola and beyond as the resort formed a long semi-circle fronted by the large high rise hotels all along the resort in front of which was the main road then a wide walkway some 12 feet wide and more in places before the beach of beautiful golden sand. It was not even noon yet as the temperature was approaching 80 degrees yet it did not feel that hot as there was a light breeze coming from the sea which appeared calm as it reflected the sun in differing patterns.

"So what are we going to do? The hotel is crap, are we all agreed?" asked Michelle taking a mouthful of braised pork with a piece of bread in her hand about to follow the pork.

"I still think we could use the beach, just look how many are and there are sun loungers everywhere," said Julie.

"No thanks, the beach is not for me," Michelle answered adamantly.

"Well if we are not going to use the beach I can only think of finding another hotel pool area to use, they wouldn't know we were not registered there, there must be hundreds of people in some of these hotels, they're massive," suggested Jill.

"Great, trust the men to book a crap hotel," Said Michelle tucking into some deep fried squid.

"If that's the best we can come up with then I suppose that is what we will have to do," Julie resigned herself to say.

"It's not ideal I grant you but what else is there?" asked Jill.

"Dunno," Michelle managed in between mouthfuls of calamari.

"Ladies, I couldn't help overhearing your conversation, I may be able to help. My name is Charles; I live just down the road about a quarter of a mile away."

The women turned as one to observe a gentleman at the table next to them, he was tall at six foot well-built but not over muscly with dark brown hair cut old style with a side parting. He was wearing a pair of khaki shorts with a smartly pressed short sleeved yellow shirt and a pair of cotton sandals on his feet, he was attractive but not overly so with piercing blue eyes and ever so long eye latches which were incredibly sexy.

The women looked at each other and back at Charles; there was a definite pregnant pause so Jill took it upon herself to talk for the others, "How can you help? And don't you know it is rude to listen in to other people's conversations?"

"My apologies of course ladies, I don't want to appear rude but then it would be rude not to help if I could, would it not?" asked Charles putting the ball back in their court.

"Your apology is accepted but I ask again, how can you help?" Jill said as she found herself looking deep into Charles's eyes.

"Well as I mentioned I live in a villa just a quarter of a mile away, it has a pool, sun loungers, it's grounds are private and are not overlooked, you may use my facilities should you so wish, it would give you another option," Charles said with no discernible accent.

"We don't know you, why would you make such an offer?" asked Jill suspiciously. Michelle and Julie were looking from Jill to Charles and from Charles to Jill.

"Why not, it is a large villa and there is just me, it seems a pity to waste it when you could make such good use of it," answered Charles.

"I'm really not too sure, thanks for the offer but I think we will make our own arrangements all the same," said Jill with again Michelle and Julie looking from one to the other and back again.

"Of course," said Charles and picked up his copy of Three Blind Mice by James Patterson just as a waiter brought him a cup of black coffee; he thanked the waiter and returned to his book.

Michelle nudged Jill sharply in the arm, "What's the matter with you? It's the best offer we are likely to have from anyone, it's better than that bloody hotel!"

"Who is he and why would he make such an offer?" asked Jill firmly.

"I don't know, maybe he's lonely," was all Michelle could come up with.

"He ain't gonna be lonely looking like that now is he!?" admitted Jill.

"Well ask him then," said Michelle.

"Ask him what?" asked Jill.

"WHY! For Christ's sake!"

Jill coughed slightly putting her hand over her mouth whilst looking first at Charles and then at Michelle and Julie.

Charles looked up from his book and smiled pleasantly at Jill as she asked, "Why would you make us such an offer, you don't know us?"

Charles placed his book on the table and turned to the women addressing all of them," The offer is there, why don't you go and have a look at the place by yourselves it is open, you go down this road to the traffic lights and turn left, it is further down the road a little on the right surrounded by a 12 foot high wall and there are two concrete lions guarding the driveway, you can't miss it, or don't go it is up to you."

The women looked at each other, Julie said, "I'm happy with the beach."

Michelle turned to the others and said, "Well I'm takin a look, are you coming?" She already had her bag in her hand as she rose from the table leaving Jill and Julie to follow in her wake.

Jill turned away from the other two saying, "We haven't paid the bill, wait there for me," and Jill walked inside past the draughts playing tables and paid the bill leaving a larger than normal tip as she liked her waiter for his patience, his bottom was pretty cute as well.

Walking towards the traffic lights they passed numerous bars and cafes as they argued amongst themselves, Jill and Julie were still against going to the villa as they suspected Michelle had her mind on Charles' body. Turning right at the lights they could see they did not have much farther to walk as the surrounding wall of the villa was visible. There were just a few shops on their left as they turned from the lights and on the opposite side of the road was open field which had recently had its crop of sweetcorn harvested leaving the white stone wall of the villa clearly on view, it looked quite old with bougainvillea trellising down the walls as if overflowing from the inside out.

After walking a few more yards they could see the concrete lions about three feet tall guarding the entrance. The entrance consisted of two large columns attached on each side of the wall holding two large open metal gates approximately ten foot tall, a gravel driveway led to the large villa directly in front of them and to the side was parked a silver Audi A4. They walked up to the large domed double front door and found it locked.

"Charles said it was open," said Jill.

"Probably is round the back," said Michelle taking the lead again around the side of the house where they found a huge garden full of lemon and orange trees along with mature and flourishing flower beds and lush green grass.

Then as they rounded the side of the whitewashed villa they glanced upon a huge oval shaped swimming pool, on the other side of the pool were two free standing showers and a large tiled floor area where eight polished varnish wooden sun loungers rested with yellow cushions sat atop the length of the loungers. Some twenty feet beyond was the surrounding wall covered again in brightly red coloured bougainvillea and further to the right near the wall was a large wooden varnished shed. Michelle walked up to the nearest sun lounger and dropped her bag on it saying, "I'm home."

"So this is how the other half live," said Jill taking in fully her surroundings, it was beautiful to say the least.

"Where is she going now?" asked Julie as she saw Michelle heading towards the rear entrance to the villa.

The rear of the villa housed a rap around balcony to the left which protruded about ten feet from the main wall which left the underneath sheltered and in shade so it housed two large bamboo settees in between which was a table made in the same bamboo. Then there were large concertina doors some sixteen feet long which opened onto a large lounge in front with a stone fireplace on the far wall in the centre and an open plan kitchen on the left with a very large American fridge and a double gas cooker against the wall, on the far left housed a sink and draining board below a window. In the far left corner of the room was an open staircase up to a mezzanine bedroom which had an ensuite bathroom and French doors leading to the balcony. To the right of the fireplace was a passageway that led to three more bedrooms and two bathrooms. In the lounge area there were three sofas and numerous small tables in the centre and on the far right a dining table with ten chairs. The villa was furnished impeccably.

Jill and Julie followed Michelle into the villa who was already inspecting the contents of the fridge selecting a bottle of nicely chilled Spanish white wine, shutting the fridge door she began opening drawers looking for a corkscrew which she found in the second drawer she opened.

"I really don't think you should be doing that, I thought we were just having a look around," said Julie heading for the open door.

"Oh chill out, he said to make ourselves at home," said Michelle as she began opening the bottle of wine looking about her for suitable glasses.

"Did he? I don't remember him saying make ourselves at home," added Jill.

"Well, if he didn't it was implied," insisted Michelle finding suitable wine glasses in a cupboard and taking out three.

"I am really not comfortable with this," said Julie from outside looking around as if she was to be caught stealing apples.

"For Christ's sake Julie will you chill out, what's the problem?" said Michelle passing a glass of wine to Jill and taking the two other glasses outside onto the veranda passing one to the cowering Julie.

Michelle and Jill sat in one of the bamboo settees clunked glasses and said cheers to each other before sampling the wine.

"Oooh, not bad wine, I don't know the make though, perhaps it's a local vineyard," said Michelle taking another sip of wine.

"I really don't think we should be drinking his wine like this," said Julie placing her glass on the table next to where Jill was sitting.

"Oh chill out Julie," added Jill joining Michelle's side of the argument now, "so what are we going to do? Do we take up this Charles's offer or not?"

"I'm all for it, where else are we going to find somewhere like this, it's perfect," confirmed Michelle.

"But we don't know the guy and why would he make such a generous offer to people he doesn't know and we don't know him," said Julie moving further away onto the grass.

"Well I'm with Michelle on this, it is pretty perfect, the hotel is horrible, Michelle doesn't want the beach, as for not knowing the guy well we will after we spend the week here, right," said Jill.

"C'mon Julie, what's the problem?" persisted Michelle.

"He didn't say to drink his wine for Christ's sake!" said Julie.

"Is that it? So if he is ok with us drinking his wine are you ok with trying this place out?" asked Michelle.

"I suppose....if he is ok with you drinking his wine....then I suppose we could try it for a day and see how it goes......I suppose," said Julie clearly still uncomfortable with the arrangement.

"Hallelujah!" cried out Michelle turning to Jill who was now smiling.

"I see you have made yourselves at home," said Charles suddenly appearing from around the corner of the villa.

"Nice wine," said Michelle blatantly.

"I am so pleased you like it, it is quite local, from a vineyard only 20 miles away," said Charles smiling as he did so.

"We didn't mean to steal it, we will pay for it," cried out Julie.

"No need, I am so pleased you made yourselves at home, now let me show you around."

With which Charles turned and began gesturing with his arms, "this of course is the living room with open plan kitchen, please tell me if I begin to sound like an estate agent, the corridor to the side of the fireplace leads to three bedrooms and two bathrooms, please feel free to use any as you wish, up the stairs is my bedroom which leads to the balcony where I spend most of my time either working or reading, I do tend to read a lot and outside of course there is the pool, the showers outside are only cold water I'm afraid, but as I've said you are welcome to use the bathrooms in the villa."

"You really have a beautiful home," commented Jill.

"Thank you, it is a little large for one person but it suits my needs amply. You must also feel free to help yourselves to food and snacks from the fridge, there is also tea and coffee....and as you have found wine. For stronger drinks there is a drinks cabinet by the dining table. Is there anything I have forgotten?" asked Charles.

"Wow no, it's great......perfect in fact." Michelle managed to say once she had taken her eyes off Charles.

"Then I will leave you ladies to your decision."

With that Charles bowed ever so slightly before walking across to the stairs and alighting them leaving the three women in silence looking at each other.

"Another wine I think," said Jill taking charge of the situation moving to the fridge and taking out another bottle of wine, "Where did you find the corkscrew Michelle?"

With their glasses recharged the three of them walked out to the sun lounges by the pool, Julie had downed her original full glass of wine in one large gulp for it to be refreshed, she felt it go to her head a little so made a mental note not to gulp a whole glass like that in future. The sun was now beating down hard on them as the temperature hit the 80's, so Jill suggested they take their bags inside out of the sun just taking out of them what they needed, they all took sun lotion out and began putting some on their arms and shoulders. Once a little sun lotion was applied Jill took their bags inside depositing them on one of the sofas by the large stone fireplace and then returning outside to the others.

"So what's the verdict?" Jill asked looking at Michelle and Julie, not that she needed an answer from Michelle her position was obvious.

"It's simply perfect and such a charming host," commented Michelle, Jill and Michelle both turned to Julie who was now playing with her wine glass debating whether she dared take another sip yet or whether she should wait a few minutes more.

"Well?" Jill and Michelle asked again in unison after waiting a couple of minutes for Julie to answer.

"Well he seems nice," was all Julie could manage as she took a sip of wine after finally making a decision.

"Right, so are we all agreed to give it ago?" asked Jill.

"Yep, definitely," agreed Michelle turning to Julie for her decision.

"Well?" Jill and Michelle again in unison asked Julie as she had not answered them.

"I guess….if you think….alright I suppose," Julie finally agreed.

"Hallelujah! Julie!" cried both Jill and Michelle laughing.

"It's a yes, thank you!" Jill said up to Charles who she could just make out sitting on his balcony.

"An excellent choice ladies," Charles returned standing and giving a little bow to the three women.

Jill suggested they make themselves comfortable then adjusting her sun lounger to take full advantage of the sun before stripping down to her bikini, the others following her lead. Michelle was positioned on the right with Julie next to her and Jill on the left. Michelle lifted off her beach dress to reveal her naked breasts which were already tanned with no white bits, she then began taking off her bikini bottoms whilst Jill and Julie looked on with disbelief on their faces, there were slight signs of some faded white bits where her bikini bottoms had previously been and they couldn't help but notice that Michelle was totally smooth below, not a single hair in sight.

Jill and Julie looked at each other and looked away trying to avoid eye contact with Michelle, Julie opened her mouth to say something but thought better of it and stayed silent, reaching instead for her sun cream.

Michelle was finishing off applying sun cream to her ample front when she noticed Jill and Julie had their bikini's on and turning to them said, "I thought you two would have at least gone topless after all there is just us here it's private."

"There is Charles," said Julie.

"Who couldn't give a damn, he's on his balcony reading or working or whatever; C'mon topless at least girls!" demanded Michelle.

Jill shrugged her shoulders and proceeded to take off her bikini top reaching for her sun cream again to cover her white breasts. Once Jill had finished applying the cream both her and Michelle turned to Julie who as yet had not moved.

"What?" she said.

"Off!" Michelle and Jill urged together.

"But….," Julie began.

"Off," Michelle and Jill instructed again.

Begrudgingly Julie began to slowly take off her Bikini top and looked around in case we had suddenly been invaded by "Boob snoopers". Julie took another large swig of wine before grabbing her sun cream to apply to her ultra-white breasts.

As all three lay back on their individual sun loungers Michelle commented, "This is just perfection."

All Michelle was wearing was a smile and her favourite pair of Gucci sunglasses which she had owned for about 10 years ever since she found them abandoned under a sun lounger at a hotel her and Tony had been staying at in Los Gigantes on Tenerife.

They had been laying in silence allowing the sun to caress their bodies for almost 20 minutes when the depth of silence was suddenly broken by the sound of Julie's snoring, Jill and Michelle both shot up from the waist turning to check that it was indeed Julie that was so ungraciously breaking the ambience of the silence. It was, Jill and Michelle's eyes left Julie's vibrating lips as they looked at each other in disbelief and burst into laughter at Julie's expense.

"Must have been the wine," Jill suggested.

"We only had two glasses," commented Michelle.

"Doesn't she look sweet……well, when she isn't snoring?" giggled Jill.

"It's a pity she isn't laying on her front; we could have stuck a flower out of her bum," suggested Michelle.

"No it's perfect how she is, where did she put her sun block?" asked Jill.

"Why what have you in mind?" asked Michelle.

"Just this," said Jill reaching for Julie's sunblock which she had spotted under Julie's sun lounger.

Opening the top of the bottle Jill squeezed much more than you would normally apply onto her hands and touched her hands together before she placed each hand onto one of Julie's breasts palm on her nipple with fingers facing up towards her neck, her whole body was white but her breasts more so as they rarely faced the sun. Julie's body had just begun to catch the sun's rays and start to pink.

"She will go absolutely spare when she notices that, how long are you going to let her ripen in the sun?" asked Michelle.

"Oh, as long as she snores seems fair don't you think?" suggested Jill.

"I guess so, but God help you when she sees it, it won't take long in this heat you know," answered Michelle.

It was nearly 40 minutes later that both Jill and Michelle were totally fed up with the constant rhythmic snoring emanating from Julie so they decided to wake her suggesting that she needed to apply more sun block to her ever increasing pinking body or turn over and tan her back.

"Oh must have dozed off for a minute, probably best if I turn over and let my back feel the sun for a while, my front feels a little sore it will need some after sun later, will one of you put some sun block on my back for me?" commented Julie.

Jill and Michelle looked across at each other and simultaneously mouthed "a minute". Their eyes widened as Julie rose to turn onto her front, white patches in the shape of two hands were surrounded by bright pink which would be exacerbated later, Jill and Michelle looked at each other again and mouthed "OH FUCK".

"Pass me your bottle I'll put some on for you," offered Jill.

After smothering after sun all over Julie's back Julie continued to spread the sun block onto the backs of her legs before lying on her stomach so that the sun could now attack her white back, she had to rise up again from the bed to lower the headrest of the sun lounger making it a flatbed to lie on, lying down again and closing her eyes to shield them from the sun's rays she did not notice Jill and Michelle looking at each other and flapping their hands about as the black and white minstrels did on TV years ago and laughing and giggling in silence as they did so.

The three of them sun bathed in silence, it was ever so quiet with just the occasional tweet of birds in the distance and the ever so quiet rustle of leaves from the trees in the garden from the slight warm breeze from the direction of the sea. Occasionally they could just make out a whoosh as a car past by outside on the road the other side of the surrounding wall and a slightly louder whoosh as a bus or an articulated lorry past by the property. After some twenty minutes or so Jill rose and sat on her sun lounger wiping her face with her hands and looking at all the sweat her hands had taken off her face, she decided to take a dip in the pool to cool down before starting to sun her back.

The water in the pool was warm but still was sufficiently cold enough for a lovely cooling effect in the heat of the afternoon as the temperature neared the 90's. Feeling comfortably cool Jill lifted herself out of the pool planting her bum on the side of the pool leaving her feet in the water, she was not sure how long she sat there with her feet moving backwards and forwards alternatively in the cool pool water but when she turned and lifted herself fully out of the pool moving back to her sun lounger she could not help notice that Michelle was missing, maybe she has gone for another glass of wine she thought as she lay on her stomach on the sun lounger after first lowering the headrest as Julie had done before her. The water from the pool still on her body had a cooling soothing effect in the slight breeze but it soon dried under the sun's powerful glare.

With Jill in the pool and Julie quiet again on her sun lounger Michelle had decided to explore a little in the villa. She walked in through the open doors as naked as the day she was born and stood quietly for a few minutes alongside the kitchen waiting for her eyes to adjust from the brilliant sunshine outside to the relative darkness of the villa's living room.

As Michelle's eyes adjusted so the room brightened and the colours returned to the room. Her intentions were clear as she now moved towards the stairs which would take her to the mezzanine bedroom and to the balcony where Charles spent his time. Arriving at the top of the stairs Michelle stayed on the last stair as she took in the ambience of the bedroom, it looked quite sparse, there was a king size bed obviously, to the right and against the far wall a large wardrobe which appeared to have been made of a dark oak and looked to be antique of quality, either side of the bed were small stands that housed lightshades and to the left of the bed a large heavy looking chest of drawers in the same design as the wardrobe, the floor was made up of red tiles approximately 18 inches square and were covered by a couple of rugs, finally on the left of the room before the double open French doors sat a round table again in the same style as the wardrobe and chest of drawers.

Michelle could not see Charles from where she stood on the top stair so she moved on up and into the bedroom unannounced and uninvited not for the first time either. She stepped one yard then two yards then stopped and looked around the bedroom, silence, eerily silence, something was not right about the bedroom but Michelle could not put her finger on it, it was impeccably clean and immaculate in every way but there was something.

Just then Charles appeared through the French doors wearing just his khaki shorts which was more than Michelle had on, Michelle froze, Charles smiled as he walked slowly towards Michelle's nakedness, he was upon her and his neck leaned towards Michelle's as she thought he was about to kiss her as his lips approached hers slowly, she could feel the warmth of his breath as his lips barely touched hers and was gone again, she stood there frozen but not in fear at least she did not think it was fear, she hoped it was not fear, she was still wet with sweat from her sunbathing whilst Charles was dry with no sun lotion on his body anywhere, she dare not move as Charles circled behind her silently and she caught the warmth from his body.

Then she felt him blowing gently over her shoulders first the left and then the right leaving her for a second to feel the pleasure before he again blew on her from the centre of her shoulders all the way down her spine to the cheeks of her bottom, Michelle shook with delight as she became instantly aroused. Turning Michelle found Charles on his knees and he began to blow gently between her legs, her legs shook as he licked gently on her lips parting them, Michelle's head flung back in sheer delight as his tongue found and caressed her clitoris, she stepped her legs further apart as her breathing became deeper and heavier, she asked herself how long she could hold on as Charles rose and turned Michelle towards the beds headboard, he gently moved her onto the bed so that she was on all fours with her feet hanging over the edge of the mattress, she waited as she felt one of his hands caressing her buttocks and heard his zip and then with her peripheral vision saw his khaki shorts drop to the floor, once more her lips parted as he entered her and began his rhythmic probing in and out slowly at first and for what seemed an age as she groaned in delight at every thrust as her throat dried and the sweat left her body dripping as it did onto the bed.

Then she felt something probing around her backside she thought at first it was his finger or thumb that was going to enter her there but it was far too big for that as it fell in with the probing and thrusting of his cock, she realised it was a vibrator that Charles had thrust into her as it tried to leave her as Charles thrust back and then it was thrust straight back inside her as Charles thrust forward again by his stomach, her cries of delight became louder and louder until suddenly Charles stopped, she felt his hands behind her and then she realised what he was doing as the vibrator began vibrating noisily and Charles re started his gyrating, speeding up, Michelle could not control herself anymore as she screamed out in sheer delight as she climaxed harder than she could remember for a long time. Charles came soon after and Michelle collapsed on the bed as Charles pulled away leaving the vibrating dildo falling to the floor as it continued vibrating around in a circle on top of the dull red floor tiles, Michelle looked around from her collapsed position on the bed to find Charles had disappeared she rose to her feet dripping wet with sweat and picked up the vibrator twisting the end to switch it off.

Michelle heard the shower starting in the bathroom and realised that she had not been invited to join Charles by the fact that the bathroom door was closed. Michelle just shrugged at the snub and decided to stand up off the bed as the sweat from her body was leaving a damp patch on the bed where she sat. Michelle placed the vibrator on the bed next to where she had been sitting, the duvet showed several wet patches of sweat and Michelle wondered how long it would take to dry in the heat.

Wondering about the room slowly Michelle looked about and considered what it was that she was missing, something did not appear right about the room but she could not quite put her finger on it. Michelle's wondering took her to the balcony stepping onto it she had to move three paces further before she could she Jill and Julie who were now sat upright on their sun loungers chatting amiably away with one another. Suddenly she heard the bathroom door open and Charles stood in the doorway wearing a wide cheeky grin on his face and a white towel wrapped around his waist with clouds of steam rising from his shoulders and behind him steam was escaping from the bathroom.

"May I?" she asked nodding towards the bathroom.

"Of course," Charles answered whilst moving out of the way and flaying his arm in the bathrooms direction.

He walked out onto the balcony and leaned with both hands in front of him on the three foot high wall that surrounded the entire balcony, it was not a solid wall it consisted of Doric type white stone colonnades at twelve inch intervals and capped with three inch thick matching stone.

Charles could clearly see Jill and Julie sat on their sun lounges chatting away and trying not to be seen looking up at him, in vain as it turned out as Charles noticed everything including their chatter quietening as they spotted him with their peripheral vision.

He turned leaving them a view of his back and broad shoulders as his pert bum now rested against the stone wall of the balcony he crossed his arms and smiled to himself as he waited for Michelle to finish in his bathroom. Some five minutes later Michelle walked out of the bathroom having dried herself also with a white towel, she thought it best to dry herself properly as she had finished her shower with cold water to cool herself down and had given herself goose bumps and seriously erect nipples.

She walked over to the bed and picked up the vibrator as Charles re-entered the bedroom, she smiled in his direction as she about turned and walked slowly back into the bathroom to wash and dry the vibrator. Walking back into the bedroom once again from the bathroom with the vibrator in her raised and turning hand she said to Charles.

"This was a surprise; do you keep it on call for all your women?"

"I thought you would have recognised it," replied Charles, "as I found it in your bag."

"My Bag? You couldn't possibly have found it in my bag as I don't own such a thing."

"But it was hanging out of the middle bag on the couch; I thought I saw you place the bag there," said Charles.

With that Michelle moved towards the stairs still shaking the vibrator in her hand and looking down towards their three bags, "The middle bag is Jill's, my God, Jill uses a vibrator, I would never have thought that she would…go Jill!" said Michelle.

"Hand it over and I will see to it that it's returned safely and discreetly," said Charles holding out his left hand.

Michelle ignored Charles's offer and said, "That's ok, I'll return it."

With a suitably sly grin on her face as she turned back to see Charles' reaction she was disappointed to see he was making his way back out onto the balcony which no doubt meant she had been dismissed.

Michelle made her way down the stairs to replace the vibrator into Jill's bag but that was never her intention. At the couch with their bags Jill's was indeed in the centre slightly leaning over but not enough to displace the contents so Michelle moved it closer to the edge of the brown leather couch and over on its side and encouraged a nail varnish and eyeliner out of the bag to lie beside it. Then she placed the vibrator in centre of the Persian rug that separated the two brown leather couches, happy with her work she danced her way over to the kitchen singing, "I should be so lucky" by Kylie Minogue and opened the large fridge door and took out another bottle of wine, as she did so she could see Jill approaching so she ducked down behind the breakfast bar with a bottle of wine in one hand and a corkscrew in the other and giggling to herself like Muttley out of Wacky Races.

Jill Marched into the villa and made her way towards the corridor that housed the two bathrooms with Michelle discreetly observing from behind the breakfast bar. Michelle thought that Jill was going to miss the vibrator lying on the carpet as she passed the couch on the other side heading towards the bathroom but Jill pulled up in a dead stop right alongside were the vibrator was positioned and looked around the room in clear despair at the thought someone might have discovered her little pastime. Michelle ducked her head back down quickly as Jill looked in her direction. When she looked over the top of the breakfast bar again she caught Jill's backside in the air as she bent over to retrieve her vibrator, she turned and buried it in the bottom of her bag and returned her eyeliner and nail varnish and zipped the bag closed and placed it against the back cushion of the couch before continuing her journey to the bathroom but before moving off again she looked around the room again to make sure she had not been observed, once happy her secret was safe she continued to the bathroom leaving Michelle in silent hysterics behind the breakfast bar.

When Jill returned to her sun lounger she found Michelle had returned also with a glass of cold white wine for each of them. Jill and Julie thanked Michelle for the glass of wine but both of them struggled looking Michelle in the eyes after experiencing the noise of her lovemaking.

It was Jill who said, "I suppose we need to think about moving and making our way back to the Hotel."

"I guess so." Said Michelle and Julie in unison.

"Finish the wine first and then wash the glasses, the glasses we used before are still on the bamboo table, I don't want Charles thinking we're slobs," said Michelle.

"You wouldn't," said Julie sarcastically.

"What do you mean by that," countered Michelle looking directly at Julie.

"Now girls, remember what we agreed.....friends....remember," said Jill a little more sternly than she meant.

"OK, ok, ok, friends," said Michelle breaking into a smile and giving Julie a friendly nudge.

"Ok, friends," said Julie begrudgingly.

Michelle turned to Jill and mimed shaking her hands at the same time, "Until she sees her boobs!"

With their wine finished Jill and Michelle headed into the villa with the glasses, Michelle picked up the glasses from the bamboo table on the way inside the villa. They left Julie outside to tidy up the sun loungers which took all of one minute; she then replaced her bikini top and dressed for the journey back to their hotel.

Jill and Michelle joined Julie outside having washed and dried the wine glasses and returned them to their rightful shelf and brought their bags with them Michelle handed over Julie's bag with a grin on her face which she did not realise she was showing, she was just thinking of Jill's face when she spotted her vibrator sitting on the middle of the Persian rug.

"What?" Julie asked.

"Nothing," Michelle shrugged at Julie's question; Jill just looked over at the two of them as she put on her flip flops.

Jill called up to Charles, "We're leaving now; we will see you tomorrow if that's alright?"

The three women huddled together waiting for a response from Charles.

"Will you be available later around 11pm?" asked Charles.

"Not sure, we don't know what our husbands have in mind, why?" answered Jill.

"Well if you are about you could meet me at Bulbous Billy's Bar, it's near Blue's the bar you said you had been to, just ask anyone around there, everyone knows Bulbous Billy's," said Charles.

"Ok we will bear it in mind, and thanks for letting us use your villa," said Michelle determined they would make the rendezvous.

They waved goodbye as they headed around the side of the villa and out onto the main road and back the way they had come heading for the hotel.

It was nearly 5.30pm when they walked through the main entrance doors of the hotel and through the lounge area, it was still hot outside and they had all began sweating again on the walk back as their idle chatter focused on where they would end up that night, they had all decided to go straight to their rooms so that they could shower before their husbands arrived back from the golf club.

They circled around the bar where they had their drink the night before to find their husbands sat at the bar with pints of larger in front of them. "It would be rude not to," suggested Michelle.

"Not for me, I really need to shower," said Jill.

"Me too," added Julie.

"Spoilsports, ok I could do with another shower," agreed Michelle.

"We'll see you upstairs," they said to their men and left them heading in the direction of the lift.

In the lift they discussed their own plan for the evening which meant leaving their husbands as soon as they could so they could enjoy the evening themselves. They agreed to see how the evening panned out but as a last recourse they would come back to the hotel with their husbands and tell them they were having a drink together in the bar whilst the men obtained their beauty sleep which they would surely need if they were to accomplish the desired score on theirs cards tomorrow. Then with their husbands tucked safely away in bed they would go to either Blue's or this Bulbous Billy's Bar and join Charles once again.

Having taken a leisurely shower and taken time over her hair and makeup Jill was more than happy with the result and had decided she wanted to look and feel sexy this evening.

A pastel yellow pleated skirt which fell to just above her knees was to be accompanied with a white bra and blouse which would show off her newly acquired tan, albeit a red tan, early days yet she thought but she was determined her husband would want her the moment he set eyes on her and then she thought why do I bother with him with what he has put me through. She walked to the full length mirror in their bedroom and thought looks great but there is something missing and then she realised she had not put on her Jimmy Choo 3 inch high heels in shiny yellow leather with a matching Jimmy Choo yellow handbag which was small and did not allow much to be carried but she had her lip-gloss and mascara a handkerchief and a small purse. Yes she thought, you look hot. Attaching a pair of small gold earrings and her gold Gucci watch she walked to the mirror again and was just admiring herself when there was a knock at her door. Answering the knock she found Michelle and Julie at the door.

"What's up?" asked Jill.

"Don't ask Julie she's not speaking to us, have you noticed your husband is missing and it is 7 o'clock?" said Michelle.

"Great! Where are they?" asked Jill.

"Don't know but I would guess they are still in the bar," answered Michele frustration showing on her face.

"Ok, so why isn't Julie speaking to us?" asked Jill.

"Well it might have something to do with my chest, do you think?" said Julie with her hands on her hips and a considerable frown on her face.

She was wearing a white blouse similar to Jill's but Julie's was buttoned all the way up.

"Ah, right, er, ok, yeah, er, sorry but you were snoring," said Jill defensively.

"So that gives you the right to put your hands on me does it, it's a bloody great way to make friends!" said

Julie her voice rising in tone and harshness as she spoke.

"Your right, your right of course, I'm sorry, it won't happen again, it was stupid, it's important we do become friends isn't it?" said Jill.

"Can you imagine how I felt when I saw it? Can you imagine what Steve will say when he sees it?" Julie fumed.

"Sorry," Jill reiterated "You won't notice it in a couple of days."

"A couple of days! What am I supposed to do, hide from my husband for Christ's sake?!" Julie said still fuming.

"I know and I'm sorry, honestly it won't happen again, we will help you with it tomorrow, won't we Michelle," said Jill.

"Of course we will, no problem, we will have it sorted tomorrow, honest," confirmed Michelle trying to hold back a smirk.

"Shit, let's go and find the men, I'm more annoyed at them at the moment," said Julie.

"God help them!" said Michelle turning to Jill and winking with a little smirk as if to say "well you were sure lucky there."

With that Julie and Michelle turned towards the lift as Jill locked her door and joining the others parting them in the middle put her arms around Michelle and Julie and gave each a kiss on the cheek. The lift descended quickly and bounced slightly as it hit the ground floor and all three alighted the lift gasping for breath as the lift was permeated with the smell of overpowering cheap perfume.

They marched straight into the bar which was empty apart from their husbands who had not moved from their earlier positions at the bar, sitting as they were on the exact same stools, it was David who noticed the wives enter and motioned the others with his head of the impending confrontation.

"Drink?" David asked.

"Drink! When are you going to change for dinner we're hungry!" Jill said angrily.

Steve and Tony looked at David in a unanimous vote electing David to be their spokesman.

"Well, er, we, er, well we have already eaten at the club you see," said David gingerly as his head began to shrink into his shoulders, probably not the best spokesperson to pick.

"What do you mean you have already eaten?" fumed Jill.

"Well, er, we, er, managed to arrange three rounds of golf tomorrow which means our first round tees off at 6am so we need to go to bed early so we thought it better to eat at the club and just have a few drinks here before retiring to bed," said David with some degree of trepidation.

"Oh really, how nice of you to tell us before we went upstairs and dressed for dinner, what have you planned for us this evening?" Julie asked struggling to keep her temper in check.

"We just thought that you were enjoying each other's company so much you wouldn't mind going out yourselves just this once," said David more hopefully than he sounded.

"Oh just this once eh? There is no just this once, for the rest of this holiday we will be going out by ourselves you three are not welcome do you understand?!" stated Jill with finality.

"Well if that's how you want it ok, fine, but if you need anything just ask, ok," said David relieved somewhat.

"What? Like a husband in the bedroom do you mean David?!" said Jill vehemently with that she turned saying, "C'mon girls, as usual the men are a waste of time!"

The three women walked silently out of the hotel with Julie looking at Michelle with her eyes wide open and Michelle looking back acknowledging what she meant; obviously the comment about David in the bedroom.

Steve and Tony looked at a blushing and bright red David as all David could manage was to shrug his shoulders.

Tony broke the silence with, "Well done David, that works better for us, they don't realise that has helped us as we now don't have to worry about rushing back from the club and we can play as much golf as we like."

"Absolutely," agreed Steve.

Meanwhile the girls were out of the hotel and stomping their way furiously towards the centre of Fuengirola, it was Michelle who was beginning to breathe heavily that decided to break the unholy silence.

"Let's stop somewhere for a drink, please!"

As Michelle stopped, stooped and bent over putting her hands on her knees as she took in deep gulps of air. Jill and Julie stopped and looked around at the prone Michelle looked across at each other and burst out laughing, grabbing hold of each other as they laughed uncontrollably as the prone and mystified Michelle looked on.

Once they had stopped laughing and Michelle had her breath back they decided to find somewhere to eat as they realised that they were seriously hungry and they soon chanced upon a Chinese restaurant so in they went and ordered a bottle of wine whilst they checked out the menu.

They had eaten at a Chinese restaurant before in Spain and knew it would not be as good as back home but they did not mind as the night was still young! As they studied their menus Jill looked around the dimly lit restaurant from the dingy entrance with ancient beige leather low chairs and Formica fake wood topped low tables and in the corner to the side of the bar again topped with Formica fake wood housed a large fish tank some three feet long, two feet deep and 18 inches wide inside of which swam a trout some 15 inches long far too large for the tank, he was accompanied by approximately 15 other much smaller fish. There were small imitation candle lights on each table presumably powered by batteries as no leads emitted from them and there was a few not illuminated at all. There was a false lowered ceiling that housed strip lights a number of which did not work and one in the corner by the fish tank flickered on and off continuously, Jill could not help wondering whether it was the light that made the trout blink. The walls finished the dismal internal decoration having been painted a deep red over wallpaper that was coming away from the wall in places especially near the false ceiling.

To make their ordering of drinks easier they had decided to drink the same this evening and their vodka and cokes arrived in tall glasses with ampules amount of ice and a slice of lemon, Jill checked her glass for cleanliness before taking a slurp and found it to be spotless as indeed she noticed was the tablecloth and cutlery, she could not tell about the chopsticks as they were encased in paper.

"It's a bit yukky in here isn't it, should we drink up and try somewhere else?" suggested Jill.

"It's the food we're here for, may as well try it now we're here," said Michele studying her menu.

"I agree, I'm hungry and I fancy Chinese now," put in Julie.

They continued exploring their menus and decided to order fried rice and noodles for the three of them then a portion of chicken and mushrooms, a portion of garlic king prawns, and finally a portion of steak canton for them all to share.

The food arrived and it was excellent, the three women devoured the lot and even left room for a custard tart for desert, these were no ordinary custard tarts but ever so delicate and tasty the way only the Chinese seem able to do.

Their original drink had lasted them for the whole meal so they decided to pay up and make their way towards Blue's and if they found a bar they liked the look of before they arrived at Blue's they would try one or two drinks there.

They left the restaurant passing the blinking trout into the early evening sunshine which initially hurt their eyes after the darkness of the restaurant. It was now close to 9.30pm and still early for a night out in Spain as they knew most people did not bother going out until after 10pm when it had cooled suitably and when the bars began to fill up.

They were open as to which direction to try but the decision was made by Julie of all people who just walked off without a word leaving Jill and Michelle by surprise and following for a change.

"Look its Lamar's bar, it has to be good for a drink," said Julie.

"It's not Foo Foo's." said Michelle pointedly knowing how Julie assumed.

"Oh," said Julie disappointed, "Let's walk on bye then and see where we come to."

"Let's move off the main drag and try the side roads, probably see better bars there," added Michelle.

With that they turned left at the next road which housed numerous bars on both sides of the street most with tables and chairs outside many with loud music emanating from their inside which mixed with each other on the street giving the air an incoherent mix of pop music, Abba, reggae and at one point Frank Sinatra singing New York New York over all the other mix of music.

There were various smells in the air from the numerous restaurants but above all those smells was that of the sea as the wind was blowing in much fresher than it had been all day. They saw a bar called "The Mancunian" across the street which they all agreed was worth a visit.

Making their way past the people sat outside on aluminium chairs that did not appear strong enough to take their weight let alone the guy who looked to be about 22 stone and five foot ten tall, he may have sat down but would he be able to release himself from the clutches of the chair once he wanted to leave, that would be interesting and possibly entertaining to see.

The bar inside was full of people trying to buy drinks which did not help that they had six bar stools all occupied, Jill and Julie pushed Michelle forward as as usual she was dressed for the ordeal of obtaining drinks quickly from an overcrowded bar.

Making it to the bar with Oasis's Champagne Supernova blaring out of the juke box Michelle strategically placed a bare boob onto the already overcrowded bar, a barman immediately asked for her order, again three vodka and cokes, paying for her drinks she picked them up off the bar and turning barged her way back to Jill and Julie.

"That was quick!" Jill said taking one of the glasses from Michelle, "Oh!" she added, lifting her free hand to help Michelle's boob back home inside her low cut V necked cashmere cream top as Michelle for the time being was stuck with two drinks whilst Julie went in search of the Ladies.

On Julie's return she in turn was lumbered with two drinks as Michelle went to the Ladies. Julie asked Jill whether Michelle had had trouble ordering the drinks whereupon Jill had recounted Michelle's ploy at the bar.

"If today is anything to go by Michelle is like a Jack Russell on heat that has taken an overdose of Bob Martins and Viagra!" said Julie with all sincerity.

Jill could do nothing but fall about laughing, it was not just what she said but the way she said it with such a straight face and so full of innocence.

They drank there drinks and took in the loud music which consisted mainly of Manchester bands and made Michelle reminisce of her Hacienda days.

Michelle turned to Julie asking, "Are you going to the bar for drinks?"

"I don't think I have the boobs for it, anyway mine have handprints on them!" said Julie.

"That's alright, I'll go," said Jill just as Joy Division's Love Will Tear Us Apart sang out from the juke box.

Barging her way to the bar Jill was beginning to wish she had not put a bra on as how could she possibly innocently place a breast on top of the bar from her bra, not that she would stoop so low but it would make her feel more liberated and free from David, just as the thoughts were going through her brain she heard a male voice from behind the bar ask, "What's yours?"

Just as she was about to say 36DD she heard herself say, "Three vodka and cokes please."

Jill managed to barge her way back from the increasingly full bar, it was louder as the increasing numbers of clientele added to the noise of the music from the juke box, there were numerous groups of men in differing numbers and with various accents from across Britain and then a like number of groups of women, both groups were in varying degrees of sobriety.

Suddenly Julie was barged past by a clearly drunken girl of maybe 18 or 19 years of age returning from the Ladies dressed in a cheap skimpy braless top and a short skirt that had been inadvertently tucked into itself at the top revealing her bare bottom to all and sundry in the bar. It was noticed immediately by the groups of men who cheered, she fell over a man sitting at a table with six of his friends who had a close up view as her bottom glanced his cheek as she tried to right herself and stay on her feet, he spilled part of his pint of lager but kept his smile on his face as he turned to her and said, "Thanks!"

"You what? Thanks for what?" she slurred back to him trying to focus.

"I've just remembered where I parked my bike," he replied and burst out laughing along with all his friends at the table amidst the continuing jeers of all the men in the bar.

"Aw fuck off!" she slurred back to him as she turned back to find her friends completely unaware of the plight of her skirt.

A woman she passed tried to pull her skirt out for her but received a slap for her efforts. She eventually found her friends who pulled her skirt straight before dragging her outside of the bar to a barrage of wolf whistles and laughter.

Jill, Michelle and Julie were becoming increasing fed up with the constant barging past them to either the bar or the toilets and with the noise levels reaching a crescendo of nonsense they decided to drink up and leave to find Blues which they believed would be a little more civilised than the raucousness of The Mancunian.

They left the bar to find the sun had retired for the night leaving the sky a deep blue and cloudless and not yet dark, it was a warm night with a cooling wind blowing in from the sea as they made their way along the street past numerous bars and restaurants which continued to fill with happy holidaymakers.

It took them ten minutes to find the pink and blue neon lights of Blues. They strode in expectantly and slowly made their way to the bar allowing their eyes to adjust to the darkness, Julie ordered their vodka and cokes as Jill and Michelle looked around for a table to sit at but found they were all occupied, they did however find a standing table that was circular and stood about three foot six inches tall and was positioned towards the left of the room away from the bar and about three quarters the length of the room away from the stage but certainly good enough to see all they needed to.

Julie found them with their drinks as they looked around and Julie pipped up, "I just managed to order the drinks before some of the bar staff left, apparently they are doing something on stage."

At which point Camp Teddie bounced onto the stage in too tight trousers again and showing off his purple chest hair, four sharp spotlights picked him up as he announced.

"People of Blues please be upstanding for your resident dancers, Men O'Pause."

With clapping and wolf whistles from all over the room the male dancers appeared in ever so tight and short pink hot pants and nothing else accompanied by Hot Chocolate's "You Sexy Thing" with Erol Brown's unmistakable voice ringing out. They danced and gyrated their hearts out to continued applause, wolf whistles and laughter from all the audience and when they had finished the shouts of encore reverberated around the room but alas they needed to return behind the bar to serve drinks. The bar crowded quickly and noisily and the tips flowed freely.

"I like it here," announced Julie.

"Yes, it's good, relaxed and a good friendly atmosphere," Michelle agreed.

"Don't look now Julie but I think that young lad is in whose gran you said looked like Lily Savage!" said Jill smirking and winking at Michelle.

"Where?" asked Julie looking all around the room in a semi panic.

"Oh, It's not him, you can relax," said Jill mischievously eyeing Michelle's reaction.

The time passed pleasantly with an array of singers taking to the stage and when Michelle checked her watch she cried out to the others, "Its 11.30pm, we said we would meet Charles at 11pm."

"You said we would, it was only an if and maybe," said Julie.

"Yes it was but it might be fun to check out Bulbous Billy's Bar, I wouldn't mind knowing why he's called bulbous Billy," said Jill.

They finished their drinks and made a move with a reluctant Julie, realising as they made their way outside into the cool night air that they did not know where the bar was.

"This way."

Michelle instructed as they walked along the now dark but brightly lit street, although the streetlights were fairly dull the street was illuminated by the brightly lit bars they passed.

They turned a corner at the end of the street and could make out a brightly lit bar with some thirty people sat at tables and chairs outside the bar and some were standing in the street with their drinks and smoking cigarettes all were chatting away amiably.

Walking inside they were again greeted with a dimly lit interior and full of customers but not quite as full and overbearing as they had found the Mancunian and there was no juke box playing here but a stage was in the far corner with someone trying to sing My Old Piano by Diana Ross and failing miserably.

They looked around as Michelle made it to the bar a little easier than she had in the Mancunian and managed to order drinks whilst remaining fully clothed.

"Look!" screamed Julie, "There's Lady Gaga sucking out Elton John's tonsils!"

"It's not Lady Gaga or Elton John, although she does have a telephone stuck to her head, I think they've dressed for the karaoke," said Jill.

There was a group of about twenty people or so milling around the stage area with some sat at the tables next to the stage in different types of attire trying to look like famous singers and entertainers. There were some who clearly took their dress seriously and had spent some money on their attire and there were others who had not or could not afford to make such an effort and others again who would never look similar to who they were trying to look like because of their size or looks but they looked as if they knew that and did not mind.

It was as much a social occasion as anything as they all appeared to know each other. There was a group of three men sitting at a small table to the left and next to the stage that appeared to be having an argument and were slapping a hitting and gouging each other. It was at this point when Michelle returned back to them with their drinks and said.

"Isn't it great! Have you seen the Three Stooges down by the stage, they're hilarious, look at them kicking and hitting each other, they even look like Larry, Curley and Moe."

"I thought they looked familiar but I couldn't place them, David loves them," said Jill with her head nodding in realisation.

"So do I, I couldn't stop laughing at them when I was a kid," confirmed Michelle.

"Never heard of them what do they sing? Maybe I've heard one of their records," asked Julie.

"What!" said Michelle incredulously?

"Not my fault I don't know their songs," said Julie a little annoyed now that both Michelle and Jill knew who they were.

Just as the DJ whose name they did not catch introduced someone singing Like A Virgin by Madonna, Charles appeared behind them having just arrived. He gave each of them a kiss on their cheeks which made Julie blush for some reason and asked if they would like their drinks refreshing which they declined explaining they had also just arrived, so Charles made his way to the bar alone.

He arrived at the bar next to Barry the barfly a harmless individual who sat at the solitary stool in the corner of the bar furthest away from the stage and drank whiskey and coke all night keeping himself to himself, all the regulars many of which were expats knew him.

The head barman Steve came over to serve Charles and prepared his drink without Charles asking, he turned back around with a glass of red wine placing it on the bar in front of Charles, Charles responded by giving Steve a five euro note gesturing for Steve to keep the change. Before Steve left to put the money in the till Charles asked where Billy was to which Steve placed a hand on Charles arm and raised his other hand with his forefinger over his lips. Charles took this to mean wait for his return, once he returned he turned pointedly to face the door so only Charles could hear him or see his lips move, well except for Barry the barfly, he began,

"He's made himself scarce, said he was going to Gib(Gibraltar) to pick up stock but I know he hasn't. Without turning do you see the big guy at the end of the bar standing in our access drinking a pint of larger, well he came in here about an hour ago and has had four pints he refuses to pay for, says he's Billy's partner, I know you know about Billy's past he told me, he had a partner back in the UK right but he was sent down for 15 years, that was ten years ago, I reckon it's him out early with good behaviour, I don't mind telling you he scares me, he must be six foot four inches tall and twenty two stones and he's becoming more and more annoyed every minute Billy doesn't show."

Just then there was a clinking noise from the other end of the bar, it was the big guy banging his glass on the bar demanding another pint. Charles waited for Steve to finish serving him and return which he did a minute later.

Charles turned to him and said," Don't worry about him, I've seen men like that before they think because of their size people will back off and probably most do but he's just a bully, no substance, and he's arrogant with it."

He winked at Steve and left the bar to re-join the women. Madonna had long finished on the stage and now there was an Elton John lookalike on stage singing Goodbye Yellow brick Road, he had clearly spent a small fortune on his outfit which consisted of a long, floor length multi-coloured overcoat made of what appeared to be a mixture of fur and feathers, the collar of which consisted of ostrich feathers, his singing was pretty damn good as well as the audience were lapping it up.

A table became free by the open front door which Charles was the first to claim so he summoned the girls over, Michelle rushing so she could place herself next to Charles.

Charles sat at the back so he had the full view of the bar and stage, he knew it was not terribly gallant but it was necessary, Jill and Julie sat opposite on stools which they moved wider and sat themselves down watching the stage having manoeuvred themselves so that Charles and Michelle had unbridled sight of the stage.

The room and bar was full and lively, Charles explained to the girls the elaborate dress of some of the karaoke singers in that they were mostly expats who sang in different bars most nights and took part in a number of competitions in Fuengirola and some of the singers took part in some competitions up and down the coastline of the Costa Del Sol.

The main competition in Fuengirola was every fortnight at the Music Bar for a grand prize of one thousand euros. He further explained it was held every two weeks traditionally because most holiday makers changed every fortnight and that it had only been the last couple of years that the prize money had escalated to a thousand euros. Just as Charles finished explaining there was a little noise at the bar and the big guy at the end of the bar had the barman Steve by the scruff of the neck with one hand whilst waving his empty pint glass in front of his face with the other. Once Steve took hold of the glass he was released but Charles began watching him closer now as it was apparent his uncontrollable temper was rising to fever pitch.

The girls decided they wanted to have a sing so were discussing what they could sing. They concluded as they were a threesome they would try a Bananarama song but they were now arguing over which song, when they came to some agreement someone would mention another song and the discussion continued. Eventually an agreement was made so Jill was sent to the DJ with their choice of song, Venus, and she was duly informed by the DJ that they would be on after Simon and Garfunkel, Jill looked all around the room for Simon and Garfunkel on her way back to her seat but could not see who they might be having concluded they must not be in fancy dress and then she laughed at herself as how or why would Simon and Garfunkel be in fancy dress. Michelle and Julie turned to Jill when she returned hoping to find out when they would be on.

Jill said, "I'm not sure how long before we're on but we are after Simon and Garfunkel, oh and the DJ is called Mad Mike."

"Why is he called Mad Mike?" asked Julie.

"No idea, unless Mike is short for microphone, Nah, no idea," answered Jill.

As a holidaymaker took to the stage with Rick Astley's Never Gonna Give You Up starting his first few bars showed he sounded more like Ricky Tomlinson, Charles made his way to the bar for more drinks, Steve noticed him approaching and began pouring him a fresh glass of red wine.

Charles nodded acknowledgement at Steve and ordered drinks for the girls whilst taking a closer look at the big man still blocking the staff entrance to the bar but who was staring at some men sat around three tables in a group of about 16, they were noisy but not overly so clearly they were having a great time and seemed friendly enough.

Charles knew what he was doing, he was selecting his prey, he was close to being tipsy and he was angry and frustrated by Billy's absence. Charles left the now sweating and bright red Steve whose blood pressure was rising by the minute to return the drinks to the girls and resume his place beside them all the while keeping an eye on the big man at the bar.

It had been some ten minutes now since Charles had collected his drinks from the bar and he was convinced the big man had selected his prey for the evening, his evening entertainment, and was waiting to make his move.

DJ Mad Mike announced the arrival on stage of the next karaoke stars, it was to be The Sound Of Silence by Simon and Garfunkel, the girls looked around in excited anticipation at who was to be Simon and Garfunkel knowing they would be called on stage next.

Two of the Three Stooges rose to their feet, the girls looked at one another in confused silence, surely not they thought. The two looking like Larry and Moe indeed climbed onto the stage, the room was strangely engulfed in a hushed and respectful quiet as the crowd expectantly looked on, were they to sing the song jokily with slaps and pokes and kicks?

The music began and they began to sing and the crowd remained silent as it sounded so eerily like Simon and Garfunkel, quite excellent in fact.

One of the men from the crowd of sixteen rose from his table making his way past everyone carefully so as not to knock anyone's drink over and headed towards the long corridor by the side of the bar and stage which led firstly to the Ladies and then at the end of the corridor on the left was the Gentlemen, straight in front was an emergency fire door exited by a bar located halfway up the door.

The corridor was dimly lit by a single small light outside the Ladies door and a further single light outside the Gentlemen which was working irregularly, flashing on for a few seconds then off again alternately. The man from the table was making his way innocently down the corridor to the Gentlemen's when the big man from the bar placed his half full pint of lager on the bar turned and followed to the corridor.

Charles had seen what was coming and was up and on his way as the big man turned from the bar. The big man was halfway down the corridor as Charles approached the Ladies, looking up to his left as he past the door of the Ladies Charles noticed a spiders web vibrating slightly from the fly which had just been caught and was still fluttering his wings in a hopeless attempt to free itself as the spider slowly crept towards it, its frustrated attempts at escape increasing in voracity at each step the spider made towards it. Charles wondered whether the fly knew it had only a few fleeting seconds of life left.

Charles was upon the big man crashing into him with his full force as they both flew through the fire escape into a rear yard with nothing but a half dozen industrial size rubbish bins randomly positioned. The big man turned furiously as the fire escape door crashed too but did not lock, he threw a huge right hand roundhouse at Charles but he was expecting it as he had been observing him in the bar and saw him use his right hand for everything, Charles thrust up his right arm instantly blocking the punch and then in the same smooth movement stepped forward thrusting his elbow into the man's Adams Apple crushing it on impact and then he followed it up with two quick punches hitting the same spot killing him instantly. He stayed on his feet for a couple of seconds in which time Charles threw open the rubber lid of one of the bins alongside him, the big man began to fall forward so Charles ducked underneath him and as he fell on top of Charles he rose himself upright quickly throwing the big man over his shoulder and into the bin.

Charles now took a handkerchief out of his right pocket and opened another bin taking out several of the full rubbish filled bin liners clutched in his hand covered by his handkerchief and throwing them on top of the body until it was covered. Then closed both lids again with his right hand covered with the handkerchief. Charles knew these bins were collected by a wagon with a hydraulic lift at the front that lifted the bin up and over the wagon's cab to deposit the rubbish into its main body and with any luck the trash would be deposited without anyone seeing the body.

Charles was not worried if the body was found anyway. Wiping his hands with his handkerchief Charles opened the fire door and once inside shut it securely wiping the bar with his handkerchief before returning it to his right pocket, all things in their rightful place. Charles turned to enter through the Gentleman's door but the door was opened for him by the man from the table who had no idea at what had just transpired some ten yards away from where he stood and which had no doubt saved him at the very least from a considerable beating; they nodded at each other as their paths crossed.

Charles once inside the Gents checked himself over, nothing unto Ord showing so he brushed his hair once with his fingers and turned to leave. Charles had been outside a total of thirty seconds. Charles re-entered the main room as the Sound Of Silence was just ending and a round of rapturous applause began to ring out, he passed Jill, Michelle and Julie who were standing by the side of the stage in eager anticipation waiting to be introduced.

Charles walked past the bar noticing the half full pint glass of the big mans was still where he had left it and Steve was busy behind the bar and evidently had not noticed Charles leaving or returning. As Charles sat down the girls were being introduced on stage by Mad Mike and were nervously taking hold of a microphone each. Charles took a sip of his red wine, returned the glass to the table sat back in his seat and clapped as the girls began singing with varying degrees of nervousness. Charles allowed himself a wry smile as he thought that he had not noticed whether the spider had devoured his fly or was leaving it to die slowly.

The girls finished their song onstage and were grateful for the applause and cheers from some of the audience, despite being their first time on stage together and indeed the first time they had sung together, they had acquitted themselves well. They bounced their way back to Charles each in turn kissing him on the cheek as he continued to clap them smiling wide.

"We should go to the Music Bar," he suggested.

"Why? What's there?" asked Julie rather surprised at herself enjoying being on the stage.

"It's where the main karaoke completion takes place in Fuengirola, there's a competition every fortnight on a Thursday, invitation only," said Charles.

"So how are you invited?" asked Jill.

"Rather simple actually, you sing on their stage and if they like you they invite you back for the Thursday of the completion, which happens to be this Thursday," said Charles.

"Let's go then, what do you think Julie, Michelle?" asked Jill.

"Let's go for it," said Julie.

"Why not, it's somewhere new," agreed Michelle.

Charles stood leaving the rest of his wine where it was whilst waiting for the girls to finish their drinks which took all of twenty seconds. Charles took a step backwards to allow the girls to walk past him and out through the open front door, he glanced towards the bar and noticed Steve nodding towards where the big man had been standing and hunching his shoulders as if to ask did Charles know where he had gone, Charles just hunched his own shoulders as he followed the girls out of the door.

The girls were excited and had begun discussing which Bananarama song they should sing next, they had turned right out of Bulbous Billy's and were some ten yards in front of Charles when Julie noticed he was walking in the opposite direction and nudged Jill and Michelle, the three of them turned and looked at Charles in some confusion.

"This way," said Charles and continued walking.

The girls turned and ran to catch up with Charles, Michelle and Jill arriving first and they linked arms with him one on each side leaving Julie to link arms with Michelle as she still had not forgiven Jill. They passed numerous people on the streets that were moving between bars or were looking for somewhere to eat, there were people in varying degrees of inebriation and rowdiness. They walked up this street and down the next street still discussing their best song options leaving Charles to his own thoughts. After ten minutes of walking they arrived at a doorway with a small illuminated sign above the doorway which simply said Music Bar.

"Is this it?" asked Michelle a little disappointedly.

"They don't need to advertise, everyone knows the Music Bar especially the expats," said Charles as he opened the door for the girls to enter.

The bar was dimly lit with no natural light at all and no windows, it took a few minutes for their eyes to adjust; the stage was by the entrance door, not perfect they thought and the bar was on the left and spanned the full length of the room and in the centre and to the right of the room were circular tables large enough for four chairs, some of which had been placed together by larger groups of people, there was Ladies and Gents rooms to the rear. There was currently a middle aged thin balding man with a bright pink face from the sun on stage clearly a holidaymaker singing Red Red Wine by UB40.

The room was full, Charles made his way to the bar leaving the girls to see if they could find a table which they did in the centre of the room next to the far wall away from the bar, Michelle made her way back to Charles at the bar to help him carry the drinks and show him where the table was they had found.

They returned to the table and Julie told Michelle that Elton from Bulbous Billy's was in at the back of the room along with Madonna and The Three Stooges; she said she had also spotted who she believed to be a Frank Sinatra once his lips had separated from Diana Ross. Julie said that she thought she had seen Barbara Streisand but was not sure but she thought she recognised the nose, Julie then turned towards the back of the room pointing towards David Bowie dressed as Ziggy Stardust talking to Lionel Ritchie.

They all sat down and took a sip of their drinks whilst taking in the ambience of the bar. The décor left a lot to be desired as all the walls had been painted a deep red some years ago by the looks of it as the shade deepened the further up the wall you looked, the tables and chairs were also ancient and mismatched whist the carpet was dark and although it had a pattern at some point it was indistinguishable now and was sticky underfoot. Michelle was listening to the girl singing on stage who appeared a little inebriated wearing a short red skirt with white socks up to her knees with red high heel shoes and a white T-shirt that had "I'm not here" written across the front in black script; she was singing "You've got Bette Davis eyes" by Kim Karns but was actually singing "You've got Marty Feldman Eyes" and was totally impervious to singing the wrong lines. Michelle nudged everyone to inform them of her findings in case anyone had not noticed.

"Perhaps she has updated it and rereleased it, they do that you know," suggested Julie.

"What with Marty Feldman eyes, have you ever seen Marty Feldman?" asked Michelle.

"Yes, he is really sexy; I loved him in Wet Wet Wet," said Julie.

"That's Marti Pellow; Marty Feldman was the hunchback in Young Frankenstein whose hump kept moving from shoulder to shoulder, with the weird eyes that never look at you," said Michelle perplexed.

"Ooh that must have been painful!" said Julie.

"What? His eyes?" asked Michelle.

"No, his humps moving from shoulder to shoulder, that must really smart, no wonder his eyes looked weird," said Julie.

"I give up!" said Michelle looking at Jill and Charles for support.

"Anyway, are we agreed which song we are singing, I'll go and see the DJ, so it's Really Saying Something, ok?" asked Jill.

"Yep," Michelle and Julie agreed.

Jill was up and heading towards the stage before anyone could change their mind. Returning five minutes later Jill informed the others she had seen the DJ but he was not really a DJ but rather Pete the owner and his wife Debbie worked behind the bar keeping a close eye on the staff.

They were up after someone singing Jolene by Dolly Parton. It seemed a long long time since Jill had been to speak to Pete and the girls were becoming a little restless as they endured streams of singers alighting the steps to the stage before them.

The room was now packed to the gunnels and the air was stale with a vague unpleasant smell, a combination of beer, cheap sickly sweet perfume and sweat from the heat of all the bodies in such a confined space with no ventilation.

They heard the music starting for Jolene and saw Pete next to the stage summoning them forward, they had been hoping the girl singing Jolene would not be too good so that they might give a good impression and the crowd would support them with a raucous applause but she was very good and the crowd showed their appreciation. They could only hope that the crowd were in the mood for more applause when they took to the stage.

After what seemed an age their turn came and so did the applause they had long been hoping for as they waved goodbye to the audience descending the steps from the stage they saw Pete approaching with a smile on his face and he invited them to take part in the competition on Thursday saying they would have to register by 10pm or they would not be allowed to take part. They barged as delicately as possible back to the waiting and applauding Charles who was smiling in anticipation and began enthusiastically applauding again once he heard that they had been invited to join the competition. It was Julie who brought the celebrations to a close by informing everyone that it was now 2.50am and they still had a full drink in front of them thanks to Charles fetching them from the bar whilst they were on stage.

"Don't worry, it's still early, the bar doesn't normally close until around 4am," said Charles winking at Julie.

"Yes but we have husbands back at the Hotel, they'll be worried wondering where we are," said Julie nervously.

"They'll be fast asleep and won't notice were not there until they wake up around 6.30am," said Jill clearly in the mood for another drink.

"That's true, but if we leave it too late we won't be up ourselves and we'll miss the Sun," said Michelle.

"Ok, we will leave when we've finished our drinks, I'm going to wake David anyway when I'm back in our room, put the arsehole off his game," said Jill quite nastily.

"You really don't like him at the moment do you?" asked Julie.

"I bloody despise him at the moment and he better change drastically and soon or he has a bloody great shock coming," said Jill nodding her head although she was not sure why.

"I wouldn't like to be in his shoes over the next few days!" said Julie as she took another sip of her drink.

"He won't like being in his shoes I can promise you!" pledged Jill.

They finished their drinks and rose to leave with Charles leading the way; they passed Pete as they approached the front door and he shook Charles' hand and smiled pleasantly at the girls as they walked through the door out into the cool night air, cool fresh night air.

The girls turned to Charles to wish him goodnight and thank him once again for his hospitality.

"I'll see you safely back to your hotel," Said Charles pointedly.

"No need we'll find it alright," said Jill.

"I insist, I would never forgive myself should something happen to you," said Charles.

"Ok, if you insist, thank you," said Jill smiling at his chivalry.

They turned and made their way slowly in the direction of their Hotel enjoying the fresh breeze that fanned their bodies. The sky was deep blue and cloudless and stars covered every inch of it, the streets were quiet with just the odd person in the distance making their way wherever.

As they turned onto the front of the resort the road was empty apart from a single council water bowser that was making its way slowly down the front with a man sat on top of the rear with a hose in his hand watering the flower pots hanging halfway down the street lights.

Everything at peace until the dawn.

Chapter 7   Monday

Jill woke to the sound of David's golf clubs crashing to the polished tiled floor, her head was pounding and the son of a bitch had opened the curtains again allowing the early morning sun's brightness and heat to explode into the room and her head. Jill was sure he had lifted the clubs high to drop them as noisily as possible in retaliation for her slamming the hotel room door when she arrived back late last night, well this morning actually.

Jill really could not be bothered making any attempt at retaliation not even bothering to look at her watch that she had taken off last night and placed on the bedside cabinet as she knew David would be leaving at around 6am, she rolled over placing her back between her and David and the door, pulling all the sheets into her body and legs and then ducking her head beneath the sheets. Her head beat loudly and painfully to the continuous beat of her heart, she thought if only she could turn it down until she returned to sleep and peaceful hibernation.

The sheets contained the warmth of the morning sun and Jill found it increasingly difficult to find the sanctity of sleep despite having forced herself out of bed to drink some warm bottled water they had bought for cleaning their teeth and closing the curtains to the increasing glare of the strong Spanish sun.

Jill became aware of the early morning sounds making their uninterrupted way into her beating head, she had heard the chatter of people as they made their way out of the front door of the hotel and people making themselves comfortable about the hotels swimming pool, there was also increasing traffic noise interspersed with the odd car horn.

Having finally admitted defeat in her attempts at returning to sleep Jill decided the next best thing was a long hot shower. Having dried herself as best she could with the hotel towel she placed it onto the towel rail in the bathroom and walked naked through the bedroom and onto the small balcony to take in the full bright early morning vista of Fuengirola through blood shot eyes.

She began to smile to herself as the bright strong sun dried her body and was interrupted in her thoughts by someone knocking on her door. At the door she asked who was knocking to be told by Michelle to open up, as Jill opened the door Michelle and Julie barged past her only briefly glancing at her nakedness.

"C'mon, dress, I'm hungry, let's go for breakfast."

"What time is it?" Jill asked.

"10 o'clock, hurry up, breakfast at the hotel has finished we can go to the tapas bar we went to yesterday if you like," suggested Michelle.

"I haven't done my makeup yet," protested Jill.

"No time for that, just dress you can always do your makeup later, bring it with you," urged Michelle.

"What's the rush for Christ's sake!" asked Jill annoyed at the intrusion.

"We're hungry!" Michelle and Julie cried in unison.

Jill opened the second drawer in the cabinet by the wardrobe and took out a pastel orange bikini and put it on, then rushing pulled up a short pleated white tennis skirt and finished with a peach blouse which she left open as she was rushing, completing her wardrobe with a pair of orange Nike trainers. Jill grabbed her beach bag making sure she had her purse with her changing the money over from the one she took with her the previous evening and room keys and they were off.

Waiting for the lift to arrive Julie turned to Jill and said, "My God your eyes are bloodshot, we'd better find you some Optrex."

"You should see them from this side!" said Jill with a hint of a smile.

As they walked through the hotel's front door and the full glare of the sun hit them all three turned away from the sun as they searched for their sunglasses, finding them they turned looked at each other and nodded and took their first steps of the new day into the bright searching sun with their short shadows following behind them.

They soon found the venta they had eaten in the day before and sat at the same table, the same young waiter with the nimble backside approached them. They ordered coffee whilst they decided on what they would like for breakfast.

They each decided on a light breakfast of omelette, Jill had hers with cheese but Michelle and Julie had theirs with mushroom and asparagus spears and of course more coffee was ordered.

Michelle took care of their bill and as they prepared to leave Julie informed Jill she was going to look for some sun cream that could help with the handprints emblazoned across her chest and she would buy her some Optrex to help with her eyes.

Leaving the venta they separated with Jill and Michelle heading for the villa leaving Julie to her shopping. On arriving at the villa they made themselves at home on the sun loungers moving them in direct line with the sun's rays along with one for Julie.

Charles had learned over the edge of the balcony and said good morning before returning to his work or reading or whatever it was he did on his balcony.

As usual Michelle stripped off completely naked and Jill joined her except for leaving her bikini bottoms on. They chatted amiably whilst they applied sun lotion to their bodies, Jill noticed Michelle kept looking to see if Charles was taking any notice of her and was not best pleased to find he was not taking a blind bit of interest in her.

Eventually Julie returned from her shopping and found Jill and Michelle in the midst of conversation and laughing together, paranoid and wondering whether they were talking about her she asked what they were laughing at.

"Oh we were just talking about some of the things we did in school to pass the time," said Michelle.

"Oh, like what?" Julie asked still paranoid.

"Oh, like "Flick the Kipper"," Michelle said and instantly Michelle and Jill began giggling like a couple of school girls.

"Did you play "Flick the Kipper"?" asked Jill.

"No, we played netball at our school," said Julie innocently.

At which Jill and Michelle fell about laughing uncontrollably leaving Julie with a totally puzzled look on her face which changed to one of annoyance at her realisation there was a joke in there somewhere.

When they eventually calmed down Michelle asked Julie where she had been for so long.

"I was trying to find a decent Farmacia; I had to go into Fuengirola before I found one," said Julie.

"Did you manage to find some Optrex for me?" asked Jill.

"I couldn't find it, I looked everywhere," said Julie.

"Oh, so you didn't bother buying me anything then?" asked Jill.

"Yeah, I bought you some, I found it eventually," said Julie.

"Oh great, thanks, where did you find it?" asked Jill.

"It was in between the condoms and the Vagisill!" said Julie.

Jill took the Optrex from Julie and opened the bottle where she sat on the sun lounger and began to fill the cap with liquid, before she began bathing her eyes Michelle turned to her and asked.

"You did check that it's Optrex and not Vagisil didn't you? You know what Julie is like, what will your eyes look like with Vagisil splashed in them?"

"I don't know but it would stop my eyes from itching!" said Jill as both her and Michelle laughed at the thought leaving Julie to take out the Ambre Soliel oil which she had just bought hoping it would help her chest to tan quickly so it would hide the blatantly obvious hand impressions covering her breasts.

Julie undressed down to her bikini bottoms but could not help herself from looking around for boob snoopers, having found none she began applying the oil onto her boobs before advancing onto her shoulders, moving on to massage the oil into her bright pink legs.

She turned to Jill and Michelle and said conspiratorially, "You'll never guess what I saw on my way back from the centre of town?"

"What?" asked Michelle as Jill was bathing her left eye with the Optrex lid filled with liquid.

"A black Labrador walking a naked man!" announced Julie.

"Seriously? Don't you mean a naked man walking a Labrador?" asked Michelle.

"No, and it was definitely a black Labrador walking a naked man," confirmed Julie.

Jill now taking the Optrex lid away from her eye and squinting, she rubbed her eye as she tried to focus.

"Ok a black Labrador, but surely the man was walking the dog," asked Michelle again.

"Oh no, that wouldn't be possible," stated Julie conclusively.

"I'm going to ask," said Michelle looking at Jill, "Why wouldn't it be possible?"

"Because the man was blind so the black Labrador was walking the naked man," said Julie.

"What? He's blind and totally naked? Was he not wearing anything?" asked Michelle.

"Only a smile and flip flops," confirmed Julie.

"Where was he going?" asked Jill.

"Don't know, but the dog looked like he was heading towards the beach," said Julie.

"I need a drink!" said Michelle as she pulled her legs from the sun lounger and rose herself up and headed towards the villa's kitchen. Jill returned to soaking her eyes with the Optrex Julie had bought for her, double checking it was Optrex. Whilst Julie finished applying the oil to her legs and laid herself prostrate on her sun lounger allowing the sun to burn away the impression of the hands.

Total silence permeated the garden of the villa as Michelle returned from the kitchen carrying a silver tray with 3 full wine glasses perched atop of it.

"Why are your nipples stuck out on storks?" asked Julie.

"I found some ice," said Michelle.

They sat in the heated solitude of the garden sipping their wine in silence, the quiet interrupted briefly by a solitary bird's wings as it took a brief respite in a branch of a lemon tree. A car horn sounded in the distance interrupting the tranquil silence, they heard steps from the villa and saw Charles walking through the open doors of the villa dressed in Khaki shorts and a white T-shirt both impeccably pressed with brown open sandals on his feet, he walked straight passed them towards his silver Audi A4 parked at the front of the villa.

Calling out as he passed, "You're with me Michelle."

"Duty calls," said Michelle as she grabbed her beach dress throwing it over her shoulders as she jogged towards the car.

She sat gingerly on the piping hot black leather seat next to Charles, he was already on the move, she crashed back on her seat lunging for the car door managing to shut it just before the entrance wall gate loomed up and they were through barely stopping as they turned right out of the entrance past the impassive staring concrete lions.

It was unbearably hot inside the car's interior as the air conditioning fought a losing battle against the latent heat. After approximately a mile of silent driving Charles checked his rear view mirror as he slowed and eventually stopped pulling over to the side of the road.

Michelle turned towards him with an awkward nervous smile as Charles reached into the side pocket of his door and pulled out a bright flowered silk scarf, he touched Michelle on her shoulders with both his hands turning her away from him as he tied the scarf around her eyes blindfolding her, he felt her nervous shiver.

He said, "Don't worry; I just want where we are going to be a surprise, ok?"

"OK," Michelle heard herself utter in almost silence.

She felt the car lurch forward and pick up speed. The seats still burned into her legs. Charles drove in silence. Michelle sat in silence. The heat from the seats was almost unbearable but the air conditioning was now cooling the air in the cars cabin, it was the only sound in the car the air conditioning working overtime to control the heat, the only other sound was that of the tires as they ground out the miles over the tarmac.

They had been driving what seemed an age to Michelle but in fact had only been 5 minutes as the car slowed and Michelle felt the car turn and jump as it now travelled over a rough surface very slowly, they bumped along for a couple of minutes as Michelle grabbed at something to hold onto for support and found the door arm rest. They came to a standstill and she heard Charles switch off the engine and open his door, Michelle could hear the air conditioning pump wheezing to a stop. Her door suddenly opened and she felt the heat immediately rush in as Charles took her arm and helped lift her out of the car, automatically raising her hands to remove the blindfold.

Charles's arm stopped her as he said, "Not yet."

Michelle felt sweat running down the sides of her face by her ears and between her breasts, she pulled at the back of her dress to release its sticky attachment to her back.

Should she be worried she thought, what did they know about Charles, nothing. Charles took her by the arm and guided her over what felt like rough ground created by tyre tracks over time, they climbed a small stone wall that could not have been more than three foot. The ground was now flat but dirt sounding and felt stony and Charles seemed to be directing her around objects. They came to a stop and Charles turned her before encouraging her backwards a step, she felt something at her back which took her by surprise as she let out a gasp immediately apologising, she was scared now, she could not hide it from herself any longer, but what could she do blindfolded against an obviously strong man such as Charles. How stupid she was to let him blindfold her, she thought. Just then she felt the bottom of her dress begin to move, over her thighs, releasing her breasts, then without thinking she lifted her arms in the air so her dress would fit over her head and off, she stood there, where she thought, naked but for the blindfold. She felt herself shake as Charles took hold of one of her arms and lifted it horizontally against something, was it wooden, it felt wooden, a tree branch maybe, and then something soft a material of some kind being wrapped around her wrist and the branch if that is what it was, anyway she could no longer move her arm as Charles took her left arm and tied it the same way.

Michelle felt herself physically shaking as if frozen to the spot, she could not believe she had allowed herself to be blindfolded by essentially a stranger and worse still then helping him to undress her and tied her arms to something, she could still not see through the blindfold. Then she heard Charles take a few steps and nothing, total silence, she could feel the sweat flowing down her body and hear her own heart beating so fast she prayed it would not burst. The silence persisted, she turned her head first one way and then the next trying to hear anything but the silence, and then she heard her voice crying out almost silently not wanting to annoy Charles, "Charles?"

After an eternity of silence she heard a faint rustle behind her, something grabbed a hold of her feet and raised her legs into the air separating them at the same time, then she felt a naked body against her naked thighs and then she felt what she hoped was Charles's cock touch her labia and entered her vagina, he began pulsing in and out, she bound her legs around him as she felt a hand around her head as it whipped away the blindfold to reveal a smiling naked Charles making love to her, she felt her whole body relax as she began to take in her surroundings once her eyes adjusted to the brightness of the sunshine. They finished making love and Michelle had relaxed enough to realise that she was tied to a thick low tree branch with more scarfs similar to the one she had been blindfolded with.

They were in a sort of sparsely populated forest with a few tall trees but the majority were small low level ones, she could make out a number of orange trees but they were not part of an organized grove as they were not being harvested rather the fruits would drop and rot on the stony course dry ground.

Looking around where she stood still tied to the branch off to the left was beautiful green grass clearly well cultivated and watered and then she realised why. It was a golf course. Charles had disappeared again. Great he could have untied me first Michelle thought. Then she heard a distant noise, a sort of whoosh and a whack, looking over to her left in the direction of the incoming noise she saw a golfer had just taken a tee shot with what appeared to be a wood. Focusing clearer on the golfer she realised abruptly it was not any old golfer, who had just thumped the ball, it was David, and not any old David but Jill's David! "Oh shit" she thought as she quickly looked around for Charles as she needed untying now.

"Charles!" she cried out, a little too loud as the sound travelled far in the silence and she noticed David looking around.

"Charles, for fucks sake Charles!" she was now screaming under her breath trying to keep the noise to a minimum.

Whoosh, whack she heard again from her left, this time it was Steve who had teed off. Her husband Tony was now manoeuvring himself into position bending to place his tee in the ground and his ball on top.

"Charles now would be a good time, Charles." Michelle pleaded,"Fuck Fuck Fuck."

Whoosh, whack. Michelle heard faint laughter as her husband sliced his ball badly sending it in Michelle's direction.

"Charles, where the fuck are you? I need you now!" Michelle cried out in total frustration.

The men were now walking towards her and it looked as though Steve had spotted her as he stopped walking gathering the others attention as he pointed directly at Michelle some 200 yards away, all she could think of to do was turn her head away hoping they would not recognise her, who was she kidding Tony would recognise her anywhere naked or dressed, tears were streaming down her cheeks uncontrollably, she could only stand there slumped over tears hitting the ground without touching her cheeks now, her hands tied to the branch, try as she had she could not release herself from her ties.

She could hear the men shouting in her direction asking if she was alright, it could not be long now before they recognised her and her humiliation would be complete along with her divorce no doubt.

Her shoulders heaved up and down in rhythm to her tears; she could not bear to raise her head. The shouts of concern from David, Steve and Tony reached a crescendo as they neared, Michelle had given up and was in total dismay when she felt something touch her skin at her left wrist and she realised it was a knife as it ripped through her torment, as her right wrist was released she turned and ran as quickly as she could without looking back, she jumped over the three foot wall and into the empty silver Audi A4 the seats heat burning into her naked flesh. Charles opened the driver's door and jumped in throwing Michelle's dress at her in one flowing movement.

Turning to her he asked, "How do you feel?"

"How do I feel? How do I feel? Are you for real? How the fuck do you think I feel?" cried Michelle, doubled over as if shielding her nakedness her hands holding her wet eyes.

She took hold of her dress and held it to her face allowing it to fall over her breasts.

"Can we please leave here now," she whispered as she wiped her face with her dress, the tears beginning to ease.

"Of Course," said Charles as he wrapped his left arm around the back of Michelle's seat.

Starting the engine with his right hand and putting the gearshift into reverse as he turned to look over his left shoulder reversing all the way back down the rough terrain of the track to the tarmacked road. Reversing onto the road he put the Audi into drive as he drove away and to Michelle's surprise away from the villa, she felt a shiver not sure if it was from the air conditioning or the fear rising again from deep inside of her, where on earth were they heading now she thought.

Charles pulled over to the side of the road leaving the engine idling which left the air conditioning without sufficient power to cope and gasped noisily in its efforts to contain the heat within the confines of the car's interior.

Turning to Michelle he said, "Put on your dress, it will help you to feel at ease."

"I need more than a dress to help me feel at ease, I need a drink, and a bloody strong one at that!" her voice surprisingly strong.

"How do you feel?" Charles asked again.

"How do I feel?" Michelle repeated looking directly into Charles' eyes looking for something, not sure what and not sure what had just transpired at the side of the golf course, certainly nothing remotely like anything she had experienced before.

Her body was tingling all over, her heart had finally found it's natural rhythm, she was aware of a glow from her body she had not experienced before, she was experiencing an anti-climax in some strange way at not being caught, she was exhilarated, and Oh My God was she Horney! A smile appeared on her face that Michelle could not control. She felt seriously Horney!

"I thought so," said Charles smiling knowingly as he put the car into drive and looking over his shoulder checking for vehicles approaching behind him, seeing there were none he moved the car back onto the road and slowly gained speed as Michelle did indeed put her dress on over her head and then shoulders having to lift her bum pulling the dress down over her thighs, all the time the smile did not leave her face.

It was only a minute later that Charles turned his Audi A4 into a large stone covered car park; the Audi ripped dust up in its wake as Charles found a spot he was comfortable with slightly behind the main group of approximately 100 cars.

They sat quietly in the car whilst the dust settled and Michelle could see the large white three storey building in front of them which housed the golf club their husbands were playing at.

Michelle looked across at Charles who just looked blankly back. Three men approached the car park from a side door of the building pulling behind them their golf clubs attached to trolleys, hands raised in salute as they separated and made their way to their individual cars. There was a large glass area in the centre of the building with large glass doors on either side of a central glass turnstile entrance doorway. The ground floor of the building housed a reception area and to the right of which were two lifts and a stairway, to the side of which was a corridor which led to a gymnasium. To the left of the reception area was the changing rooms for the golf course and a shop which contained everything golf, from clubs to knickers and all in between. The second floor consisted of a large bar and restaurant area and to the rear of which was an even larger function room. The second floor consisted of a few infrequently used offices except for the exceptionally large office of the club chairman; the rest of the space was used as storage.

Fernando Torres Marquez was the grand self-important chairman, whose only qualification for his gratuitous position was he was a school friend of the owner some 30 years prior. He was a rather plump individual of close to 20 stones in weight for his height of five foot 2 inches. He was bald with a rib of black hair around the rim of his head and a small black moustache. He wore a dark blue suit, always, with a matching waistcoat and a white open necked shirt, sometimes with a cravat but he always carried his Romeo y Juliet cigar whether lit or not.

"C'mon," Charles summoned and opened his car door and climbed out shutting it again as he stood waiting for Michelle.

There was a pregnant pause, if you can call it that, as Michelle sat where she was watching Charles stand waiting for her. Michelle opened her door and pulled down the rear of her dress which was stuck all the way down her back and legs with sweat and the heat from the leather seats as she stood and closed her door behind her. Charles held out his hand so Michelle walked around the front of the car's bonnet to reach Charles and took his hand as they began to walk towards the glass entrance, Michelle's curiosity aroused.

"As we enter you will see lifts on your right, walk to them and wait for me, do you understand?" asked Charles.

Michelle nodded her understanding as they walked through the glass turnstile, the coolness of the interior hit immediately as it was like going from one climate to another, she shuddered from the cold air making her way to the lifts as Charles had instructed, he walked straight on to speak with the pretty young Spanish receptionist. Michelle could not quite hear but she thought Charles was conversing in Spanish and he was certainly flirting with the young girl.

Michelle shook her head as she thought "don't be silly, how could you be jealous?" so she turned away so she could not see Charles or the receptionist. "Damn." She thought as she heard the receptionist giggling, "She's flirting with him too." Standing there with her back to reception she looked down to see her foot tamping in impatience. "Damn it girl," she told herself "control yourself!"

A middle aged man in a waiters uniform walked directly to the lift pressed the call button and stepped inside as the doors opened looking decidedly unimpressed by Michelle's now shabby appearance, she wore no makeup which in itself was sacrilege to Michelle, her hair was in total disarray, and as for her dress, well it was only meant for the beach and was saturated with sweat in places and was also clinging to her body especially around her breasts which accentuated their shape and size and to Michelle's great consternation around her hips which did not need any further accentuation.

Michelle felt extremely self-conscious as she waited rather impatiently now and a little worried as she was aware this was the clubhouse the husbands frequented and could walk through any number of doors any moment. Charles appeared besides her startling her and pressed the call button for the lift, as they entered the polished stainless steel interior Michelle could not contain her curiosity any longer.

Turning to Charles she asked, "What are we doing here?"

Charles smiled as he hit the button for the second floor, "You'll see."

The lift doors opened onto a reception area that was deserted and deathly quiet, they turned left out of the lift walking past the reception area to the end of the corridor and tried the large double wooden polished varnished door in front of them only to find it was locked.

Charles looked at Michelle and smiled lifting his eyebrows as he took what appeared to be a flattened crooked nail from his pocket and manipulated it in the lock releasing the mechanism, he turned the door knob and the large door opened silently, he beckoned Michelle inside.

The door opened onto a huge opulent room which was overly warm and airless, Charles walked directly over to a set of French doors on the far wall and opened them which led to a small balcony, there was another set of matching French doors some twenty feet away which Charles opened as well letting both air and natural light into the room.

Michelle closed the door and walked slowly into the room taking in each component slowly. To the left as you entered were a pair of large brown leather sofa's facing each other with a small coffee table in between sat atop a Persian rug, in front of the sofa's rested a huge solid mahogany desk with an equally huge matching mahogany and green leather chair, in front of the desk was a couple of matching but smaller chairs. The wall to the right had a couple of mahogany sideboards with a number of photographs in silver frames. All the walls housed a number of oil paintings trying to impress but failing in their quality. The wall to the left housed a solitary cabinet with a variety of liquor bottles on top and a number of crystal glasses sat on top of a silver tray, next to which was a modern fridge which looked totally out of place. On the same wall was a door which led to a bathroom complete with bath, shower, washbasin and toilet all made of marble and was immaculately spotless.

Having opened the French doors Charles walked slowly over to the drinks cabinet, not seeing what he was looking for he opened the fridge and took out a bottle of chilled white wine and finding a corkscrew on top of the drinks cabinet opened the wine.

Michelle's curiosity aroused yet again she asked, "Is this your office?"

Once Charles had stopped laughing he said, "No it's the chairman's of the golf resort, that's what I was finding out from the receptionist, he is away on business for a couple of days."

"What if someone comes in?" asked Michelle.

"There is no one to come in with the chairman away, we have it to ourselves," Charles confirmed.

Michelle took the glass of wine offered by Charles smiling as she took it and wandered over to the balcony; it was about ten feet wide but only four foot deep but with a view to die for out over the golf fairways to the mountains beyond. There was a practice putting green directly below with half a dozen golfers knocking balls towards the hole in the centre and to the left further forward a pitching green again with half a dozen golfers pitching until there round of golf was to commence.

The sun beat down on the unprotected golfers as some returned from their excursions with varying degrees of satisfaction showing on their faces whilst others walked to begin in excited anticipation at being able to show their prowess without falling flat on their faces.

"So do you know the chairman whose office we are occupying?" asked Michelle.

"I wouldn't say I know him, he is more of a slight acquaintance with the emphasis on slight," said Charles.

"What's he like?" asked Michelle curious as to who would want such an opulent and large office.

"In terms of looks then you only need to observe the portrait over the drinks cabinet," said Charles.

Michelle walked over to take a closer look before saying, "He looks like the Spanish equivalent of Toad of Toad Hall, what's the medal for he's wearing around his neck?"

"That is without doubt the best description of him I've heard, as for the medal he probably found it in a Lucky Bag, I'm not aware of him being awarded a medal for anything," Charles answered chuckling at Michelle's description.

"He must be good at his job though, to be running the whole golf complex," said Michelle.

"Well not really, the golf manager actually runs the resort; the chairman's position is really in name only, he is a social and events manager but he was a school friend of the owner who appears to owe him for something so he now has this very well paid job for doing very little," explained Charles.

"Well do you think Senor Toad of Toad Hall will mind if I take a shower in his ever so immaculate bathroom?" asked Michelle.

"There is very little he can do as we are here and he is not. Therefore you should help yourself," suggested Charles.

"Ok then, see you in five."

With which Michelle made her way towards the open door of the balcony and stripped off her dress, struggling as she did so as it steadfastly stuck firmly to her back from the still sticky sweat, once off she flung it over the door.

"It may dry a little, I can hardly hang it over the balcony, It would be like a flag, someone would be bound to investigate," with which she turned naked and walked into the bathroom.

Charles heard the shower turned on and a shallow scream from Michelle, Charles laughed to himself at the thought that Michelle had been surprised by the water being too hot or too cold.

He sat on the wall of the balcony taking in the view whilst drinking his wine; a light wind blew in the room flicking the bottom of Michelle's dress against the door.

Hearing the shower stop Charles decided to freshen their drinks but could not see Michelle's glass so assuming she had taken it in the bathroom with her he filled a new glass for her and placed it on the top of the wall of the balcony next to his.

Michelle wandered in through the main room from the bathroom wearing a white towel wrapped around her but it was ever so short reaching only slightly beyond her navel.

She approached the balcony reaching out with her left hand feeling the bottom of her dress to see if it had dried any.

Charles lifted and offered her glass of wine saying, "Nice boob tube."

"Thanks, I don't know why he has such small towels," said Michelle.

"Perhaps he doesn't have much to dry," commented Charles.

Michelle let out a giggle as she moved closer to the edge of the balcony enjoying the sun on her still damp body; she sipped her wine and placed her glass atop the balconies wall allowing her neck to fall all the way back as she closed her eyes to the sun's rays.

She heard a faint sound behind her which she took to be Charles' shorts hitting the tiled surface of the floor; she brought her head forward in anticipation as her eyes took in the tranquil scene of a vaguely empty golf course, which clearly it was not. She felt the warmth of Charles' body as he closed in on her slowly keeping just out of touch. She leaned forward a touch placing her hands atop the balconies wall and moving her left foot a few inches further out. Charles' breath caressed her neck as she felt the gentle touch on her buttocks of his semi erect phallus as it slowly increased its strength and size.

His breath was stronger and pulsated quicker against her neck as she realised her own breathing had become deeper waiting impatiently now for the inevitable pleasure of his entry. Charles took half a step forward as he entered between Michelle's wet and expectant lips thrusting himself deep inside of Michelle. He heard her slight gasp as he began his slow rhythmic thrusting motion; she looked below her at the golfers practicing their putting actions and wondered how many spent as much time practicing the putting actions with their wives. Charles increased the speed of his thrusting and Michelle matched him smiling as a golfer bellow caught her eye he almost waved but instead turned to try and put another ball. Finishing their lovemaking Charles took a sip of his wine and ventured into the bathroom and ran the shower until he felt the desired temperature and jumped underneath the fierce luke warm water.

Charles walked back into the main room naked to find Michelle sat at the desk with one leg on the floor and the other resting over the leather covered arm of the chair with the towel now abandoned over the back of the chair. Michelle smiled in pleasure at Charles's naked form as he walked over to the balcony to retrieve his glass of wine returning to rest his buttocks on top of the desk to Michelle's left. His eyes looked down at Michelle's naked body to find the end of a Cuban cigar protruding from her vagina.

"Where did you find the cigar and what is it doing down there?" asked Charles seductively.

Giggling Michelle informed Charles, "I found them in the box on the desk and I'm flavouring it, It was good enough for a president it should be good enough for a chairman."

"The box is called a humidor it helps keep the cigars moist and I'm sure El Sopo will appreciate your efforts," said Charles.

"Well I hope you're not going to call me a humidor because I'm helping to keep it moist, and what is El Sopo?"

Charles explained, "El Sopo is a toad, you did say he looked like a Spanish Toad of Toad Hall."

"I did and he does," insisted Michelle.

"Don't you think you should take it out of there now, if it stays in there too long it will go limp?" suggested Charles.

"Why, is that what happens to you if you leave it in too long?" asked Michelle with a cheeky glint in her eyes.

Charles rose from the desk and walked to the open humidor and took out another four cigars and turning walked back to Michelle holding out his hand he said, "C'mon follow me."

With which they walked over to the balcony and he positioned Michelle onto the corner of the wall so she could sit on it similar to the desk's chair with one leg on the floor and the other raised onto the balconies wall.

As Michelle made herself comfortable on the wall with one leg akimbo Charles pulled out the damp Cuban Romeo Y Juliet cigar from inside Michelle and put it on top of the wall to dry whilst replacing it with a cigar from the four in his hand. Michelle manipulated the cigar further in and out and twisted it as she did so and when she thought it was sufficiently flavoured she replaced it with another from Charles' hand, repeating the process until they had five cigars drying on the wall, turning them occasionally so that they dried evenly.

Happy with the dried cigars Charles left Michelle to return them to the humidor, she did so with extravagant gestures placing each one in turn and giggling each time one was returned with a final grand gesture of closing the lid tapping it gently as she did so.

Looking up at Charles she noticed rather disappointingly that he had not been watching her but instead he had dressed and was in the process of closing the balcony doors, grabbing her dress as he did so and throwing it over to Michelle he said, "It feels much drier, we should be leaving, your friends will be wondering what I have done with you."

"Don't worry; I think they have a good idea." Michelle said smiling as she pulled the dress over her head and for a change it did not stick whilst pulling it over her boobs and then her hips.

Finally Charles collected the wine glasses they had used and placed them on the tray of the drinks cabinet and put Michelle's towel back in the bathroom alongside his.

Michelle asked Charles if she could sign the chairman's portrait, "El Sopo", Charles did not answer her as he held the main door open for her and produced the nail like tool he had opened the lock of the door with, now locking it as they made their way towards the elevator.

They walked through the main doors of the golf club out into the bright sunshine beaming down upon them from a clear cloudless Spanish sky; the warmth hit them as if an oven door had been opened in stark contrast to the cool air conditioning of the clubhouse. Walking through the main doors as they did they had not noticed the three men walking through from the changing rooms to take the lift to the bar, David, Tony and Steve.

The drive back to the villa was uneventful by comparison to the drive out as Michelle began to relive the panic and sheer terror she had felt at being tied to the tree with her husband walking sprightly towards her. Then by complete contrast she had enjoyed the experience and ambience of their trespass of the chairman's office, she smiled at the thought of the chairman taking her in his mouth in total ignorance. Charles smiled across at her as he made the left hand turn in through the gates of the villa.

Michelle walked straight towards Jill and Julie stripping her dress over her shoulders as she walked, Jill rose to a prone position as she noticed her.

Jill asked quite annoyed, "Where the hell have you been until now, we were worried."

"Aw how nice, no need to be we were fine, just been for a drive," answered Michelle with a wink.

"Some drive," commented Julie thinking about adding to it but deciding against.

Jill remained quiet expecting Michelle to elucidate more but she also remained quiet as she sat on her sun lounger.

The silence was interrupted by Charles arriving with a wooden serving tray bearing four glasses of chilled white wine; he placed the tray on the ground by the side of Jill's sun lounger and distributed the glasses of wine out. Jill looked upon him with suspicion etched deep into her eyes; Charles noticed but said nothing just smiled politely.

"Drinks, aw goody!" said Julie.

"Thank you," added Jill.

"I guess we should be thinking about going back to the hotel after we finish our drinks, I need a long hot shower before dressing for tonight," said Jill still eyeing Michelle.

"A shower would do me the world of good too and I need to rub some after sun into my front as I can feel it burning," agreed Julie.

"I'm starving, where does everyone fancy eating?" asked Michelle expectantly.

"I don't know but somewhere new, Italian maybe?" suggested Julie.

"I'm easy," said Michelle.

"We know that!" said Jill with a mischievous grin on her face, "but where do you fancy eating?"

"Oh I don't know, why don't we walk into town and see which restaurant is the busiest, that's normally a good sign isn't it and that way it is what it is, German, French, Italian, Chinese whatever?" suggested Michelle scowling at Jill.

"Yep, good idea, I'll go along with that," agreed Julie.

"Ok good, what about after we've eaten, shall we start at Blue's?" asked Jill keenly.

"Oh yes please, I like Blue's," said Julie.

"Ok with me," agreed Michelle.

Charles just sat quietly sipping his wine whilst the girls decided on where to eat, he took his shirt off to reveal his near white chest, he was not one for sunbathing as he did not like to stand out whenever he needed to travel to the UK. As Charles was taking his shirt off Julie was putting on her bikini top on, although now relaxed in Charles' company she still did not feel comfortable bearing her breasts in front of him, well this close anyway, when he was on the balcony was different, it seemed impersonal then in some way. Jill was noticing Michelle's eyes on Charles she seemed to be looking upon him in some different way after their so called "drive", she had clearly been besotted with Charles since their first meeting but now whilst still clearly besotted she was apprehensive in some way. Jill made a mental note to keep an eye on the two of them.

"What of later ladies, shall I see you at Bulbous Billy's?" asked Charles matter of factly.

"Sure, what time are you thinking of being there?" asked Jill taking the decision from Michelle.

"I'll probably be there around 10pm," confirmed Charles.

"Ok, but it depends whose on stage at Blue's," Julie put in as she enjoyed the time they had spent so far at the bar.

"Take your time, the night is still young at 10pm after all this is Fuengirola," said Charles.

They began to dress and collect their things together, Julie put the sun loungers back in the positions they had found them whilst Michelle took the wine glasses back to the kitchen to wash them and put them away. They said their farewells making their way out of the villa's garden and onto the pavement turning left walking slowly in the late afternoon sunshine towards the Hotel of ageing zombies.

Nearing the resorts front with the main road in front of them and the beach beyond Julie asked if they could walk the rest of the way on the beach as she still had not been on it and she would not like having come all the way to Fuengirola to leave without once having strolled down the renowned golden sands. Jill and Michelle agreed so they made their way across the busy main road and sat on the short retaining wall next to the beach to take off their shoes.

The beach was still extremely busy with the holidaymaking sun worshippers tanning their almost naked bodies; there were some cooling themselves in the tranquil Mediterranean Sea others playing football alongside it but the majority lay still and silent. There were some that had turned a deep mahogany and there were the new arrivals that were turning a bright shade of pink; pinkies as the expats called them. Some had decided they had enough sun for the day and were packing up or shaking there towels free of sand, it was one such group that they were passing close to when Julie asked, "Is she wearing a G-string?"

"No" said Michelle," she's just not shaved!"

At the Hotel they went their separate ways to their individual rooms agreeing to meet at the Hotel bar at 7pm before venturing towards the centre of Fuengirola in search of somewhere to eat.

Michelle opened the door to her room and was hit by the heated stuffiness as no air had made its way in all day so she immediately opened the balcony doors taking in a deep breath of fresh air before ripping off her dress and kicking off her shoes and collapsing on the bed, closing her eyes she thought to herself, just an hour and then I will shower and change.

Jill opened her door to be greeted with a gentle breeze blowing through the curtains from the balcony doors she had left ajar, she searched her drawers for the attire she would wear that evening, once she was satisfied with her choice laid out on the made up bed she undressed and walked into the bathroom to shower.

Julie walked into her room and was hit by the stuffiness Michelle had encountered so opened the balcony doors before stripping off and taking a cold shower to cool down her burning front, having showered she looked at her naked front to be pleased that the hand prints although could just about be seen were all but covered by her bright red appearance. Her front was painful and she knew she had overdone the sun today in her determination to hide the handprints covering her breasts. Sitting on the edge of the bed she unscrewed the cap of the bottle of Nivea after sun and plastered liberal amounts all over her breasts, shoulders, stomach, legs and feet and then laid back to feel the delightful breeze from the open balcony door brush over her body with a pleasing cooling effect.

Meanwhile Jill was taking an extended shower as she had made a decision during the day, she was going to try something she had not tried before but what the hell she had thought she had nothing to lose, certainly not the husband who had not deemed to touch her wanting body for two whole years. Searching through her husband's toiletries she had found what she needed as accompaniment in the shower. Moistening and lathering her whole body under the hot shower she turned her back to the shower allowing it to hit her back and drip down her buttocks whilst taking her husband's razor and ever so gently began to run it through her pubic hair, starting at the top and running the razor down in between her legs slowly picking the hair off the blade before starting again. She found that she was sweating and not from the heat of the water. Finally she finished and looked at the result, "Hmm, different" she thought, then she cleaned the razor under the shower before turning the temperature of the water to cold staying under as long as she could take it. Turning the shower off she looked down at her erect nipples and smiled as she grabbed her towel and began to dry herself, when she was satisfied she was dry enough she laid her towel back on the wall heater and walked naked into the bedroom to the full length mirror.

Standing before the mirror in all her naked glory she nodded in satisfaction at her work and walked over to the chair in front of the vanity mirror with the intention of starting to put her make up on but stopped herself instead she turned and returned to the full length mirror to admire her work once again, smiling in satisfaction she returned to the bathroom and picked up her husband's razor returning it to where she had found it.

Whilst applying a thin coat of makeup she had decided she would follow in Michelle's footsteps for once and daringly for her, wear no underwear at all this evening. Walking to the balcony naked she was feeling more self-assured as she looked out over the still busy beach, there were still men by the sea shore playing football, a number of men and women throwing a Frisbee between themselves and to her right she could see two couples playing badminton over a makeshift net. There were a number of people packing up for the day to return to their hotels in preparation for their evening entertainment whatever that might be.

Jill was killing time as she was still deliberating exactly what she was to where for the evening, having decided to where a brand new pair of turquoise high heel Jimmy Choo shoes which she had paid far too much for but had fallen in love with at first sight. What was troubling her was what to wear with them, she had a lovely pleated shortish turquoise skirt that fell about three inches above her knees and a white blouse that would certainly show off her breasts perfectly but she was not sure it would be see through, to hell with it she thought, "I have just shaved the most intimate part of my body and I am worrying about whether my nipples will show through my blouse, really, go for it!"

Dressing slowly as she was enjoying the intimacy of nakedness beneath her clothes and the unusual erotic feel of pure smooth skin between her legs, once she had pulled on her shoes she walked in front of the full length mirror and she could not help but smile at her seductive reflection.

Putting her money and a hankie with a lip gloss into her satin black Gucci handbag she strode vibrantly to the door picking up her key on the way, opened the door and stepped through into the hallway that lead to the lift and suppressed a little shriek as a gust of wind blew down the corridor and she felt it through her legs where the hair used to be. Striding to the lift she did not notice the wide grin on her face.

Arriving in the hotel bar Jill noticed that she was the last to arrive and Michelle and Julie were sat with drinks waiting for her, as she approached their table Julie announced, "We've decided on the drinks for tonight, it's Bacardi and coke, ok?"

"Yes that's fine with me," and taking a sip of the drink in front of her said, "Oh, that's good!"

"So after we grab something to eat it's straight to Blue's, is that ok with everyone?" asked Julie eagerly.

"Yep, cool," agreed Michelle.

"Fine with me," agreed Jill.

Having finished their drinks the three of them made their way through the front entrance of the Hotel out into the early evening sunshine and made their way towards the centre of Fuengirola. They only met a few people walking the opposite way to themselves which tended to be the late stragglers from the beach either making their way back to their hotels to change or some going directly to a bar to start their evenings drinking early.

Michelle suggested they stop somewhere on the way into Fuengirola for a drink but Julie was against it as she wanted to go to Blue's as soon as they could so Jill and Michelle agreed they would find somewhere to eat and then go directly to Blue's.

They happened upon a Spanish restaurant with some fifteen or so tables outside in front that were about sixty percent occupied so they decided to try it. The large black and silver sign announced the name of the restaurant,"Rafa's"; they found a table directly under it that shielded their eyes from the strong low lying evening sun. They ordered a glass each of house white wine to drink whilst they looked at the menu which appeared quite extensive for a relatively small restaurant. The waiter returned with their white wine and brought them a bowl of green olives and slices of Parma ham to nibble on whilst they made their selection from the menu. Julie decided on a prawn salad and sat impatiently as Michelle and Jill took their time deciding on slow cooked garlic lamb with French fries and swordfish with lemon mash respectively.

"Why do they call chips French fries for Christ's sake, the French wouldn't know a chip if it sat on them!" asked Michelle.

"Dunno, not really one of those questions of life that I have bothered to waste time on," answered Jill.

Michelle looked at Jill quizzically and then burst out laughing, saying, "No, I guess not."

Clearly Julie was impatient for the food to arrive so that they could go to Blue's and had already said they should not have picked a Spanish restaurant as they took so long over everything. Their food arrived eventually and it was worth the wait, the seafood was fresh as you would expect and the lamb as Michelle described it was, "to die for".

The waiter approached the table to clear their plates and to prevent Michelle ordering any more drinks Julie thrust a 50 Euro note into the waiters hand saying, "I guess we can go now."

"What about your change?" asked Jill.

"The waiter can have it for a tip," suggested Julie.

"Some tip, Julie," said Jill.

Jill and Michelle followed Julie out of the restaurant as she made a bee line for Blue's; Michelle turned to Jill and said, "I'd laugh if it was shut tonight."

"Aw don't, I think she would sulk for the rest of the week," said Jill.

A little over ten minutes later they were walking through the pink and blue neon lights of the entrance to Blue's. They were hit by almost total darkness apart from four spotlights focused on the stage where Men O'Pause were dancing to "Don't leave me this way" by the Communards, wearing blue ripped denim hot pants and nothing else but their shoes, rapturous applause greeted every gyration and over the top camp mannerisms. The girls stood at the entrance and watched as they knew they would not be able to buy a drink until they were finished and returned behind the bar. Julie was in her element enjoying every raucous moment of their dancing, they eventually finished and after a considerable number of bows accompanied with shouts of encore they returned to their normal duties behind the bar.

Michelle made her way through the assembling crowd at the bar to be served by Christobelle the campest of the camp dancers with a considerable penchant for facial makeup and one of the nicest men in the bar who wore a permanent smile for any and all the guests of the bar. He quickly despatched Michelle with her three Bacardi and cokes and when she returned to the others she found them sitting at a table just three tables away from the stage.

Camp Teddie was bouncing onto the stage and welcoming everybody in his usual way, he continued, "We have tonight a guest who has come all the way here from a grand tour of their own back garden, just as well as it's the only place she hasn't been barred from, so please be upstanding for the one and she is one believe me, it's Elviise!"

With the background music to Queens "Flash" booming out she walked on stage wearing a long floor length white fun fur coat which she discarded to the floor to reveal her black satin dress that was open from her neckline down to her cleavage, she wore a collar around the back of her neck similar to an Elvis neckline, her jet black hair was up in an enormous beehive with a silver medallion attached to the centre and her dress barely made it past her bum revealing jet black suspenders and stockings with high heel black shoes. She walked silkily forward to the edge of the stage waiting for the applause to crescendo and at that point started to sing Flash in the voice of Barry Gibb to tumultuous applause.

Julie was looking decidedly confused by this time and trying over the loud sound system asked, "Why is he dressing like a female Elvis and singing a Queen Song like Barry Gibb?"

It was too much for her to take all at once but someone behind her had heard her and said, "She loves Elvis but try as she might she can't do his voice, the best voice she can do is Barry Gibb so that it what you have."

"Well why doesn't he, sorry she dress like Barry Gibb?" asked Julie of the man behind her.

"Would you want to go on stage in a dress wearing a beard?" he asked.

"No, I guess not," said Julie.

Michelle and Jill were laughing at Julie's consternation and clapping and singing along to "Flash" which as it happened was very good, she then went on to sing "Saturday Night Fever" which always went down well. Just over an hour later she finished off with "Dancing Queen" by Abba and was replaced on stage by Men O'Pause again this time dancing to "I Will Survive" by Gloria Gaynor. Just as the song started everybody in the audience rose to their feet as Men O'Pause appeared from all over the club summoned to the stage by the music, the majority of them left customers at the bar in their wake, all four spotlights followed their gyrating hips as the crowded audience danced and sang along to the deafening music. The music ended with the audience remaining on their feet clapping in unison to the beat and shouts of "More, More, More", although the members of Men O'Pause were returning to their chores they were forced back onto the stage for an even rowdier encore of "I Will Survive".

Jill checked her gold Gucci watch to find it was 11.15pm and thought they had agreed to meet Charles at 10pm at Bulbous Billy's Bar, she nudged Michelle and Julie pointing at her watch, Michelle nodded whilst Julie just shrugged her shoulders. Jill and Michelle picked up their handbags and rose out of their rickety chairs turning to leave, Jill elbowed Michelle's elbow nodding at Julie so Michelle took the hint and unceremoniously grabbed Julie by the arm and yanked her off her seat nearly knocking the table over as she did so.

Outside in the warmth of the evening and relative quiet after the rousing dancing to "I Will Survive" Michelle said, "I thought they were never going to let Men O'Pause back behind the bar, they are seriously good aren't they?"

"Absolutely brilliant," agreed Julie.

"Yes, I like them; they are really nice behind the bar as well, so polite," added Jill.

"Do you think Charles will be annoyed at our being late?" asked Julie.

"I shouldn't think so; it wasn't a definite time he just said he would be there around 10pm that's all," said Michelle matter of factly.

"Are we going to have a couple of songs, we need the practice before Thursday, we should think what to sing," suggested Jill.

"I'm game," said Michelle.

"We know that but are you going to have a sing with us!" giggled Jill.

"Cheeky!" laughed Michelle giving Jill a friendly shove.

"I like "Really Saying Something"," said Julie.

"Yep that's good I'll go along with that," agreed Jill.

"What about, "Robert DeNiro's Waiting"?" asked Michelle.

"Yep another good one," agreed Jill again.

There discussions continued until their arrival at Bulbous Billy's Bar, they made their way past the people stood outside drinking and smoking, there was a definite smell of cannabis in the air. The inside of the bar was crowded and there was a young girl on stage wearing the miniest of miniskirts in bright red with no knickers much to the delight of the men who had crowded around the stage and not for the singing as she was trying to sing "I will always love you" by Whitney Houston but was killing it and most of the unruly crowd were letting her know despite her friends and new found men friends at the front of the stage willing her on.

Jill, Michelle and Julie slowly made their way to the bar whilst taking in the crowd, Jill noticed the Three Stooges sat at the same table they had occupied the evening before and were again prodding and poking each other. It looked as though Elton John had made it with Lady Gaga who was refreshing his tongue inside her throat, they certainly made an effort to dress up, there was a guy Jill thought was trying to look like Bryan Ferry but it could have been Frank Sinatra she would have to wait until he sang to verify which he was trying to be. There was two Cher's in different dresses thank God; she thought one could be male but again was not sure so once again would have to wait for the song. There was a Freddie Mercury, obviously a Dolly Parton, a Barbara Streisand, a Cliff Richard; someone said Prince was on his way whilst someone else responded "I hope he doesn't use the lift as he may be stuck again!" There were so many people who had taken the trouble to dress like their favourite stars; Jill even saw Laurel and Hardy making their way over to the Three Stooges.

They managed to buy drinks at the bar thanks to Michelle and as they made their way from the bar into the centre of the room Julie saw Charles sat at a table beckoning them over, it was some four tables from the stage. Charles gave each of them an air kiss as they approached and sat themselves at the table.

The room was dimly lit and the décor was drab which did not seem of importance to the customers as they had come for the karaoke and to see and hear the numerous lookalikes who congregated amongst themselves towards the front of the stage alongside the bar.

Despite the hour the evening was just starting to liven up as Larry and Moe from The Three Stooges took to the stage with the backing music to "A Bridge Over Troubled Waters", they were clearly well known by the expats in the crowd as loud applause greeted them.

The crowd was very much a mix of regular expats and the costume singers with holidaymakers who had heard about the bar from their holiday Reps. The crowd was also a mix of varying degrees of intoxication from relatively sober to some on the edge of having too much to drink.

Jill turned to Charles saying, "I see Barry the barfly is sat at his usual spot at the bar."

"Yes, he's normally in just sits at the bar with his drink and only lets on to someone if they let on to him first, he just considers it manners, he won't force his attention onto anyone, although he is very intelligent and knowledgeable, he's a really nice guy," said Charles.

Jill now turned to Michelle and Julie, "So are we agreed on "Really Saying Something"?"

Both Michelle and Julie nodded their agreement so Jill gestured with her hand that she was going to see the DJ Mad Mike to put their names down for a song on the stage, they all nodded in agreement as she stood up making her way carefully in between the crowded tables towards the bar and then turning left towards the stage. Passing one of the tables she was nudged forward and crashed slightly into a young woman sat with a glass raised to her mouth at the table next to the aisle by the bar, she turned in a vile torrent of blasphemous personal abuse aimed at Jill who just looked at the drunken woman in disgust continuing on her way to put their request in with Mad Mike.

Mad Mike recognised her and smiled at her saying, "I have a Dolly, a Cher, a Frank Sinatra, a Stevie Wonder, it goes on and on, I tell you what, I'll put you on after Stevie Wonder he's not that good so the crowd will be glad to hear you after!"

"Oh brilliant, thanks Mike," said Jill as she turned to make her way back to their table.

Walking back along the aisle by the side of the bar she noticed someone behind the bar she had not seen before, he was a relatively tall man maybe 5 foot 10 inches bald with a large beer gut hanging over his trousers with a perpetual frown and a day's growth of facial hair and the largest hooter she had ever seen, it must be Bulbous Billy she thought, his nose reminded Jill of a Proboscis monkey.

Again she passed the drunken young woman who swore again at her as she passed by but again Jill ignored her abuse.

Sitting herself back down at their table she turned to Charles pointing towards the bar, "Is that bulbous Billy?"

"Yep, that's him," confirmed Charles.

"My God that's some impressive nose!" stated Jill at which all four of them looked towards the bar.

Michelle and Julie stared open mouthed until Charles felt obliged to say something on behalf of poor bulbous Billy.

"The bar may be called Bulbous Billy's and he does have a good sense of humour but he can be sensitive about it, you must remember he dealt drugs out of London and was a hard man at one time, alright a good number of years ago but he can still be dangerous you wouldn't want to upset him."

"I wouldn't dream of it," said Michelle whilst Julie still gazed upon him.

Jill gave Julie a nudge saying it was her round, poor girl looked really apprehensive about going to the bar. Picking up her handbag and forcing a smile as she rose to make her way to the bar she walked past the drunken young woman who assaulted her verbally, duly noted by Charles again.

At the bar she lost her footing somewhat and nudged into Barry apologizing profusely he turned to her and smiled saying, "My dear how else would we have met."

She returned his smile saying, "Of course."

As she turned back to the bar Bulbous Billy was leaning directly in front of her she could smell his beer fuelled breath, her eyes opened wide in fear as she froze.

Billy said, "You're with Charles I see."

"Err yes, could we have three Bacardi and cokes and a red wine for Charles please."

Bulbous Billy turned to gather the drinks as the drunk young woman from the table barged in between her and Barfly Barry putting her elbows on top of the bar pushing Julie further along the bar, Julie thought she could smell stale sick on the woman. They stood in silence as Julie noticed the woman surreptitiously deposit some bluish dust into Barry's drink and stirred it with her finger as Barry looked to his right out of the bar at a slight commotion on the street, Julie's drinks arrived so she paid for them and left the bar quickly so she would not have to pass the woman returning to their table.

Julie placed the drinks onto the table from her tray, a woman on the table behind asked for the tray as she rose making her way to the bar. Sitting back down and looking around her to make sure no one overheard what she was about to say she beckoned everyone closer as she explained what she had witnessed the drunk woman do to Barry's drink, they all looked to the bar and to the woman and then to Barry and then leaned back knowingly. They put the knowledge to the back of their minds for the minute as they enjoyed a Dolly Parton suitably stuffed in the right places singing "Jolene".

It was as "Jolene" was finishing that all four of them noticed Barfly Barry making his way back along the bar side aisle from the Gents with an erection protruding from within his trousers which were now deeply damp around the groin. Making it back to the bar and onto his stool he summoned Bulbous Billy over to ask him what the hell he was putting in his whiskey, Billy just shrugged his shoulders as he wiped down the bar. Behind him Barry could hear a table full of drunken women in screams of uncontrollable laughter. Jill rose to go and confront the women only to be pulled down on her seat by Charles quite sternly looking directly into her eyes saying, "What goes around comes around, believe me." And she did. It was clear to Charles and Jill that the drunken woman had laced Barry's drink with Viagra. Jill fumed in total disgust whilst Charles patted her hand and looked upon her to calm down.

Stevie Wonder was starting his song which seemed to meet a luke warm response from the rowdy audience. Jill turned to Michelle and Julie in turn warning them to ready themselves as they were on next and that they should make their way to the stage before the current song finished.

Having given it a minute since Jill's warning she nudged Michelle and Julie for them to follow her turning to Charles to once again confirm they were going to the stage to prepare for their song; Charles smiled and nodded in response. Jill, Michelle and Julie made their way through the crowded tables and chairs coming to the last table in the row occupied by the noisy and drunken young women, as they made their way carefully past them the drunken woman who had laced Barry's drink grabbed Julie by her arm saying, "Watch who you're pushing you fucking old slapper!"

Fortunately Bulbous Billy was at the next table up towards the entrance door and saw and heard the woman, he immediately took the woman's arm and slightly twisted it so she released her grip on Julie. He admonished the woman and warned her to calm down or she would be asked to leave, she swore something under her breath whilst lifting her right hand as acknowledgement and shook her head in compliance. Meanwhile the girls had arrived at the stage and Jill and Michelle were telling Julie to ignore what the drunken woman had said as they each in turn gave Julie a hug as she was clearly upset with her cheeks being flushed and she was holding her hands clenched into fists.

Jumping onto the stage as DJ Mad Mike introduced them Julie seemed to change rapidly and relaxed when the music began to "Really Saying Something".

They began to dance in unison as they had practiced, for not very long, and the words burst forth as the crowd began clapping and roaring in approval. They clearly delighted with their time on stage and were bonding well together if not dancing too well together but the excitable crowd seemed delighted with their singing as the song ended all too quickly for the girls.

Returning to their seats they pushed Julie in front of them so that should the drunken woman start anything again Jill and Michelle could protect Julie from the woman's diatribes. As if on cue just as Julie passed the drunken woman's table off she went on one, swearing and rising up out of her chair swinging her arms as her three friends drunkenly joined in but before Jill and Michelle could wade into them Bulbous Billy appeared and picked all four women up from their table and frog marched them out of the front door of the bar to tumultuous applause all around the bar even

DJ Mad Mike interrupted his introduction of the next singers to throw his twopenneyworth into the ring.

The whole bar looked on as they witnessed Bulbous Billy waving his arms in good riddance outside as the drunken women held each other together and up as they tried walking along the darkened street. The ringleader managed a few yards before falling over and Billy looked on amused at the laughable drunken attempts of the other three women of picking their ringleader up off the floor. A second one fell to the floor in a heap grabbing a hold of a third member of the abusive team who in turn fell on top of the other two already collapsed women leaving the fourth women looking on bug-eyed trying to focus through her drunken stupor shutting one eye as if it would ease her focus. Bulbous Billy turned back to the bar's entrance shaking his head in disgust at the women's behaviour which he had seen all too often before and he knew would see again before too long.

Walking back inside to receive the odd slap on his back in recognition of his quick actions he shrugged them off as he slumbered behind the bar to muted applause and began serving a customer.

Ten minutes passed with the bar returning to its usual raucousness as singers of varying talents took to the stage, Charles excused himself as he rose and passed the girls walking through the mass of people sat around the tables drinking and talking loudly to be heard above the volume of the karaoke singers on stage.

Arriving in the fresh warm evening air outside of the bar he took a deep lungful and looked around for the women who had recently been forcefully removed from the bar by Bulbous Billy. They were not on the street so having noticed they had turned right on removal from the bar he walked briskly to the end of the street and on looking both ways saw them staggering holding each other up towards The Hotel Angeline a three star establishment that catered solely for package holiday companies. He made his way to the opposite side of the road to the hotel and sat on a small wall that surrounded an ice cream parlour that was closed for the day and watched the impending slow progress of the women.

They stumbled onto the grounds of the hotel and carefully edged their way to the entrance and disappeared inside but still Charles sat on the wall watching. It was nearly ten minutes Charles sat on the wall until he saw what it was he was waiting for, high up on the tenth floor a light appeared in one of the rooms, he could barely make out the shadows from where he observed but experience taught him what he was looking for, the group of women had congregated around the first bed in the room indicating they were putting the drunk women who had spiked Barry's drink and had put her hands upon Julie into that bed, within a minute the light went off. Another minute later a light went on in the room next door and again a minute later the light went off, he was not interested in that room tonight.

Charles walked briskly back to Bulbous Billy's Bar walking straight in to the almost toxic smell of warm bodies that had been suffocated too long without fresh air and whose deodorants had long since expired mixed with the smells of warm beer and alcohol, whilst sitting back down next to Jill he explained that he had just been refreshing his lungs in the fresh sea breeze outside.

Just as he sat down one of the Cher's was starting to sing the "Shoop Shoop" song wearing a black sequined see through oh so short dress with black suspenders and stockings with six inch black satin stiletto's. The crowd appeared to love it but the appreciation seemed mainly to come from the male side of the audience which was probably more to do with the costume rather than her vocal capabilities.

The evening was beginning to draw to a peaceful close as a number of customers began to leave the heat and stagnant air of the bar behind them with Jill, Michelle and Julie rising to join them. Charles accompanied them and this time the girls just accepted his gracious offer to escort them safely to their hotel.

They clearly enjoyed their evening together showing as it did in their demeanour as they sang all the way to their hotel hoping to encourage Charles to join in even if it was just the choruses but to no avail. They mockingly chastised him for his noncompliance to be returned with Charles' blank expression. They duly arrived at the grounds entrance to their Hotel and the girls lined up behind Charles as each in turn kissed him goodnight, first naturally enough was Michelle who tried to encourage Charles tongue out to play unsuccessfully, second was Jill who planted her lips fully upon Charles' if only for a second and finally Julie approached Charles but tripped on her heels and fell into his arms her head encroaching his chest as she straightened herself in his arms she kissed his right cheek. Grabbing Jill on one arm and Michelle on the other she linked their arms as they walked together through the front door and out of sight.

Charles glanced up at their hotel and noticed most of the lights were off, there was very few people left on the street just a few stragglers finding their way home or back to their hotels. There was a short stone wall outside the hotel so Charles sat on it whilst he gazed along the darkening street as the lights from various bars were shut off and a silence and stillness engulfed the resort. The silence was only interrupted by the distant sound of a wave as it found the shoreline and died.

Charles rose and took a 360 degree look around him as he took his white ironed silk handkerchief from his right pocket and wiped his hands before returning it. He began to move slowly strolling towards the entrance to the hotels grounds, once inside he took another look upwards to find all the windows were now dark on all fifteen floors. Satisfied he walked slowly through the main entrance to find an empty entrance hall and reception area, there was a bar area to the left of reception which was now in total darkness, the only area of light was the main entrance and reception areas and a large corridor next to it which housed two lifts one for odd numbered floors and the one on the right for even numbered floors.

Charles made his way to the lift on the right. Pressing the button to call the lift the doors opened immediately as the lift was already on the ground floor, the doors fully opened to the sound of a bell indicating the doors were open, the bell shattering the total silence and sounded extremely loud although in truth it was not. Once inside Charles pushed the button for the tenth floor and checked himself out in the mirror which occupied the wall opposite the door, patting his hair down slightly to the side of his ears, the doors opened accompanied by the what seemed excruciatingly loud bell. Out of the lift Charles turned immediately left and counted down the number of doors, standing outside the required door Charles once again put his hand in his right pocket and drew out his handkerchief. With his right hand covered by his handkerchief he turned the doorknob and found the door opened. He walked through the door and closed it again silently behind him. He waited silently by the door not moving allowing his eyes to adjust to the darkness, the only light came from a quarter moon shining through the French doors to the balcony as the curtains had not been drawn. Four minutes had passed slowly as Charles stood motionless, now satisfied his vision had adjusted as much as it would he stepped forward towards the French doors turning the lock and opened the door fully. A breeze blew in and ruffled the curtains slightly as Charles turned back to face the room, the breeze slowly released the stale booze ridden air. The first bed on his left he could make out a woman face down fully clothed in a deep sleep breathing heavily with every other breath almost a snore, ignoring her he approached the second bed. The second bed housed a woman fully dressed and on her back. Charles manoeuvred himself alongside her leaning in on top of her; he slowly slid his arms underneath her. One arm beneath her knees and the other around her shoulders and down underneath her bosom, he lifted her gently and slowly off her bed, she felt his arms about her and drew herself into his chest nudging her cheeks firmly between his arm and chest, a slight comforting murmur came from her lips. He moved slowly with the weight of her between the beds. Once free of the beds he moved towards the open French door to the balcony. He twisted as he moved through the door careful not to disturb her on the door jamb. On the balcony with her in his arms the slight breeze blew her hair onto her face, she moved, drawing herself up further into his arms her face now nestling into his neck. He looked down into the closed eyes of the drunken woman from Bulbous Billy's Bar as he moved forward against the balcony wall leaning over, her eyes opened wide in fearful sudden realisation a split second before he dropped her allowing her to fall ten floors. Without looking at the result he turned walking back into the room and observed the woman on the first bed still on her stomach breathing heavily unaware of her friend's fate. Charles walked to the door and taking his handkerchief back out of his right pocket opened the door walked through and closed it again behind him. He turned back towards the lift but ignored it taking the stairs instead. He walked down the stairs normally in no rush at all. Making it to the bottom he took the back exit which led to a fire escape which he took into a rear yard that was occupied with twelve industrial size garbage disposal units in two rows leading to a large double gate. The large wooden gate was padlocked so Charles clambered over it into the rear of a darkened street with yellowed street lights every thirty yards.

Dusting himself down he walked to the end of the street and turned right so that it would take him to the main street the hotel was on, he had no reason to hide. A woman had been out drinking all night and had witnesses to her excessive drinking; she was helped back to her hotel by her friends who also happened to be drunk. At some point during the night she had made her way out of bed for whatever reason, perhaps to go to the bathroom and in her drunkenness had mistaken the balcony for the bathroom.

An unfortunate accident, one that has happened before and would no doubt happen again.

Charles walked home in the dark of the evening through empty street after empty street; it took twenty minutes at an easy pace. Approaching his villa he turned as he heard the sirens of a police car and an ambulance in the distance. He walked around to the rear of the villa and opened the doors, walked through to the kitchen and took out a bottle of red wine, a glass and a corkscrew and took them outside to the bamboo table and chairs. He opened the bottle and poured himself a glass of red wine whilst he sat back and relaxed in the night air.

Chapter 8   Tuesday

Jill woke to the sound of a door slamming shut and realised it was their door and it was her husband David who was responsible. "Son of a bitch" she thought as she felt the brightness and warmth of the early morning sun shining through the windows as her husband had once again drawn the curtains for the desired effect. A glance at her watch, once she could focus, informed her it was 7am, reluctantly she moved over to David's side of the bed as it was still in shadow, the smell of his pungent aftershave lingered on his pillow making her gag, she was sick a little in her mouth and looking around decided to swallow it again which made her gag again.

Rising from the warmth and comfort of the bed she strode into the bathroom and cleaned her teeth before once again collapsing into bed, this time her side of the bed as the whole of it was now totally covered in bright sunshine. Jill's eyes wanting to remain shut she allowed one to partially open whilst she kneeled on the bed reaching for the curtains behind it pulling them shut, the relief from the sun's rays was immediate as she collapsed back onto the bed burying her head firmly into the middle of her pillow. Jill could feel her heartbeat through the pounding pain in her head, she silently prayed for the release of sleep.

Jill woke again some time later to the unwelcome noise of someone knocking on her door; she thought that if she ignored it it would disappear but to no avail as it continued unabated.

Reluctantly Jill rose out of bed squinting her eyes from the now fearsome sun as it gained attention through the wide gap between the curtains, moving slowly and hesitantly as she tried to focus towards the door her hand was on the lock turning it slowly to open sure in her knowledge something was wrong, she stopped whilst taking the time to look around the room, it was not the room so she turned back to the lock just at the point of realisation, she stopped and walked to the bathroom. Returning with a towel wrapped around her, she had been naked which she had realised just in time before opening the door which someone was still persistently knocking.

Jill opened the door to view Michelle in front of her dressed for the day ahead; Jill motioned Michelle inside with her hand not wanting to add to the noise in her head with talk. Jill just turned about and walked straight into the bathroom shutting the door partly to prevent the possibility of talk. She remained in the bathroom for 15 minutes. The bathroom door opened with Jill walking through a cloud of steam into the bedroom with a white towel about her torso and steam rising from her head and shoulders.

"Take it the shower was hot!" asked Michelle.

"It needed to be, my bloody head was throbbing for England!" said Jill.

"We're meeting Julie at the venta for breakfast," stated Michelle.

"Oh ok, why meeting her there? We could have gone together from here," asked Jill.

"You don't remember do you?" Michelle asked.

"Remember? Remember what?" asked Jill.

"Do you not remember the obnoxious drunken girl last night abusing Julie and spiking that guy's drink at the bar?" Michelle asked.

"Yeah ok, it's coming back to me slowly, I need food and coffee and not necessarily in that order," said Jill as she dressed.

It was a little after 10am as Jill and Michelle sat at a table outside the venta under one of the large yellow Mahou beer advertising umbrellas, both Jill and Michelle kept their sunglasses on as they ordered coffee explaining they were waiting for a friend and would then order food for their breakfast.

Jill asked Michelle, "So why are we meeting Julie here?"

"Ok so you remember the obnoxious drunk bitch that abused Julie and spiked that guy's drink with Viagra?" asked Michelle.

"Yeah, yeah what's that to do with meeting Julie here?" asked Jill.

"Well, she's gone to buy the bitch something," said Michelle.

"You're not making sense, why would she buy her something?" asked Jill.

"It's Julie, she wants to be prepared in case she sees her again so she's gone to the Pharmacia to see what she can buy to make a suitable concoction she can slip into her drink," explained Michelle.

"Oh I see, I can't believe we sent Julie though, she'll probably come back with tampons and a packet of Fisherman's Friends!" said Jill chuckling at the thought.

"Yeah she could knowing Julie, I suggested she buy a length of rubber tubing, a jar of honey, itching powder and a thousand red soldier ants when she asked what for I suggested we give the bitch an enema; she really looked confused at that so I hope she doesn't meet someone called Emma!" Said Michelle laughing uncontrollably at the thought of Julie asking everyone their name in the faint hope of coming across someone called Emma and then not remembering why she was looking for someone called Emma in the first place.

They were still smiling at the thought of Julie shopping for an "Emma" when the waiter approached them with their coffee held high on his black plastic tray. The waiter placed their cups of coffee silently in front of them as he tried to ignore the frozen smirks emblazoned on Jill and Michelle's faces.

They sat in silence sipping their coffee awaiting the foragers return. It was going to be a very hot day as the temperature was already beyond 80 degrees and there was currently no breeze. It was quiet in the venta just half a dozen people sat outside near to Jill and Michelle with no customers inside except for the Spanish regulars playing checkers silently. They had nearly finished their second cup of coffee when they saw Julie approaching some 200 yards away, they both smiled as they noticed she was walking alone so no "Emma".

Julie sat down quietly next to Jill placing her beach bag under the table, Jill and Michelle exchanged glances and Michelle nodded at Julie's bag now resting under the square heavy timbered table, Jill raised her shoulders as if to say, "I don't know". Michelle nodded directly at Jill and then at Julie's bag again, Jill shrugged her shoulders again. This was repeated several times interrupted only once by the waiter whereby more coffee was ordered along with croissants.

Michelle started tapping her nails atop the table trying to draw the attention of Jill so she might yet again nod to Julie's bag under the table, Jill ignored the annoying nail tapping despite it not helping her headache. Michelle extended her right leg under the table in an unsuccessful attempt at toe poking Jill, instead her bum slid forward at the precise moment her wooden chair slid backwards leaving Michelle to crash heavily to the concrete ground on her bum, Jill and Julie looked upon her simultaneously and broke into uncontrollable laughter. Michelle looked about her to see who had seen her unfortunate crash to the deck to feel the arms of the waiter under her armpits trying to raise her, only Michelle's right leg was now twisted around one of the table legs which made Michelle crash back onto the floor once halfway up with the waiter now crashing on top of her with his head buried into Michelle's voluminous chest. The waiter moved his arm to help raise himself back on his feet but he missed his intended target and instead grabbed a handful of Michelle's left breast, whereupon Michelle twisted with her right hand outstretched and hit the waiter across his left cheek forcing him to crash down on top of her again. By now three more waiters were rushing outside from watching the game of checkers, one approached slightly ahead of the other two but unfortunately trod on a large piece of discarded lemon which raised both his feet high into the air and with both his arms flaying uncontrollably his tray lofted high into the air as he came crashing down on top of his colleague who in turn crushed Michelle further, the waiters tray was falling rapidly back to earth and one of his colleagues stretched to catch it which he managed to one handed but he had overstretched himself thereby losing control of his momentum and crashed headfirst into the laughing Jill who although stayed in her chair it tipped backwards and so she finished on the floor with the waiter firmly attached to her looking straight into her tearful eyes.

There was a silence whilst everyone took in their positions at which point they became aware of thunderous laughter coming from Julie who had remained untouched and who now could not control her laughter. Again everyone looked at each other in turn and everyone in turn laughed at each other's predicament before slowly raising themselves up and dusting themselves down. The waiters cleared the table of now upturned cups and spilt coffee remains; they replaced the table cloth with a fresh clean one and brought fresh coffee along with their croissants. It took a good few minutes for the girls to settle down again and begin quietly to eat their croissants as the waiters looked on from the relative safety of inside the restaurant.

Finishing her croissants first Michelle thought it prudent in light of the earlier calamity to take control of Julie's interrogation. She first asked, "Did you buy anything interesting on your trip into town?"

"Just a few things," Julie managed before taking another mouthful of croissant.

"Oh, for instance?" Michelle tried.

"I bought more after sun; I've gone through so much," replied Julie.

"You can never have enough after sun, anything else?" pushed Michelle.

"I felt very decadent and I couldn't resist,"

"What!" cried Michelle.

"I bought a Cadbury's Flake, I do like to suck on a Flake," teased Julie.

"I thought you were buying something for that bitch from the bar last night," straight to the point from Michelle.

"Well I wouldn't buy here a flake that's for sure," said Julie.

"No, of course not, so what did you buy her?" asked Michelle trying to keep control through her frustration.

"Nice coffee, isn't it?" stated Jill.

"Great… Julie?" Michelle redirected starting to lose her temper now.

"Yeah, coffee's great," said Julie.

"Not the bloody coffee, what did you buy for the bloody bitch from the bar for Christ's sake!" said a seriously irritated Michelle.

"Ok, keep your hair on, um that's where I started I suppose, hair remover, I bought hair remover to start with," said Julie.

"Hair remover? What the hell did you buy hair remover for?" asked Michelle confused at Julie's purchase.

Meanwhile Jill just sat listening enjoying her head finally recovering.

"All in good time, I also bought eye drops," said Julie stringing her answers out as she was enjoying Michelle's frustration.

"Eye drops!" Michelle exclaimed.

Julie raised her hand for Michelle to keep quiet as she continued, "Heat rub."

"Heat...." Michelle tried to interrupt but Julie's hand was up again.

"Heat rub yes, wasabi paste and syrup of ipecac, oh and of course a laxative," finished Julie.

"Well that's more like it, a laxative, what's all that other stuff for, and what the hell is syrup of ipecac?" asked Michelle.

"If you don't know what syrup of ipecac is well, that is for you to find out, the rest is part of the concoction to be administered surreptitiously, the eye drops contain visine and could be deadly, could be, the laxative is magnesium sulphate or Epsom salts, the heat rub is not for internal use but what the hell she's annoyed me, the rest are just little extras for her benefit," explained Julie.

"Holy Shit!" said Michelle, "Where did you learn that?"

"Ah, well that's a different story and I would need to know you a hell of a lot longer and better to explain that one," said Julie with a wink to Jill.

"Don't you think you're going a little over the top there, wouldn't just a laxative do the job just as well?" Jill asked with a little concern showing in her voice.

"Oh don't worry, the concoction will be fine once mixed and will certainly have the desired effect," answered Julie with a satisfied grin on her face.

"You really are a surprise Julie; Jesus I wouldn't want to upset you," added Jill.

"People really should be careful who they annoy," stated Julie whose face had become stern and determined.

Jill and Michelle exchanged glances and silently agreed to leave the subject alone hoping Julie would calm down during the day. Julie had surprised and shocked them both by her determination at buying the ingredients and seemingly knowing what ingredients to buy in the first place, who the hell had heard of syrup of ipecac? They thought it best to make their way to Charles' villa and relax which they hoped would put Julie in a more tranquil frame of mind, it was clear they really did not know Julie at all. Jill was now regretting her trick on Julie's boobs and hoping she was not to suffer from Julie's formula.

They arrived at the villa some fifteen minutes later after walking in relative silence from the venta; Julie's shopping spree was still a little puzzling and somewhat uncomfortable for Jill and Michelle. They walked through the lion guarded gates into the silence and tranquillity of the villa's gardens making their way towards the swimming pool which remained as they had left it the previous day. They took out what they needed from their bags and laid their towels over the sun loungers before repositioning them in line with the sun's rays,

Michelle took their bags inside the villa and deposited them on one of the sofas by the vacant chimney breast. Michelle returned to the sun loungers immediately having not bumped into Charles and began to undress whilst Jill and Julie rubbed sun lotion into their bodies.

Jill had been thinking how Michelle and Julie were coping with not seeing much of their husbands as with herself she had nothing to miss, well nothing more than she had missed for two years but with Michelle and Julie it was different they were clearly close to their husbands.

"How are you two doing not seeing much of your husbands, is it bothering you?" asked Jill a little awkwardly.

"Not me, Steve woke me before he left this morning," said Julie with a warm smile on her face as she reminisced.

"He woke you, what on earth for? You must have been dead to the world," asked Jill.

"Oh, he was so gentle."

"How did he wake you?" asked a curious Jill.

"I felt him kissing my forehead to start with."

"He kissed your forehead?" asked Jill.

"He did, he kissed my forehead and as I began to wake he kissed my eyes then my nose and ever so slowly my mouth. He moved down to my neck caressing it with his lips and then he moved down to my nipples first my left taking it slowly in his mouth and leaving it erect before moving on to my right nipple which by this time was also erect. He then slowly made his way down to my navel licking all around and inside it before moving further down all the time I could feel his warm breath against my body as I began to tremble at the pleasure; he moved between my legs brushing over my labia a spasm took hold of my body as he did so. He moved further down kissing my knees and then my feet he caressed my toes with his tongue before moving slowly back to my knees and then his hot breath caressed my inner thighs; his nose split my lips apart as he moved slowly upwards first his hot breath touched my labia before his lips touched my wet labia my back arched as I longed for more. He moved up to my nipples again sucking them in turn as I writhed in pleasure and then he made his way back down quicker now his tongue separating my lips as it searched for my clitoris, his tongue found it and circled it and his lips joined in sucking as they drove deeper. He moved back up to my nipples and as he did so I could feel his erection pass over my knees and then my upper thighs as it approached and then entered me sending spasms all over my excited body; he began his rhythmic surges slowly at first and then became more urgent as he began to lose control of his urges and then cried out in delight as he came inside me, he kept on pulsing in and out waiting for my climax; I eventually cried out in delight allowing him to heave his hot and sweating body off me as he crashed wearily and exhausted onto the bed with an enormous smile emblazoned on his face."

"Did you have an orgasm?" asked Jill.

"No, but he worked so hard, he needed to feel his work was not in vain," said Julie.

"I have!" said Michelle cheekily.

Both Jill and Michelle watched Julie as she reached under her sun lounger her hand searching in the cool shade, she grabbed a hold of something and as her hand returned to the sunshine she revealed a Cadbury's chocolate Flake which she slowly unwrapped before touching the edge to her lips; Jill and Michelle gasped at the symbolism as Jill wiped a little drool from the side of her mouth. Jill and Michelle looked at each other and without a further word lay themselves prone leaving Julie to her chocolate.

The minutes passed in silence as the three friends bodies soaked up the sun's soothing rays until Jill's patience failed her. She turned her head towards Michelle her lips moved with no sound as she further considered her words. Eventually she released the following words, "How are Tony and you doing as you haven't seen much of each other have you?"

"Oh we're fine, you know, same old same old," replied Michelle.

"Oh good, good," said Jill having expected more from Michelle.

"Yes he woke me this morning also, too damn early by the way," said Michelle.

"Oh?" asked Jill.

"Yeah, I woke to find him on top of me making love to me whilst I was still asleep!" said Michelle.

"What, while you slept, what did you say to him," asked Jill a little too eagerly.

"I told him he could have woken me up."

"What did he say to that?" said Jill as she sat herself up as if it would improve her hearing.

"He said that I looked so cute with my eyes shut."

"Nice," said Jill.

"As if, I told him to hurry up as there was no chance of my catching up with him."

"What? You didn't mind?" asked Jill.

"Mind? What was there to mind about, I like to see him enjoy himself especially with my body. I've done the same to him, there's many a time he has woken to find my mouth around his erection. He wasn't too pleased once though when I woke him early one morning when we were staying at a hotel in Stratford Upon Avon, it was last year in May I think. Anyway I woke him shaking his arm with mine with my mouth firmly fixed around his erect penis, as he realised what I was doing he began to smile which was soon wiped of his face when I pretended to have lockjaw, his facial features moving from delight to shear panic within seconds was priceless. Unfortunately it didn't last long as it was so funny I couldn't keep a straight face. As soon as he realised I was joking he jumped out of bed and chased after me as I tried to lock myself in the bathroom until he calmed down; he caught me before I made it into the bathroom I was laughing so loud but that stopped as soon as he opened the door to our room and threw me naked into the corridor."

"My God what did you do?" asked Jill.

"About the only thing I could do as I knew he would not let me back into our room without first teaching me a lesson, so I walked along the corridor to the stairs, I thought the lift was too risky even though it was only 6.30 in the morning. I took the stairs to the ground floor and made my way to the back of the hotel where they had a gymnasium and a swimming pool, I arrived without seeing anyone so I made my way through the gym to the pool thinking I might have found a towel which had been left but no such luck so I jumped in the pool and swam a couple of lengths before hanging at the deep end waiting for Tony to find me, I knew he would look for me eventually. A couple of older guys went swimming at about 7am; they had a pretty good view of my backside until Tony showed at about 7.15am with a towel for me, as I wrapped the towel around me I couldn't help but notice how wrinkly the water had made my extremities, it was Tony's turn to laugh and he certainly made the most of it. We both had a good time when we returned to our room though and we missed breakfast!"

"I bet you haven't done that trick again," said Jill.

"Oh God yes and worse!" said Michelle, "anyway, enough of Julie and I what about David and yourself, how are you two doing together on this holiday?"

"Well I must report David woke me this morning at 6am," started Jill.

"No way, what was he after?" asked Michelle noticing Julie's ears had pricked up.

"He asked me rather pointedly and with considerable annoyance in his voice whether I had been using his razor," said Jill nodding her head at Michelle.

"Really, as if," said Michelle all ears.

"I denied it of course," confirmed Jill raising herself off her sunbed and bending slightly taking hold of the top of her bikini bottoms and with one swift downward movement lifting each leg in turn ripped off her bikini bottoms revealing her newly acquired ever so white shaved area and sat back down on her sun lounger.

"Yes!" cried out Michelle, "Go Jill....your turn next Julie!"

"It most certainly is not," Stated Julie defiantly.

After a few quiet minutes with Jill now lying naked full length on her sun lounger clearly a little self-conscious as she had never been fully naked in public before Michelle sat back up and turned to her and asked, "So what is really happening with you and David?"

"Absolutely nothing, that is the problem, he has no interest in me at all, it's as if he resents my presence, I really don't deserve this I have done nothing but he clearly has, so enough is enough when we return home he won't be, he will have to find somewhere else to live I am kicking him out I've had enough, I am going to find a job and to hell with him."

"You can't mean that, you love him," protested Michelle worried now at what she had contributed to.

"Maybe, but it's no good one way, my mind is made up," said Jill with tears forming in her eyes.

"I'm sure he will change, I'm sure he loves you, he must know how much you love him," reassured Michelle.

"Well we'll see over the next few days won't we?" concluded Jill tears now flowing freely down her flushed cheeks.

Michelle fell silent as she lay back down on her sun lounger and began laying the foundations of a plan to rescue this sad situation.

They had been sunbathing in complete silence for a little over twenty minutes when Julie piped up, "I wonder if the black Labrador is walking his naked man today?"

"Where did that come from?" asked Michelle.

"Don't know, I was just wondering that's all," said Julie.

"Well wherever they are it's nothing to do with us," said Jill.

"But are you not just the least bit curious?" asked Julie.

"Curious about what?" asked Michelle.

"Well, what is the Labrador doing with the naked man?" said Julie.

"Even if we were curious there is no way we could find them," said Jill a little bored.

"Maybe not, I suppose, just thought it might have been fun to see what they were up to today," said Julie clearly disappointed.

Charles had been listening to the conversation from his balcony, he put his book down on the table in front of him and rose himself up moving his chair behind him as he turned and walked to the edge of the balcony and leaning forward on the wall said, "It's quite easy to find them as Bob the black Labrador loves Chinese food so he always walks Peter, that's the blind man, to Fu's Chinese Restaurant at 12 midday when they open for business. The owner always saves him some food from the previous evening; you can set your watch by Bob arriving at Fu's."

"But Bob's a dog," said Julie questioningly.

"He still likes Chinese food," replied Charles.

"Oh right, thanks Charles, shall we go and see them?" asked Julie ever so eagerly.

"What for?" asked Michelle knowing it would wind Julie up.

"Oh come on, it's something to do, better than just laying here all day," pleaded Julie.

"If that's what you want to do then that is what we will do," said Jill, which sounded more like an instruction, so with that Michelle began to dress and Julie followed suit with a huge grin on her face.

They recovered their beach bags from inside the villa and shouted up to Charles what they were doing as they began to walk around the villa to the front. They walked out past the concrete lions and all three of them stopped at once and looked at each other showing the same confusion on their faces and it was Jill who spoke first, "So who knows where Fu's is?"

They looked blankly at each other and both Jill and Michelle looked at Julie volunteering her with their eyes to return and ask Charles for directions to Fu's, after all it was Julie's idea. Julie looked blankly back at Jill and Michelle for a few seconds before realising she had been seconded to ask Charles for the appropriate directions to Fu's so she turned on her heals and stomped back around the villa.

Jill and Michelle smiled and winked at each other as Julie stomped back around the villa after a pause of a few seconds they could hear Julie asking for directions which were soon forthcoming and thankfully simple.

Julie returned to the girls after a few minutes and marched straight past them turning right out of the villa's entrance, Jill and Michelle looked at each other in surprise at Julie's purposeful stride and they both jogged to catch up to her.

There was a left turn and a right turn and a further walk straight ahead but they soon arrived at Fu's Chinese restaurant, a whitewashed stone fronted building standing alone with a small car park in front and what appeared to be a small garden area to the rear.

It was 11.50am when they walked past the car park entrance, they stopped and turned to look in both directions both up and down the road but there was no sign of Bob the dog or his naked owner. They began to look around more closely to their position as they needed to find somewhere to wait that was not as conspicuous as where they were now standing.

The solution surfaced across the road as directly opposite was a bus stop which they made their way to. Julie's eyes were locked onto the restaurants front door and she did not have to wait long to witness activity. The front door opened and a middle aged Chinese man in black trousers white shirt and a black waistcoat walked outside and stretched his arms aloft and when he brought them down he placed a cigarette in his mouth with one hand and then cupped it as his other hand lit a lighter against his cigarette.

It was now 11.57am and still up and down the street there was no sign of Bob the dog. Julie was looking nervously around her; she had taken to biting her lip. Michelle was looking decidedly bored as she leaned against a lamppost whereas Jill stood boldly on the pavement her head flicking rapidly from left to right; the speed of the flicking seemed to increase as the seconds rapidly approached midday.

Michelle's right foot had begun to tap impatiently as she looked down at it she noticed a black Labrador sniffing the base of her lamppost as her eyes rose she noticed a man's bare legs then his limp heavy canvas man bag hid his midriff, he was totally naked but for his flip-flops and sunglasses.

Bob now ignored the lamppost as he positioned Peter the nudist on the pavement edge ready to cross the road, the Chinese man had spotted Bob and called inside the restaurant.

A diminutive old Chinese lady appeared wearing white coated overalls and held a large oval shaped stainless steel dish which had some kind of food on it which Jill could not make out from where they were. Bob waited patiently for a gap to appear in the traffic and when one appeared began to walk Peter across the road as they approached the other side Bob's tail began to wag, and the old Chinese lady bent over from her waste and gently placed the tray in front of Bob, it was precisely midday.

Julie jumped up and down on the spot with excitement clapping her hands as she did so whereas Jill looked on in total amazement frozen in time with her mouth wide open as she gasped; Michelle apparently still bored just turned to Jill suggesting she shut her mouth "as you don't know what will fly into it."

Bob lead Peter directly to his dish of Chinese leftovers and as he began wolfing down his food Peter just stood silently looking around apparently in some confusion as to why they had stopped, perhaps he did not think they were stopped at the edge of a road waiting to cross.

The Chinese man continued smoking his cigarette as he looked on whereas the old Chinese woman had said something in Chinese to the man and had returned inside the restaurant. Bob finished his food and looked up at the Chinese man as if in thanks before moving off with a silent Peter by his side.

Julie was still looking on excitedly as Michelle silently motioned her head in the direction of the villa at Jill in an attempt to ask if they could now move on back to the villa at which point a tall thin bald headed man with gorgeous deep blue eyes dressed in a silver grey summer suit with an open necked white shirt and wearing highly polished black brogues appeared in front of them and asked if they had seen enough.

The girls looked at one another in slight confusion as to who the man was and indeed what gave him the right to question them in such a way. He remained standing in front of them motionless looking directly at them, well not looking at them more as though he was looking through them. Jill was quite unnerved by his presence and said, "We were just leaving."

Jill needed to take Julie by the arm to encourage her to move from her observation position whilst Michelle needed no encouragement to move.

Michelle was keen to return to the villa as she was fully expecting Charles to ask her to accompany him again for the afternoon. Julie mumbled her disapproval at being made to move on as she was somewhat proud of herself for finding the Labrador that walked a naked man.

They walked slowly back to the villa in silence on arrival Jill and Michelle immediately stripped off and lay on their sun loungers whilst Julie tried calling up to Charles on his balcony.

On receiving no reply she made her way inside the villa and tried calling up from the stairs that led to his mezzanine bedroom again no reply was heard so she tentatively put a foot silently on the first step of the stairs then her other foot still calling out. Julie continued in the same vein until she reached the last step and upon calling out Charles' name again received an answer from behind her, she jumped out of her skin in fright and nearly fell off the stairs, slowly regaining her composure she smiled down to Charles who reciprocated her smile whilst holding out his right hand expecting Julie to lower herself down and take it. Taking Charles' hand as she lowered herself to the ground she said to Charles, "We found the Labrador with the naked man."

"Oh good, you mean Peter and his guide dog Bob?" said Charles walking Julie to one of the sofas and sitting her down whilst he sat next to her.

"Yes yes that's right, we found them where you said at Fu's restaurant but then a strange man appeared near us and asked us if we had seen enough, he was really spooky, I was wondering if you knew who he was?" asked Julie hopefully.

"No one seems to know who they are or where they come from, they all dress the same in silver grey suits and all appear to have piercing blue eyes, but they appear to be protecting Peter and Bob from nuisances and unwanted attention," explained Charles.

"But who are they and where do they come from?" asked Julie impatiently.

"Unfortunately I cannot answer you as I really don't know and furthermore I know of no one who does," reiterated Charles.

"Oh ok, thanks anyway," said Julie forlornly standing up to join her friends outside.

"I shouldn't let it worry you," said Charles reassuringly.

Julie smiled at Charles and thanked him again before joining Jill and Michelle outside.

On reaching them Jill asked her what she had learned from Charles, "Oh nothing, he said no one seems to know who they are," said Julie.

"How strange," said Jill whilst Michelle just shrugged her shoulders.

"Someone must know who they are and what they are up to; it was strange how he suddenly appeared as if out of thin air, he was spooky don't you think?" asked Julie.

"I shouldn't worry about it; it's no concern of ours," said Michelle disinterested as she was more interested in Charles putting in an appearance and asking for her company again for the afternoon.

Julie undressed to her bikini and sat on her sun lounger as she took her sun lotion out of her bag having forgotten to leave it inside the villa. Squirting some lotion onto her hands she began applying it to her shoulders before smoothing lotion all over her front enabling her to lie on her back.

Thoughts drifted to the mysterious men in their silver grey suits as Julie lay in the silence of the afternoon sun with the heat penetrating her still body. Julie could feel herself drifting off to sleep and was content to allow herself to when she heard steps from the villa, declining to open her eyes she assumed it was Charles which was confirmed by his words, "Jill you're with me," as he disappeared around the corner of the villa heading for his car.

Jill fumbled to her feet at first falling off her sun lounger she grabbed her skirt and blouse whilst putting her sandals firmly on her feet, as she moved off she caught a glimpse of the disgust and disappointment on Michelle's face.

Jill continued to fumble forward as she tried putting first one leg then the other through her skirt before she could raise it and then fasten the zip at its side. Jill's arms swung wildly as her blouse firmly refused to allow her arms to thread into the holes designed for them, Jill stopped dead as she asked herself why she was in such a flustered rush, if Charles wanted her to accompany him he would surely wait.

Now standing still the arms of the blouse now threaded through easily and she slowly fixed her buttons before adjusting her skirt correctly from its current position with the zip to her front. Charles smiled from his position in the driving seat as Jill now approached in a as she thought restrained and ladylike manner but she could not hide the fact her cheeks were blushed bright pink.

Charles opened her door from his seated position and she sat onto the hot leather seats pulling down her short skirt as much as she could to save her legs from the heat of the seat. Jill became very conscious she was virtually naked apart from her ever so short tennis skirt and her blouse was all but see through. The engine started and they reversed allowing Charles to drive out through the gates stopping as he approached the road allowing a bus to pass before moving out onto the road.

Jill turned and faced Charles asking, "Why me?"

"Why not," was Charles' only response.

"Where are we going?" Jill asked.

"You'll see," Charles responded abruptly.

Jill half smiled and sat back to await the answer to their destination, despite the air conditioning on full it struggled to cope with the latent heat of the car so Jill opened her window half way and allowed the immediate breeze to blow at her hair.

They passed a lonely venta on their left whose carpark was half full of local traffic from farm trucks to a police car, Jill made a mental note that it was probably a good place to eat with so many local people partaking of its cuisine.

They had not been driving long when Charles turned right off the road into a small side road that led to a golf complex, Jill's curiosity aroused but she refrained from asking Charles what they were doing here as his previous responses had been blunt to say the least.

The car park was relatively full but Charles managed to locate a lonely spot to the rear and side next to a walkway that led directly to the main entrance. The carparks drab appearance contrasted sharply with the view in front of them, the carpark being covered in stone chippings and was a lonely grey appearance whereas the building itself was painted bright white and beyond lay the green surface of the golf course interspersed as it was by areas of green leafed trees and multi coloured flowers whilst in the distance lay the mountains topped with a smattering of snow.

Leaving the stifling heat of the car's interior behind them Charles took Jill's hand in his as he led her down the concrete path towards the clear glass entrance to the golf complex. Twenty yards from the entrance

Charles instructed Jill that as they entered they would walk to their right heading for the lifts.

"Intriguing," was all Jill responded as she looked on at the approaching entrance.

They walked through the large glass revolving doors into the lobby and felt the air conditioning hit them immediately as they continued to the lifts; Charles pressed the button to summon the lift. The lift doors opened with a loud ping from a bell to reveal a large full length and width mirror in front of them as Jill gasped in horror at her appearance.

Her blouse was buttoned up wrong as she had buttoned from the second button hole down but had used the second button in the third hole and with the amount of sun lotion she had rubbed all over her front it had soaked into the material of her blouse making it totally see through, her nipples exposed for all to see. Her skirt was still pulled down at the rear where she had tried to save her legs from being burnt by the extremely hot leather car seats; she had not noticed the zip had partially opened allowing the skirt to slip further giving her a "builder's bum" exposed more than she would ever dare.

Blushing profusely she adjusted her skirt as best she could and then ran her fingers through her hair which was sticking up every which way from the blast it was exposed to from the gusting wind from the half opened car window. Charles looked down upon her discomfort with considered amusement.

The lift stopped accompanied by a ring of a bell and the doors opened, Jill followed Charles out of the lift and left down a long corridor. They arrived at a large wooden door in front of them and Charles reached into his pocket and brought out what Jill at first thought was a key but on closer inspection realised it more resembled a bent and squashed nail.

Charles opened the door with his homemade skeleton key to reveal an extremely large and opulent office that felt oppressively muggy and hot, clearly no air conditioning at work here. Charles walked in and turned to his right reaching out to a dial on the wall adjusting it then turned to Jill bidding her to follow him through the threshold; he closed the door behind her as she did so. He now marched straight in front of him to two large French doors and opened them both allowing a flow of fresh air to slowly engulf the room.

"Is there a bathroom in here?" Jill asked as she was desperate to do something with her appearance especially her unruly hair.

Charles motioned with his arm and Jill disappeared into the grandeur of the offices' bathroom undoing her blouse as she walked. Having damped down her hair and brushed through it with her fingers as best she could she took off her blouse and looked around the bathroom in the forlorn hope of finding a method of drying her blouse, having found none she walked back into the now cooler office with her blouse in her hand and turning to Charles whom she found by the drinks cabinet opening a bottle of Champagne asked, "Any ideas how I can dry this?"

He smiled that Charles smile and took her blouse over to the nearest French door and hung it over its top allowing it to blow gently in the breeze. He then returned to the drinks cabinet and picked up the bottle of champagne pouring the bubbling liquid into two Chrystal champagne glasses passing one to Jill as he lifted his glass to his lips and tasted the chilled wine, he nodded his approval. Jill took a sip of her wine as she rotated 360 degrees taking in the sheer scale and decadence of the office and turned to face Charles asking, "I take it this is not your office judging by the way you entered it, so what are we doing here?"

"I thought it would be nice to spend some time together away from the others, I thought it would help you to relax more as you seem to have to look after Michelle and Julie, well perhaps not look after them more help them with their decisions and arbitrate between them, I thought you should have some Jill time," Charles said as he then finished his champagne.

"How kind of you to think of me, were you not also thinking of yourself in some way?"

"Of course, always."

"At least you're honest," Jill said following Charles back to the drinks cabinet.

"One thing you can be certain of is my honesty at all times, more champagne?" asked Charles.

"Yes, please, so what or whose is this place?"

"It is a slight acquaintances office who happens to be the chairman of the golf club," said Charles matter of factly.

"So why isn't he using his office, is he aware you are borrowing it?"

"He is away on business for a few days and if he knew it wouldn't be half as much fun, would it?" Charles said handing Jill her replenished glass of champagne back.

"You have used this office many times before then?"

"Not many no, but before yes," said Charles again with that smile he has and a definite twinkle in his ever so blue eyes.

He walked over to the balcony with his champagne glass in his hand and stepped onto it saying, "It has a wonderful view of the course and mountains from here, you should try it."

With that Jill stepped closer but not onto the balcony motioning towards her bare breasts, "But nobody will notice them, we are on the third floor people do not tend to look up, they are either starting on the first tee which faces away or finishing on the 18th green which is to our right and side, you are perfectly safe I assure you," advised Charles.

With that Jill finished her Champagne and placed her glass on a trestle table which stood at the side of the French doors and stepped tentatively onto the balcony and took in the contrast of the greenery in front of her and the duller pale brown of the earth beyond the boundary of the golf course in the distance. She basked in the brilliant sunshine as it hit and warmed her bared breasts she leaned forward placing her palms onto the wall; she threw her head back closing her eyes allowing the suns powerful rays to hit her face.

She heard a dull sound to her rear as if something light had fallen to the floor at first she thought her blouse had dropped from its perch overhanging the French door but she could see its movement in the breeze. Then she felt Charles' deft touch and spun round in surprise as she noticed Charles had allowed his shorts to drop to the ground and his erection was obvious, she fell backwards, falling over the balconies edge, her hands scrambled in open air trying to grab hold of something that would stop her motion over the balconies edge, her legs flew into the air. Her right hand grasped behind Charles neck followed rapidly by her left, she struggled to hold on. She felt Charles move imperceptibly forward in between her flaying legs and her grip behind his neck took hold as she realised Charles' erection had entered her vagina, "Oh no, dear God no," she screamed in shock and surprise, "no, oh why, oh, ooh," she began to realise this was two years, two years since she had felt a man inside her.

Charles began slowly motioning in and out, Jill's head fell onto Charles' shoulder as her legs raised further up resting her feet above Charles' bottom. Her long lost feelings were emerging from the depths they had been hiding as she began to join in with Charles' thrusting motion, her fear of falling over the balconies edge had all but disappeared. Their bodies were so in tune with each other's as their writhing became quicker and quicker until they both could take it no longer and cried out their delight together.

They stayed in each other's arms both spent, breathing heavily, their sweat mixing together where their bodies joined; sweat flowed from them onto the floor of the balcony. Not a word was said between them as they stayed clinging to each other on the balconies edge. Jill could only think of why her husband could not have released her from her two years of chastity and a tear formed in her right eye away from Charles gaze. Jill untangled her feet from around Charles' body and allowed them to drop to the floor as she wiped the tear from her eye she moved silently around and away from Charles, walking slowly through the office to the bathroom closing the door behind her. Jill unzipped her skirt allowing it to drop to the marbled floor of the bathroom as she walked to the shower cubicle and turned on the shower holding her hand under the flow of water until she was happy with the temperature and then stepped under the hot flowing water. The water flowed freely over her body as she stood silently and still, reflecting on why she had allowed her husband to neglect her body for so long and the tears came flowing freely as she sobbed openly her shoulders heaving as she did so.

Then the realisation dawned that it was not her that had allowed her body to be neglected but her husband, it was her husband that had been and was still neglecting her and her tears stopped immediately. Turning the water from hot to cold she forced herself to remain under it until her body and soul had chilled. Jill turned the shower off and looked around the steam ridden bathroom for a towel, finding a white one in a rack full of clean white towels she dried herself and rubbed her hair as dry as she could before racking her fingers through it in a half-hearted attempt at styling it.

She folded the towel and left it neatly on the sink then turned picked her skirt up off the floor with her left hand and walked over to the door opening it and walked through accompanied with a cloud of steam following her into the office.

Jill was rightly proud of her naked body and she wanted Charles to see it close and in all its glory as she vowed he would never have it again. Charles handed Jill a fresh glass of chilled champagne which she took and clinked it against his as she half smiled at him. Charles gulped his full glass of champagne down in one and walked into the bathroom leaving the door open whilst he turned on the shower adjusting the temperature knob from cold to hot. Jill sat in the large leather chair of the desk as Charles took his shower she even opened the cigar box, which she thought was called a humidor, on the desk in curiosity, she sat in silence naked and sipped her champagne.

Hearing the shower stop Jill rose and made her way slowly over to where her blouse hung on the French door, it had dried somewhat but was still immersed with oil, it really did not bother her any more whether her nipples could be seen through it or not, she put it on. Then returning to the desk she picked her skirt up of it and pulled that up zipping it fast at the side. Then she sat back down at the desk's leather chair again and waited for Charles.

Jill picked up her glass of champagne off the desk top where she had left it just as the shower stopped; steam had been flowing freely from the open bathroom door. Jill's back was to the bathroom door from where she sat at the desk; Charles emerged from the bathroom walking slowly through the cloud of steam disturbing its slow rhythmic passage. Jill could feel but not see his naked presence which did not bother her and it certainly did not arouse her anymore, Charles sensed Jill's remoteness having expected a warmer welcome to his return to the office's interior. He turned on his heels returning to the bathroom to recover his polo shirt and then walked over to the balcony in silence and put on his shorts and sailing shoes. He closed the French doors locking them into position and began walking towards the front door; Jill placed her glass gently onto the desk in front of her and rose herself walking slower than Charles had to the front door making him wait for her, all in absolute silence.

Charles had made no attempt at clearing the office leaving the champagne glasses where they were, the now empty champagne bottle remained in the open atop the drinks cabinet and he had left his wet towel where he had dropped it on the marbled floor of the bathroom, Jill's remained folded on the sink. They both stood silently in the corridor awaiting the lifts arrival from the ground floor, it arrived and the doors opened accompanied by the single ring of an electronic bell. They stepped silently inside; Jill brushed the hair of her fringe aside with her right hand before turning and facing the closing stainless steel doors.

The lift bounced slightly as it arrived at the ground floor and they again heard the single ring of the bell as the doors opened, Charles was first through them walking brusquely to and through the glass revolving front door leaving Jill in his wake walking slowly taking her time knowing he would have to wait for her at the car. Jill approached Charles Audi and noted with some amusement Charles' impatience as he sat in the driver's seat tapping his fingers on the steering wheel.

Jill entered the Audi and quite purposefully sat a little forward in her seat which pinched the bottom of her skirt in place and exposed the top of her thigh and a small amount of buttock, she then raised her left knee resting it on the dashboard which gave a tantalising glimpse of the very top of her thighs and even more so when she rocked her right leg slightly towards Charles as her skirt fell ever so slightly closer to her waist. Charles inadvertently let out a groan which he tried to hide by starting the engine. Jill smiled to herself. They drove back to the villa in silence. Jill walked defiantly back to her friends whilst Charles walked back inside the villa in silence and alone.

Jill was greeted by knowing looks from Michelle and Julie which she ignored and although she sat on her sun lounger she remained clothed which in itself drew looks from Michelle and Julie. Even Julie refrained from saying anything as they all remained in silence. The silence remained awkward for a few minutes until Jill broke the silence with, "I need a drink!"

Michelle immediately responded with, "I'll open a bottle of wine."

"Not here, let's go find a bar somewhere," suggested Jill.

"Ok, I'm game," said Michelle who was more interested in finding out what had happened than in the drink or finding a suitable bar.

Michelle and Julie nervously began to dress whilst Jill needlessly adjusted her skirt and flicked and brushed her hair with her fingers, just needing something to do while she waited for the girls. Julie finished dressing first and jogged to the villa to retrieve their beach bags. There was no sign of Charles.

They tidied their immediate area moving the sun loungers back to how they had found them then picking up their bags they followed Jill as she began walking to the side of the villa towards the entrance. Michelle made a slight detour to call up to Charles on the balcony assuming him to be there, "We're going now, see you later?"

"Of course," Charles replied.

They turned left out of the gate and walked slowly taking Jill's lead. They walked in silence and the atmosphere was strained to say the least, Michelle felt as though they were walking on eggshells which she knew made it difficult for Julie. Suddenly Jill's pace increased as Michelle and Julie looked at each other as if the other could furnish the answer, not receiving one they rushed to catch up each one smiling nervously at Jill as they came level with her, there was a slight pregnant pause as they waited for Jill's response. The smile was returned as Jill held her arms out to be linked with Michelle and Julie on each arm. The three strode purposely forward arm in arms in pursuit of a bar and a much needed drink.

They came upon The Mancunian Bar the noisy overpopulated bar they had frequented before each of them responded by shaking their heads and saying in unison,"Nah."

Next they came upon a small Spanish bar with maybe eight or ten tables outside each table covered by a large advertising umbrella for Martini in plain white with the name Martini circling the umbrella several times, there were only three tables occupied, they each nodded at each other and then followed Jill to a table furthest away from the door and the other customers. They sat quietly putting their beach bags under the table out of sight taking in their surroundings as they sought the attention of a waiter.

A waiter appeared from inside and strode up to them with his empty black plastic tray in his right hand, "ladies?" was all he said.

"What are we drinking today?" Julie asked.

"Vodka, I need vodka today," said Jill.

"Ok, can we have three vodka and cokes please," asked Julie.

With that the waiter smiled and withdrew leaving the women in silence again. It was bright sunshine as normal, there were a few people walking about but most were still on the beach or arranged around their hotel pools as it was still not quite 4pm.

The waiter returned promptly with their drinks balanced on his outstretched black plastic tray, he place three small paper matts on the table one in front of each woman and then placed a drink on top of them nodding politely and returning inside the bar.

Jill was the first to lift her drink saying, "Cheers," as she did so. Michelle and Julie followed suit. They took a sip of their drinks and looked at each other nervously, Michelle and Julie showed clear relief as Jill smiled in turn at them both.

Julie took it as an indication she could ask, "So what did you and Charles do this afternoon?"

"I am not going to answer that and I will never answer that so don't ever ask again, is that clear enough for you, now change the subject," said Jill quite chillingly.

Julie looked to Michelle with her eyes wide open as if to say "what do I ask now? Help."

Michelle responded by asking, "Are we going to have a couple of drinks then find somewhere to eat before going back to the hotel to change or do you want to change and then eat?"

"Now that is a good question," said Jill pondering a response.

"I'm quite hungry; I wouldn't mind finding something to eat and then changing," said Julie.

"Then that's what we will do, a couple of drinks, eat, change," confirmed Jill.

"We could see what the menu is like here when we order our next drink, I quite fancy paella," suggested Michelle.

"I quite fancy Leonardo Di Caprio!" said Jill.

To which both Michelle and Julie laughed which seemed to settle the atmosphere a little. They continued in idle chatter whilst sipping their drinks until Michelle ordered more drinks from the same waiter and asked him for menus as well. The menu was relatively short but had all the main Spanish items from tapas to paella, the waiter had brought green olives and slivers of Parma ham to the table which the women thought was a nice touch, so made their minds up to order from the menu.

They decided to start with a number of tapas as it was still so early and they had started drinking vodka early so best to have something in their stomachs more or less straight away. When they asked their waiter for details of the tapas on order it became apparent the choice was gargantuan so they asked their waiter to make the choice for them maybe six to eight and then they would see how they felt and either order some more or order their main meal.

Jill allowed the waiter to enter the door before asking, "Tell me what you think of Charles?"

Michelle answered first, "I like him, he's kind, attractive, I love his eyes, generous, sexy, what else is there to know?"

"What about you Julie, what do you think of him?" asked Jill ignoring Michelle's answer.

Julie sat silently for a minute with both Jill and Michelle looking on before saying, "He's a little too mysterious for me."

"What do you mean exactly?" pushed Jill.

"Well, what do we know about him, absolutely nothing, if you ask him a question he either avoids the answer or answers a question that hasn't been asked or changes the subject, it's like talking to a politician."

"What's the matter with that? He's just a very private person; he likes to keep himself to himself is all," protested Michelle.

"And he doesn't like his picture taken, look at his reaction when that woman tried to take his picture with her mobile," added Julie.

"A lot of people don't like their picture taken, look at Bianca for instance," pointed out Michelle.

"That's because she's pregnant and hates the weight she's put on; it's not the same thing at all," said Jill quite annoyed.

"The villa seems strange to me, it doesn't fit somehow," continued Julie.

"In what way?" asked Jill.

"I can't put my finger on it, it's too neat, as if it doesn't belong to him, there's nothing personal, no pictures of family or friends anywhere, there's nothing built up of his do you know what I mean? Like no books he has read or magazines or DVD's he's watched, it doesn't appear to me to be a home as he is making out it is," said Julie picking up her glass and taking a long slurp of vodka and coke.

"Michelle?" asked Jill.

"Ok, I can see what Julie is saying, I mean I said the other day about his bedroom and bathroom pretty much the same thing, also there's nothing intimate or personal for instance no aftershave, no deodorant, no shaving foam just a cheap Bic razor, no shampoo just a cheap odourless bar of soap. And his bed sheets doesn't fit," said Michelle.

"His bed sheets don't fit? What they're too small, too big, what?" asked Jill.

"No not size, they are the sort of bed linen a woman would buy yet he purports to be single, a gent of the world as it were," said Michelle quizzically.

"Anything else?" asked Jill looking pointedly at Michelle and then at Julie.

"Well there is him, I mean he's kind of average in a sort of a way, he doesn't stick out as seriously handsome although he is handsome, his eyes are kind of special but nothing else, he seems to want to blend in everywhere, there's that term they use on TV in detective programmes "no distinguishing marks", he has no scars, blemishes or anything and he doesn't really have a tan."

"There's a lot that doesn't add up when you begin to think about it," said Jill nodding her head to herself.

"So what are you saying Jill? That we shouldn't go back, we should avoid him? What happened to you this afternoon?" asked Julie.

At which point they were interrupted by the waiter who appeared at their table with his tray held high full of tapas, he began lifting each one off his tray and placing them on the table with some flourish and clearly with some pride as well, he bowed slightly wishing them "Bon appetite" before turning and disappearing inside once again.

Michelle did not need an invitation as the tapas dish with king prawns barely touched the table her fingers had already picked one up and had stuffed it deep inside her mouth.

"Oh my God, they are out of this world," said Michelle licking sauce from her fingers.

"Forget this afternoon, I shall, no I may be wrong and he may well be just a nice guy but I also think we should be careful and maybe we can dig a little....this does smell good!" said Jill helping herself to a prawn.

"Dig how?" asked Michelle putting her hand over her full mouth as she did so.

"Well tomorrow he is bound to ask one of us to accompany him again in the afternoon probably your turn Julie....try the pork in tomato sauce, it melts in your mouth," said Jill.

"It won't be me I can tell you, I won't be going anywhere with him," stated Julie flatly.

"Then it will be you again Michelle, he certainly won't ask me," said Jill.

"That's ok with me but what are you two going to do?" asked Michelle licking sauce from her fingertips.

"We will take a good look around the villa and that shed in the garden," said Jill taking a piece of fish and watching it break apart in her hand.

"Ok that's a plan," agreed Julie.

"Shall we just order some more of these tapas rather than a main meal, they are absolutely gorgeous!" asked Michelle nodding at Jill and Julie.

"Ok that's a plan," said Jill smiling as she did so and finishing her drink, she looked up for the waiter to see he was already on his way to their table with drinks held high on his tray.

"He's certainly going to have a tip from me!" said Michelle smiling at the drink bearing waiter.

"And me!"

"And me!"

They took the opportunity to order more tapas which were duly dispatched with suitable zeal as they discussed their plan of attack for the evening which incorporated more singing practice for them as they were determined to do well on Thursday.

They unanimously decided on starting at Blue's as it was a favourite for them all and if they had not met Charles they would no doubt have spent their entire evenings there.

Having finally finished their voluminous plates of tapas they sat for half an hour chatting idly allowing their stomachs to slowly recede. It was just gone 6pm when they finally paid their bill and made their way slowly back to their Hotel.

They decided to meet at the hotel bar before setting off for Blues. Michelle made her way back to her room still devising her plan in her head; she needed to speak to Tony.

Jill opened the door to their room and was immediately hit by the heated stale damp odour from her morning shower and opened the doors to their balcony and was grateful for the rush of warm fresh air into the room. She sat on the bed and looked around her forlornly and thought "is this my future? Walking into an empty room every day, worse walking into an empty house. There was of course Bianca and in time her child making me a grandmother, good God, a grandmother. I hadn't even considered it."

And so came the tears, what had she done wrong? Absolutely nothing. She shook herself and thought, "No bloody way, I'll be damned if I am going to feel sorry for myself. I have everything to look forward to, a grandchild a little sooner than I had thought but nonetheless a little beauty to treasure. I will find a job, in itself a new adventure and independence. No everything is looking up not down."

With that she wiped away the tears and stripped off her clothes, well skirt and blouse, throwing them wildly into the air allowing them to fall where they might and strode purposefully into the bathroom turning the shower tap on fully. Having showered and brushed her teeth Jill walked out of the steam filled bathroom naked into the much cooler bedroom and shivered for a second from the warm breeze echoing in from the balconies open door. She walked to the wardrobe opening its doors fully and stood with her arm folded and right forefinger to her lips as she contemplated her attire for the evening. Should she or shouldn't she? She should she decided.

So sitting at the dressing table she began blow drying her hair, once complete she took great care over her makeup using a new Gucci eyeshadow and lipstick she had bought especially for the holiday, the lipstick being a deep red and the eye shadow a very pale blue.

She stood for a second in front of the open wardrobe
as if about to change her mind but she did not and took
out the brand new dress on its hanger covered still with
the polythene bag it was sold in. She began to
carefully tear the polythene bag open revealing the
silkiness of the material, it was lined with thin white
paper to protect it, she tore it loose.

Throwing the hanger onto the bed she held it to her
naked body as she looked into the dressing tables
mirror, now she could not wait so stepped into it
carefully and pulled it up her body, she bent her head
forward and caressed the strap over it allowing it to
fall and rest on her shoulders. It felt divine, it looked
very much like the Marilyn Monroe dress that was
blown up from the drain beneath her feet and she had
to hold it down. It was a delicate very pale blue with a
loosely pleated bottom half with the top backless, it
looped from the lower back around in opposite
directions coming up the front just past the naval
before splitting open over the boobs and then looping
around the back of the neck. She had bought shoes
especially for this dress and now took them out of their
box throwing it back into the wardrobe and sat on the
bed to put them on. Looking in the mirror again she
was absolutely delighted with the result, "Knickers,
knickers!" she exclaimed as she realised she had even
bought special pale blue silk French knickers for the
dress. She took them from out of her drawer and
admired them for a second before flipping off her

shoes and pulling them up, it was the final finishing touch. Taking her money out of her beach bag she placed it into a darker blue handbag four inches deep and about ten inches long, with a lip gloss, her perfume, a small vanity mirror and a handkerchief. Feeling a million dollars she grabbed her room key and skipped out of the door along the corridor to summon the elevator.

Arriving at the hotel bar to find that Michelle and Julie had beaten her there, as they noticed Jill they looked on open mouthed. They had a drink waiting for her so she sat and immediately took a sip. Michelle could not resist saying, "My God Jill you look amazing, I love your dress where did you buy it?"

"Why thank you honey, I bought it at Chantelle's, it's a little gem of a shop just off Deansgate in Manchester," said Jill.

"Very stylish and sexy," agreed Julie.

There was an elderly couple having a drink three tables away and the man was being hit by his wife for not taking his eyes off Jill, Michelle noticed and thought "he won't be the last tonight".

They sat chatting sipping their drinks in no rush as it was still early as Jill mentioned how much she was enjoying herself away from David which made Julie chirp up, "Well I'm missing Steve, I've hardly seen him, when I return to the room at night he's asleep and when he wakes in the morning I'm fast asleep but I have to say and I never thought I would, I'm really enjoying this holiday."

"I sort of miss Tony as well in a way, I even left him a message, I couldn't find a pen so I had to write it in lipstick, I had no paper either so I used the mirror in the bathroom," said Michelle.

"What was the message?" asked Julie.

"I'm HORNY! No just kidding, it was personal," said Michelle mischievously.

Having finished their drinks they left the hotel to find there was a warm breeze blowing in from the direction of the sea which made the evening perfect for walking. Taking their time walking along the front there were a few holidaymakers making their way to their evening's destination as well as some stragglers still on the beach, mainly youngsters playing football, there was a game of volleyball taking place as well, boys verses girls.

As they walked the conversation came around to song choices and they all agreed on "It aint what you do it's the way that you do it" so as they walked they now sang the song to each other and received numerous strange looks from pedestrians they passed. They approached Blues and could see an A advertising board had been placed outside on the pavement but as yet they could not read it. Their pace increased with their curiosity. They arrived at the bar to find a large six foot by four foot advertising poster had been placed on the wall of the bar as well, it announced that for tonight only they had a Bette Midler tribute act and she was called D'Oris Clit; The Divine Miss C and her Kiss My Arse Tour.

"This should be good, I absolutely adore Bette Midler," said Jill excitedly.

"Be a bit tame won't it?" asked Julie.

"You have to be joking, Bette Midler Tame! You do know who Bette Midler is don't you Julie?" asked Jill as Michelle giggled beside her.

"Wasn't she in Gone With The Wind with Clark Gable?" said Julie at which Jill could not answer with rolling about laughing with Michelle bent double her stomach hurting she was laughing so hard.

They did not bother trying to explain to Julie they just said she would have to experience the act to understand as they marched her inside and up to the bar, Jill and Michelle were still trying to contain their laughter as they ordered three vodka and cokes from a barman wearing his usual pink hotpants.

They made their way with drinks in hand to the only table they could find that was still free which was on the opposite side to the bar and three quarters of the way back away from the stage but they still had a good view and they had arrived just in time as it was now standing room only.

The crowd were becoming a little restless as they waited for the show to start; Jill noticed the bar staff making their way towards the stage and nudged Michelle and Julie. The bar staff disappeared behind the stage as Camp Teddie the DJ attempted to jump on the stage and missed falling flat on his face to raucous laughter and applause, he then tentatively walked up the steps to the stage waving his hands in the air in an initially futile attempt to stop the audience's laughter and applause. He decided to give up and instead stood where he was taking bow after bow.

Eventually the noise abated to allow Camp Teddie to announce the arrival at Blues of D'Oris Clit.

He began, "We have with us tonight and unfortunately only tonight an entertainer known not only along the coast of the Costa Del Sol but also from Blackpool to Cleethorpes. She has entertained royalty, well Pearly Kings and many Queens so please be upstanding for D'Oris Clit our Bathhouse D'Oris!"

With that the audience as one stood as the music started for Boogie Woogie Buggle Boy at which point Men O'Pause crashed quickly onto the stage in their customary hotpants but with the addition of white T-shirts with a huge rubber or plastic pink nipple at its centre. As they began to dance D'Oris Clit made her entrance behind them singing, "Boobie Woobie Boobie Boy." The crowd were going wild with excitement as D'Oris wore a tight white bodice and fishnet stockings with white high heels she also brandished in each hand a large boob and nipple on the end of a stick. At the end of the song it took a good two minutes for the applause to die down as D'Oris began to tell some very rude and explicit jokes, far too rude to repeat.

She ended by advising everyone not to use the toilets here as there was no toilet paper she said, "I had to wipe my arse with a wet tampon!"

The music started again this time it was the Wind Beneath My Wings and she sung it straight and very well, again it ended to loud applause. It continued in the same vein a song then a few jokes then a song again.

Michelle went to the bar for more drinks and Julie turned to Jill and said, "She wasn't in Gone With The Wind was she?" Jill just shook her head smiling as she did so.

"She's very good though isn't she?" said Jill nodding to herself.

"Yes she certainly is and what's even better that bitch from last night isn't here," said Julie.

"I know but I wouldn't expect to see her here anyway, maybe Bulbous Billy's later," said Jill.

"Oh I do hope so, I'm fully prepared," said Julie taking a small plastic bottle half way out of her bag just enough for Jill to see it.

"What's that?" asked Jill concern written all over her face.

"My little concoction I prepared especially for her, I told you I would," said Julie with a deviously mischievous determined grin on her face.

"Oh Christ! You're surely not thinking of using that?" asked Jill with even more concern written all over her face.

"No I'm not thinking, I am going to use it and don't even think about stopping me," said Julie kissing the bottle before returning it to her bag.

At which point Michelle returned from the bar placing all three drinks on the table at once before sitting down. She then leaned down to pick up her handbag so she could return her change to her purse, as she was still bent over Jill bent beside her and recounted what Julie had just told her. Michelle rose back up straight and just shrugged her shoulders as if agreeing with Julie; Jill raised her eyes up despondently.

D'Oris finished on stage at just gone 11.00pm and rushed off stage and out the front door to be driven to her next gig. With her leaving there was an anti-climax that surfaced within the club with a number of customers leaving for venues new. Michelle looked at her watch and motioned for them to move on to Bulbous Billy's Bar, Julie was the first to move smiling at her handbag as she did so which prompted Jill to nudge Michelle and point with her eyes towards Julie's bag. Michelle again just hunched her shoulders.

They all walked silently to Bulbous Billy's Bar with Jill in particular wondering what on earth she was going to do to prevent Julie from using her concoction should the drunken woman once again be there, clearly not knowing Charles had already provided a solution.

They arrived at Bulbous Billy's without Jill finding a solution in her mind. On entering the bar they found it was packed to the gunnels with the usual lookalikes surrounding the stage, they eventually managed to edge their way to the bar.

Steve the barman served them and threw his head in the direction of a table informing them Charles was already in and had a table for them so they ordered an additional drink for Charles, his usual red wine. They then tried nudging their way over to Charles which proved difficult as they were pushed and shoved here and there. Julie being the smallest was pushed into a man sat a table with three other men who spilt a little of his pint of lager and turned hurling abuse at the startled Julie, she apologised and moved on.

Eventually they sat themselves alongside Charles who asked Julie what the man had said, she shook her head to say that it did not matter but Charles pushed so she told him. Julie clearly enjoyed watching the different lookalikes with their variety of dresses and clothes, it was not long before she was announcing who she had now seen and pointing she said, "Look at that Betty Boo, she'll mess her lipstick if she keeps doing that to Buddy Holly!"

"Julie, that's supposed to be Liza Minelli and the guy is supposed to be Elvis Costello," said Jill.

"Oh.....who's Elvis Costello?" asked Julie.

"Never mind," said Jill shaking her head whilst smiling.

DJ Mad Mike was just introducing a new arrival on stage this time a holidaymaker dressed in jeans and T-shirt and barely looked eighteen but had her whole left arm draped in tattoos, one of which was an alligator about to eat a teddy bear or it was a badly drawn koala, who was about to sing Barbara Streisand's Evergreen. Applause as always greeted the start of the music and the girl sang very well perhaps trying a little too hard to reach the high notes but apart from that she was very good.

"I need to give Mad Mike our choice of song so we can have our place in line but I don't fancy walking all the way up to the stage in this crowd," said Jill to both Michelle and Julie.

"That's alright I will go, what's your choice of song?" offered Charles.

"It aint what you do it's the way that you do it," said the girls together.

"Ok and what's the name of the group?" asked Charles.

"Bananarama!" said the girls again in unison.

Charles began inching his way along the row of tables and when he came upon the table with the man who had said something to Julie he made a point of kneeing him in his side just below his ribs. The man jumped to his feet and tried to push Charles but Charles sidestepped quickly and the guy missed, he threw a wild punch which Charles ducked easily. Bulbous Billy was out from behind the bar in seconds and had pushed the man back down into his seat with his arms around him leaning the full weight of his body onto him whilst he spoke into the man's ears. The man nodded and sat still as Bulbous Billy released his hold and returned to the bar, Billy smiled at Charles as he walked past him. His mission to Mad Mike accomplished Charles returned to his seat through total hatred showing in the man's eyes. Charles had discovered what he wanted to know about him.

"What was that all about?" asked Michelle as Charles took his seat.

"No idea but you're seventh in line for the song," Charles said taking a sip of his wine whilst he totally ignored the stares from the man.

They all thanked Charles for his industrious efforts on their behalf and sat back waiting for their turn on stage. They seemed to have to wait forever before Mad Mike called them up to the stage for their rendition of "It aint what you do it's the way that you do it". They had been waiting impatiently but with a great deal of trepidation, not about singing but rather about passing the man that both Julie and now Charles had had an altercation with. They passed him with great care and noticed his eyes never wavered from them sending a shiver down Julie's spine and a rather mischievous look on her face which neither Jill nor Michelle noticed.

They arrived on stage to their usual applause until Jill burst into her position between Michelle and Julie and then all the men in the audience wolf whistled strenuously until the music began. They danced and sang their hearts out enjoying every minute until they had to return their microphones back to Mad Mike and force their way back through the crowd to their table and Charles.

Julie offered to go to the bar and buy drinks for them all which in itself was slightly unusual in as much as Julie detested having to go to the bar to order drinks, Jill and Michelle did not think anything of it at the time just smiling in thanks at her as she left. Neither did they notice Julie taking out a small vial from her handbag alongside her purse.

Julie made her way slowly and purposefully towards the bar and as she arrived alongside the unruly man she had previously had the altercation with she inadvertently on purpose slipped into his lap, apologising profusely she kissed the man full on the lips whilst unobtrusively administering her homemade Mickey Finn into the man's almost full pint of lager. What she did not see as she rose out of the man's aroused lap was one of his friends swapping his half-drunk pint of lager for his friend's almost full one. Julie triumphantly made it to the bar and ordered their drinks from Bulbous Billy whilst the man was extolling his sex appeal to his friends.

"I see you've made your peace with Bob The Builder!" said Bulbous Billy jokingly.

"Bob The Builder? Is that his name?" asked Julie never learning when someone was joking.
"No but it's what I call him, he's in the building game, steel erector I think," said Bulbous Billy.

"I might have known, not the nicest man I've ever met," said Julie smiling at Bulbous Billy as she collected her drinks together in both hands and carefully turned to return to her table.

Passing Bob The Builder she received an enormous smile and a wink which she had no option but to half smile to knowing what was to become of him once he finished his drink.

Arriving at their table she carefully placed all the drinks down on the table and took her purse and half empty vial from under her left arm where she had been clutching them and returned them to her purse, she could not help but giggle as she sat down.

Charles leaned into her and said, "Nice work," smiling knowingly as he did so, Julie just shrugged her shoulders and returned the smile.

Having thanked Julie for his drink Charles excused himself from the table and ambled over to the bar where he found Bulbous Billy in his favourite position, at the opening of the bar which led from the bar area to the front of house, he stood there leaning on the bar with a pint of lager in his right hand checking out his customers looking for where trouble may come from if any. He nodded as he noticed Charles approaching and they began chatting idly as old friends do. After what Charles considered to be a sufficient time he brought up the subject of the four men and within conversation he milked all Billy's knowledge of them.

He learned they had been frequenting Bulbous Billy's bar for approximately three weeks, that they were steel erectors between contracts and that they were prodigious drinkers spending a great deal of time and money in the bar. They arrived at Bulbous Billy's Bar every day at approximately 2pm and did not leave until around 4am but what most interested Charles was the information Billy had about what they did when not in Billy's Bar.

Billy recounted, "The big guy the leader thinks himself a bit of a hard man, he might be where he works but we both know he hasn't met a really hard man he's just all mouth. Anyway he was saying when they leave here at 4am they make their way down to the water park, they've found a way in they reckon, anyway they strip off jump in and mess about for a bit. Well he says it sobers them up, so then they duck back to their hotel and sleep for about three hours then go down to the hotel pool for a couple of hours lying in the sun and then they're back here. Ok with me they're spending all the time they're in 'ere."

"I haven't seen too many hard men with beer guts that size," commented Charles.

"Like I said all mouth," said Bulbous Billy.

Charles stayed chatting with Bulbous Billy for another five minutes before leaving him to return to the table with the women, happy now he had the information he wanted.

Charles just sat down and took a sip of his wine when the DJ Mad Mike began, "We have a special request which is on behalf of nearly half the men in the audience for the women singing the Bananarama hit It's Not What You Do It's The Way That You Do It, and it's certainly the way that you do it with that dress, so come on girls up you come."

Jill, Michelle and Julie were at first surprised, then astonished and then grateful as they had not bothered to put their names down again as there was so many people waiting for their turn on stage. All three of them skipped and smiled their way to the stage as they did not need asking twice. The applause and wolf whistles was deafening as they began their number. The whistles continued throughout especially from the table of four which halfway through the song became a table of three as one of their number was taken short and needed to dash to the toilets rapidly. Julie's concoction was beginning to take what would be a dramatic effect.

They returned to their table after singing again through continued appreciative applause and wolf whistles, Charles was still applauding as they sat down and they took deep gulps of their drinks through large smiles on their faces, Jill stood to take another bow to the loud acknowledgement of the appreciative men in the room.

The karaoke continued unabated as the expats who dressed up as various lookalikes chatted amongst themselves whilst they waited their turn on the stage. The largest applause was reserved for the Elton John lookalike who clearly spent a fortune on his outfits but also sang very well and very like Elton John.

The next couple of hours past uneventfully except the man in the group of four was clearly in some distress and pain which was being ignored by his three companions as he continually visited the toilet time and time again. Julie was now convinced her Mickey Finn had gone astray and had no idea how whereas Charles did.

It was a little after 3am when Jill, Michelle and Julie decided to call it a night and as usual Charles walked them to their hotel. They all walked in silence as their minds individually were elsewhere, Jill having nothing to look forward to returning to her room, Michelle needed to speak to Tony and Julie was confused as to how her plan had gone amiss. They said their farewells and left Charles to walk home alone and the women departed for their individual rooms.

Julie entered her room to find Steve sound asleep so she quietly rounded up his clothes he had been wearing and put them in his suitcase out of the way. Then she took out clothes that he would need later, she placed a pair of golfing trousers over a chair and then placed his shirt around its back whilst leaving a pair of socks and underwear on top of his trousers. Satisfied she walked into the bathroom and cleaned her teeth before returning to the bedroom and undressing left her clothes on another chair before creeping gently into bed without disturbing Steve.

Michelle entered their room and threw off her clothes and let them fall where they might as she then crawled naked under the bedclothes and edged her way towards Tony's sleeping naked body. She began to tease Tony's limp penis with her lips and smiled at her growing success. She continued her arousal of her husband until he woke groggily and uttered, "Shit Michelle, what time is it?"

"It's late or early, whatever, listen we need to talk so wake up!" demanded Michelle.

"Well finish what you started, that should do the trick," instructed Tony.

So Michelle indeed went back to what she was doing and once finished she sat up straddling his knees and said," OK now are you listening?"

Tony raised himself up on his elbows and asked, "Yes, so what's the problem?"

"You're not playing golf tomorrow..."

"Now wait a minute..."

"Shut up and listen, Jill's going to kick David out when they return home, she thinks he's having an affair, apparently he's not touched her in ages and she's had enough," explained Michelle.

"But what's that have to do with me, and playing golf tomorrow?" asked Tony.

"We have to stop them separating, so tomorrow you take him to Gib and you make him buy something seriously expensive and exquisite for Jill, jewellery and gold preferably with diamonds would be better, you make him see what he's been doing is wrong and tell him he has to stop," said Michelle demandingly.

"Why is it our problem? It's between the two of them, nothing to do with us," protested Tony wanting his sleep.

"What do you think will happen if they split up? I can tell you one thing, the golfing holidays will stop, you can't bring David by himself. So if you want the golfing holidays to continue you do what I suggest, Gibraltar, gold, expensive, preferably with diamonds, right?"

"If you put it that way I see what you mean, do we know who he's been seeing?"

"Not a clue!" lied Michelle straight faced.

"Leave it with me, I'll try and catch a quiet word with Steve before we set off and put him in the picture."

Jill walked into their bedroom to find David asleep in their bed so she undressed and carefully hung her dress in the wardrobe before going into the bathroom to clean her teeth. Returning to the bedroom she instinctively carefully and quietly manoeuvred her way into bed hit her pillow with her fist before placing her head on it and shut her eyes.

She had been lying still with her eyes closed for a couple of minutes when she realised she had not done something really important, "shit" she thought as she flung her legs out of bed and strode purposefully back to the bathroom. Once there she shut the door and put the light on moving over to the sink, she found Davis's toothbrush and rubbed it across her palm with the brush in her right hand. Then she looked down as she moved her legs apart and inserted the toothbrush inside her vagina moving it up and down inside her a couple of times before returning it to where she had found it and switching off the light she opened the door and returned to bed. The mischievous grin remained on her face until morning.

Charles walked back to his villa alone in the early morning darkness on arriving he made his way around the side of the villa and through the stillness of the garden to the wooden hut in the corner. He opened the door and felt around in the dark until he found the box of matches he left towards the edge of a lower shelf, striking one he took the glass top off an oil lamp and lit it replacing the glass. In the dim light the oil lamp provided he searched for the items he would take with him, once found he placed them inside a small black leather pouch which he threaded through his belt to his right side and then blew out the lamp closing the door of the hut behind him.

He now left the grounds of the villa turning left at the guarding concrete lions. He walked alone along the road not passing anyone and not being passed by any vehicles. A little over 15 minutes later he arrived at his destination, the water park; it was dark, empty and unlit. Entering was much easier than he had anticipated a large industrial sized rubbish bin had been left outside the main entrance which meant he only had to climb on top of it and then climb the remaining height of the wall and he was in.

Once inside he needed to find the electrical control box which he found without any problem, then he began flipping switches on and off to establish what each switch controlled. Leaving a couple of lights on he looked around the water park for the best location to set his trap, it was staring him straight in the face.

The largest slide was perfect, it lay in the centre of the pool and had a couple of bumps in it that you slide over at speed and could not see over the bump until you were over it. He turned off the light he did not need and set about working on the slide. It took him a little over ten minutes to complete his task and when he finished he remained dead still and listened, complete silence, nobody about still. He was not sure at what precise time the four steel erecters from

Bulbous Billy's Bar would show up for their early morning swim.

He left one set of lights on which covered the slide he had been working on and he turned the water pump on that supplied water down the slide. The only light showing now was on the slide all the way down to the water and an eight foot circle of water immediately beyond the edge of the slide, the remainder of the pool was in total darkness and the only sound was that of the water charging down the slide and hitting the pool at its bottom.

Charles now checked his leather pouch and once happy everything was accounted for he returned it to his belt and made to leave. Arriving back at his villa a little after 4.10am, having returned his pouch to the wooden hut in the garden he then opened the rear doors leading into the living room and kitchen and turned on the lights in the kitchen. He then took a bottle of his red wine and opened it with the corkscrew which had been left out by the women. He took a single glass out with him and sat down on one of the bamboo chairs and waited.

The four men left Bulbous Billy's at 4pm their usual time despite having to wait for the one that was ill, having spent most of the evening in and out of the toilets. When they arrived at the water park they did not use their usual method of entry as they saw the rubbish bin and decided to climb onto it and over the wall as Charles had done.

On entering the pool area they were delighted at
what befell their eyes, someone has left the slide
running for them. They rushed to strip naked and
climb the stairs, only one of them left to find a toilet
having thrown up when he climbed over the outer
wall.

The three men made it to the top of the stairs
simultaneously and being the leader "Bob the Builder"
jumped off first screaming with delight as he rushed
down the water slide over the first bump. The other
two followed on directly behind him only a second or
two before they also hit the first bump. Their speed
accelerated as they approached the second bump. Up
and over the second bump the first man landed heavily
and immediately knew something was wrong, he could
feel blood pumping out of him as he lost
consciousness, the second man over felt something as
he landed and instinctively his head fell back rigidly
and was sliced open by the layers of blades Charles
had inserted into the slide. The third man over felt his
heels being sliced open and shredded also his bottom
and then his back. The three men hit the pool in rapid
succession one after the other.

The first man lay unconscious in the water blood
oozing from his gapping wounds. The second man was
also unconscious and bleeding profusely whilst the
third man remained conscious for a minute although he
wished he had not as the realisation of the seriousness
of his wounds dawned on him as his hands found their

way to bones through his bottom, he screamed uncontrollably until he too lost consciousness.

The pool was now a mass of red as the three inert bodies floated gently away from the stream of water pulsating into the pool from the slide. Charles had inserted three rows of Stanley knife blades onto the slide just below the second bump being out of sight as you slid down, each row was set off from the next, 12 blades in total, two inches long and razor sharp.

Ten minutes later the fourth man emerged from the toilets with a cigarette sticking out of the side of his mouth as he did up his flies. He looked up and his jaw dropped leaving the cigarette dangling from his bottom lip. The bodies had now sunk to the bottom as their hearts has stopped pumping blood out and their lungs filled with chlorinated water. The fourth man stood frozen as he watched a testicle float past in the blooded red water he began heaving uncontrollably but his stomach was empty by now, once the retching stopped he began screaming frenziedly as he fell to his knees tears flowing freely from his eyes. He could not move, all he could do was scream.

Charles sipped his wine as the first signs of sunrise appeared accompanied by the sounds of police and ambulance sirens in the distance. He stood up walking through to the kitchen and placed his wine glass in the sink. He turned the lights off and made his way to bed.

Chapter 9   Wednesday

Jill woke in the usual way by the door being slammed shut by her husband leaving; the curtains had been drawn allowing the early morning light and heat of the sun to penetrate the room. As usual Jill crawled out of bed and shut the curtains darkening the room again and as usual she crawled back into bed. This morning though she rose out of bed again and without opening her eyes fully as they hurt from the suns glare through the curtains she ambled into the bathroom and picked up David's toothbrush. Satisfied at its dampness she turned and sauntered back towards the bed crashing onto it and crawling to her side and painfully pulling the covers from beneath her and throwing them back over her shoulders, she groaned as her head found the dimple her head had left in her pillow.

The three friends David, Tony and Steve assembled in the hotel's restaurant as planned at precisely 7.30am. Tony appeared subdued as he had been racking his brain as to how to broach the subject of David's infidelity. Having come up with no solution he had decided to speak with Steve on the subject hoping he may have an answer.

The hotel provided a buffet style help yourself breakfast and David and Steve having returned to their table with their selection looked quizzically at Tony shrugging their shoulders forcing him to his feet to attend the smorgasbord selection of varying breakfasts from around Europe. Returning to their table with a bland bowl of Weetabix instead of his usual full English his two golfing partners puzzled looks emerged again. Tony waited as patiently as he could for an opportunity to speak privately with Steve, his chance came when finishing his breakfast David excused himself and left to locate a toilet.

As soon as David was out of earshot Tony related Michelle's account from the previous evening and her apparent solution and therefore their proposed trip today to Gibraltar. After Steve's initial incredulity he agreed it was a possible solution and that they must persuade David that if he is to avoid the dire consequences of Jill's intentions he must in part buy Jill the most expensive gift they could find from an establishment that took credit cards. That was another problem for them; they would need to make sure David was carrying his credit cards. They decided not to mention anything to David until they were on their way, it would not take David long to realise they were not taking their usual route in their hire car to the golf course. Once he realised they were heading in the wrong direction that would be the time to tell him of what their mission was today. They agreed just as David was returning.

Tony and Steve stood up from their table together and joined David before he could return to their table, they turned him and walked him out of the restaurant and out of the hotel directly to their Enterprise Vauxhall Astra hire car. Tony drove with Steve sitting in the front passenger seat leaving David in the rear behind Tony. Both Tony and Steve looked across at each other and kind of shrugged their shoulders with their eyes as Tony took the plunge and started the engine. Pulling out into the deserted side street Tony wondered at what point David would question the fact that they were not heading towards the golf club.

They were not even on the carreterra when Steve asked, "Are we going to stop off in Marbella on the way back?"

Tony's eyes opened wide in shock as he looked across at Steve who in turn looked skyward whilst shrugging his shoulders and David asked, "On the way back from where?"

"We've decided to go to Gibraltar today to try and help you find a solution to your problem," answered Tony taking the lead.

"A solution to my problem, what problem?" asked David.

"Come on David you've been having an affair and Jill's found out about it," explained Steve.

At which point David's whole demeanour changed, his face turned bright red as he put his head in his hands, he began to wonder just how much Jill knew and therefore how much Tony and Steve knew. He prayed to God that Tony did not know it was Michelle he had had the affair with, he knew then just how serious this could be, he could lose his wife and his best friend at the same time.

The realisation of his stupidity struck him at once, at what he could lose, he knew straight away that he did indeed love Jill and always had, how could he have been so stupid and selfish and limp brained. He looked forward through his fingers but he could not see Tony only Steve, he knew what he had to ask and so he went for it, "Who does she think I had an affair with?"

"She doesn't know but that's not important right now, what is, is that she is going to throw you out when you return home unless you can sort it out now and here, hence our trip to Gibraltar, by the way you do have your credit cards with you don't you?" said Tony bluntly.

"What, yes of course," answered David sighing with a great deal of relief they did not know who he had been partnering.

It was quiet in the car as they pounded out the miles towards Gibraltar, all that needed to be said had been said all that needed to be done was ahead of them in the not too distant future. The traffic began building as they approached Marbella and thinned again once they were through. The silence in the car was unnerving and eerie between the three good friends. The Rock of Gibraltar was in sight in front of them and to their left still some ten miles away. The air conditioning was annoyingly loud as it pumped out cool air to combat the heat of the early morning which was building by the minute. They trudged out the miles in silence as their destination grew before them. The traffic was building with many coaches full of bargain hunting holidaymakers and those searching for cheap booze and cigarettes. They had missed the worst traffic build up which was between 8am and 9am as workers took their daily pilgrimage to wait indefinitely at the border crossing. Depending on how the Spanish border guards felt about the British on any given day determined the length of time it would take to cross the border either into Gibraltar or out.

It was nearing 10.30am when they saw the first sign indicating they needed to take the next slip road off the carreterra, Tony sat up in his seat as his eyes scanned for further signposts that would direct him to their destination. They found the border crossing checkpoint without encountering any problems and decided to park in the large carpark and walk across the border.

None of them had been to Gibraltar before and were a little wary as to what to expect, as they vacated the hire car Steve was the first to notice that the carpark was a pay and display. They had not prepared for the journey and therefore had not prepared for the pay and display carpark so they stood around one of the machines and pooled their change, luckily they found enough for six hours which they all agreed would be sufficient time for David to locate his marriage saving gift. They all knew they had their passports on them as they needed to show them at the golf club each day which was a pain in the backside but they were grateful for it now as no one had thought of passports until they saw the border crossing.

They walked along the rough stoned surface of the carpark to join the end of the long queue managing to do so before a fresh coachload of tourists arrived behind them. They felt a little self-conscious in their golfing regalia until they noticed the dress sense of the majority of the coach passengers. There was a bunch of about fifteen directly behind them in shorts and football club T-shirts that was two sizes too small for their beer guts and was totally insufficient to hide the motley selection of tattoos emblazoned about their bodies, and that was just the women.

There was a gang of men behind them that must have only arrived a couple of days ago as parts of their skin appeared bright pink from sunburn and other areas where they had worn different size T-shirts were white still. Another coachload was disembarking elderly tourists and the driver was opening the underneath of his coach that was normally reserved for suitcases and other luggage but now housed a number of Zimmer frames and a couple of wheel chairs.

Tony, Steve and David's eyes now concentrated on the front of the queue which appeared static, they could just about make out a number of Spanish border guards who appeared to be standing about chatting and smoking and were for the time being ignoring the stationary queue.

"Oh this is hopeless, it will take forever to pass through, perhaps we should shop somewhere else, Marbella for instance?" David asked in his clear nervousness.

"We're here now so we'll wait, anyway you don't want to be paying Marbella prices, it's a waste of money," insisted Tony.

"Hey you two have you noticed those two guys behind us about three paces behind, they look a bit dodgy, keep your eyes on them, I don't like the look of them," asked Steve whispering discreetly who kept looking all around him at the various characters.

"Yeah they do look a bit iffy, keep away from them," confirmed Tony.

The two men they had been talking about were called Shifty and Sam, two inveterate expat's who made their living anyway they could and generally not legally. Shifty was taller than Sam and thinner he stood about five foot ten inches tall with a long slim face and wore a short sleeve non-descript shirt with a pair of stone coloured shorts and well-worn trainers on his feet with no socks. Sam was about five foot five inches tall and slightly overweight with a rotund puffy face that showed old acne scars and had a discernible beer gut, he also wore a non-descript shirt with blue jeans and sockless sandals on his feet. They were both tanned but not from sunbathing rather by just being in the sun most days looking for their next scam.

Shifty had a nervous twitch in the form of rapidly blinking every few seconds and he could not keep his head still looking from side to side constantly. Sam was a little calmer but was developing his own twitch as when Shifty's head moved rapidly from side to side Sam's head would look in the direction Shifty's had just looked as if he did not want to miss seeing an opportunity or more probably a policeman. They could set each other off and it was becoming a perpetual motion of head turning which gave them a particularly devious look which really did not help their cause.

The queue began to move as the Spanish border crossing officers had put their cigarettes out and decided to do some work. A great sigh seemed to lift from the entire queue which was now nearly 200 strong. Tony, Steve and David eventually made it through customs with just showing their passports and followed the irritable throng of holidaymakers as they made their way along Winston Churchill Avenue towards the runway crossing, where flashing red lights were holding the line of people up yet again.

It was five minutes before a British Airways A320 Airbus landed and the lights changed to green allowing an onslaught of tourists to descend at once into the town centre of Gibraltar. It was now nearly midday and they had been travelling and queueing all morning therefore they were in dire need of caffeine so decided to stop at the first café they came to.

The first café happened to be Barbara's British Butty Bar and not being able to fault all the B's entered into a typical British café you would find in any city in the UK except perhaps for the air-conditioning which was very welcome. Tony nudged Steve and David and nodded to the centre of the table where there was alongside the salt and pepper pots a jar of red sauce and a jar of HP brown sauce. The décor was worn and a little drab but it smelled good so the signs were hopeful. They sat at a table by the window waiting to be served, a youngish early twenties girl finished taking an order at a table of four a few tables away and approached them asking for their order whilst still several feet away from their table. They ordered coffee each and when they did not ask for food the waitress piped up, "There's Lancashire hot pot today being Wednesday, it'll be gone if you try and come back."

The three men looked at each other and shrugged their shoulders so the waitress took it as an order and yelled, "Three pots by the window! I'll be back in a mo. with your coffees."

"So have you thought about what you're going to buy Jill?" Tony asked.

"Dunno, some earrings maybe," suggested David.

"And for how much?" pushed Tony.

"Couple of hundred pounds or so," said David nonchalantly.

"A couple of hundred pounds? Are you taking the piss? Your wife is kicking you out and leaving you and you're going to fix it with a couple of hundred pounds?" Tony said sarcastically.

"No I guess not," said David sheepishly still worried Tony would find out who he had been with.

"£5000 that's what you're going to spend and it's not me telling you its Michelle and she should know, she suggested a gold and diamond necklace, so I hope your credit card is good for it," demanded Tony.

"Fine, fine ok £5000," confirmed David, with the mention of Michelle's name he would have agreed to twice that as he was not sure whether it was a threat coming from Michelle through Tony.

The waitress arrived with their coffee's which was instant; well they thought what would you expect from an English café. Just behind the waitress was a rotund middle aged woman with three plates crammed with Lancashire hot pot on a large black plastic round tray, she smiled as she waddled towards them placing each one carefully in front of them and handing them knives and forks wrapped in paper napkins. They ate what turned out to be a delicious hot pot and drank their coffee whilst watching people passing by through the window.

They noticed Shifty and Sam walk past following a couple of middle aged women with large open handbags. They paid their bill which they thought was very reasonable and left a decent tip before leaving to head towards the port area where they thought they may find the better deals.

David was now resigned to spending £5000 so he led the way thinking it best to buy it and have it done with instead of wasting time and resisting as he knew Tony of old and if he said he was spending £5000 he had better spend it and be done with it.

They found a street which led down to the port area and it housed a number of jewellers none of which were household names and began to wonder whether they would know what they were buying was kosher. The first three shops they tried they left without buying anything as nothing looked to be in Jill's taste, no point buying something just to buy something it must also have the desired effect, it must show Jill exactly what he feels about her with no ifs or buts. The next shop was a little more encouraging for one thing it was larger but it also had a section where you could have items made to order which they did not have time for but they thought it showed a level of expertise that the other establishments did not have.

They began inspecting the various cabinets and although David found something he thought would be perfect on enquiring about the price found it was £20000, a great deal more than he could afford. By asking about the over indulgent item they began explaining to the shop assistant what they were looking for and the assistant turned out to be the owner who showed them over to the made to order section. David explained they did not have the time to wait for something to be made especially but Michael McCarthy, the owner, held his hand up as if he was stopping traffic and then put his right forefinger to his lips before disappearing behind a curtain into the rear workshop.

He returned after a few minutes with a broad smile on his wizened face and began to place a square case on top of the display cabinet. It was wrapped in a dark blue silk cloth which he uncovered slowly to reveal a light polished and varnished wooden box which he opened slowly to reveal the most exquisite gold necklace. It was quite thick but would lay flat on the skin, it rolled down from the rear becoming thicker and developing into a triangular shape at the bottom. Within the triangular shape lay five clear diamonds, David smiled and whispered, "Perfect," "but how much is it?"

"Well," Michael said, "It's £7000 but I made it to order and took a deposit, the gentleman has not returned therefore his deposit is forfeit, I could let you have it for £6000."

"It is perfect for Jill, my wife, but it's just that little bit too much I'm afraid," said David not able to take his eyes off the necklace.

"So tell me what you will give me for it?" asked Michael.

"£5000 is all I have," said David looking as sheepish as he could.

"Shake my hand at £5500!" said Michael holding out his hand.

David shook his hand and was delighted to do so, the necklace was perfect in every way and looked every penny of the £5500. David put his hand in his pocket to retrieve his wallet and took out his credit card handing it to Michael as both Tony and Steve gave him a congratulatory slap on his back with great sighs of relief from them both. Michael took David's credit card over to the PDQ machine and lifted it off its charging cradle returning towards David whilst pressing £5500 onto the numbered keys and waiting patiently while the machine rang through for authorization which came through within a minute as it then printed out two receipts, one for Michael and the second for David.

All three of the friends looked highly delighted and greatly relieved with David's purchase so whilst Michael placed the necklace back in its case and wrapped it placing it in a yellow plastic carrier bag that was only just large enough at twelve inches square Tony suggested they find the nearest pub and celebrate. All three agreed.

The first pub they happened upon was The Lord Nelson, a more apt a name for a pub in Gibraltar they could not think of, it was located just 100 yards from the jewellers. It was a rustic Tudor style establishment which could easily have been located in Portsmouth, the exterior appearance was a little tatty and in need of some much needed TLC. Nonetheless they crossed the threshold to find the interior fared no better.

They approached the bar whilst still taking in their surroundings which consisted mainly of a stone slabbed floor and imitation oak beamed ceilings with walls to match, there was still an odour of tobacco although smoking in public places had been banned for a number of years and the walls and ceiling still showed the scars of tobacco staining. There were several of what appeared to be regulars stood about and leaning on the bar whilst talking about some football match that was to take place at the Victoria stadium.

Tony caught the eye of the barman and ordered three pints of Stella Artois which they took and sat at one of many empty tables by the front of the building by the front open door, they hoped that a breeze would freshen the rather stale air of the room. They decided against taking the necklace out of its newly wrapped case considering their surroundings as it would arouse unwanted interest. Having completed their mission ahead of schedule they decided to partake of a couple more pints and then take a cable car ride to observe the Barbary apes which would round off their day in Gibraltar nicely before driving back and detouring to Marbella for dinner.

They were in excellent spirits, laughing and joking, discussing golf and the best methods to improve one's swing; before they knew it they had had four more pints of Stella Artois and so decided the cable car should now take precedent over the lager.

They left The Lord Nelson much more inebriated than they had intended but nonetheless still found the cable car station at the southern end of Main Street alongside the Alameda Botanical Gardens and paid for their tickets and waited patiently for the next cable car to arrive. It was a short wait of ten minutes and they just made the cut for the car as the tourist numbers waiting for the cable car was mounting. It was a slightly sweaty, smelly six minute ride to the top of the rock at 412 metres above sea level as a number of the tourists personal hygiene was called into question. Great gulps of air were inhaled as people pushed and shoved their way out into the glorious blue clear skies above the Rock.

They made their way out towards the viewing platform that gave the most extraordinary views along the coast and mountains of the Costa Del Sol and the coast of Africa could be seen across the Mediterranean.

The apes were as expected excited by a new wave of fresh victims and they took about relieving as many as possible of any food foolishly brought up to them. Steve was in hysterics having witnessed a woman being molested by one ape with its hands down her bra and as she was endeavouring to retain control of her bra another ape stole her hat and flew at great speed over the parapet and disappeared from sight, the woman was left holding her breasts as the other monkey left looking for another victim.

It was not long before the ape's attention was drawn to David's bright yellow plastic bag containing his necklace, he was nervous enough as it was as he had noticed Shifty and Sam on the cable car and had been nervously looking around him to locate them.

An ape pounced on to his rear holding on by his belt, whilst he spun trying to force the ape off another grabbed at his plastic bag with neither ape nor man letting go, the bag tore and the necklace box fell, the ape grabbed it before it hit the ground and was off over the parapet out of sight. David ran to the handrail looking over for the offending ape followed closely behind by Tony and Steve, they looked at each other in deep shock and consternation which was rapidly followed by sobering panic. They could not see the ape; it was a hopeless situation as there were hundreds of the darn things rapidly darting here there and hither. Then Steve spotted it foraging in a woman's shopping bag way down below them, the woman was none the wiser as she chatted to another woman in the queue for the return cable car back down the Rock. The ape dropped the necklace box into the woman's shopping bag swapping it for a bag of food it had found.

"There, there, there, it's there in that woman's bag, quick we need to go down there before she can jump on the cable car," cried out Steve.

Steve grabbed the other two by their shirts as they were trying to see what Steve had seen shouting they did not have time to look they had to move quickly. They knew that if the woman managed to ride on that tram they would have little chance of catching up with her and the £5500 necklace would be lost. They ran as quickly as they could but arrived just as the cable car was leaving.

It would be some 15 minutes before the next cable car would leave which meant they had no option but to run down the Rock as quickly as they could. They looked at each other with forlorn distain at the inevitability of having to run so far but at least it was downhill and sharply downhill. They set off with David taking the lead, he ran like a girl with arms flaying from side to side and his bum stuck out as he kind of flicked his legs forward alternately. Tony and Steve were right behind him and Tony began laughing loudly at the strange site of David running turning to Steve saying, "He's running as if his haemorrhoids are bleeding!"

"Oh Christ! Don't make me laugh!" cried out Steve with which he pulled up at the side of the road and threw up just missing one of the Barbary apes in the process.

David and Tony continued their run downhill which turned out to be quicker than they expected because of the sharp incline. Their feet, muscles, knees and lungs were paining them with each stride they took but they continued through the pain not noticing they had lost Steve who was now walking nonchalantly down the Rock. After what seemed an eternity of increasing pain they made it to the bottom and to the cable car station with no sign of anyone just a line of people walking away from them on main street so they turned to ask Steve what the woman looked like and what she was wearing to find no Steve.

"Holy shit! Where is he?" David just managed to croak out between his heaving chests attempt at breathing.

"Don't know." Managed Tony doubled over resting his hands on his bent knees, himself trying to breathe in the heat and through the sweat which had now overtaken his entire body.

Meanwhile back in Fuengirola Jill, Michelle and Julie were having breakfast at their now usual venta, Spanish restaurant, and discussing their plans for the day after Jill's usual early morning rant and rave at David's apparent morning ritual of opening their curtains to allow the early mornings suns glare and heat to penetrate their room and more pertinently their bed where Jill escaped her reality and then he has the extreme audacity to slam the door shut on his way out.

Her rants were becoming a little boring for Michelle and Julie but they sympathised and empathised and ooh'd and ahh'd in all the right places or so they hoped. Once Jill had finished they welcomed the next round of coffee brought to them by their favourite waiter, Jesus Dai Jones, apparently his mother married a Welshman from Prestatyn, and began discussing the days agenda.

Their priority was to have Charles out of the way for a significant time to allow Jill and Julie to snoop out clues to exactly who and what Charles really was or is; Michelle was assigned to Charles to her delight. The longer Michelle could keep Charles away from the villa the better as they had decided only one of them would do the actual snooping and one would keep watch for Charles and Michelle should they return early.

They all felt a little trepidation as they a little reluctantly left the safety of their now favourite restaurant and made their way in temperatures approaching eighty degrees to Charles's villa. They arrived alongside the villa's pool and first manoeuvred their sun loungers into position in direct line with the sun's rays. Although they thought they were acting normally they were in fact not, they were not talking but miming to each other so as not to attract Charles's attention which indeed did attract his attention.

"Good morning ladies, you're very quiet today," Charles observed from his balcony.

Jill piped up by way of explanation, "We've just finished breakfast, I think we ate too much."

"Easily done, you have another beautiful day for sunbathing," added Charles.

"It's glorious, must be so nice to live here?" said Jill.

"It is, anyway enjoy your day," said Charles turning to resume whatever he was occupied with.

"Thanks," finished off Jill but Charles could no longer be seen.

They stripped off, Jill and Michelle naked with Julie in her bikini and began applying sun lotion to their tanned bodies sharing knowing looks between themselves.

Time seemed to drag by as they kept glancing at each other as if it would hasten Charles departure. One hour passed nothing. Two hours, nothing. Still hardly a word spoken between them, they were becoming fidgety, applying more sun lotion than was necessary for something to do. Michelle was wishing she had not given up smoking, Julie was wishing she had started smoking. Then on close to two and a half hours Charles walked to his car carrying a white tarpaulin bag a little larger than a shopping bag, they heard the car boot slam shut and thought he might leave on his own. They saw his head pop around the corner of the villa as he said, "Come on Michelle, what's keeping you?"

With which Michelle jumped up off her sun lounger grabbing her dress and throwing it over her head bending down to pick up her beach bag but Charles shouted over that she did not need it. Putting on her shoes she looked at Jill and Julie in turn with her eyes wide open as if to say, "We're on."

On hearing the car leave and accelerate onto the road Jill jumped up off her sun lounger and began to run to the entrance to confirm their departure, she was halfway there when she heard Julie screaming after her, "Jill, Jill, JILL!! Don't you think I should go?"

"Why?" Jill asked.

"Because you're naked!" observed Julie.

"Oh. Ok might be better," said Jill returning passing Julie on the way, she began putting on her bikini, just in case, whilst waiting for Julie to return.

Once Julie returned confirming their departure Jill explained that Julie was the lookout and that Jill was starting her search in Charles bedroom then the living room and breakfast area, then the spare rooms which should be empty, once she had finished those she would come and fetch Julie and they would look at the shed in the garden together as being outside they should hear the car should it return. Julie not wanting to look too obtrusive at the villa's gates she grabbed a jacket and put it on before returning to her post.

Jill set about her task with a great deal of glee and enthusiasm taking the stairs to Charles mezzanine bedroom two at a time. She sprang into the bathroom which only housed a bathroom cabinet over the sink; she opened the mirrored door expectantly to discover it was empty. Her shoulders dropped slightly in disappointment as she looked around her, it was bare, a single toothbrush and a single throwaway Bic razor blade accompanied a lonely Simple fragrance free bar of soap.

She moved onto the bedroom itself starting with the wardrobe and found it contained three pairs of trousers, three pairs of shorts and seven shirts. Moving onto a set of drawers, the first draw contained underwear and a pair of swimming trunks, nothing concealed underneath them. The second drawer contained 13 pairs of socks, nothing concealed underneath. The third and final draw contained six T-shirts of varying colours, nothing concealed underneath. There was a small cabinet beside the bed with a small table light sat on top, its draw was empty so was the inside of the main draw. The whole bedroom was clinical; it contained nothing and therefore nothing personal, no photographs, or diaries or notepads, nothing.

Walking onto the balcony there was a circular wooden table and four matching chairs and on top of the table sat a laptop, eureka! On opening it the screen lit up but asked for a password, she closed it again moving downstairs.

Beginning in the living room there were a couple of cabinets but again Jill found nothing of interest and nothing personal, in fact there was nothing anywhere personal, no discarded magazines or newspapers or pictures or books, nothing. The kitchen was the same, looking in every cupboard there was nothing but what you would expect to find in a kitchen but again it was not quite right. There were just basics, coffee, tea, sugar but no opened packets. For instance no half eaten packets of biscuits or opened packets of spaghetti or rice, in fact there was not any, so it was clear the kitchen was not being used for cooking, he must eat out always. That was the other thing all the bins were empty and clean as if they were never used. Jill moved on to the spare rooms which took all of two minutes, nothing.

Frustrated Jill walked outside and around to the front entrance to inform Julie of her findings or more correctly lack of them. Julie asked if she had looked under his bed and mattress, she had not so they did together, nothing. Jill informed Julie about the laptop and its need for a password in case she happened to be a closet geek, no.

They moved outside and looked inside the wooden shed but that housed nothing out of the ordinary just normal garden tools and a lawn mower and other bits and pieces of tools, nothing strange or sinister. Closing the garden sheds door they each instinctively shrugged their shoulders and looking at each other they both said at the same time, "Drink!"

They found a chilled bottle of Chardonnay in the fridge and opened it with the corkscrew, taking their glasses outside with the bottle to the shaded area with the bamboo furniture; they sat down and poured each other a glass of what they thought was much deserved wine. Although they had found nothing that in itself was something.

Jill said to Julie, "Not even a passport, nothing."

Julie said, "That's strange in itself, isn't it?"

"I would say so, definitely."

"I wonder what Michelle is up to?" asked Julie.

Michelle jumped into the passenger seat alongside Charles and the latent heat in the car exacerbated by the leather seats hit her all at once, the sun lotion seemed to make her body retain the heat and she began to sweat profusely. Charles accelerated away from the villa at speed as though he was in a hurry to reach their destination, wherever that may be. Michelle's nervousness pervaded every sinew in her body as she began to ponder their destination as they sped past the turning for the golf course.

Charles turned to Michelle and asked, "You're all very quiet this morning, is there a problem?"

"Problem? No, there's no problem....we... er... had a little too much for breakfast, that's all," answered Michelle a little unconvincing.

"Too much breakfast. Oh, I see, well that's easily done; you'll feel better when we reach our destination," said Charles smiling as he eyed Michelle.

"And where exactly is our destination?" asked Michelle.

"You'll see," answered Charles with that grin come smile of his.

They drove along in silence, mile after boring mile on the main carretera that threaded along the coast; the signposts suggested they were heading towards Malaga. After what seemed longer but only half an hour had passed before they began entering the outskirts of Malaga and off to their right they could clearly see planes on their final flight paths coming into land.

Michelle began to fidget nervously as she sensed they were approaching their arrival point, her thoughts began to drift to her first afternoon foray with Charles at the golf course and the fear and dread she had felt at being tied up, the feeling of helplessness and the inevitability of being caught, then escaping and the exhilaration and excitement. She wondered with both fear and trepidation at what Charles had planned and what was in the tarpaulin bag?

Charles sensed Michelle's nervousness but kept his peace allowing Michelle's fears to grow and become more pronounced in her mind with every passing second. The traffic slowed as they drew further into the centre of Malaga and then they came to a stop at the end of the slip road which leads into the centre of Malaga. Moving off slowly from the slip road they approached a roundabout and Michelle noticed Charles take the second exit which was signposted for the airport, it prompted her to ask, "Are we going to the airport?"

"You'll see," answered Charles.

At which all Michelle could do was frown her frustration and fold her arms in contempt. At the next junction they again followed the signs for the airport but all Michelle did was look a question at Charles and when no answer was forthcoming she looked the other way out of her side window. They now saw a sign approaching that showed a right turn ahead for the airport, Michelle turned and stared at Charles as if she knew he was going to turn right, when he drove straight on her features turned to that of surprise.

Charles allowed himself a smile and Michelle noticed and Charles noticed she noticed. They both began to laugh and it broke the tension that was building within the confines of the Audi. In the midst of their laughter Charles turned right onto a narrow lonely road that ran parallel to the runway some 150 or so metres away, the runway was hidden by trees and shrubs but they could see a plane coming into land. It appeared to be an Airbus A320 with its tailgate emblazoned with EasyJet in bright orange. Michelle now sat up straight in her seat as it was now obvious they were near their final destination. Charles pulled the car over to the side of the road and onto the grass verge where he turned off the engine and turned to Michelle smiling and asked, "Ready?"

Michelle nodded before opening her door and strode out into the fresh air and bright warm sunshine with a slight breeze coming off the ocean which was yards away at the start of the runway. Michelle took a good look around and all she could see where the trees and shrubbery to their right along with the runway which they could not see and the desolate road they had just driven down which was empty apart from their Audi.

Charles was at the back of the car opening the boot and taking out the white tarpaulin bag which he hauled across his shoulder whilst motioning Michelle to follow him. They made their way to the end of the line of trees towards the ocean and then made their way down the other side back away from the ocean which gave them an uncluttered view of the runway except for the security fence which was chain-link and about twelve feet high and ran the length of the runway as far as the eye could see.

Michelle's curiosity was driving her insane so she asked, "What are we doing here?"

"You'll see," was all Charles answered.

They walked up about 100 metres from the chevrons that started the runway and Charles dropped his bag as another plane was coming into land. Michelle waved at the plane and was pleasantly surprised that she could see some of the passengers in the windows waving back at her; they were about 50 meters away and could be clearly seen. Charles bent over his bag and unzipped it bringing out a large white inch thick rope with two eight inch wide strips of black rubber about forty inches long.

Charles laughed out loud at Michelle's confused look as he spread it out on the ground. Once spread out Michelle could see that it was one long loop, circular the way it had been spread, there was a connection showing where the two ends had been sliced together, Michelle held her arms out and then slapped her thighs in confusion. He pointed up at one of the branches of a tree protruding next to them and Michelle noticed there were two wear marks where the bark had been rubbed away at the top of the branch; Charles has been here before she thought. He then grabbed an end of rope with one of the rubber flanges; the other was at the other end of the rope, and running it back and forth to give it some momentum threw it over the branch and then pulled it down so the two rubber parts of the rope were level with each other. He then adjusted the two ends of rope over the branches so that they were about four feet apart, so the rubbers now dangled about three feet off the ground.

Michelle was beginning to see what the contraption was for and began to strip her dress off in readiness. Charles turned and smiled at Michelle's eagerness at wanting to try his oversized sexual aid, well swing.

Charles instructed Michelle in the best way to position herself, one of the rubber flanges went around her shoulders with her arms through and the other was for her lower back to rest on. She managed to climb onto the contraption on the first attempt despite being in hysterics at the way she looked.

Once comfortable Charles began to gently push her so she was travelling through the air in an ark, Michelle loved the feeling with the breeze from the sea hitting her wet sweaty body, she was feeling herself wanting Charles inside her, she was watching him undress as another plane came into land and giggled as she noticed some of the passengers had seen her.

Charles was now alongside her naked as he gently massaged her whilst pushing her through the ark. He looked behind him to check on the position of the next plane as he wanted the timing to be perfect. Michelle hung onto him as she swung gently making him harder and then pushed him towards his position between her legs as she could wait no longer to feel him motioning inside her. The next plane came into land and she found herself waving at it again although this time she felt she should have had a hat in her hand as she felt like a rodeo rider, only she was the one being ridden. She had to laugh at some of the expressions on people's faces when they suddenly stopped waving as the realisation at what they were doing dawned on them.

They continued their rhythms with the next plane coming into land and then they heard the scream of a siren and saw a blue flashing light rapidly approaching from the far end of the runway. Charles pulled out and Michelle awkwardly jumped down off the rubber flange that was sticking to her shoulders and buttocks, they both bent down at the same time and picked up their clothes and shoes and ran as quickly as they could down the 100 metres back to the end of the line of trees all the time with the siren becoming louder as the police car caught up to them. The rope was left in place dangling with just a little motion in the ark left. The run back to the Audi was hampered as they were both laughing so much. They arrived back at the Audi and jumped in naked as Charles searched in his pockets for the key, finding it he ripped it out of the pocket throwing the trousers onto the back seat and put the key in the ignition and turned, the engine fired up straight away and Charles pushed the gear knob back into reverse gear and sped backwards, turning the steering wheel abruptly and applying the handbrake at the same time he now rammed the gear knob into drive and sped away looking in his rear-view mirror as he did so. They were both out of breath and sweating profusely so Charles engaged the electric windows and opened all of them to let in a draft until the air conditioning could cope.

They arrived at the T junction at the top of the desolate road and as Charles waited for a break in the traffic so he could join the main road he checked his rear view mirror again and found the road behind them was clear. He pulled out into the mainstream of traffic and turned to see Michelle low down in her seat pulling her dress over her head, he looked down at himself, laughed as he realised he was naked. He continued driving as he was until after about a mile he pulled into a St. Dunne's store car park and stopped his car away from the mainstream of parked cars and dressed himself.

Before carrying on he turned to the windswept Michelle and said, "We didn't have to rush so much you know."

"Really, why, the police were right on top of us," asked Michelle.

"Yes I know, but what were they going to do? Climb the fence? They were on one side and we were on the other," said Charles.

They both laughed while Charles once dressed turned the car around and re-joined the main road. On the way back to Fuengirola Charles rued losing his rope fancy and determined to make another.

Charles closed the windows and let the air conditioning take over as they enjoyed a cool ride back to the villa. They arrived back a little over 3.30pm to find Jill and Julie both in their bikini's on their sun loungers enjoying the heat of the sun's rays on their tanned oiled bodies.

Charles left them and went to his bedroom and took a much needed shower. Michelle stripped off and jumped straight into the pool and wishing she hadn't as the water was freezing and hit her body like a sword. Jill rushed to the edge of the pool and laid down beside it asking Michelle what was in the bag but all she received from Michelle was giggles. Eventually she said she would tell her when she told her what they found out about Charles from the villa.

David and Tony were still sweating profusely but their breathing had relaxed somewhat as they looked desperately upon the disappearing throng in front of them. Turning and glancing up the hill they saw the lackadaisical shape of Steve strolling towards them without a care in the world.

David turned on him saying, "Where the hell have you been, all the passengers have disappeared and you're the only one who knows what she looks like."

"Well, after I'd thrown up you were so far in front there didn't seem much point rushing down after you," said Steve somewhat hurt by David's reaction.

"But you're the only one of us that saw the woman and knows what she looks like and what she is wearing and more importantly what her bloody bag looks like," said David rattily.

"Oh," said Steve apologetically.

"Alright, alright, what's done is done, Steve take a look around and see if you can see her, let's walk to the left which is where the majority of people walked when they left the cable car station," suggested Tony.

They walked on for about 5 minutes without any sign of the women as all three of them were becoming more and more desperate. There was no conversation between them as their eyes darted from one direction to the next unsuccessfully. They rounded the corner of an old building and Steve saw a woman dressed in a blue skirt and carrying a beige canvas shopping bag entering through large glass entrance doors to a huge five story high building, "That's her, that's her there going through those doors, the woman dressed in the blue dress."

David turned to Steve putting his hands onto Steve's shoulders and looking him straight in the eye asked, "Are you sure? Are you one hundred percent sure?"

"Yep, one hundred percent," confirmed Steve.

Tony meanwhile had been watching the woman and more pertinently the building as he now turned to both David and Steve and said, "So you're sure it's the woman, dressed in blue, like a nurses uniform, going into that building with the Hospital sign above the entrance."

David still had his hands on Tony's shoulder as both he and Tony said as one, "Oh Shit!"

All three of them turned and ran up to the building and up the steps leading to the entrance, they all shoved their way through the heavy glass doors into a large reception area that led through to the various departments. They stood frozen as one as they were met by a cavalcade of nurses passing through, entering and leaving the building.

Now all three said openly, "Oh Shit!"

"We have to split up and check everywhere," David demanded.

"Everywhere! Are you taking the piss! It's a fuckin hospital; we don't know what she looks like, oh except she's wearing a blue dress, in a hospital full of nurses in blue dresses!" said Tony.

"We have to try, what else can we do?" pleaded David now close to tears.

"We could buy you a Happy Divorce card," suggested Steve.

"Really? That doesn't help Steve, we'll split up and look around different floors each then meet up back here in half an hour, ok?" instructed Tony.

"Sorry, ok," said Steve.

They split up in the reception area; David would take the ground floor, Steve the first and Tony the second. They went their separate ways although Tony thought David was unlikely to accomplish anything as he had pretty much lost hope, he was pale and tears had appeared in his eyes. Stranger things had happened at sea; unfortunately they were not at sea.

A little after half an hour Tony and Steve met up again in the reception area but there was no sign of David, they gave him another five minutes then decided to search for him. Tony and Steve split up to search the ground floor for David, after ten minutes Tony heard Steve calling after him, he turned to find Steve running up to him.

After gaining his breath back he said, "I've found him, he's sitting outside Herpes ward with a nurse."

"Herpes? Don't you mean Hermes ward?" asked Tony.

"What, oh yeah, this way, c'mon," said Steve as he turned and rushed back the way he had come.

On arriving outside Hermes ward they found David with his head on a nurse's shoulder with tears streaming down his face. The nurse said that David was upset about losing his wife and that a colleague had tried to find more information about his wife's case but they could find no record of her ever being in the hospital. Tony began explaining their day's exploits finishing with the ape stealing David's gold necklace and their resulting search for the mystery woman in blue.

"That could be Suzie Mathis; she goes up the Rock every day in her lunch hour, I'm not saying it is but it could be, I'm Lorna Done by the way," said the nurse.

"Great, so where can we find this, er, Suzie Mathis?" asked Tony ignoring David's obvious distress.

"Wait here and I'll see if I can find her for you," said Lorna.

She returned after ten minutes minus Suzie Mathis explaining she was just scrubbing up for theatre but she said I could check her bag and I found this, she held up the wooden necklace case. David fell to his knees grabbing it out of her hand and on opening the case found the necklace unharmed within.

"Oh thank you, thank you, thank you, thank you," David whimpered.

Tony thanked Lorna for her help and offered her and Suzie Mathis a reward but she would not take one and said neither would Suzie and that they were just happy to help. After saying their thanks again and farewell they picked David up off the floor and returned outside to continuing glorious sunshine.

They walked happily in the warm air chatting happily except for David who remained quiet, embarrassed at his breakdown. Passing the Lord Nelson Steve expressed his need for refreshment as he had left his previous drinks on the path at the top of the Rock on his aborted jog down. Steve agreed and although David was clearly against the idea he kept his silence whilst Tony and Steve marched into the pub and up to the bar.

With drinks in hand they sat at the same table they had occupied earlier although the conversation was somewhat more subdued this time. In their attempts at bringing David into the conversation they began to discuss their plans for dinner and it was decided they should stop off in Marbella and find a restaurant. Tony also mentioned he had heard that there was a casino in Marbella which they could try and locate later as they were in no rush to return to either Fuengirola or their hotel as their wives were not expecting them. It was 5pm before they found their way back to their hire car after spending a sultry half hour waiting in the burning sun to proceed through the passport control on the border, the delay once again being the Spanish officials.

Michelle still smirking slightly at her afternoons romp with Charles climbed out of the swimming pool with goose bumps all over her body and walked quickly over to the outside shower located by the pool. Standing underneath the shower jets she turned the control knob to hot and switched the water on, she screamed as the freezing water jetted over her already cold body and was less than impressed when a smiling Charles appeared on his balcony to inform her the heating on the shower was not working.

Turning the shower off she walked quickly over to her sun lounger and picked up her towel off it and wrapped herself in it until some warmth returned to her body. Having finished drying herself and noticing her nipples had returned close to normality she began to put her dress over her head, this she hoped Jill and Julie would take as a sign of their impending departure.

Jill and Julie noticed Michelle dressing and followed her lead quietly, having packed their belongings away into their beach bags and returned the sun loungers to their original positions they shouted up to Charles saying their goodbyes and agreed to meet at Bulbous Billy's Bar at 11.00pm. No sooner had they left the confines of the villa Julie turned to Michelle and asked, "Well c'mon tell us, what was in that tarpaulin bag?"

This just set Michelle off giggling again, "I need a drink, wait until we are sat comfortably with a vodka and coke."

"You're winding me up now," said Jill frustrated at having to wait longer to find out the contents of the mystery bag.

"I don't know why you're so interested in the contents of that bag; it's probably just his washing," said Julie disinterestedly.

"I don't know what planet you're on sometimes," said Jill.

They continued walking in silence, Julie silent as she had not liked Jill's comment and Jill impatient with Michelle, Michelle was still smirking and thinking of Charles and herself running naked back to the car and the comical sight they must have made especially to the chasing police seeing two retreating backsides bouncing up and down as they ran.

They walked on in silence enjoying the sun's warmth and although no one had suggested where they should go for a drink each one of them knew they were walking to their venta.

Arriving at the venta Jill motioned them towards an outside table closest to the sidewalk and away from prying ears. They were approached by an elderly waiter they had not seen before; he must have been easily over sixty years old but still had a full head of black hair and was short at five foot five inches and walked a little stooped forward with a curvature in the top of his spine. He smiled brightly revealing two missing front teeth and excusing himself for the lapse as he had left his false teeth at home so his wife could use them because their daughter was visiting with their grandchildren.

They ordered three vodka and cokes, as the waiter left they waited until he was safely inside the restaurant before laughing at his storey. They each people watched whilst waiting for their waiter to return which he did shortly with their drinks setting them down on the table gently in front of each of them and then he placed a generous plate of green olives on the table for them before introducing himself as Pepe, and to his family he was known as Papa Pepe and when he had his own pizza shop some years prior he was known as Papa Pepe Pizza's and his shop was called Papa Pepe's Pizza Palace. He smiled politely as he turned and made his way back inside the restaurant leaving the girls to ponder Papa Pepe.

"I wouldn't want to ring his place for a pizza when I'd had too much to drink!" said Michelle laughing, which they all did but they liked Pepe he was a nice old guy.

"Right c'mon Michelle what was in that bloody bag?" asked Jill expectantly.

"You first, I want to know what you found in that villa after all I was the diversion," demanded Michelle.

"Absolutely nothing, isn't that so Julie?" said Jill sighing slightly.

"Nothing at all," confirmed Julie.

"Hang on, there must have been something, in that whole villa you found nothing at all, I don't believe it," said Michelle incredulously.

"Well the fact that we found nothing says something, there was absolutely nothing not even a passport. There was a laptop but it is password protected so we couldn't look at it, but apart from that, nothing," confirmed Jill.

"Well that says something in itself doesn't it, I mean who has nothing personal and no passport? Strange," Michelle said.

"We looked everywhere as well, all we found were some mushrooms he is growing in that shed and some plants but other than that there is just tools and gardening stuff. Oh and that big barbeque thing at the side of the villa, its massive about seven foot long and eight foot high and about three foot wide, he must have massive parties with that thing," added Julie.

"But you didn't find anything at all personal? Like magazines, a diary or pictures or books or anything?" asked Michelle.

"Not a dicky bird!" confirmed Jill.

"It's all a bit strange but not very conclusive of anything is it?" asked Michelle.

"I know…but," said Jill. "So at last, what was in the bag?"

"The bag, yes, a rope! Not just any rope though, a rope with two rubber sort of flanges on it, the ends had been tied together and he threw it over a branch of a tree so the two rubber bits were at the bottom for me. I climbed on it with shoulders through one end and my bum on the other and then he pushed me like a swing," informed Michelle.

"He pushed you, that's it, he pushed you?" asked Julie.

"Well not exactly, I mean we were both naked at the time," confirmed Michelle.

"And where exactly were you both naked at the time?" asked Jill.

"At the airport."

"The airport?"

"Yes the airport."

"And where abouts at the airport?"

"Well, by the runway."

"By the runway, at the airport, how close?"

"About 50 yards."

"You're lucky the police didn't come for you."

"Ah, well they did."

"And what did they say to you."

"Don't know."

"What do you mean you don't know?"

"We ran and they didn't catch us," Michelle could no longer keep a straight face and burst out laughing.

"You think that's funny? Really?" asked Jill.

"Well it was hilarious actually, both of us running back to the car naked and then driving off naked," Michelle said still laughing.

"And what if they had caught you," asked Jill.

"That was the funny thing, they couldn't have caught us, there was a twelve foot high fence in the way!" said Michelle in-between guffaws.

"Really Michelle, I can't believe you would do that, what if someone saw you?" said Jill.

"Funny you should ask that, there were the people on the planes."

"The people on the planes? What people on the planes?"

"Well we were alongside the runway and there were these planes landing and…"

"And what people Michelle?"

"Well as I said there were these planes landing and people were looking out of the windows, like they do, and waving at us…."

"They were waving at you? While you were…."

"As I said they were waving at us until they realised what we were doing…."

"And when they realised they stopped waving…."

"Well yes some stopped waving….but others were cheering…I think they were enjoying it."

"But there would have been children on that plane, did they see you also?"

"Oh, I don't know, probably, but they wouldn't have realised what we were doing, not that far away."

"But the parents did know what you were doing, obviously."

"Yeah, it would have been pretty obvious to them."

"I don't believe it, and you ran away naked?"

"Yep, back to the car, it must have been funny for the police following our naked bums bouncing up and down."

"It wouldn't have just been your bums bouncing up and down though would it."

"Well no but they wouldn't have been able to see them though as I was running away from them."

"You really don't see a problem with what you were doing do you?"

"Well no, not really…oh except the rope."

"The rope?"

"Yeah the rope, we left that behind in the rush, we just managed to grab our clothes off the ground and run…so we forgot about the rope."

"Well that is a loss isn't it? The rope…." said Jill sarcastically.

"Yes it is….Charles will have to make another one now."

"Christ Michelle, I really can't believe you at times," said Jill shaking her head from side to side.

"Just a second here little miss righteous! It was you who suggested I go with Charles as a distraction so you two could look around the villa in solitude, wasn't it? What the hell did you think we were going to do?

Tiddlywinks for two on the beach?" said Michelle a little aggrieved at Jill now for her attitude towards her.

"No, no your right Michelle I'm sorry, of course I knew you would erm, do something but I just didn't expect sex at the airport, that's all."

"So are you a swinger now?" asked Julie.

"What?" asked Michelle.

"Well you know, now you've had sex in a swing as it were, does that make you a swinger?"

"Don't," said Jill.

Changing the subject Michelle asked, "So what's the plan with Charles now?"

"Unless we can find out his password for his laptop I don't see what else we can do, ideas anyone?"

"Food!" said Julie.

"Top idea, I'm starving," said Michelle.

"Must be all the running you've done!" said Jill with some degree of sarcasm in her voice again.

"Jill!" said Michelle.

"Sorry," said Jill, "where's Pepe?"

With which Michelle caught Pepe's eye as he stood inside the restaurant keeping a casual eye on his customers and ordered more drinks and mimed opening a book which she hoped he would understand as a request for menu's. Pepe marched out to them with his black plastic circular tray outstretched on his right arm carrying their drinks along with three menu's, he placed their drinks gently on the table and then proceeded to open each menu in turn as he handed one to each of them, he took his leave by bowing slightly saying he would return shortly to take their orders. They did like Pepe, they thought him sweet.

Tony, Steve and David were driving along the careterra in the direction of Marbella, Tony was driving and Steve sat next to him with David in the rear, the silence prevailed. They were travelling at a steady 70mph in the middle lane as the nearside lane was full of articulated lorries of varying sizes with different loads expected in locations across Spain. In the outside lane Tony became aware of a dirty old brown Ford Mondeo which inched its way alongside them at maybe 72mph leaving in its wake a trail of impatient drivers waiting to pass them at much beyond the speed limit. Tony could make out the old couple in the front seats of the Mondeo and was surprised to see the elderly woman driving, not because she was a woman but rather that she did not seem to be able to see over the steering wheel properly although her seat was positioned as far forward as it would go and she bent forward as she drove but seemed to look through the steering wheel rather than over it. Tony could see in his rear view mirror cars slowing as they approached the increasing queue behind the Mondeo.

Tony nudged Steve next to him and threw his head back in the direction of the car following the Mondeo for Steve to keep an eye on it. The car following behind the Mondeo was an old silver Mercedes which Tony could not make out the model but he did note it was speeding closer and closer to the old Mondeo. Steve was now turned in his seat with his eyes directly on the Mercedes when he noted the occupants and turned back to Tony to inform him they were Shifty and Sam whom they had seen in Gibraltar, although they did not know their names. It was Shifty who was driving and Steve could clearly see his head rapidly moving from side to side in his nervous twitch. Shifty was moving his Mercedes closer and closer to the unaware Mondeo until he buttoned up onto it and began accelerating much to the angst of the confused and clearly frightened elderly woman driver who now veered her Mondeo towards the centre lane and Tony's car. This forced Tony over towards the inside lane but he was blocked by an articulated lorry, he saw in his rear-view mirror he had a car directly behind him so he had no choice but to accelerate hard himself, which he did only to bang into the old Mondeo forcing it all the way back into the fast lane and in turn forced forward by the speeding Mercedes which was still buttoned up to it. Tony knew his hire car was damaged where the Mondeo had bounced of it but was more concerned with avoiding the inevitable accident that must surely come so sped off in front of the Mondeo and into the fast lane as his speed quickly rose above 90mph.

Not seeing any accident in his rear view mirror Tony was shaking and decided to leave the careterra as soon as possible to cool down and inspect the damage on his car. A road sign appeared indicating the next slip road would take them to the west of Marbella which suited him so he slowed down and eased into the middle lane hoping to find a gap in the nearside lane so he could take the slip road off. A gap appeared just in time for him to take the slip road off. A mile later on the much quieter road they saw signs for a restaurant so Tony made the decision to stop, he drove onto the stoned car park and stopped the car exhaling deeply, he sat still for a minute taking deep breaths as the dangerous nature of what they had just survived hit him.

Opening his car door a wave of fresh warm air hit him and began to revive him as he closed his door and began to inspect the damage. There was a scratched line midway up the car which ran the full length, it could have been much worse and with a little elbow grease with the aid of some T-cut it probably wouldn't look too bad but would no doubt still cost them with their hire company.

All three of them walked slowly towards the restaurant in much need of some refreshment, as they were halfway to the restaurant a battered old brown Ford Mondeo clattered slowly past at barely 20mph with a little old lady driving without a care in the world with her husband waving at them through the passenger window. Tony, Steve and David all instinctively waved back with incredulity emblazoned on their faces and as they passed began to laugh although none of them knew why.

The restaurant itself was a reasonable sized stone built build with red tiles to its roof and whitewashed walls. Outside were a number of tables enclosed by a three foot high wooden fence, a smell of warm oil, garlic and coffee permeated the air from an extractor fan to the side of the building. They chose one of the outside tables and were greeted by a waiter who had observed them pull up onto the gravelled carpark. They ordered coffee and sat back under the large Mahou beer advertising umbrella and enjoyed the cooling effects of the breeze coming in from the east. Their coffee arrived and once the waiter had left Tony piped up,"I don't believe what that idiot did, trying to push that car out of the way at that speed, it's a wonder we weren't all killed."

"It was those dodgy looking two from Gibraltar in the Merc," said Steve.

"I didn't see much just felt that old Mondeo hit us," said David feeling a little more like himself again.

"They are a pair of lunatics, what the hell could the rush have been about?" asked Tony.

"Who knows with that two?" said Tony shaking his head finishing his coffee and looking for the waiter so he could order some more.

Jill, Michelle and Julie could not make their minds up from the menu as Pepe stood silently awaiting their order; he smiled knowingly as he informed the women that they had slow cooked lamb shanks which had been marinated for 24 hours in their chef's secret formula which obviously included garlic. The three of them folded their menu's handing them back to Pepe nodding as they did so.

They chatted idly for five minutes or so until the topic of Charles came up again and although they chatted for a further ten minutes on the subject until their food arrived they did not reach any conclusions.

The lamb shanks placed before them were enormous and as they dug in their faces creased up in sheer delight as the lamb melted in their mouths. Try as they might they could not finish all the food placed in front of them which caused some consternation for Pepe, his distress was apparent and needed stern persuasion from the women that it was just because there was so much on their plates and that nothing at all was wrong with the food. Eventually Pepe accepted their pleas and took their plates away leaving them to return to their conversation about Charles. They concluded that as they had no concrete information to the contrary they should take Charles at face value as the exemplary host and friend he had shown them to be. Until facts suggested otherwise.

The three women left the restaurant slowly and began walking along the wide pedestrian walkway alongside the beach, their stomachs were full and they all felt bloated so were in no particular rush to reach Blues.

They decided on a quick change at their Hotel, 15 minutes tops. Having changed in rapid time they walked silently along with each to their own thoughts as they observed people still on the beach, some playing football, some volleyball, some just walking. A warm breeze blew in from the sea.

They noticed a half dozen small fishing boats with a single yellowish light on the bow making their way along the coast for their favourite hunting grounds for the evening, they would return in the early morning.

They walked all the way into the centre of Fuengirola and walked around the marina aimlessly before Julie suggested it was time to make their way to Blues, they said nothing just changed direction and walked on. They did not notice their pace picking up as their stomachs eased. Their whole deportment changed as they walked with a spring in their step with hips swinging and they were talking again, not making a great deal of sense but talking anyway.

On approaching Blues they noticed that the A sign which normally sat outside on the pavement advertising the evening's entertainment was absent therefore they thought it would be karaoke for the night.

On entering they made their way directly to the bar which was unusually absent of customers. The lights dimmed and music blasted from the speakers, Tainted

Love by Soft Cell, and Men O'Pause jumped onto the stage, the girls looked at one another with huge smiles as they scattered to find a table, the drinks would have to wait. All the customers were clapping and cheering as they began their routine. Finishing to a huge standing ovation the dancers rushed back to their duties behind the bar.

Jill volunteered for bar duty and returned shortly with their vodka and cokes which had become their mainstay. Camp Teddie was on the stage when Jill returned halfway through his introduction of Miss Ellie a very blue comedian. She was a transvestite of ample proportions with a gregarious overlarge black wig and long flowing cream diamond covered dress.

She began with, "What's the difference between a G spot and a golf ball? A man will look for a golf ball!" which went down well with the women.

Then came, "What's the difference between a hooker and a drug dealer? A hooker can wash her crack and resell it!"

"What's the difference between your wife and your job? After 5 years your job will still suck!"

And so on and so on it went for half an hour before Camp Teddie returned on stage to say they were having another number by Men O'Pause, Like a Virgin by Madonna, then they would be having karaoke so anyone wanting to sing should come to the front of the stage to see him.

They left Julie to look after the table whilst Michelle bought drinks from the bar and Jill put their names down with Camp Teddie before Men O'Pause again took to the stage. Before the music to Like a Virgin started Camp Teddie announced the first three karaoke singers and Jill, Michelle and Julie were on third.

The lights dimmed and the applause rose and the music began with Men O'Pause stripped to just their hot pants as they began dancing. As the music died away the applause rose along with raucous cheering, it was clearly obvious that Men O'Pause were a clear favourite with the crowd.

The women now sat back to await their turn and struggled through the first singer who was attempting to sing "Simply the Best" by Tina Turner unfortunately she sounded more like Tiny Tim. The next singer was better in his attempt at New York New York by Frank Sinatra, it helped him as he did not try and do an impersonation he just sang it his way.

The women now made their way to the stage and jumped up onto it with glee and excitement; they took their microphones off Camp Teddie and waited for the music for Bananarama's Love In The First Degree to start. They were a little out of synch with each other to start with but recovered well and earned a warm applause when they had finished.

The waiter picked their empty coffee cups up off the table and replaced them with full fresh cups of strong coffee, the smell of fresh ground coffee rose quickly to their nostrils and as they were enjoying the smell Steve began laughing, puzzling Tony and David.

"We're going to the casino right? Have you seen the state of us? We look like hod carriers for Rodney Dangerfield in Caddyshack!" said Steve taking off again in another bout of laughter.

They each looked at each other and joined in the laughter as they had not noticed their clothing which was their golf attire, David with bright red trousers and a very obnoxiously bright red and white Hawaiian shirt, Tony with pastel yellow trousers and a light green short sleeve shirt and then Steve with his Tartan plus fours and a stripped lengthwise black and yellow shirt. They looked like some 1970's pop group; Steve could certainly have been in the Bay City Rollers.

After they eventually calmed down they thought all they really needed for entry to the casino would be their passports which they had in view of their visit to Gibraltar.

They decided to find the casino and eat there as most casinos' had a fairly decent restaurant, it was in the casinos' best interests to keep their customers happy and refrain from leaving.

They paid their bill and made their way back to the damaged car inspecting it again before climbing inside. They decided to make their way into the centre of Marbella and hoped to find a road sign for the casino or they would stop and ask someone for directions. They were about two miles from the centre of Marbella when they saw the first sign for the casino which was part of a large hotel complex. After a further 15 minutes winding their way through the centre of Marbella and out the other side they pulled into the hotels large very neat and tidy tarmacked car park.

Tony and Steve climbed out of the car and stretched whilst David remained in his seat; Tony leaned down looking through the window at David and said, "C'mon, what are you doing?"

"Nothing, I'll just be a minute," answered David.

Their curiosity aroused both Tony and Steve rested an arm on the roof of the car whilst they both leaned down and looked through the window at what David was doing, Steve said," Your kidding me!"

"Well I'm not leaving it here, I nearly lost it once," pleaded David.

David was caught placing Jill's necklace around his own neck and trying to tie the top button of his Hawaiian shirt to hide it but it would not work, he stopped in vain trying to hide it from view totally, it showed somewhat but not too badly.

David climbed out of the car and ran to catch up to the laughing Tony and Steve; Tony turned and flicked the key fob to lock the car.

They arrived at the casino reception area with Tony and Steve still chuckling with each other whilst ribbing David and learned that in addition to seeing their passports they needed to pay ten Euros each for admittance. They walked through a short corridor and pushed open a large stout highly varnished wooden double door and entered into the casino.

The doors were at one end which meant walking through the casino to the bar or restaurant, the bar being on the end right and the restaurant at the end and full width. Walking through they passed numerous blackjack tables some occupied some not, then roulette tables and French roulette, to the back of them was a long twenty seat Punto Banco table and alongside that a solitary craps table.

They ignored the tables and made their way to the restaurant where they were seated by a maître de. He left them with menu's to inspect and sent over a wine waiter, they ordered a bottle of French wine much to the obvious disgust of the waiter which amused Steve. Once the wine waiter had returned with the ordered bottle and had poured it and left the food waiter arrived at their table looking down his nose at them again much to the amusement of Steve.

They ordered steaks with various sauces and sautéed potatoes with asparagus spears. Once the waiter left they looked at each other in the waiters eyes and laughed quite loudly bringing a sneer from the maître de.

The food waiter eventually returned with their steaks which looked enormous sat alone on the plates with the sauce, the potatoes and vegetables were placed onto the table in separate dishes to be helped onto the plates by the diners.

They were nearly halfway through their meal when Steve tapped both Tony and David on their hands and nodded at them both to look. They followed his eyes and saw an enormous man, not tall maybe five foot six inches tall but very round and powerful looking, he looked to have the strength of a weightlifter. He looked similar to Oddjob out of James Bond's Goldfinger. He strode down the casino floor with his legs kicking out to the side, the only way he could walk as his legs were so big. He linked three gorgeous beauties on each arm and walked straight ahead his head and massive neck solid and immobile, his eyes unblinking, he was oriental looking although which part of the orient was unclear. He wore an overlarge long shirt with gold cufflinks, and a large thick gold chain hung off his uncompromising neck. His thick legs were covered by black trousers and he had open sandals on his feet with no socks. He was totally expressionless as he made his way to the bar area and sat his six women down at a low circular table and he sat at another table by himself next to it.

Before Tony, Steve and David had finished their meal one of the women had disappeared none of the men saw her leave. They did see the next woman leave, a man bent down and whispered in the Oddjob looking man's ear, he nodded his head; the man went to his pocket and lifted out a wedge of money handing it in total to the enormous man. He then turned and took one of the women by the hand and walked her out of the casino. During the next hour further men approached the enormous man and sometimes he nodded agreement straight away sometimes he shook his head at which there was further whispers in his ear until agreement was found and the man would leave the casino with a woman. This continued through the next hour until all the women had left the casino, all the time the enormous man remained expressionless. Once the last woman had left the casino the man turned to the barman and smiled, that was all. The barman collected a bottle of champagne and filled a small silver bucket with ice placing the champagne into it. The barman then walked around to the bars exit and walked through with the bucket of champagne held high in one hand and a small Champagne glass in his other hand. He placed the bucket on the table and placed the glass in front of the enormous man, he opened the Champagne with a loud Plop and filled the glass, the enormous man gave the barman a number of Euros, he returned behind the bar. The enormous man lifted the Champagne glass and seemed to salute the ceiling before taking a drink and then let out an enormous smile.

"Why's he so happy all of a sudden?" asked David.

"You really can be pretty dumb at times can't you?" said Tony.

"What?" asked David.

"All his women are now working....so they are making him money.....Christ!....They're prostitutes David!" said Tony pointedly.

"Oh...Oh I see," said David.

Tony and Steve left David alone at the bar with his gory Hawaiian shirt for company as he thought that he had spent enough money for one day whilst they searched the gaming floor for a suitable blackjack table. Having found one they sat at one of the six stools available next to one another and Steve watched Tony throw 300 Euros onto the table for the dealer to change into chips. The dealer placed twenty 5 Euro and 8 25 Euro chips in front of Tony who moved them closer to him whilst placing a single 5 Euro chip into the box marked on the table in front of him. Steve followed his lead but with 100 Euros and the dealer duly placed 20 5 Euro chips in front of him, he asked the dealer for one Euro chips only to be informed by the dealer that the minimum bet was 5 Euros, his chin dropped but he recovered quickly placing a 5 Euro chip in the box in front of him and managing a smile for the dealer. The dealer dealt two cards for each of them in quick succession leaving one of his cards turned over so the card could not be read. Tony had 13 and took another card which was a queen, bust, Steve had 15 and stuck only for the dealer to reveal his hidden card which was a king which went with his other card of 10, they both lost.

After half an hour of play Tony was down to 160
Euros and Steve was up to 310 Euros, Tony was
frowning whereas Steve was smiling. David remained
at the bar. Tony was playing each hand with 5 Euros
whereas Steve was letting his bets ride for two
sometimes three hands, he lost some but when he won
he was winning more than he lost.

They were joined by an elderly man probably in his
70's who walked with a cane; he wore a brown
stripped suit with an unbuttoned at the neck white shirt
and had an unlit Cuban cigar protruding from his
mouth. He nodded to Tony and Steve but remained
silent as he threw 5000 Euros onto the table, he was
given 20 one hundred Euro chips and three one
thousand Euro chips, he placed two chips into his box.
After a further half an hour Tony had no chips left
whereas Steve had 540 Euros in chips in front of him
which kept him smiling. The old man now had 8600
Euros in chips in front of him, he also was smiling.

Tony left the blackjack table to join David at the bar.
Tony had been listening to David's bland conversation
for some twenty minutes when he noticed Steve and
the old man at his blackjack table chatting away during
their game; with his curiosity aroused he excused
himself to David before wandering over to Steve's
table. Arriving at the table he patted Steve's shoulder
letting him know it was him standing behind him
watching and nodded at the old man. He stood there
silently observing and listening. Steve and the old

man's conversation continued unabated. Tony was at a loss as to how the two men were conversing. Steve spoke English and only English, the old man was speaking French and only French; yet they were happily conversing and nodding and shaking their heads in the right places. They were even laughing at each other's jokes. Confused Tony shook his head knowing Steve did not understand or speak a word of French, he turned and returned to the bar and David's scintillating conversation.

Tony was totally bored listening to David and thought their conversation was not going nearly so well as Steve's and the old man's and they did not even speak the same language.

The Punto Banco table was now in full swing and sounded a little rowdy compared to the blackjack tables so yet again he excused himself from David, in mid conversation, and walked over to watch what Punto Banco was all about. Although there was twenty seat positions available at the table there was currently only ten players seated. Tony was curious as to how the game was played having vaguely heard the name before.

Michelle pushed her left arm under the noses of Jill and Julie pointing at her watch which was showing the time at just gone 11.30pm and suggested they make their way to Bulbous Billy's Bar. This always produced a frown from Julie as she had made it clear that Blues was her favourite drinking hole. They bumped each other out of the front door to Blues, it was a double door but someone had locked one of the doors so they had barged into each other leaving as they expected both doors to be open as usual.

Outside once again in the fresh air they brushed themselves down, adjusted their clothes and began their walk towards Billy's. Their excitement was rising now for the karaoke competition that was only one day away now and they wanted as much practice as possible although none of them thought they had a chance of winning but pride was at stake.

They rounded the corner of the road that led to the street that Bulbous Billy's Bar was on and were met with Blue flashing lights, the road had been cordoned off by blue and white polythene police bunting. There were three police cars parked within the bunting parked directly outside Bulbous Billy's Bar, there were also two unmarked cars which the women assumed were also police cars. There was a crowd gathered the entire length of the bunting on both sides of the road where the police had cordoned the area off. There were people from differing bars circulating and adding their suppositions as to what had happened, there were local Spanish people looking on as well some of the elderly women were wearing their customary long black dresses and stood silently watching. Julie had heard someone saying an ambulance had just left with a body in a black body bag and relayed that information to Jill and Michelle.

They saw Charles walking towards them from the opposite pavement. As he approached them they all asked at once what had happened. He raised his arms for them to calm down and said, "All I know is they have found a body in one of the refuse bins in the back of the bar when it was being loaded onto the council refuse wagon, the wagon was lifting the bin in its front forks and apparently the body fell out of the bin and landed on the floor alongside the wagon, they've taken Billy away for questioning."

"Who was it?" asked Julie.

"I really don't know, the police are still inside questioning the staff," said Charles.

"Was it a customer?" asked Jill.

"I really don't know, there's no point all of us hanging about here, does someone want to stay and see what they can find out while the rest of us go…erm..where?" asked Charles.

"I'll stay if you want and meet you back at Blue's later," offered Jill.

"Great but I believe we have the perfect person for information gathering and nosing about, what do you say Julie?" asked Charles.

"Yes, sure, I can do that," said Julie a little surprised and more than a little pleased that Charles had asked her, she waved them off with the flick of her hand as she walked straight up to the first policeman at the line of the bunting.

"C'mon then let's leave her to it," said Charles turning to walk in the direction of Blues and expecting Jill and Michelle to follow his lead.

Michelle turned and trotted after Charles in her high heels and when she caught up to him asked, "Why on earth did you ask Julie to find out what was going on? You know how stupid she can be."

"Wait until she reports back and then see how stupid she is," said Charles looking directly at Michelle lifting a knowing eyebrow.

Michelle stomped along quietly at Charles's put down which left Jill with a smirk as she walked alongside silently. Arriving at Blues Charles walked directly to the bar whilst asking the women to find a table. It was quite dark in Blues as the karaoke was in progress and spotlights were pointed at the singers on stage, it was quite full but Jill and Michelle found a table on the far left of the room away from the bar and about three quarters of the rooms distance away from the stage. It was very warm and clammy as there were no windows and nowhere for air to distribute around the room, there were some air conditioners but they were ancient and were not serviced so could not cope when the bar was busy hence the smell of stale beer and a fainter smell of old sweat mixed with cheap perfume which you surprisingly became accustomed to.

Charles arrived with their drinks placing them on the table, vodka and cokes for Jill and Michelle, red wine for himself. He immediately seemed attentive to what was happening on the stage so Jill and Michelle took it that he did not want to talk about what was happening at Bulbous Billy's.

There appeared to be an atmosphere in the bar as if news of what had happened at Bulbous Billy's was filtering through. Jill and Michelle just looked at each other and drank their vodka and cokes whilst pretending to be interested in the karaoke. Thoughts of themselves taking to the stage again did not enter their heads and anyway they were one down until Julie returned, they were far more interested in what Julie may find out.

Jill and Michelle kept looking at their watches amid bouts of conversation which amounted to either bitching at the karaoke singers or acknowledging some when they sang well. Charles just sat quietly, without a care in the world. Every time the doors behind them opened Jill and Michelle turned around expectantly whereas Charles stayed motionless. The bar continued to fill and soon it was standing room only as still no sign of Julie. Michelle took herself to the bar for more drinks and returned with them a few minutes later having to barge her way through the increasing throng. Jill took herself to the toilets a minute later looking back at the front door in case she missed Julie's return.

Jill was returning to her seat adjusting her skirt as she walked when she looked up and saw Julie walking in through the main doors with Steve the barman from Bulbous Billy's Bar. They met at their table together and looked around the surrounding tables for a seat for Steve as they had only saved one for Julie. Charles stood and instructed Steve to sit in his seat whilst he went to the bar to buy drinks for Julie and Steve, he returned with a Vodka and coke for Julie and a Bacardi and coke for Steve. Another chair had been found so Charles sat at it leaving him next to Julie, with Julie next to Jill and Jill next to Michelle and Steve next to Michelle. Jill and Michelle looked at Charles expecting him to start grilling Julie as to what she had found out, Charles nodded at Steve whilst turning to Julie and asking her, "What did you find out?"

Julie sat herself up on her stool and looked at everyone in turn before saying, "Well the police are flustered, they are shocked at having another murder on their hands. I brought Steve back so he could tell you what he knows about Billy's but it seems the police have their hands full. Did you know that there was a triple murder last night, well, early this morning I suppose at the water park? All their attention has been on that as they are receiving a great deal of pressure from the Mayor to find the culprit before it has an adverse effect on Fuengirola's tourism. Apparently four men went to the water park for an early morning dip before it opened, anyway apparently one of the slides was booby trapped with some kind of razors that shredded their backs as they went down the slide."

"Just go back a second Julie, you said a triple murder? But there were four men at the park? Is that right? What happened to the fourth man?" asked Charles.

"Yes, four men. Well, apparently one was ill and was in the toilets when his friends went down the slide so he didn't see anything until he came out, not a pretty site apparently, the police found the fourth man screaming on his knees in tears. They took him to the hospital where he still is, they pumped his stomach as he was still ill and losing consciousness and the police wanted to question him straight away, they think he was poisoned in some way and don't know if it's connected. They know they were English and where they were staying but they don't know if they were the targets or whether the water park was the target. Apparently that's their priority, to find who was the target, the men or the water park, obviously they want it to be the men as if the water park was the target it beggars the question will there be another attack and the other question will it be limited to the water park or will they attack somewhere else. The police are totally flummoxed and the last thing they needed was this body at Bulbous Billy's," explained Julie taking a long breath then downing half her vodka and coke.

Charles nodded approvingly and looked at Jill and Michelle who in turn nodded approvingly at Julie who was in her element smiling back at them all proud of her report and bringing Steve back with her.

Charles smiled at Julie as he said, "Well done Julie, that's a great report," then turning to Steve he asked, "What can you tell us?"

"Not a lot really, the council binmen turned up at about 5.00pm and began lifting the bins into their truck as usual, then one came running in saying they had found a body in one of the bins, well it fell out actually when the bin was being lifted over the trucks cabin. Anyway the driver called the police whilst one came in to tell us, well Billy was shocked like the rest of us and we went outside to look. Well Billy turned green, looked really ill and shocked, said it was John his ex-partner, he didn't even know he was out of prison. Billy was really shocked, you couldn't fake his reaction, he ran back into the bar and grabbed a glass and filled it with whiskey and drank it down in one, haven't seen Billy drink shorts before, you know Billy he's a lager man. Anyway the police turned up and shut the bar and took Billy away for questioning, I don't know if they know the dead man is Billy's ex-partner or not. They questioned all the staff before taking our addresses and then letting us leave."

"Did you say that the guy was Billy's ex-partner to the police?" asked Charles.

"No, of course not but I did say he had been in the bar drinking, thought it best in case someone else saw him," said Steve looking around for agreement from someone.

"You did the right thing, no point denying he had been in the bar, anything else?" asked Charles.

"Well the coroner turned up obviously and said that the guys thorax was crushed, well we could see that, it was bloody obvious, it was all bruised and purple and black in colour, anyway the police are treating it as murder and they aren't pleased about it I can tell you, they have everyman working on that thing from the water park. I heard one of the detectives ask if it was connected, the senior detective said he didn't think so."

"I forgot that you speak Spanish, did anything else come up?" asked Charles.

"Yes Billy takes advantage of me speaking Spanish, I do all his ordering and sort his bills out, nothing else really came up, they asked if I noticed anyone talking to him or taking an interest in him, obviously I said no but I have the impression that they are not that interested, that's probably the wrong word, they have other priorities in other words the murders at the water park," said Steve.

"Right, well. That's great Steve thanks for....." Charles almost finished.

"It's strange though isn't it? The four men at the water park at that time, I think it's the four steel erecters that came in the bar, they've not been in today and they come in everyday at the same time, strange isn't it?" asked Steve.

"What are you saying Steve?" asked Charles.

"Only that it seems to me that the guys killed at the water park must be the steel erecters and obviously the guy at Bulbous Billy's is billy's ex-partner, the common denominator is Bulbous Billy's. Therefore I would be asking is the killer a Bulbous Billy's Bar customer. Wouldn't you?" said Steve.

"Holy shit!" cried out Julie.

"And did you mention this theory to the police?" asked Charles thinking it was also obvious to him, well it would be.

"No of course not, makes you think though, doesn't it?" said Steve.

"It was that steel erecter I....." Julie began before Charles interrupted.

"Jill take Julie to the bar with you to help with the drinks, do you want another Bacardi and coke Steve?" asked Charles.

"No, I'd better go back to the bar and see if they will let us open up tomorrow but thanks anyway," said Steve saying his farewells as he left.

"Bloody hell, it all goes on here in Fuengirola doesn't it," said Michelle.

Jill had indeed taken Julie to the bar and they were now returning silently in anticipation of Charles' conclusions.

"I sent you two to the bar to stop Julie from telling someone else that she slipped one of the steel erecters her Mickey Finn," said Charles.

Jill and Michelle stared at Julie as Jill said, "Tell me you didn't, Julie."

"Well he asked for it, he was a complete arsehole, I didn't do that thing at the water park though," said Julie.

"Jesus, Julie, how could you? What if the police find out?" said Jill.

"I'm not sorry and anyhow how will the police find out?" said Julie.

"Julie, they will find out if you let it slip as you nearly did just then in front of Steve," chastised Charles.

"Oh Steve's ok, he wouldn't say anything," said Julie.

"Rubbish, if the police have him in for questioning and push him he will tell them whatever he knows, so make sure you never mention it to anyone, understand," said Charles sternly.

"Yes ok, alright," said Julie.

"Bloody hell! Julie the poisoner!" said Michelle.

"See what I mean Julie, Michelle cut it out, understand?" instructed Charles.

"Sorry," said Michelle.

"I can't believe it, four men dead and one in hospital and the one connection we know about is Bulbous billy's Bar, and Julie connected to the steel erecters, good job we're leaving Saturday," said Jill.

"Still gives us two full days though," said Michelle.

"Yeah but tomorrow night is the karaoke competition at the Music Bar, keeps us away from Billy's," said Jill.

It was the first time that they had thought about the competition for some time and Jill asked Michelle and Julie if they were up for a song, which they were, so Jill made her way towards the stage to find Camp Teddie so she could put their names down for a song. They had not really noticed the bar and what had been happening but Jill now noticed that there were a number of Bulbous Billy's Bar regulars in. No doubt because of those customers there were eight people in front of them before they could hope to grab hold of the microphones. As Jill approached their table she noticed Charles leaning in close to Julie who had a strained look on her face, she was curious as to what Charles was saying to her, she would have to bide her time to ask she thought.

Steve had decided he had ridden his luck long enough so he gathered his chips together to leave the blackjack table. He was having trouble gathering his chips together, he had shoved as many as would fit into his trouser pockets but still could not safely gather all the chips into his hands, he looked around confused.

The dealer and the old man looked at each other in amusement. The old man threw his chin up towards Steve with his eyes on the dealer, as if saying we have laughed enough. The dealer asked Steve if he would like him to change his chips for higher denominations so it would make it easier to carry them, Steve just smiled at the dealer and nodded as he realised they had been laughing at him, even though silently. Steve began emptying the chips out of his pockets replacing them onto the table. The dealer gathered them together and began to line them up in columns of 100 Euros; once he had all the chips lined up he counted them under the watchful eye of the pit boss. In total there were one thousand eight hundred and forty Euros, the dealer gave him one one thousand Euro chip, eight one hundred Euro chips, a 25 Euro chip and three 5 Euro chips.

Steve thanked the dealer picking up his more manageable chips and said goodbye to his new friend the old man making his way back to the bar with a huge grin on his face. On arriving at the bars lounge area he saw David sitting at a low table with three other empty chairs, his head was leaning back as if he was looking at the ceiling. Steve went to the bar and ordered a pint of Stella and looked back to ask David if he wanted one but noticed a full pint in front of him on the table. Paying the barman for his drink with the wide smile still stuck to his face he turned and was about to tell David of his luck when he noticed he was fast asleep.

He took a slurp of his lager whilst he looked around the casino floor for Tony, he found him on the second slurp. He put his pint down next to David's and walked quietly away not wanting to wake him. He strolled over to the Punto Banco table where he had seen Tony sitting with curiosity. Having not seen or even heard of Punto Banco before he stood silently behind Tony watching the game unfold. He noticed Tony had a fair number of chips in front of him and began to wonder whether he was ahead which would depend on how many chips he bought to start with which obviously Steve was unaware of.

Observing for a few minutes Steve concluded it was a simple game which consisted of just two bets, the Punto or the Banco, he could see people betting on either one or the other. Face cards and 10's did not count and it appeared the hand closer to 9 won with either two or three cards being dealt to each. Tony felt someone standing behind him and turned to see Steve smiling down on him; he nodded and turned back to the table as a hand was in the process of being dealt. Tony won and once he was paid out by the dealer he pushed four hundred Euro chip to the centre of the table asking the dealer to change them for 100 Euro chips, he watched as the dealer counted them into columns and placed four hundred Euro chips in exchange in front of him, he nodded thanks and left the table.

Walking back to the bar Steve told Tony of his windfall as Tony explained he had made his losses back and was a couple of hundred Euros up so was happy. Back at the bar Tony bought himself a pint of Stella whilst Steve picked his pint up off the table where he had left it noticing David was still asleep and thought he would awake with a sore neck. Tony and Steve stood in the centre of the bar area watching the gaming floor and the mass of varying gamblers of different nationalities playing different games.

The only other people in the bar area was "Oddjob" who was accompanied by one of his women who had returned from her customer and was now no doubt awaiting another. Oddjob was still drinking Champagne but the woman did not have a drink before her, well she was working. Tony and Steve looked over at David and laughed together saying that they could always leave him but they were only joking and then they thought about the necklace. David had been sleeping alone in the bar area so Steve checked under his gaudy shirt to make sure it was still housed around his neck, it was, Tony and Steve both sighed relief. Tony checked his watch to find it was 2am, "We're teeing off at 8 o'clock, we'd better make a move, wake sleeping beauty will you while I take our glasses back to the bar."

Steve gently nudged David awake; he looked around asking himself where he was. He was a little drunk and realisation slowly dawned on him he was in a casino, his right hand moved to rub the back of his neck which was sore, he felt the necklace and further realisation dawned. Tony and Steve picked him up and half carried him out of the casino. The old man waved to Steve as he noticed him leaving, Steve smiled and waved back at his new friend whom he would probably never see again. They made their way to the cashdesk to change their chips before leaving.

Arriving at their car in the dark car park they man handled the murmuring David full length into the back seat and closed the door on him. They could see the bright lights in the distance of the waterfront bars and restaurants as they ducked into the car and drove off joining the now quiet main road hoping it would lead them back to the careterra and Fuengirola.

They enjoyed an uneventful drive back to their hotel with the roads scarce of vehicles. They found a parking space on a side road next to their hotel and turning off the engine Tony turned to look at the again sleeping carcass of David. "We're going to have to wake him, I'm not bloody carrying him, he'll weigh a ton," said Tony opening his car door.

"We need to take that necklace off him and put it back in the box as well," added Steve.

"Great! Open the rear door on your side as you're next to the pavement," instructed Tony.

They man handled the irritable and drunk David out of the car and while Tony held him up against the front passenger door Steve ducked into the back looking for the necklaces carry box, he found it under the front driver's seat and stretched to retrieve it. He placed it on the cars roof shutting the rear door behind him and whilst Tony held the now sleeping again David up against the car Steve endeavoured to undo the necklace so that they could return it to the box.

"Hold on," said Tony, "We need to move him a bit towards the engine before you undo the necklace."

"Why?"

"Because he's standing directly over a grid and knowing our luck the bloody thing will drop down it, I don't want to spend the rest of the night trying to retrieve it from down the bloody grid."

"Ok, ok."

They moved him to the noise of David drunkenly murmuring his undying love for Jill and woe betide anyone who said otherwise. Tony and Steve just looked at each other shaking their heads in laughable disbelief as they had never witnessed David quite so drunk before. Back to their task in hand, David now in a safe position and thankfully unconscious and quiet again Steve put his hands behind David's neck and undid the necklace saying as he did so, "I hope no police come by as it looks like we're mugging him."

"We could hide the necklace and watch him panic in the morning," suggested Tony.

"Would David do that if the roles were reversed?"

"No"

Walking on each side of David they stumbled and dragged him along the street eventually reaching the hotels entrance but before dragging him through the door Steve said, "Wait" and wandered off back the way they had come. Tony saw him bending over a flower bed rich with colour and retrieving a bright red flower that resembled a rose but was closer to bougainvillea. Returning he dumped the flower in David's shirt pocket and picked him up again and pulled and pushed David through the front door. Both Tony and Steve were sweating profusely as they sat David in a chair in the empty reception area whilst they both took a breather; David sat still asleep with a stupid smile across his face.

They picked David up again and dragged him to the elevator, it pinged as the doors opened and dragging David inside they looked in the mirror on the wall of the interior, Tony and Steve looked as though they had been dragged through a bush backwards kicking and screaming, they looked bedraggled and full of sweat with their shirts sticking firmly to their torso's, and David, well David looked as though he was ready to go out, except he was unconscious.

They made it to David's room but then Tony and Steve argued about who was going to put their hand into David's pocket to retrieve his key. It was decided by the toss of a coin which Tony lost. Once in the room they crashed David onto the bed and left him there fully clothed. They placed the necklace box on the pillow next to David and Steve placed the flower above it. Leaving the room Tony said to Steve, "7am?"

"7am," Steve agreed as they separated for their own rooms.

Jill, Michelle, Julie and Charles left Blues at just gone 3.30am and noticed a slight chill in the air as the breeze flowing in from the sea was cool for a change. They walked slowly back to their hotel accompanied as usual by Charles, silent as he walked looking deep in thought.

The women chatted idly about tomorrows karaoke competition at the Music Bar and realised it was actually today. They continued chatting about which song they should start with until they reached their hotel. They said goodnight and gave what appeared to be a brooding Charles a kiss as he turned and walked silently away in the direction from which they had come.

The women grew more excited at the looming competition and had decided on their walk home to venture to the Fuengirola outside market tomorrow afternoon to buy outfits that Banannarama would have been happy to adorn. They considered it worth the effort as they knew they would be competing against the expat regulars who would also be dressing up extra specially for the occasion as there was money at stake for them.

Taking the lift to their floor they burst into song looking at themselves in the mirrored wall of the lift, giggling like little schoolgirls. The lift pinged as the doors began to open and the singing and giggling ceased. They said their goodnights with exaggerated air kisses and separated towards their rooms.

Jill entered her room and tutted as she forgot to slam the door to as David usually did in the mornings, she thought about opening it again so she could slam it but decided against it, she switched the light on instead. She noticed David prostate on the bed, "slob", she thought on her way to the bathroom. She undressed and had a pee, washed her hands and brushed her teeth, picked her clothes up and gave herself a quick rub between her legs, "have to shave again to stop the itching" she thought, as she dropped her clothes into the bottom drawer of the wardrobe.

Turning towards the bed she tutted to herself again as she remembered the light, she walked towards the door and the light switch but before she switched it off she turned back, she had seen something on her pillow. She walked curiously back towards her side of the bed and on her pillow was a red flower and a beautifully crafted small square wooden box.

She picked the flower up and smelled it as she smiled looking over at the comatose David; she placed the flower on the bedside cabinet and picked up the box. She pulled at the little catch on the box's lid and slowly opened it and froze in shear abject delight at the sight that befell her. It was a beautiful gold necklace with five diamonds, her eyes bulged and her jaw dropped. She was frozen in awe. Slowly her senses returned, her eyes returned to normal and she managed to close her mouth as she looked first upon the necklace then on David. She felt the tears welling in her eyes; she sat on the bed with the box on her knee and allowed the tears to flow. She cried uncontrollably. Eventually the tears stopped, she wiped them away with the backs of her hands.

Picking the necklace up gently out of the box she admired it as she held it up in front of her and turned it through 360 degrees. She allowed herself a smile. Overwhelmed by the thoughts flowing through her brain, all she kept asking herself was, "does this mean David is back?" "Oh dear God let it be so," she thought.

She put the necklace on and ran into the bathroom putting the light on, turned to the mirror and said out loud, "Perfect." She walked out of the bathroom switching the light off and walked over to David, bent down and kissed his cheek and felt the tingle she had known years ago. She also thought, "Oh my God you stink of beer!" She grinned mischievously as she thought about it and walked over to where she had left her handbag, taking out the lipstick, a subtle red, perfect. She took it and walked over to David and grew a large heart on his forehead with the lipstick, giggling to herself as she did so. Returning the lipstick to her bag she switched off the light and jumped happily into bed for the first time in two years. Taking hold of the top sheet she folded it over David turned over and slept happily.

Chapter 10   Thursday

Jill woke to the sound of gentle tapping on wood. It took her a minute to realise it was someone knocking on their room door. It took her a further minute to realise where she was. Her left arm raised and her hand felt around her neck. A further minute and she realised she was wearing a necklace. Tap, tap, tap. Her left arm now stretched to her left at the warmth she felt, it was a body. Tap, tap, tap. Her eyes struggled to open; the light was bright although the curtains were drawn shut. She rolled to her left, the body was motionless, she tried to focus, she recognised the clothes, it was David. Tap, tap, tap. She sat up in bed, she fell back down. She sat up again this time putting one of her legs out of bed and forcing her foot to rest on the cold tiles of the floor. She grabbed her knee with her right hand to stop herself from falling backwards again. Tap, tap, tap. She bent forward at the same time forcing her other leg out of bed and using her momentum of leaning over to stand upright. She put one leg in front of the other and slowly arrived at the door. Tap, tap, tap. She put her left hand on her forehead to help keeping her head up whilst undoing the lock and turning the door handle. The door creaked open and she came face to face with Michelle and Julie who were fully dressed unlike Jill.

Michelle was the first to speak, "Nice of you to dress."

"What?" asked Jill.

"Nice of you... oh never mind, are you coming?" asked Michelle.

"Coming? No, I erm I, I'm staying with David this morning."

"What's that around your neck?" asked Julie.

"David bought it yesterday...I think...you go, I've some talking to do, I may catch you later," said Jill closing the door on Michelle and Julie. She walked slowly back to the bed and collapsed onto it turning her head into the pillows to hide her eyes from the sun.

Tony and Steve met in the hotel's restaurant for breakfast at precisely 7am as agreed. It was a buffet style so Steve followed Tony with his plate in hand as Tony bunched bacon, sausage, eggs and beans high on his plate, Steve's portions were a little more moderate. They returned to their table with their plates setting them down whilst they returned to the buffet for coffee. Tony had nearly finished his coffee by the time he had returned to their table so he about turned to refresh his cup leaving Steve to sit down and start his breakfast.

As soon as Tony returned Steve asked him, "How do you think David did last night?"

"How do you think? He was unconscious when we left him, probably won't come to till later," answered Tony a little impatiently.

"But Jill must have found the necklace after all we left it on her pillow."

"She probably did but it doesn't follow that she liked it or that it has solved anything," said Tony.

"But it's a good necklace isn't it Tony, I mean it should do the trick shouldn't it?" asked Steve.

"We can only wait and see, best if we just go and play our rounds as planned, we'll find out soon enough whether it has worked or not," said Tony a little bored with the conversation.

Steve took the hint and did not mention David or the necklace again turning the conversation back to golf and any ideas Tony had for their next golfing holiday. Tony said he had not thought about it and wanted to enjoy what was left of the golf here on this holiday, Tony was being a little abrasive as if he had something on his mind.

They had finished their breakfast by 7.30am and were on the road by 7.35am. The roads as usual at that time in the morning were quiet and they arrived at the golf club at 7.50am perfect timing for their 8.00am tee off. Tony was looking forward to the round as being one short meant they could complete the round quicker than normal and may, just may sneak in an extra round.

Jill's eyes opened again at a little after 10.00am and her arm wandered over the bed to where she remembered David had been. Nothing, she turned all the way over to see if he had fallen out of bed and noticed the bathroom door open and steam flowing out, the shower was running. She threw he legs out of bed and sat hunched for a minute running over in her mind returning to the room last night and finding David comatose and then finding the flower and necklace on her pillow. She turned her head slowly to the right the flower was right there where she had left it, she could still hear the shower running. She stood up and began taking heavy steps, a smile creased her face as she realised she had been completely naked when she had opened the door to Michelle and Julie, she had thought the guy walking behind them was staring at her necklace but now realised he had been appraising her nakedness. Her shoulders shrugged involuntarily.

She continued her zombie like walk towards the steam. She remembered the shower scene from Psycho, she saw herself pull the shower curtain back and stab David and stab, stab, stab, stab uncontrollably and when she looked at her hand she was holding her lipstick, David's body was covered in lipstick stabs. She shook her head and pulled back the shower curtain, David turned and jumped his head and hair covered in shampoo, he blinked as the shampoo irritated his eyes, then he smiled. David put his head directly under the stream of hot water rinsing the shampoo away and then moved slightly allowing Jill to drench herself under the powerful jet of steaming hot water, it refreshed her immediately. She turned allowing the hot water to stream down her back and put a hand on David's chest to steady herself. David took the bar of soap in his hand and began to rub it over Jill's breasts, she felt her nipples react as he reached over her stomach, she turned and he rubbed soap all over her back then reached lower and caressed her buttocks, Jill moaned quietly almost to herself. She turned again and David's hands automatically touched the lips of her vagina, Jill now groaned out loud as she noticed David's arousal. He put his hands between her legs, spreading them as he lifted her against the wall of the shower and entered her with his full erection, Jill's arms swung around his neck as she clung on in delirious delight as David's thrusting movement forced her legs further into the air. It did not take Jill long to orgasm and she thought the whole of Fuengirola must have heard her. They both smiled into each other's eyes as David held her in place, her back on the wall with her legs wrapped around David's waist and her arms around his neck, the hot water pouring over them. Jill felt the tears as she asked, "Why?" and put her forefinger over David's lips to prevent him from answering, wishing she had said nothing as it spoiled the moment.

They reluctantly turned the gushing jet of steaming hot water off and left the confines of the shower drying each other with their towels, enjoying touching each other's bodies albeit through the cloth of the towels.

They cleaned their teeth before leaving the bathroom and walked naked out onto the balcony, David opened the curtains before joining Jill.

David chose to talk first, "I didn't thank you for the heart."

"The heart?" Jill asked.

"The one you drew on my forehead with your lipstick."

"Oh, that heart, your welcome."

"Are we ok?"

"I don't know David, are we?"

"I want us to be."

"So do I David, more than you can imagine, but…"

"But?"

"Oh David, two years, two bloody years David."

"I know and I'm sorry, I…I…"

"Don't…don't even think about justifying it or explaining, I really don't want to hear."

"But…"

"Don't"

"I do love you Jill, you must believe that."

"If I didn't you wouldn't be here now."

"So what do we do now?"

"Well…we could take another shower."

"I have a better idea."

With that he bent down and lifted Jill up into his arms and carried her inside and gently placed her on the bed and climbed on top of her taking her head in his hands as he kissed her gently on her lips. Her body was still hot from the shower and her hair was damp as he threaded his fingers through it moving his head lower as he kissed her neck his hands searching out every sinew of her hot and sultry body. He raised himself up on his elbows so he could take in the fullness of her breasts before diving head first into them, sucking each nipple in turn, relishing the taste of her as he lowered himself further his tongue searching her inny belly button. He could hear Jill's slight groans as his tongue worked harder, he went lower ever so slowly until his mouth searched for her clitoris and found it, her groans grew lounder immediately. Jill's nails dug into his shoulders as she struggled to control herself, she wanted him inside her, she wanted him inside her now, dear God inside me. She pulled at his shoulders as she opened her legs wider pulling him closer to her she could feel his erection as it passed up her thighs and then, there, it was inside her and David was writhing in and out of her he was groaning louder than Jill now as they both cried out together they both knew they had climaxed together. David collapsed on top of her his sweating face next to hers, their bodies were wet with sweat, their heated exhaustion was sweet.

"God, I've missed that," said Jill.

"Me too, I didn't realise how much until now," David climbed off Jill and collapsed on his back next to her.

"Guess we need another shower now!" said Jill laughing.

When David stopped laughing too he asked," When did that shave thing down there happen?"

"A few days is all, I can't believe you didn't notice."

"Neither can I, I kinda like it; are you going to keep it like that?"

"If you like it, yes, I like it as well, but it's starting to itch so it needs doing again."

"Did you use my razor?"

"Of course!"

They both began laughing again together, another first for two years. They had a lot of making up to do but Jill was loving the start of it.

Michelle and Julie left Jill in her room and could not stifle a giggle as the door to Jill's room slammed in their faces, "Guess she's not had time to dress," said Michelle mischievously.

They turned towards the lift and noticed the man who had just walked past them harbouring a seductive smile. They discussed what they were going to do without Jill and decided to discuss it over breakfast at their favourite restaurant.

Arriving at the restaurant some 15 minutes later they took a table outside as there was little breeze in the early morning sunshine as the temperature neared eighty degrees. The large advertising umbrella kept the suns aggression at bay as they ordered coffee and croissants; a light breakfast was called for as it was the day of the karaoke competition and despite Jill's absence they had planned on going to the large market that was open on Thursdays to buy costumes for the evening. They decided they would still buy costumes and would have to buy Jill's hoping that it would fit. They needed something for the three of them and hopefully they would find something that Banannarama would have worn.

They then contemplated what they should tell Charles, they worried that he would be annoyed that Jill had not showed up but then dismissed the idea as absurd. They realised they were procrastinating as neither of them wanted to explain to Charles where Jill was, it was silly really unless they were scared of Charles, Michelle scoffed at the idea as she summoned the waiter to ask for their bill.

They then found themselves walking the long way to Charles's villa and then realised they were walking slowly. They walked past the concrete lions taking in the lack of detail; their heads were bowed as they almost crept through the grounds to the sun loungers, placing their bags delicately down on the ground so that they would not make any noise.

"Good morning ladies," greeted Charles stooping over his balcony his hands resting on top of the rails.

"Good morning," replied both Michelle and Julie.

"Really hot today isn't it?" added Julie.

"It is, no Jill today?" asked Charles.

"No, she's spending some time with David; they have a few issues to sort out," explained Michelle.

"Oh good, I hope they manage to sort things out," said Charles turning back to whatever he was doing and disappearing from the sight of Michelle and Julie.

In turn Michelle and Julie looked each other in the eyes and sighed audibly. They placed their towels on top of the sun loungers and lined them up with the sun before sitting on them and then rubbing sun lotion all over the front of their bodies, Michelle naked as usual and Julie in her bikini.

Julie turned to Michelle leaning close and whispering, "You didn't tell him we were leaving early to go shopping on the market."

Michelle leaned towards Julie and whispered back, "Neither did you."

"You won't leave me here by myself will you?" asked Julie.

"No honey, I won't."

Jill and David took another shower together, a long relaxing touchy feely shower which inevitably culminated in their making love again. They dried each other off with their towels before cleaning their teeth again and wondered out of the steam laden bathroom together naked. They sat quietly on the edge of their bed, their bodies glowing bright pink with the latent heat from the shower.

They sat quietly for a few minutes allowing their bodies to cool in the slight draft from the open door to their balcony. Jill lay back on the bed with her arms outstretched above her head, her knees bent and her feet on the cold tiled floor. David was sat with his elbows resting on his knees.

Jill turned her head slightly towards David and asked, "Hungry?"

"Hungry," he said.

They both jumped off the bed simultaneously to dress, Jill went straight to the wardrobe picking her selection deciding she would not bother with makeup, whereas David was stood still looking perplexed.

Jill asked, "What's up?"

"What do I wear? I've only brought my golfing clobber."

Jill smiled shaking her head at his indecisiveness as she searched through the wardrobe finding a pair of stone coloured shorts and a grey T-shirt for him.

"Feet?" He asked but Jill turned as he asked with a pair of brown sandals in her hand, David smiled taking them from her and sat on the bed to put them on. Both fully dressed for the outside world Jill grabbed her handbag and opened the door asking David if he had his room key.

In the lift on the way down David asked Jill what she fancied to eat and after a cheeky smirk from Jill she said she was not too bothered but needed coffee and suggested the venta that her and the girls had been frequenting.

Leaving the front door of the hotel the heat of the sun hit them as they felt the slight welcoming breeze on their faces; they could hear numerous voices and commotion from the crowded beach. Turning left onto the pavement David took Jill's hand in his as they walked together along the front of the resort.

They walked in mutual silence both content with their sudden closeness. Arriving at the venta Jill guided David to one of the outside tables and they were greeted by a waiter who had just served a table nearby, they ordered coffee whilst they perused the menu. The waiter returned with their coffees whilst they were still deciding on the menu when the waiter informed them that the chef had just taken the slow cooked lamb out of the oven, it having been in there overnight. The decision was made for them, slow cooked lamb for two. Ten minutes later the waiter arrived with two steaming large plates full of lamb and thin chips cooked in garlic oil which were to die for.

"Oh, I've not told you, have I?" said Jill tantalisingly.

Charles marched out of the doors to the villa with a large brown leather bag in his right hand; it looked like an old style cricket bag the sort cricketers kept their bat and pads in, which looked heavy as Charles stooped to one side. "I've a few errands to run and may be some time, if I'm not back when you leave just pull the door to, it will be fine, see you later at the Music bar for the competition."

"Ok, bye," Michelle and Julie muttered, relieved at not having to explain they were leaving early.

They heard his car turning on the gravel of the driveway before it accelerated onto the road.

"We can relax now he's gone, should we leave a little earlier and see what's happening at Bulbous Billy's?" suggested Julie.

"We could but Charles said to stay away from the place," said Michelle.

"Well we don't have to go in, just look and anyway we don't have to tell Charles we've been."

"We can do that."

"We can. Shall we go now?"

"I don't see why not."

They both jumped up excitedly off their sun loungers, dressing quickly and moving the sun loungers as they had found them. They were giggling and smiling at one another as naughty school girls about to embark on an adventure to be kept secret.

They walked swiftly out of the villas garden past the guarding concrete lions along the concrete pavement towards Bulbous Billy's Bar. They walked quickly looking about them as they walked to check if they were being observed by anyone, of course they were not and were ignored by all they passed but they felt they were on a mission and needed to check.

They turned into the street that accommodated Bulbous Billy's Bar and stopped dead in their tracks. Had someone seen them? Were they to be reported to Charles for being near the Bar? No of course not, they walked on slowly now looking all around them as they inched forward.

"Hiya!"

Shit, who is that? They froze where they stood. They saw a puff of smoke from behind a streetlight and a head popped around after it. Michelle and Julie sighed with relief as they saw the friendly face of Steve the barman who had slipped out for a fag break.

"You scared the crap out of us! What are you doing hiding behind the lamppost?" said Michelle with Julie standing slightly behind her as if to protect her.

"Sorry, I wasn't hiding, I was just leaning on it having a fag, not much going on inside," said Steve.

"Oh, are you open then now?" asked Julie moving from behind Michelle.

"No, not yet, there's a couple of policemen inside but just for presence, we are waiting for the ok to open from the main detective, but I think we're in for a wait as we are not his priority. It's that murder up at the water park that they are more concerned with," said Steve apparently bored with the waiting.

"Have they let Billy out yet?" asked Michelle.

"Not yet, apparently they've questioned him and he's just waiting for them to release him but everything takes so long here, it is Spain after all," said Steve throwing his cigarette into the road.

"Well we were just passing on our way to the market; hope they let you open soon. See you, bye," said Michelle.

"Bye," added Julie.

"So what do you make of that?" asked Julie her face a mask of curiosity.

"Make of what? He didn't exactly reveal the name of the killer did he?" said Michelle shrugging her shoulders as they walked on.

"Oh, no, suppose not." agreed Julie disappointedly.

"Anyway we need to think about what we are going to buy for tonight, what look are we trying for?" said Michelle.

"80's Bananarama?" offered Julie.

"Great! C'mon let's mooch!" suggested Michelle.

"You've not told me what Jill?" asked David with some concern in his voice.

"About the murders! Have you heard about them?" said Jill excitedly her eyes wide open.

"Murders, what murders? No I haven't heard, where? When?" asked David with some relief and then more concern for a different reason.

"Well, umm, which do I tell you about first?"

"Which? How many has there been?"

"Three, no four, yes that's right four."

"Christ four, when? Where?"

"Suppose I should start with the ones at the water park, they found four men there early yesterday morning before the park was open, apparently three of them went down a booby trapped slide, it cut them to ribbons, there were knifes or razors on the slide and they died. The fourth guy was ill in the toilets, well when he came out he found his friends like that, all cut up and dead, lucky he was ill I guess."

"Who would do such a thing? Some sick individual, I mean it's mainly kids that use that water park, it's unimaginable if kids had gone down it. You said there were four murders what was the other one?"

"The binmen found that one; it was in a rubbish bin outside a bar, the binmen came for the rubbish and when they were lifting the bin into their wagon the body fell out so they're not sure how long it was in there."

"Bloody hell, sounds like we picked the wrong week to come here, four murders in a week, bloody hell!"

"Yeah and apparently the police are flummoxed, they are worried the ones at the water park was against the park itself, if they were they think they maybe more, I think they are hoping it was an attack against the men but who knows?"

"How do you know about it?"

"The one the binmen found was in a bar we went to, it's quite well known."

"Oh just great, you go to bars where they find dead bodies, what the hell were you doing there?"

"Like I said it's well known, it has good karaoke there, we were singing there a few times."

"A few times, oh just great. Does Steve and Tony know?"

"I don't know, there your friends."

"Jesus Jill, I don't believe this, you've been singing in a bar where a murder was committed! Next you'll tell me you know the murderer."

"Don't be so melodramatic, as if, well we think we know the four from the water park."

"What! How the hell do you know them?"

"Well not know as such but ran into them sort off."

"Explain."

"We were in Bulbous Billy's Bar, that's where they found the dead man in the dustbin, anyway one night there were these four men in and we think they are the ones from the water park."

"Why?"

"Well we think Julie poisoned one off them."

"Holy shit, this story just becomes better and better, one of your friends is a poisoner, you'll tell me next she killed someone."

"It's not a story and of course she hasn't killed anyone, not that we know of anyway, it was just a

Mickey Finn she made that she slipped into one off the guys drinks."

"Bloody hell Jill, have you heard yourself, one off your friends makes, makes mind you Mickey Finns and slips the bloody things into people's drinks, Jesus Christ Jill I wouldn't even know where to start making a bloody Mickey Finn, what the hell did this guy do to her to justify her going away and making such a thing."

"She didn't go away and make it silly, she brought it with her, we told her not to, but she made it for a woman that was being obnoxious to her the night before anyway she didn't show but this guy with the other three, well he started being obnoxious to her so she slipped it in his drink, we didn't know about it until after when she told us, she only told us because we heard that one of the men at the water park was ill so we think it was him that drunk her Mickey Finn."

"I need a drink," said David looking around for the waiter, he pushed his plate away from him, he had hardly touched the food but he had suddenly lost his appetite.

Jill just smiled at him whilst she tucked into her meal ravenously. The waiter arrived with concern written all over his face with the meal hardly touched by David, David assured him there was nothing wrong with the food and that he had just lost his appetite. The waiter suitably assured he ordered himself a whiskey and coke whilst ordering Jill a vodka and coke.

The drinks arrived just as Jill finished her meal leaving a solitary bone on her plate; she smiled at the waiter as he placed her drink in front of her and barely managed a thankyou as her mouth was still full of food. David took a long slug of his drink downing half of it whilst looking quizzically at Jill. He was for the first time in his life lost for words.

After a few minutes of reflective thought David said to his wife, "From what you've told me I think we should look for an earlier flight home."

"Oh don't be silly David, we'll do no such thing and anyway we have the karaoke competition tonight, the girls are no doubt out as we speak selecting costumes for us," said Jill decisively.

"Costumes? What sort of karaoke completion is it?"

"A very popular one, the expats dress up all the time, you should see them, there's allsorts from Elton John and David Bowie to Dolly Parton, oh and Simon and Garfunkel, it's utterly brilliant."

"I think we'd better come along then, keep an eye on you after what you've told me, I'm sure Tony and Steve would agree."

"Like hell you will, you've had your golf, well this is what we have had, it's our night not yours."

"But…"

"No buts, it's our night and that's final."

"Ok, ok but be careful ok, suppose I should tell you about tomorrow night then."

"What about tomorrow night?"

"Let me order another drink first," said David putting up two fingers politely and pointing at our drinks, the waiter nodded and turned walking back inside towards the bar.

"Well c'mon you have your drink now, what about tomorrow?" asked Jill with her brow furrowed.

"Hot out here isn't it?" answered David taking a handkerchief out of his pocket and wiping his sweating face.

"Stop stalling, what about tomorrow?"

"There's a dinner dance at the golf club and we thought you would like to come so we've booked a table."

"You've booked a table without asking us?"

"We weren't exactly talking were we and we did think you would enjoy it, you used to enjoy them didn't you?" asked David wiping his face again with his hanky.

"I think that would be very nice, thank you, and it will give me a chance to wear my blue dress."

"Oh good, I do so like you in your blue dress."

"Why David that's the nicest thing you've said to me in two years."

David smiled with relief and stood up moving closer to Jill, he bent down and kissed her gently on the lips, Jill smiled and touched his cheek with the tips of her fingers as he pulled slowly away sitting back down.

"You're excused David."

"Excused? Excused for what?"

"You may leave, Michelle and Julie have just turned up, we have to discuss tonight, you don't mind do you David?"

"No, no of course not, I'll go and see if I can find Tony and Steve, they're probably still at the club."

"Oh and David."

"Yes?"

"Buy yourself a toothbrush."

"I have a toothbrush in our room."

"You need a new one dear."

"Oh ok."

With which David jumped back to his feet and kissed his wife goodbye with the on looking Michelle and Julie giggling in the background. The women rushed over to Julie's table putting down bags and bags of shopping as they both began talking at the same time, they looked at each other and began laughing sitting down and looking around for the waiter. Magically the waiter arrived within seconds of Michelle and Julie putting their bags on the floor, they ordered vodka and cokes all around and sat silently looking at Jill waiting for her to tell them of her morning.

When Jill remained silent looking inquisitively at the shopping bags Michelle could no longer wait, "Well? C'mon tell us, what have you been up to all morning? And what was that quip with the toothbrush all about?"

"Making love and none of your business," said Jill nonchalantly.

"All morning?" asked Julie with a beaming wide smile emblazoned onto her face.

"All morning!" confirmed Jill.

"That's not good enough, give, c'mon all the intricate little details," pushed Michelle.

"We made love in the shower twice, no, three times, in bed and very nearly on the balcony."

"Holy Shit! What was it like and what the hell brought it about?" asked Michelle leaning in closer almost drooling.

"Well you saw this little number this morning, right?" asked Jill lifting the bottom of her necklace up with her outstretched fingers, the sun reflecting off the gold and diamonds.

"That's not all we saw but go on," said Michelle excitedly.

"David bought it for me yesterday and left it on my pillow last night with a single flower for me to find when I arrived back at our room; he was comatose on the bed by the way."

"So what did you do?" asked Julie.

"I put it on and went to sleep."

"Boring, so when did you first make love?" asked Michelle.

"This morning and it was great."

"So does this mean everything is ok between you now?" asked Michelle hoping she had helped to fix what she had helped to break.

"We are a long way from perfect but we have made a great start."

"Oh that's brilliant," said Michelle.

"Yep brilliant," added Julie.

"But I slipped up a few minutes before you arrived, can we look at what you've bought now?"

"Not yet, what do you mean you slipped up?" asked Michelle with concern showing in her voice.

"I was telling David about the murders at the water park and the one at Bulbous Billy's Bar, he hadn't heard anything about them and that's when I let it slip."

"You let what slip Jill?" asked Michelle.

"That we thought we knew the guys that were murdered at the water park and that Julie slipped one of them a Mickey Finn."

"Oh Shit Jill, how could you?" asked a rather worried looking Michelle.

"It's worse, I then told him we went singing in Bulbous Billy's Bar and that's where they found the other murder victim."

"Shit, what did he say?" asked Michelle.

"He wanted to arrange an early flight home but I told him no way as we have the karaoke competition tonight. Then he wanted to come with Tony and Steve, anyway I told him that wasn't going to happen as they had their golf and the karaoke was ours."

"Yes and then he told me about a dinner dance at the golf club tomorrow night that they have booked a table for, I don't suppose they've asked you two either as yet?"

"No I know nothing about it," said Michelle.

"Nor me," added Julie.

"Listen Julie, I'm so sorry to have dropped you in it with Steve."

"Don't worry about it, I know Steve he won't say anything to me about it, he trusts me explicitly," said Julie taking another sip of her vodka and coke.

"Now can we look in the bags?"

"Sure ok," said Michelle handing Jill the bag that lay closest to her feet.

Jill dug her hands deep into the bag and began pulling out the contents which appeared too big for the bag, she had to tentatively pull the sides of the bag slowly down around the contents. Eventually she freed three pairs of what would be on them very tight jeans almost leggings, one pair was white, one a pale sky blue and the third red. Julie passed her the bag which lay by her feet. Taking it Jill again dug deep but this time the contents flowed freely out in her hands, she looked down on three silk tops which were very short and V necked and baggy and of all things rainbow coloured from top to bottom.

"Is this it? We will look like a cross between the Spice Girls and the Muppets!" said Jill aghast.

"We could call ourselves the Spice Muppets," suggested Julie.

"That's not funny Julie; it's not a good look."

"Oh," said Julie.

"Christ our arses will look massive in those, we're in our forties not twenties."

"Oh stop being a piss party pooper snicker. They'll be fine, it's one night and we'll be on stage and anyway everyone is going to be dressed up tonight no one will pick us out," said Michelle.

"I take it we are all going braless with the tops; I hope they cover our boobs."

"I'll wear a bra if you don't mind," said Julie prudishly.

"Well yes we do mind you're not wearing one," stated Michelle leaving no room for argument.

"Did you see Charles at the villa?"

"Briefly, he was on his way out somewhere with a big brown leather case, don't know what was in it," said Michelle.

"Did he say anything?"

"No nothing, oh I mentioned we thought you and David were back together, he just said good," said Michelle.

"Oh ok, we'll probably see him later anyway, did he say what time he would be there?"

"No, didn't mention it, oh we walked past Bulbous Billy's earlier and saw Steve the barman," said Michelle.

"Is anything happening? Is Billy out?"

"No and no, he said they are still waiting for the ok to open again but he's not holding his breath as he said, it is Spain," said Michelle.

"We'll probably be home when it's all sorted."

"Where are we starting tonight?" asked Michelle.

"Blues," instructed Julie leaving no room for discussion.

David forgot all about the toothbrush as he walked along the road opposite the beach to the taxi rank and jumped in the first one which happened to be an immaculate white Mercedes. He gave the driver the golf club as his destination and sat back in his seat in the rear of the plush leather air conditioned interior of the taxi and pondered what his wife had just told him.

They arrived at the golf club a little over ten minutes later as David jumped out of the taxi and paid the driver he looked around the car park for their hire car, he could not spot it in the multitude of vehicles parked. Giving up his search he walked towards the main entrance thinking he would check the bar first in his search for his friends.

The air conditioning hit him as usual as he entered the main building through the large glass entrance doors making his way swiftly to the bar where he immediately saw Tony and Steve sat at a table with half-finished pints of lager in front of them. He walked past them briefly saying hello and patting Tony on the back as he approached the bar where he bought another three pints of Stella Artois, he picked the three pints up in his hands and walked carefully back to the table placing them down before sitting down.

"I take it the necklace worked then?" asked Tony with a glint in his eyes.

David was taking a huge slurp of lager downing nearly half his pint before answering, "I'll say, what a morning."

"So you're back together and all is hunkey dorey in the Jones household?" asked Steve.

"I guess, she even told me to buy a new toothbrush, don't know what that was about, but yeah things look really good," said David not able to hide his excitement.

"I'm pleased for you and I'm glad the trip to Gib was worth it, you two should be together you are a great couple together," said Tony thinking their next golf ho;iday was now more secure.

"Thanks it sure feels good, I've just left Jill with Michelle and Julie, she was telling me about the murders in Fuengirola, do you know about them?" asked David.

"We heard some of the guys in the changing room mention them but no not heard anything specifically, why?" asked Tony.

"It's just what Jill has been telling me, they have been going to the bar where they found one of the murdered men, she said it's well known and they have been singing karaoke there."

"Well it's bloody well known now! It's not their fault they found a dead man at the bar they've been going to, there must be loads of people go there," said Steve.

"Yes I suppose so but then she said that they thought they knew the other murdered men from the water park."

"Men? Just how many were murdered?" asked Tony now a little concerned.

"One at the bar and three at the water park."

"So what exactly makes them think they know these men?" asked Tony abruptly.

"Well apparently Julie made a Mickey Finn and gave it to one of the men and it made him ill but he's the one that survived."

"My Julie?" asked Steve incredulously.

"Yes your Julie, Jill said one of the men said something to her so she slipped it into his drink."

"Bloody hell, my Julie?" asked Steve again.

"Your Julie Steve."

"I'm gobsmacked; I mean she wouldn't say boo to a goose, my Julie....bloody hell!" said Steve looking towards the ceiling.

"I need another beer," said David leaving his two friends to ponder over what he had just imparted whilst he made his way to the bar.

David returned with the beers placing them on the table and picked his up removing the head. The three of them sat in silence for a few minutes looking at one another in turn. It was Tony who first broke the silence, "So what did you say to her?"

"To who?"

"Jill, your wife," said Tony a little abruptly, "and it's to whom being pedantic."

"I said we should look for early flights home but she wouldn't hear of it, they are in some karaoke competition tonight which she said they are going to."

"I think we should go with them," suggested Tony decisively.

"That's what I said but she wouldn't hear of it, she said we have our golf and that they have had their karaoke and we were not welcome, period."

"Oh just great, you're being quiet Steve what do you think about this?" asked Tony.

"If they want to go by themselves that's fine by me, like they said we have our golf, they have needed something as they haven't exactly been the best of friends have they but they seem to be now, so that's a positive step, isn't it?" said Steve raising his eyelids questioningly.

"So you're alright with Julie making a Mickey Finn, how the hell does she know how to make one? I wouldn't have a clue."

"No of course not but I trust her implicitly it's that simple," said Steve.

"So that's it is it? We just leave them to carry on as normal."

"I don't know what else we can do, if I try and tell Michelle she can't go tonight she'll just ignore me and go anyway," said Tony despondently.

Silence descended on the three of them again as they pondered their plight. The silence was only broken by some acquaintances walking into the bar which they acknowledged by a grunt each. Tony noticed a local English paper the Sol Sur had been left on one of the tables and went to retrieve it. The murders were detailed on the front page and again on the second and third pages. It speculated on the motives behind the murders at the water park and only briefly mentioned the murder at the bar; it said the police were currently at a loss for a motive but that all their personnel were involved in solving the case within days.

"Look on the bright side," said Steve, "We'll be home by the time they solve it."

"I almost forgot, I told Jill about tomorrow night's dinner dance, I wasn't sure if you had already mentioned it to your wives."

"No I hadn't but Julie will be fine about it," said Steve confidently.

"I haven't either but Michelle should be ok with it," said Tony less confidently.

Jill lay on her bed fighting like mad to pull the jeans that had been bought for her over her bum; she had been fighting for over five minutes and was losing. She felt herself beginning to sweat so stopped as she did not want to spoil her makeup which she had been applying for half an hour.

She was rapidly becoming annoyed with Michelle and Julie for buying such an absurd costume; they had said the jeans would stretch but clearly not enough. Jill had tried everything from going to the toilet to farting but nothing helped, she was about to give up when there was a knock on her door. She waddled off the bed with the jeans stuck around her thighs and threw one leg forward followed by the other and she hopped, skipped and jumped her way as her naked boobs flew from side to side as she edged forward.

Eventually at the door she called out asking who was there and was relieved to find it was Michelle and Julie. Opening the door and letting them in they looked despondently at Jill's predicament. Jill in turn was surprised to see Michelle in her pair albeit with a little belly flab hanging over. Michelle took charge telling Jill to lie on the bed with Michelle and Julie on either side of her; each had one hand on the back of the jeans and another on the front.

"Right Julie when I say pull, pull with all your might with both hands….Pull!" said Michelle.

They duly pulled with all their might and all three landed on top of each other on the floor having pulled Jill off the bed, as they began to stand they saw that the jeans were miraculously around Jill's hips, all they needed to do now was zip them up and fasten the button. Another five minutes of pushing and prodding Jill and her stomach the jeans were finally fastened.

"I told you you should have bought a pair the same size as mine and not yours Julie," said Michelle.

"What! These are the same size as yours Julie, no bloody wonder I couldn't pull them on," said Jill annoyed and frustrated at the same time.

"I thought they would have fit, you're in them," said Julie innocently.

"What do I do when I want to pee?" asked Jill.

"We'll have to go with you," suggested Julie.

"It's no good they'll have to come off, I'm putting my own jeans on, how the hell do I take them off?" asked Jill with a huff.

Jill lay on the bed again whilst they reversed what they had done before, another five minutes passed and Jill was free of the jeans but with scars, well white marks where the jeans had been digging in. Finally in her own jeans Jill was ready to leave as she noticed their tops she began to smile then laugh.

Jill said, "We look as though we should be supporting the Jamaican bob sleigh team with these tops, and you can see your boobs at the bottom of your top."

"We might win a few more votes then," said Michelle with a naughty giggle.

"At least we're still red, white and blue, good job you had the blue ones Jill," observed Julie.

"I can't believe this is what you bought and I can't believe you let her buy these Michelle," said Jill looking at the three of them.

"Better than what I would have bought, my choice was X rated!" said Michelle pointedly.

"I'm not going to ask," said Jill.

Michelle was dying for Jill to ask as she grinned from ear to ear but she waited in vain. They had exaggerated their makeup applying more than they normally would and had blow dried their hair and applied enough hairspray to make them a fire hazard, their hair was puffed out all over as some people wore it in the 80's. They all wore high heels, to say they were happy with the look would not be quite accurate but they walked out of the door anyway.

As they walked along the corridor to the lift Jill could not help herself from observing, "We look like the three slappers!"

"Please," said Julie, "I'm no slapper."

"We certainly would if I'd bought the outfits," said Michelle still trying to tease Jill into asking.

"I'm still not asking," said Jill.

They walked through the reception area of their hotel with the clientele all stopping in their tracks and staring at the three of them striding towards the front door, one poor old resident nearly tripped over his Zimmer frame, another old guy walked straight into a wall and banged his head, he turned around rubbing his wound and was rewarded with a slap from his wife.

Exiting the front door they were greeted by the heat of the early evening which drew around them as there was no breeze at all with the air being perfectly still. As they walked along the road opposite the beach they became aware of the stares from all they passed, they found they enjoyed the attention; as such their gate became exaggerated as they waggled their bums from side to side. Their smiles grew more pronounced.

They even waved at the odd passer-by. Their smiles turned into the odd giggle as they now flirted with the stares of the men passing by. They pondered whether to go straight to the Music Bar thinking they might be able to sing a song or two in practice but then dismissed the idea as they thought all the "professional" expats would be hogging the stage so they decided to stop by their favourite venta for a drink and to cool down a little as it was such a warm night with the air being so still. Arriving they found the restaurant quite busy but managed to find a table outside and sat under the now familiar advertising umbrella. They were smiling and looking beyond the clientele of the restaurant as with their dress sense they seemed to be the centre of attention. They were served briskly by a young waiter named Rafa who was barely twenty years of age and Michelle as usual could not keep her eyes off him as she said "he has a delightfully tight bottom", Michelle was not the only one, he garnered quite a lot of attention from numerous women of all ages.

They sat quietly enjoying the early evening sunshine, perhaps nerves had a little to do with the lack of conversation. Julie suggested they stop off at Blues for a drink before finally making their way to the Music Bar but Jill said they were best going straight to the Music bar as she knew Julie would not want to leave. They were also taking time over their drinks and were all clearly a little bored so Jill took the initiative and announced they were leaving for the Music bar.

They started off walking sluggishly but it was not long before they began to strut the way they had before with their bums pertly marching from side to side, their smiles had returned too.

It did not take them long to reach the Music Bar strutting as they were. Once inside they felt blind by the darkness, it took their eyes a few minutes to adjust, Pete and Debbie greeted them and informed them that as soon as all contestants were present their names would be put into a hat and drawn randomly, as they said it was the only fair way to do it. They also informed them that once everyone had sung they picked out the best six for a final sing off.

Pete advised them not to try and be the best initially as all they needed to do was make the final six. They gave Pete their song choices all of which were by Bananarama and then made their way to the bar looking around the room in search of Charles.

The bar was already crowded and as they suspected the expats were hogging the stage and had taken control of the tables around the stage both for themselves and friends that would cheer them on.

With drinks in hand and not being able to locate Charles they found a vacant table just past the halfway point in the room, the table was central so when they had to leave for the stage they would not have to pass too many tables. They recognised most of the acts which were quite easy to recognise in their costumes, there were just a few they were not sure of.

People continued to pour into the bar and it became apparent they had needed to be early. It was extremely noisy in the bar with the acts practicing on stage and the crowd chatting loudly to each other. The stale pungent smells once again filled their nostrils, the mix of stale beer with cheap perfume and long forgotten smoke. As the time slowly crept by the excitement and expectation built.

The time edged towards 10pm and still no sign of Charles. Pete and Debbie took charge of the stage as the singing stopped the crowds chatter seemed deafening. Pete was handed a silver bucket, well a bucket wrapped in silver foil, by one of the bar staff.

Pete's hand disappeared inside the bucket and waved about and immerged with a piece of paper, he announced into his microphone, "The first singer tonight will be Carole Swettenham singing as Cher and Believe, let's hear it for Carole."

The crowd leapt to their feet shouting and cheering as Carole walked onto the stage almost wearing something. She was wearing a black mini skirt that was shorter than a mini, a good job she was wearing matching knickers, and a black glittering boob tube. What made the look worse was the amount of gaudy makeup plastered onto her plump rotund face and the fact that although she was only 50 years of age she was 18 stone and at five foot five inches, needless to say she bounced around the stage but her voice sounded good and the audience certainly enjoyed her performance.

Next Pete introduced Kevin Gilbert and Peter Jones who would be singing Simon and Garfunkel's A Bridge Over Troubled Water, who turned out to be two of the three stooges, Larry and Moe and a firm favourite of the crowd. They began to sing and the audience fell to silence listening intently, they would certainly take some beating. Halfway through their song Charles arrived at the girls table with a fresh round of drinks and a beaming smile.

The girls welcomed him nervously, they thought they would know when they were on stage but Pete was introducing people as he went along dipping into the hat each time. As the song came to an end to tumultuous applause the girls fell into a nervous silence until they heard Pete announce,"Thankyou for that now we have Raymond Choudhry singing Elvis's Blue Suede Shoes, let's hear it for Raymond!"

He literally jumped on stage, an Indian Elvis with a costume to match which must have cost a small fortune, it appeared to be white leather with hundreds of multi-coloured stones stitched onto it, he had long black hair quaffed back and long sideburns, he was about forty years of age and six foot tall and very slim. Again he was given a tumultuous welcome and the rowdy applause continued throughout the song. During the song Charles asked how everyone was and struggled to obtain answers from the more and more nervous women as they waited anxiously to be called on stage, they were wishing they had practiced more.

Elvis finished his song to extraordinary applause as his gyrating hips finally slowed and then stopped; he passed Pete as he exited stage left. Pete put the microphone to his lips and spoke over the still applauding crowd, "Thank you, thank you, Elvis is still in the building!" he shouted, "and now we have Jill Jones, Michelle Pemberton and Julie Anderson singing Bananarama's Love In The First Degree."

Jill, Michelle and Julie jumped to their feet nerves forgotten as they rushed forward to the stage just making it at the end of their introduction, the music had already started as Pete handed them three microphones. They just had time to start their dance routine before echoing the first words into their microphones over the deafening shouts and applause from the overexcited crowd. They were slightly stunned at how quickly their song ended but left the stage to continued applause and wolf whistles from a number of men, they bounced quite literally, boobs in motion, back to their table not able to hide their delight as they smiled from ear to ear.

They also did not hear Pete introducing John Musket as Elton John singing Candle In The Wind. The crowd cheered wildly until he started singing at which point a deathly hush gripped the room, as he approached the end of the song there were even tears in some people's eyes. Pete had almost to kick him off stage as he hogged the short-lived limelight.

Jill was still gently tamping her face with a handkerchief to mop up the sweat that was attacking her makeup; she struggled to stop it running from her scalp and now regretted using so much hairspray. Michelle turned to her and said, "We've no chance of beating him."

"I'm really not bothered, I think we've swam the Channel if we make the top six, I never thought we would win," said Jill.

"You were very good; I'd like to see you make the top six, you would have to sing again and if you think the crowd is loud now just wait until later," said Charles with a wink to Michelle.

On stage there were two women singing Abba's Dancing Queen as Julie observed that she thought Men O'Pause should dance to that.

Michelle left the table announcing she was off to the bar. The uninterrupted noise in the bar was becoming unbearable as the heat rose and so too the pungent odour of sweat and cheap perfume permeated the room. Michelle's return from the bar was welcomed with drinks cooled by multitudes of ice. Jill continued her losing battle with her dripping sweat, her hankie now soaked through. She looked at Michelle and Julie wondering how they looked so cool and noticed they too were suffering.

The minutes dragged by and slowly turned into hours as singer after singer took to the stage, Jill, Michelle and Julie had followed other people's example and to cool down had left the bar for some cool outside fresh air, people stood in groups free to talk quietly for a change, smokers on the left, the Bee Gees around a lamp post talking to someone who looked like Richard Nixon thankfully not singing, Dolly Parton was adjusting her inflated boobs in front of an interested Tom Jones who looked to be about 25 years of age. It must have been a strange sight for anyone that did not know what was happening inside the bar.

There was a constant stream of people walking in and out of the bar in various forms of attire and attempted lookalike shapes and sizes some bearing uncanny resemblances others who should not have bothered. The overall atmosphere was jovial and becoming more so as the night progressed and the alcohol consumption increased.

As 1am approached and then faded into memory people were discussing the merits or not of their personal top six singers and arguments ringed out around the overcrowded bar. It was clearly obvious how the bar could put on a top prize of one thousand Euros as the bar had not stopped serving all evening and the six staff had not managed a single break between them.

Finally at 1.45am Pete less than energetically bounced onto the stage with a piece of white paper clutched into his hand as he bade for quiet, "Please, please, we have, I said we have the names of the six acts which have made the sing off and I will announce them in no particular order, their names then will go back into the hat and will be drawn again randomly…..are you ready?….I said are you ready? The first act in the sing off is Cliff Richard and Liza Minelli singing The Pogues The Fairytale of New York. Next is Elton John and Candle In The Wind. Next Simon and Garfunkel and A Bridge Over Troubled Waters. And then we have Bananarama with Love In The First Degree. Next it's the Bee Jees and Stayin Alive. And finally and no way last is Tina Turner and Simply The Best. Thank you all who didn't make the final six but this has been so difficult to separate everyone, we'll have a five minute break and then we'll draw the first name out of the hat!"

With that Pete stepped off the stage leaving it empty for the first time all evening, the noise from the crowd was even more deafening as the six acts were announced and now people were arguing over the final six as their choices had or had not been chosen. Jill, Michelle and Julie were deliriously happy at making the final six and began to think that they should have perhaps slowed down on their drinking.

They had suddenly made new friends all over the bar as people they did not know waved at them and some came over to congratulate them, they received numerous pats on their backs both welcome and unwelcome. Charles just sat by smiling at the girls' undoubted joy.

Pete was no sooner off the stage than back on again with a rowdy and uncontrollable audience to contend with. It took several attempts by Pete to quieten the noise to at least a level where he could be heard as he announced the first of the finalists to take to the stage, Bananarama.

Jill, Michelle and Julie rose to their slightly unsteady feet to be hustled and bustled to the stage, it was now nigh on impossible to hear anything coherently as the noise from the audience reached a crescendo as the music began and the girls began swaying their hips hoping they would remember the words in the correct order. Although a karaoke competition no words were shown on screen for the competitors. They sung their hearts out as best they could but even so they struggled to hear themselves over the now overexcited and largely drunken audience, so God knows how the judges were to come to a decision.

They gratefully made their way back to their seats at the end of their song smiling all the way and being slapped on the back as they walked slowly accompanied by applause and quite a few wolf whistles.

As they sat down they downed what remained of their drinks as the crowd now concentrated on who would be the next to sing. Pete announced Elton John. Charles left them pointing at his glass in his hand to indicate he was going to the bar for drinks.

The heat inside the bar was now overpowering along with the smell of stale sweat and beer. People were up on their feet jumping up and down applauding and cheering as the Elton John singer began.

It was a further three quarters of an hour before all of the finalists had sung and Pete once again ventured onto the stage to announce the winner. Pete now took his time to announce the winner, he tried several times asking for quiet all to no avail until he stood still in the middle of the stage quietly waiting for silence to prevail. Once satisfied it was as quiet as it was going to be he announced by a clear majority the winner was…..A Bridge Over Troubled Waters.

John Musket immediately threw a tantrum and physically hit one of his friends sat at his table before storming out of the bar. Although only two of them sung the Three Stooges took to the stage to take their cheque for 1000 Euros and immediately gave an impromptu Stooges performance by hitting and poking each other whilst stealing the cheque from one another, it was an hilarious site and was a suitable ending to what had been for everyone a great night, well all except for John Musket.

It became apparent to Jill, Michelle and Julie that the end of their holiday was now within sight, Charles felt their mood and asked what was wrong as he knew it was not about winning the competition as they had never expected to win indeed they were deliriously happy at reaching the last six.

Jill again felt nominated to speak from the looks of Michelle and Julie, "It's just our holiday is rapidly reaching its end, this is our last night with you as tomorrow our husbands have bought tickets for a dinner dance at the golf club, I think we all just wish we had a few more days."

"All good things come to an end but you have your memories and you can always come back," said Charles.

"Yes I suppose we could and we no doubt will at some point but it's never the same," answered Jill.

"Still, it's no reason to be sad you still have tomorrow at my villa."

"But not long, I've said I will spend the morning with David now we're close again, maybe a couple of hours of sunbathing in the afternoon when he plays his final round of golf," said Jill.

"Julie and I will make the morning though, won't we Julie?" said Michelle expectantly.

"After breakfast yes," added Julie.

"Let's then make the most of your time left by not being sad, agreed?"

"Agreed," said Jill followed closely by Michelle and Julie.

Charles made himself scarce as he again took himself to the bar leaving the women to discuss the remainder of their holiday. They chatted about the positives of this over the other holidays they had shared, they all agreed that they had now indeed become not just friends but close friends who would be happy in each other's company at home as well as abroad. Then there was the fact that Jill and David were back in each other's arms once again, a major plus everyone agreed. Then there was Charles, they knew they were still not one hundred percent sure of him, there was definitely something under the surface with him, perhaps there always would be, but he had said he would welcome their return. Then Michelle suggested that they could come back by themselves when their husbands went on their next golfing holiday, why not let them go wherever by themselves and we come back here by ourselves.

They were giving the idea some consideration when Jill lifted her empty glass and said in frustration, "Where the hell is Charles with the drinks?" And they all fell about laughing.

Charles returned moments later smiling with the drinks and could not help notice the women's improved demeanour. Placing the drinks on the table the three women were still laughing uncontrollably, Charles was unsure why and so were the women, perhaps it was a release of tension. Although the hour was late they were all reluctant to leave as it also meant an ending.

Chapter 11   Friday

Jill awoke to the sound of water crashing at speed and realised it was a shower; one eye opened reluctantly, her left and took in her surroundings. Her head remained firmly attached to her pillow on her right, she could feel warmth penetrating through the closed curtains as she began to realise where she was. Her head felt somehow detached, it throbbed relentlessly, her eye closed, it did not help.

The water stopped, someone was singing, it was David singing. Her head tried to burrow itself deeper into her pillow. What was that song? Where had she heard it before? It was familiar but she could not fathom out why. Something heavy had landed on the bed and the singing was louder now. She knew she knew that bloody song, what was it? David was in the room, she turned to look at him, her eyes hurt as she opened them to witness her husband's bare backside as he bent over to open the bottom drawer of the cabinet and take out a clean pair of underpants.

She fell back onto her pillow closing her eyes again. David said something in between singing, she could not be bothered to make out what he said, the pain in her head persisted. The singing grew louder as did the pain in her head. David was by her side of the bed, her left eye opened again, oh God, not only was he singing he was also dancing swaying his hips from side to side. Unfortunately David could not sing and his dancing was worse. What was that bloody song? David handed her a glass of water and two aspirins, thank God. He cheerfully told her to take the aspirins and to take a shower; it will make you feel better. You stopping being so bloody cheerful and singing would help she thought. David stripped the covers off the bed and opened the curtains in almost one move. You bastard...she thought. She was naked lying prone on the bed with the ever so bright rays from the sun blaring down on her. The song, of course, it was Leave Your Hat On sung by Tom Jones in the film The Full Monty.

The shower Jill had taken was extremely hot, her thinking was the hotter the shower the quicker her headache would leave her still pounding head. Drying herself quickly, she began brushing her teeth; she began to feel slightly better with her mouth refreshed until she looked in the mirror as she swilled her mouth out with bottled water. Are my eyes really that colour she thought taking a closer look, bloodshot just does not even begin to describe this look, she thought, and when did I age so much?

She trudged miserably into the bedroom, her shoulders arched downwards as she almost tripped over her own feet, she glanced up towards the naked windows bleached by the powerful sun, she realised her eyes still hurt. She plonked her bum down on the stool in front of the dressing table, another mirror confirmed her earlier prognosis, she reached to her right and dug in her beach bag finding her sunglasses, she put them on and exclaimed, "Ready!"

"You might try putting some clothes on," suggested David.

"Shit."

Walking along the front of the resort with David beside her Jill's demeanour had only slightly improved, her jeans seemed a little tight and her T-shirt loose, at least her Nike's fit her.

They walked silently along David happily following in Jill's wake. Jill although she did not realise it was following the route she took with her friends as she walked into the venta and sat instinctively at a table, she noticed David sitting down beside her as she looked up for a waiter, "Hello, coffee, I need coffee." She said.

David ordered coffee for them both from a passing waiter whilst he inspected the menu. Jill Placed her arms on the table in front of her and allowed her head to crash on top of them, she remained in that position until the waiter arrived with their coffee. David ordered croissants for them both and more coffee.

After another half an hour Jill began to mutter her first words of the day grateful that her head had ceased its pounding. It emerged David was meeting Tony and Steve at the golf club at 1.00pm for a round of golf before returning to the hotel to change and meet up with everyone to leave for the golf club again at 7.00pm. David left the table and strolled inside the venta to pay their bill and was a little surprised to see Jill had risen to her feet unaided as he returned, she even managed a smile but David was not sure, it may have been a grimace. They kissed briefly on the pavement outside the venta before David left to find a taxi to take him to the golf club. Jill turned in a circle as she decided where to go, just before she turned a second circle she thought villa, Michelle and Julie will be at the villa and off she trekked.

Arriving at the villa some time later, Jill had walked slowly in rhythm with her mood; she walked past the concrete lions and straight through the open gates. She found Michelle and Julie lying quietly on their sun loungers, Michelle as usual naked and oiled whilst Julie wore one of her bikinis. Both Michelle and Julie sat upright as they heard Jill's hello greeting.

Jill walked straight up to a sun lounger and plonked her bum down throwing her bag nonchalantly next to her. She asked, "Have you seen Charles?"

"No, it's been very quiet, not sure if he's here," answered Michelle.

"His car is here so he can't be far," said Jill.

"He's not here, it's too quiet and anyway he always says hello when he hears us," said Julie.

"No doubt he'll turn up, my head was bad after last night, it's only just coming round," said Jill.

"Mine was a little tight but not too bad, not like little miss cheerful here, full of the joys of spring all morning," said Michelle.

"Well I can't help it if I don't have hangovers, never have, probably wouldn't drink if I did," answered Julie.

"Morning everyone, I do hope you've made yourself at home, been shopping, thought we would have a light lunch, I've Parma ham, cheese, prawns, chicken, salad and French bread, is that ok for everyone?" asked Charles as he marched past them through into the kitchen.

Jill, Michelle and Julie looked at each other with their eyes widening as if to say, "Oh, that's where you've been."

Charles immerged from the kitchen with a red and white chequered table cloth, utensils and began setting the outside bamboo table smiling as he did so. Michelle began to throw her dress over her shoulders followed by Julie putting her bright pink blouse on over her bikini along with a matching pair of pink shorts. Charles made his way in and out of the kitchen bringing plate after plate of food to the table; the women looked at one another asking how much more. He finally returned to the bamboo table and began pouring the wine into the glasses whilst the women just hovered around their sun loungers not sure if they should make their way over to the table and sit down.

As he finished pouring the last glass of wine he turned to the women and said, "C'mon ladies what are you waiting for?"

Michelle needed no second invitation as she was starving, sitting down she began pilling food onto her plate which became overburdened quite soon. Charles looked pleased at her eagerness as he broke off some French bread and took some salad. They chatted amiably as they ate in the solitude of Charles's garden paradise.

The ambience of the relaxed atmosphere was somewhat strained when Julie asked Charles, "Have you heard anything about the murders or Bulbous Billy?"

"Nothing about the murders par se but I did see Billy earlier," said Charles matter of factly.

"Where did you see him? Is he out? Did he do it?" asked Julie stubbornly.

"Julie! Really, how can you ask that? Did he do it, really?" admonished Jill.

"That's alright, Jill, no he didn't do it, I saw him at his bar and he is fine although a little nervous," said Charles.

"So who do they think did it then if not Billy?" pushed Julie.

"Well, according to Billy they don't know but they said if Billy had done it they didn't think he was stupid enough to hide the body in a rubbish skip outside his own bar even though he is English," said Charles.

"Not very nice of them," said Michelle.

"Do they think it's connected to the murders at the water park?" asked Julie.

"Billy is of the opinion that they are treating it as a separate incident as they are concentrating on the water park murders as that is where all the pressure is coming from and where all the media attention is," continued Charles.

"So have they let him open the bar now then?" asked Michelle.

"Yes the bar's open from this morning, Billy was drinking when I saw him at 10.00am this morning, Steve was there as well to help him clean up a bit before they open to the public," said Charles.

"He must be alright if the police are letting him open the bar, I mean they mustn't suspect him anymore or they wouldn't have let him open the bar would they?" asked Michelle.

"As Billy said they are more interested in the water park murders, they need to make sure there won't be anymore. The murders have hit the national newspapers now although not our English ones as yet," said Charles.

"Perhaps we could go to Billy's bar for a quick drink as we're leaving tomorrow we could say goodbye," suggested Michelle.

"Certainly not, I've told you to stay away; you don't want any gossip starting about Julie's involvement," instructed Charles.

"I'm not involved!" insisted Julie.

"You're very much involved as you drugged one of the men at the water park so you must remain silent about it, whatever you do do not discuss it in public, you never know just who is listening," reiterated Charles.

"Probably saved his life more like," said Julie almost to herself but loud enough to be heard.

"It probably did save his life but the police wouldn't look at it that way, they would probably keep all of you in for questioning and they certainly wouldn't let you return home, at least not for a while, so best to keep very quiet about it as I say, don't say anything in public, agreed?" asked Charles looking at Jill, Michelle and Julie individually until each in turn had nodded in agreement.

"What time does your dance start this evening?" asked Charles changing the subject.

"Around 7.00pm I think," said Jill.

"You must be all looking forward to it, a chance for you to dress up and relax before you leave tomorrow?" said Charles.

"Yes I suppose so, I just can't believe how quickly the week has gone, it's a pity we didn't book ten days," said Jill.

"Probably best you didn't in the circumstances but still you can always come back," suggested Charles.

"I do hope so, I was thinking of asking Jill and Julie if they would like to come over when the men next go for a golfing holiday, they could go wherever and we could come here," suggested Michelle not for the first time.

"Well I'm not sure; I'll have to see how it transpires with David and me first," said Jill.

"I'm sure I would be able to," said Julie.

"Just leave your Mickey Finns at home though won't you," said Charles with a deliciously cheeky grin on his face.

"That's not fair," said Julie with a sulky expression on her face.

"Just joking Julie," said Charles.

"Yes so anyway that still gives us a few hours to kill, any ideas Charles?" asked Michelle seductively.

"I'm afraid you'll have to leave me out of your plans, I promised an old friend that I would call by later today, sorry," said Charles.

Michelle looked totally dejected and Julie was about to say something, one of her not so prudent statements, when she received an opportune dig from Jill, she turned indignantly looking at Jill as if to say what was that for. Jill returned the stare saying you know damn well what that was for.

Charles stood and began assorting through the dinner plates returning some to the kitchen; the women took the hint and joined in. The atmosphere had quite suddenly become morose as Jill began running some hot water in the sink to wash the plates and wine glasses. Nobody seemed to know the right thing to say so instead they said nothing.

The silence became awkward. Jill looked to the others but it was clear she had been silently nominated again to say something. She was annoyed, why did she accept being the spokesperson all the time so she took out her feelings on the pots which did not go unnoticed by Michelle and Julie. With Michelle and Julie erratically trying to look busy and failing the pressure on Jill to speak was mounting as the time ebbed away.

Charles excused himself and climbed the stairs to his mezzanine bedroom presumably to change before visiting his friend.

At which point Jill stopped what she was doing in the sink and turned to face Michelle and Julie with her hands on her hips and frown on her face she said, "Why is it always up to me to speak? Why couldn't you say something Michelle as you were eager enough to go for a little tryst with him or you Julie? It's not fair you expecting me to do the talking all the time."

With her short lived rant duly dispatched Jill turned back to finish the dishes leaving Michelle and Julie to look at each other and immediately shrug their shoulders in silent "whatever". Their chores complete they walked over to the sofas in the middle of the room and sat down in abject silence as they waited for

Charles. Jill sat still staring straight in front of her with her arms folded whereas Michelle and Julie sat opposite to Jill and stared in every direction but that of Jill's.

Charles appeared and was halfway down the stairs when Jill sprang to her feet leaving Michelle and Julie fumbling pathetically to regain their feet and composure.

Charles approached with a warm smile as Jill reciprocated before saying, "before you leave and we leave we just wanted to thank you for your hospitality and warmth this week, I am not sure what we would have done had we not met you but I'm sure we wouldn't have had as much fun, so thank you Charles." Jill stepped forward and kissed him briefly on his lips. Julie stepped forward and managed an air kiss, whilst Michelle went gung ho and tried losing her tongue.

Once Charles managed to break away from Michelle's grasp he said, "Thank you ladies, that's sweet of you to say, I am really so pleased that you have enjoyed your week, I can only hope that you come back and see me some time, that would be nice, now I really must be off, just pull the door to when you leave and have a pleasant flight home, bye now, bye."

That was it he walked out through the doors and was gone from their lives; they heard his car start and move over the stones of the driveway and then silence. Jill sighed with relief as she sat down on the sofa again.

"What was that for?" asked Michelle.

"What was what for?" asked Jill.

"You know what that bloody great sigh," said Michelle.

"I'm relieved that's all, it's over, that's the last we'll see of him, we still know nothing about him but I suppose in his way he's been ok," said Jill knowing she had not told them what he had done to her.

"Well I think he's been great, let's face it this would have been a pretty crappy holiday without him," said Michelle.

"We know why you think he's been great, but I'm sure we would have managed without him," said Julie pointedly.

"What's that supposed to mean?" said Michelle her eyes blaring at Julie.

"Right, that's it, stop it you two, we've been great together all holiday we're not falling out now, do you hear?" said Jill.

"Ok, ok, ok," said Michelle.

"Ok, sorry," said Julie.

"Let's gather our things together and go to the venta for a drink, what do you think?" suggested Jill.

"Sounds like a plan," agreed Michelle.

"Oh yes please, I could murder a coffee," said Julie.

"Just a coffee this time!" said Michelle sarcastically.

"Michelle!" protested Jill.

"Sorry Julie," said Michelle.

They arrived at their favourite venta some twenty minutes later, they could have arrived sooner but they walked slowly people watching and bitching which Michelle excelled at. They had a half competition at who could spot the most ridiculous tattoo but they had to give up as there was so much competition they would never have agreed on a winner.

They collapsed into their chairs at an outside table as Michelle spotted another tattoo which she insisted would probably be the winner. Julie trotted off to the toilets leaving Jill and Michelle continuing their search of tattoos until a waiter showed up, with tattoos, they eventually took their eyes off his tattoos long enough to order three coffees.

They chatted lightly but amiably and all agreed they were quite pleased to be going home tomorrow as they could do with the rest. Eventually they agreed to leave which Jill was rather pleased about as she was eager to return to her room so that she could take a long relaxing shower before she needed to concentrate on her makeup, and then put on her incredibly sexy blue dress, she knew it was sexy, everybody said so, so it must be, right?

Jill showered with her favourite shower gel which foamed excessively and smelled of freshly cut strawberries all for the princely sum of £1 from her local pound shop. Jill also took her husband's razor into the shower, well, she thought, apart from under my arms I have other areas to shave now and anyway it's started to itch and I don't want to be scratching it in my dress especially as I'm going knickerless. She giggled at the thought. Jill had been looking forward to the dance since David had told her about it; they had not been dancing together for an awful long time, longer than she could remember. It would be good to dance again with David, it would be romantic, just what they both needed and a great opportunity to show off her new necklace which she had not as yet taken off and would not until back home in England.

She took her time shaving as she did not want any little nicks that might bleed and certainly nothing like she gave herself at the airport coming, she shuddered at the thought. The shaving complete she rinsed herself all over before smothering herself with the strawberry scented shower gel again to wash away any remaining hairs she told herself but she knew really it was because she found the odour intoxicating. She felt herself all over and happy with the smoothness all over her body she rinsed off again. Realising that she was beginning to sweat in the heat of the shower she turned the control to cold and stayed under as long as she could. With Goosebumps all over her body and her nipples erect she jumped out of the shower before turning to switch it off. She dried herself as best as she could leaving her hair damp so that she could blow dry it and walked into the bedroom naked.

Feeling the draught from the open door to the balcony she walked out onto it and enjoyed the heat from the blistering hot sun's rays. She felt she wasn't alone and looking to her right saw a man on the balcony from the room next door, she grimaced in his direction and turned to her left to re-enter her room pulling her face as she did so at the sight she had just given her neighbour.

She took her hairdryer out of her suitcase and sat in front of the mirror as she blow dried her hair, just as she was halfway through she heard a key in the doors lock and looked in the mirror to see David walk in the room. He threw his key onto the bed whilst walking towards Jill, he bent over and kissed her remarking at how nice she smelled, then he stripped his shirt off whilst walking into the bathroom and turned on the shower. He walked back into the bedroom stripping himself naked before returning to the bathroom.

Within seconds he was back out, "have you been using my razor again?" he asked.

"Well you did say you liked me smooth, it's in the shower," said Jill with a sulky expression on her face.

David swore under his breath as he returned to the bathroom and showing his displeasure shut the door, Jill just tutted. I thought men liked their toys played with, she thought mischievously.

Jill was busy with her makeup when David surfaced from the bathroom with steam still rising from his shoulders; he sauntered over to her and tried nuzzling her ear, "No..shower…cold..now..go," Jill instructed.

He mumbled something inaudible and went and sat on the bed with the steam still rising from his shoulders. He sat and watched his wife carefully and meticulously applying her makeup through the mirror.

Jill could tell he was bored so she asked, "How was your game?"

"Diabolical, couldn't hit a ball straight to save my life."

"You should have asked me, I'm good with balls, or so you tell me."

"Very funny, all this sodding money on golf and I'm not improving, I've a good mind to give it up."

"Oh don't do that, you'd soon miss it, what would Tony and Steve do without you?"

"Yeah, suppose."

"Look, why don't you dress and go down to the bar for a drink, I'll finish up here and join you as soon as I'm ready."

"Yeah ok, I could do with a pint."

David duly dressed and picking his key up from the bed gave Jill a quick kiss on her lips and left for the bar, Jill tutted and rearranged her lipstick from an ever so slight smudge from David's kiss. This was the first night out where she could dress up for well over two years and she was determined to be immaculate and to damn well enjoy herself, she deserved to. She sat still for a minute observing herself in the mirror from all angles and checked her nails, she had applied a very subtle blue nail polish which she had not used before, unusual she thought blue nail polish but it worked and would do more so when she put her dress on.

She could not prolong it anymore so she lifted herself up taking a final look at herself in the mirror; she liked the look of her body naked more so now she was shaved. She climbed into her dress and put her shoes on; she transferred her money and odds and ends into her matching handbag, now she was ready to take a final look in the mirror. Satisfied, more than satisfied, she noticed she was smiling at her reflection and she so liked the look of her necklace, she just knew some women would be jealous. She strutted out of the room and down the corridor to the elevator that would take her down to her husband.

Jill walked into the bar in all her splendour to find her husband sat alone at one of the lonely tables, she immediately deflated with her shoulders dropping as she took a seat next to him answering vodka and coke to his question.

She looked around the dank and odorous bar area as she adjusted the skirt of her dress as it was a nightmare to keep straight and free of creases. Her gaze fell upon an old gent sat in a corner she had missed when walking into the bar, he sat by himself with an absent expression and an empty glass on the table in front of him, he wore a black dinner jacket with white shirt and black tie but was also wearing a pair of beige shorts and of all things Adidas trainers without socks. His Zimmer frame rested beside him. David returned with her drink as she nodded at him towards the old man but David just shrugged his shoulders. The old man suddenly noticed Jill and smiled imperceptibly whilst nodding his head ever so slightly, Jill returned his effort with a full on smile and a wink. Julie and Steve entered the bar with Julie going straight over and sitting next to Jill, she was wearing a long pale peach dress with an open back and Jill noticed it was one of the few times she had seen her wear something without a bra. As Steve brought their drinks over to the table Michele and Tony entered this time Tony went to the bar whilst Michele sat next to Julie, she wore a black sleeveless dress that just covered her knees and only just covered her ample breasts, typical Michelle Jill thought. They agreed that when they finished their drinks they would walk down to the taxi rank and take three taxis up to the golf club, they had not seen a taxi that could have taken all of them. Two elderly ladies entered the bar with a pair of black trousers and a pair of black brogues. They positioned themselves on either side of the old man and proceeded to take his shorts off, as they began to pull them down it became apparent he was not wearing any under garments but rather than stopping they just tutted at each other and without changing expression continued to take his shorts off and replace them with the black trousers of his dinner suit. They continued with his trainers taking them off and only stopping for a second when they realised they had not brought any socks, they put his shoes on without them. Finished they collected his shorts and trainers together and turned to leave, noticing the group of people in the opposite corner of the bar they must have thought they owed them some sort of an explanation so turning one of them said, "He's the magician for tonight's show, he's on in an hour."

With that they left leaving the magician once again on his own with only his Zimmer frame for company. Jill and David, Michelle and Tony, Julie and Steve looked at one another trying very hard not to laugh and keep a straight face; they decided it was time to leave.

As they walked slowly along the front of the resort in the early evening sunshine with a warm breeze blowing in off the sea they passed a street mime artist who had just completed his rendition of the Ten Commandments. There was some consternation from his crowd of onlookers as they were arguing that he had only presented nine commandments and not the complete ten, there was some in the crowd who were becoming more heated in their argument when the artist began verbally arguing, they seemed to think as a mime artist he should not talk.

They continued on leaving the argument to flourish. Early evening was a strange time of day in some ways on the Costa Del Sol. There were people extracting themselves from bars where they had spent the afternoon drinking, there were people still on the beach who would remain there until the final rays of sunshine had dissipated, and there were people who were just leaving the beach heading for their hotels to change before heading to bars and restaurants for the evening, then there were the people heading out from their hotels for the evening now.

As the six friends continued towards the taxi rank they encountered one small group who had clearly been drinking all afternoon. The group consisted of three men and one woman who was so intoxicated she could barely control her legs, falling to the ground several times to be ignominiously raised again by the three men. It became apparent the three men were in some heated discussion as to which of them would escort her to her hotel room for their rather obvious if slightly disturbing reward. One individual suggested that they should all escort her back to her hotel and share the reward, this suggestion went down well until the argument immerged as to who would go first, then second and finally last. As the argument became more and more heated the girl collapsed onto her bottom again on the side of the pavement and defecated herself both front and back, the three men noticed turning away whilst agreeing to go back to the bar leaving the girl lounging on the pavement.

Arriving at the taxi rank they found they had a choice of eight taxis, they were all white, they were all Mercedes and they were all the same model. The three couples each chose a white Mercedes taxi to transport them to the golf club. They arrived some twenty minutes later passing by the crowded car park and alighting from their taxis outside the front door. There were taxis in front of them and more arriving behind them and there was a steady stream of people immerging from cars in the car park.

Entering the golf club they were offered a glass of champagne as they waited to be introduced to their host Fernando Torres Marquez. Jill heard Michelle behind her involuntarily say "El Sopo" Tony asked her what she had said but Michelle ignored him. Jill recognised him from the picture in his office but she knew nothing about him. It took some twenty minutes to eventually be introduced to Senor Fernando Torres Marquez who seemed charming but was clearly prone to sweating profusely; no doubt his weight did not help.

Inside the main entertainment room the multitude of large circular tables, which could accommodate 12 people, looked magnificent with their white table clothes and all had silver cutlery and glasses with a central flower montage. The men left the women whilst they trotted off to the bar for drinks, it was now Jill who asked Michelle what it was she had said whilst they were in the queue.

"Oh, it was just El Sopo, is all, it's nothing."

"C'mon explain, why would you say that which I assume is Spanish, now I know you don't speak Spanish Michelle," demanded Jill.

" Alright, I came here with Charles one day and we used his office for you know, anyway there is a painting in there of him and I said to Charles he looked like Toad of Toad Hall, so Charles called him El Sopo, which is Spanish for toad, that's all," explained Michelle.

"Oh my God I thought I had seen him before, he was in the pantomime two years ago we took Trevor and Daniel to see," said Julie.

"Who was? Fernando Torres Marquez?" asked Jill.

"No, at least I don't think so, no Toad of Toad Hall!" said Julie innocently.

"Back to the present Julie, ok?" said Jill.

"I hope he smokes one of his cigars," said Michelle.

"Why would you hope that Michelle?" asked Jill curiously.

"Oh, no reason, I'll tell you later if he does," said Michelle with a wink and a wicked grin.

With that the men returned with much needed drinks from the bar. There was a group of musicians warming up in the far corner of the room and the rumble of their instruments permeated the air. The room was cool as the air conditioning worked at full capacity it would no doubt warm up as the room filled with guests. More and more people kept entering and as they did so they inspected the seating charts by the doors. The band were now playing relaxing music quietly making it easy to talk and be heard, the sound of idle chatter filled the room along with the many air kisses and handshakes as people greeted old friends, it was clear that a lot of the guests were expats. Jill was pleased with herself as she noticed the admiring looks she was receiving from men and women, the men clearly admiring the way she looked in her dress and the women no doubt admiring her necklace. An announcer asked people to take their seats which took some time as a number of guests had ignored the seating instructions and now were waiting around the crowded signs at the entrance to discover their table number.

Finally when everyone was seated a myriad of waiters appeared with a first course of a Spanish lentil soup, other waiters were bringing bottles of opened wine to the tables which were included in the price of the tickets.

Jill's group found they were sitting with a group of three couples from Redditch near Birmingham who were in their 50's and were also on holiday. They were friendly enough and had decided for the first time to rent a villa for their two week stay, this being the end of their first week. Julie immediately asked if they had heard about the murders and when they said they had not began exhaustively telling them all about them thankfully leaving out her part in them. Jill quickly moved the conversation on asking about their villa, where it was, how big and how much it had cost.

They found the food adequate and warm rather than hot which they could understand as there must have been 300 guests sat to dinner.

"El Sopo" wandered from table to table talking to his guests making sure the food was agreeable and making idle chatter. It was while he was at their table talking to Michelle and Tony that a young waitress who looked younger than her 18 years was serving churros to the table, her larger serving tray became unbalanced and fell from her hand spilling its contents of four dishes on the floor. Fernando Torres Marquez turned on her with a tirade of abuse and as he was talking in Spanish it was difficult to tell but it sounded as though he was swearing at her. The poor girl ran in tears from the room, Fernando turned to his guests apologising for the spillage and left to arrange a clean-up party.

The outburst took everyone at the table by surprise and shock, the vilification of the young girl was totally over the top and worried everyone, Julie in particular remained quiet as the rage built inside of her. Three waiters came over to clear the mess which took all of a few seconds, hence why such a tirade? Jill asked the three waiters how the young girl was to be met with three hunched shoulders. Jill rose to her feet determined to find the young girl and make sure she was alright.

The conversation at the table had died after the incident. With Jill gone from the table Michelle was talking with Tony and did not notice the steely determination in Julie's eyes. Julie picked up her handbag and excused herself to the table as she rose to leave. She made her way to the bar where she had observed Fernando leaning against it with a drink in his hand and a handkerchief in the other which he used to continually wipe the sweat from his puffy face.

Fernando noticed Julie walking towards him. Julie used all her skills and charm as she slinked towards the bar, her face was open and she wore her sexiest smile, the effect on Fernando was immediate. He immediately offered to buy her a drink as she sidled up to him making sure her breasts just touched against his belly. He turned to find a waiter waiting for his order, they knew not to keep him waiting, asking Julie what she would like she seductively opened her eyes wider whist asking, "To drink?"

Fernando's sweating profergated as his use of his hanky went into overdrive, Julie's vodka and coke arrived followed shortly after by a Campari, vodka and tonic which he took in a long glass. Julie picked up her drink and Fernando picked up his, they clinked glasses together before taking a sip of their drinks. Julie put her drink down on the bar hoping Fernando would follow her lead which he did. She looked Fernando directly in his eyes without blinking which Fernando found mesmerising. With her left hand she deftly touched his lapel seductively which prompted an impulsive wipe of his sweaty face with his hanky again, he was entranced by Julie's beauty as he struggled to find words. Whilst she had Fernando under her control her right hand was reaching into her handbag, she found the vial by touch and unscrewed the top with her fingers holding the small bottle in her palm. Once she had the top off she dropped it in her bag and slowly moved her hand towards the Campari, vodka and soda spilling the remaining drops into it. Then she reversed the action, screwing the top back onto the vial and dropping it in her bag. She smiled ever so seductively at Fernando as she picked up her glass and took a large gulp hoping again that Fernando would follow her lead which he did. Julie then called the waiter over and ordered another round of drinks; Fernando began to protest but thought better of it and accepted the drink gracefully. The drinks arrived so Julie picked up the first drink and drank down the contents closely followed by picking up the second drink and waiting for Fernando to follow her so she could again clink glasses. He took the hint and downed his first drink in one picking up the second to clink glasses with Julie. Julie put the glass back on the bar before clinking it against Fernando's saying, "Sorry, my husband's calling me."

With that she turned on her heels and walked back to her table with such a sly satisfied grin on her face. She did not realise she was slinking back with her bum strutting from side to side but a good number of men did to their pleasure.

Julie sat back down on her seat as Jill was explaining to Michelle that she had found the young waitress who was now fine, she had said they were all accustomed to Fernando's taunts and tantrums. Jill now turned her attention to Julie as she had seen her with Fernando but could not see much else, turning to Julie and them Michelle she said, "Meeting in the Ladies now, please."

Once in the Ladies powder room they waited for two women to finish their makeup adjustments in the mirror and leave before checking they were alone. Once satisfied they were by themselves Jill snatched Julie's handbag from her grasp and opened it and searching found the vial of her concoction which was now drained of all its contents. Jill held it up in front of Julie and said, "I thought we agreed no more of this, you put it in his drink didn't you?"

"It isn't more, it's the same one and there wasn't much in it and anyway he deserves it, treating that young girl like that, he's just a bully and deserves all that happens to him," said Julie.

"You can't argue with that," said Michelle.

"I don't need you agreeing with her, you can't keep doing this, it's dangerous and wrong," said Jill.

"It's the last of it, I won't make any more, I promise, I just couldn't let that arsehole abuse that girl with no comeback, I just couldn't Jill," said Julie.

"Ok, ok but no more, you promise?" said Jill.

"Promise," said Julie crossing her heart with her right hand.

"Don't say anything to anyone ok, not even to Steve, agreed?" said Jill.

"Agreed," said Julie.

With that final word on the subject they hugged each other, then Jill threw the vial in the bin looking at Julie pointedly before returning to their table. They arrived at their table to find Tony and Steve missing, David explained they were at the bar buying drinks. They looked over to find Fernando had left the bar and as they scanned the room they found no sign of "El Sopo".

The music was in full swing now and a singer had joined the musicians as people made their way to the dance floor. David knew Jill was longing to dance, he knew she wanted to show herself off and he hoped she wanted to show her necklace off, he thought she liked it; she certainly had not taken it off as yet. As the dance floor filled so did the heat in the room as the air conditioning struggled to cope but Jill did not mind she was enjoying herself, she was enjoying dancing in her husband's arms. Soon Michelle and Tony with Julie and Steve joined in the dancing. They danced in the arms of their husbands blind to the knowledge of what had happened to Fernando.

When Fernando began to feel unwell it hit him like a rocket, his sweating increased if that was possible, his stomach became bloated and he felt as though he was going to vomit. He rushed upstairs to his office so that he could throw up in his own bathroom. He did not make his office let alone his bathroom before he soiled his pants, it oozed out of his backside and dribbled down his legs, he did not have a spare pair in his office. He opened his office and walked slowly doubled up with the pain from his stomach.

In the bathroom he took his soiled trousers and underpants off as he vomited from the stench, he missed the toilet as it spread across the tiled floor. He managed to sit on the toilet as his bowels released more contents. He wondered what he had eaten to make him feel so unwell. He suffered with high blood pressure and tachycardia, he felt weak as he sat with his elbows on his knees. Twenty minutes later he died.

As Jill danced in her husband's arms she saw Charles walk into the room and shuddered involuntarily, David noticed her shudder but did not say anything he just held her closer. Jill tried to catch Michelle's eye which she eventually did nodding her head in Charles's direction. Michelle nodded back to show she had seen him. Jill smiled at her husband saying she needed a rest and then walked over to where Julie was dancing and grabbed her hand pulling her away from her husband as she did so. They walked towards the Ladies powder room and Michelle followed some yards behind. They entered to find the room full and far too busy for them to talk so they found a quiet area just outside as Jill asked, "What the hell is he doing here, did he say anything to you Michelle?"

"No, nothing, he does know Fernando maybe he invited him, it shouldn't be anything for us to worry about," said Michelle.

"Maybe not, I just thought we had seen the last of him," said Jill.

"Let's go to the bar for a drink, maybe one of the barmen knows him," suggested Julie.

"Good idea, let's go," said Jill.

They sauntered casually over to the bar but Jill's eyes looked everywhere for their husbands and for Charles. She found their husbands who were sat at their table chatting amongst themselves quite amiably. Then she spotted Charles, she nudged the other two nodding in the direction of Charles who was pulling up a chair to join a table of 12 elderly women, they were between the ages of fifty to probably seventy. Julie was ordering drinks from the barman who had served her when she was with Fernando and clearly recognised her, when he returned with their drinks she asked him, "Do you know that man over there sat with the 12 women?"

"Of course, that is Senor Charles, we see him quite regularly."

"And what about the women he is with, do you know them?" asked Julie.

"Of course, everyone knows the golf widows; they are expats whose husbands died out here, some of them on our very own golf course."

"What is Senor Charles doing with them?"

"I thought that would be obvious, let's just say, he services their needs," he winked knowingly at Julie.

"Oh, right ok, thank you."

They returned to their table and their husbands who were sat together talking in a huddle, they barely acknowledged their wives and continued talking. The women sat down and nursed their drinks saying nothing. The singer finished her song which was Love On The Rocks by Neil Diamond and was interrupted from starting another number by a man dressed in a dinner jacket which they assumed was a member of the clubs management.

He began to address everyone using the singers microphone, he was clearly Spanish and was heavily accented, "Ladies and gentlemen, may I have your attention for a moment, I am sorry to interrupt your entertainment but I have a sad announcement to make, Senor Fernando Torres Marquez was found dead a few moments ago in his office, we have called for an ambulance and the police which is standard practice but I hope you agree it would respectful to bring this evening to an early close, thank you, have a safe journey home."

There was a shocked silence in the room for a minute as the information sunk in; Fernando Torres

Marquez had welcomed everyone personally at the beginning of the evening so everyone knew him. The silence turned into rapid chatter and speculation as people began to gather their belongings and slowly make their way outside, there were numerous taxis arriving as a member of staff had called them in response to ending the evening early. Jill, Michelle and Julie walked quietly behind their husbands towards the entrance; David, Tony and Steve were discussing where they should go to finish their last evening. Just as they were about to walk through the doors Jill stopped suddenly exclaiming, "Shit!"

She grabbed hold of Michelle and Julie by their arms and dragged them back inside calling to David as she did so that they would be back in a minute. David, Tony and Steve just shrugged their shoulders as they looked at one another and positioned themselves outside to wait for their wives to return. Once away from their husbands Jill pulled Michelle and Julie to one side and looking around her to make sure she could not be overheard said," the vial, we threw the vial in the bin in the Ladies powder room, we need it back just in case they investigate Fernando's death. I really can't believe this, you bloody well killed him Julie, shit, c'mon we need that vial."

"It couldn't have killed him; it didn't kill that other guy," protested Julie.

"Yeah right! There must be over 20 years age difference between them and Fernando didn't look the healthiest individual, he must be at least 15 stones overweight, bloody right you killed him!" said Michelle.

"No time to argue we need to find that bloody vial," said Jill.

As they walked into the Ladies powder room they were greeted with a multitude of women waiting for stalls to become vacant and others rearranging their makeup in front of a large mirror. Jill pulled Michelle and Julie close as she whispered, "Stand in front of the bin while I look in it for the vial."

With that they all moved forward as one, they must have looked a site, two women in front and Jill bent over double with both hands inside the bin searching. Finding it towards the bottom she had to search through discarded handtowels, when she brought her arms out they felt damp and dirty but she did not want to wait for a sink to become free so they left immediately walking as quickly as they dared back to the entrance and their waiting husbands. They bitched and bickered as they walked along until Jill pulled them together and warned them not another word to be spoken about it whilst their husbands were near, it was to be kept amongst themselves solely, they solemnly agreed.

The taxi rides back towards the centre of Fuengirola was decidedly quiet in each cab. The men had agreed to find a bar in the centre of Fuengirola where they could have a couple of drinks before walking back to their hotel, it was not the final night they had planned but they would make the best of it. As the taxis pulled up outside the Bishop's Nipple Bar the men gathered looking about them as to the most suitable pub.

Michelle and Julie looked on as Jill squatted over a drainage grid by the side of the road where the taxi had just pulled away from and surreptitiously deposited the vial down into it, they each acknowledged mission accomplished with a barely perceptible nod of their heads.

They walked down the street a little before deciding on a bar that was open fronted with about 15 tables outside, the men sat the women down whilst they went to the bar.

Jill took the opportunity to issue instructions, "Right now listen up, not a single word about tonight with anyone, agreed? And certainly not until we are back home and even then I don't want to hear about it. Most importantly, when we are safely back home with our mobile phones back in our possession do not mention it over the phone and certainly no texts, agreed? And definitely no mention of our holiday in any way, shape or form on Facebook, agreed?"

Michelle and Julie both agreed just in time as the men returned with drinks, Julie drank half hers down in one gulp, as she finished she belched loudly bringing floods of laughter from Jill and Michelle, Julie never belched. They sat in the bar for the remainder of the evening enjoying light conversation and the odd bitching at some of the people passing along the pavement but all the time in the back of their minds was the demise of Fernando Torres Marquez and their need to make it back to the safety of England and their homes.

It was a little before 2am before they decided to call it a night and walked slowly back to their hotel in the warm air of the evening. The evening had ended a little unexpectantly and subdued due to the demise of Fernando Torres Marquez. They walked along the front of the resort slowly and quietly all a little sad to be at the end of their holiday. Jill walked along hand in hand with David, Michelle and Tony were laughing and joking about something as they playfully pushed and shoved each other whilst Steve walked along with his arm draped around Julie's shoulder.

At the hotel they took the lift up to their floor together and tiredly said goodnight to one another as they entered their own rooms.

Jill walked into their room first with David closing the door behind him, he grabbed Jill's shoulder turning her towards him as he took her in his arms and kissed her long and lovingly searching her tongue with his. Jill thought it was the last thing she needed, a randy husband, with her thoughts on Fernando and Julie's seemingly lack of emotion at what she had done. She would not deny him though not with how close they had recently become again. David slipped the shoulder straps down her arms as Julie pulled her arms through

David reached around the back of the dress around the top of her bottom for the short zip and undid it, Jill stepped back allowing the dress to fall leaving her naked as she kicked her shoes off forcing a smile.

David rushed to catch up, throwing his shirt off up into the air, then undoing his trousers he tried nonchalantly pulling them down and over one leg using the other leg to flick them away but he became caught up in them and tripped himself up landing thankfully prone on the bed. Jill could not help herself as she fell onto the bed alongside him laughing at his attempts to be sexy and cool. David too saw the funny side and when their laughter died away they kissed again long and passionately. David grew more eager along with his manhood. Jill could feel him harden against the warmth of her leg as he manoeuvred Jill onto her back he entered her, pushing deep inside her as he pulsed in and out. Jill found herself checking her watch; she noticed a multitude of abandoned cobwebs on the ceiling wondering where the spiders were now and what had made them abandon their webs, and why had the cleaners not cleared them away. She made sure she smiled politely whenever David moved his head to look at her, oh and groan too hopefully in the right places; well she was out of practice. David almost caught her looking at her watch but an exceptionally sweet smile and groan in the right place seemed to placate him and encourage his thrusting. He made it obvious to everyone in the hotel when he came as Jill inadvertently patted him on the back, she realised immediately what she had done and prepared the sweetest of all smiles for when David raised himself up on his elbows and looked into her eyes.

He talked for a few minutes about how he loved Jill but all she could think about at that moment was the previous two years and then she became determined to find out just who he had been seeing behind her back. She took herself to the bathroom and cleaned her teeth before returning to the bed where she found David was already asleep, on her side of the bed!

Chapter 12   Saturday

The journey back to the UK proved uneventful and rather dull, as the women were somewhat downbeat and not just because their holiday had come to an end. At Malaga Airport the men huddled around the bar drinking an early morning pint of lager as they asked each other about their wives lackadaisical approach to the day, they remained clueless.

Jill, Michelle and Julie instead of joining their husbands in the bar were wandering aimlessly around the duty free shops with absolutely no intention of buying anything. Jill was still concerned at Julie's apparent indifference to Fernando's early demise. Jill was still worried they would be able to take their seats on the plane, whenever she saw one of the airport policemen she thought he was looking directly at her, she shuddered at the thought. Whereas Julie, for a change, was the most talkative amongst them, Michelle too seemed to be distracted in some way. Jill forced herself to be realistic about the possibility that should they become implicated in Fernando's death they would need to plan in advance their combined response, as with currently being in the EU the

Spanish police could no doubt question them and ultimately extradite them back to Spain.

They needed to meet once back in the UK and once they had time to think of the consequences of their actions. Julie obviously administered the fatal dose whereas Jill and Michelle were complicit as knowingly they had aided and abetted Julie's "escape" and had helped her to rid herself of evidence, namely the empty vial. Jill explained her thoughts to Michelle and Julie and then suggested they meet somewhere they were not known, just in case they were overheard, she suggested the Gay Village in Manchester on Tuesday evening, they all agreed on 8pm.

Julie's quip, "Does that mean I have to be gay for a day."

Did not even bring a smile to Jill's or Michelle's lips.

Indeed Michelle became a little despondent as she had thought, incorrectly, that once they were back home the whole sordid mess would be over. It brought everything back to the three of them; it was not just Fernando's death that concerned them but Julie's involvement with using her Mickey Finn on one of the four steel erectors. If the police suspected Fernando's death was not natural causes and ordered a post mortem then surely Julie's drug would be discovered in his body and then it may be linked to the steel erectors deaths. The more they thought about it the more they worried. They finally decided to join their husbands in the bar for a drink but as they approached the bar their flight was called for boarding.

Arriving back at Manchester Ringway Airport there was little for them to say, they had collected their luggage from the carousel and had progressed through customs. Now awaiting their turn at the taxi rank the girls air kissed goodbye as the men shook hands. The taxis followed each other onto the M60 motorway and did not separate until they took the off ramp signposted for Ashton Under Lyne.

Jill was grateful to open her front door and rushed through and up the stairs to Bianca's bedroom where she was certain she would find her daughter. She was not there and checking the house they found it to be empty. Jill went back upstairs to her bedroom, she heard David's protest behind her as he said she could have taken one of the cases up with her, she stripped discarding her clothes on the floor and walked into their bathroom and jumped into the shower.

She dressed quickly into something warm, for a change, she grabbed her mobile phone off the dresser where she had left it for the duration of the holiday and switched it on quickly typing in her password, the phone bleeped uncontrollably as texts and messages loaded themselves, she then grabbed her car keys which were next to her phone and rushed downstairs shouting behind her to David that she was going to Lidl shopping as there was nothing in fresh for their supper. Before David could answer she had disappeared out of the front door slamming it behind her, within a minute her key was in the door as she rushed up the stairs to her bedroom.

She heard David quip "that was quick." "I forgot my purse." She answered as the front door again slammed closed behind her.

David being David he just shrugged his shoulders whilst he grabbed himself a beer and sat himself in front of the TV and switched on the sports results programme, it was just turning 4.30pm.

Jill arrived back home a little before 6.00pm and looked on David sat with his beer in front of the TV with disdain asking, "Have you unpacked?"

"No, I'll do it tomorrow, won't take long, it's mainly washing," said David nonchalantly.

"Any sign of Bianca?"

"Not yet, do you want a drink?" asked David.

"That would be nice!" said Jill from the kitchen unpacking her shopping.

"Wine, vodka or Bacardi?" asked David.

"Wine I think, have we any Cava?"

David appeared in the kitchen with a glass of Cava for Jill knowing she was a little annoyed at him for not unpacking whilst she was out shopping. He put his hands around her waist and raised up the glass of wine for Jill to take whilst nibbling her ear before kissing her neck, whilst Jill rose up her right hand which housed a chicken. She had just cut a full bulb of garlic in half and stuffed both halves up its rectum, "very becoming," David chirped "but I think I prefer baby oil."

"Chicken, salad and French bread for supper, is that ok?" asked Jill.

"Sounds great," said David returning to the living room and his TV.

Jill joined him five minutes later having put the chicken in the oven. David was sat on the end of the sofa so Jill sat beside him lifting her feet onto the sofa and resting her head on his chest. Whilst shopping she had hatched a plan to find out who he had been having the affair with, part one consisted of putting him to sleep, in other words allowing him to think Jill was over the affair and let him carry on as normal. In the meantime Jill would be checking into everything she could, their bank accounts, credit card statements and when she could she would check his phone for numbers and messages and pictures. Then she would move onto part two, but she had not decided on part two yet, it depended in part what she discovered from part one.

Jill felt tired not from the travelling but the late nights of their week away, they had not returned to their rooms before 3am throughout the entire week. The drinking too had taken its toll, Jill enjoyed a drink and drank at home but nothing to the extent they had in Fuengirola, but the drink there did not seem to have the effect it did at home even though the measures were far larger abroad.

Jill's mobile phone rang; she jumped up and ran to the kitchen where she had left it in her bag. It was her mother making sure they had arrived home safe, once Jill assured her and told her they had a great time asked about Bianca. She informed Jill Bianca had been fine and spent most of the week in her room on her laptop, she did add that she had gone to visit with her friend Nicole today and had said she would be back about 10pm. Jill was back in the living room relaying the information to David with that mime that women do, similar to Les Dawson's Ada.

Jill hung up her phone and threw it on the sofa where her feet had been, she was just about to sit down when David held up his empty glass for refreshing. After taking a sharp intake of breath Jill reminded herself of part one of her plan and so just smiled at David as she took his glass to their bar in the living room. Returning with David's pint glass filled with Stella Artois and hers with more Cava she placed her glass on the coffee table and resumed her prone position on the sofa resting her head once again on David's chest. Jill asked David if he had anything planned for Tuesday once he said not she informed him she was out with Michelle and Julie. He muttered something which was incomprehensible so she ignored it whilst she snuggled closer to David; he took the hint and put his hand inside her blouse resting his hand on her warm boob within the cup of her bra.

She asked whether he had enjoyed the holiday, when she did not receive an answer she turned to find him asleep. Not able to stop herself she gently lifted David's hand from her bra and rose up from her position not making a sound. With a sneaky little grin on her face she tiptoed from the room and ever so quietly climbed the stairs making sure she placed her feet on the extremities of each riser so as to shrink any sounds she made. Walking along the landing and into her bedroom she rummaged in her makeup bag for the brightest and reddest lipstick she could find. With the lipstick in hand she retraced her steps without making a sound. Back in the living room she found David still asleep, she undid her lipstick and began to draw two red circles, one on each cheek as one would see on an old wooden toy soldier. David's head moved as she applied the lipstick and at one point she was fearful he would wake but she managed to complete the task with more than a little silent giggling along the way. Once complete she hurried into the kitchen to give full vent to her laughter.

Whilst there she checked on the chicken which was cooking away in the oven, the strong odour of garlic filled her nostrils as she opened the oven door, she had to force her head away sharpish to avoid the rush of steam escaping the oven. She moved to close the oven door but her fingers slipped and the oven door crashed noisily shut. She rushed to the doorway to see if the noise had woken David and was relieved to discover him still sound asleep. She took the time to prepare the salad, washing the lettuce, tomatoes and cucumber, then stripping the spring onions. Jill then returned to the living room and took a slurp of wine whilst she gazed upon her sleeping husband with his rosy cheeks. She gave him a dig in the ribs and said, "So putting your hands on my boobs now sends you to sleep does it? Well thank you very much!" She jokingly chastised him.

David groggily pulled himself upright and rubbed his eyes much to the chagrin of Jill who thought he would rub part of his ruby red lipstick circles off his cheek, but he did not. She smiled affectionately at him turning her head to one side as she did so, her cute look, but she found she had to turn about as she began to giggle.

"What's up?" asked David leaning forward to take his drink off the coffee table.

"Oh nothing, I was just thinking of something Julie said when we were in Fuengirola."

"Oh, ok, she can be bloody thick at times can't she?" said David.

"Only at times? Oh yes she can, she doesn't realise what she says, she speaks without putting her brain into gear that's all."

"That garlic smells good, are we having any chicken with it?" David chuckled.

"Ha, ha," laughed Jill sarcastically, "Taken is starting on Film4 in a minute, do you want to watch it?"

"May as well there's nowt else on, he's really good in it isn't he, Liam Neeson?" said David.

"'bout as good as my Aunt Fanny's fart!"

"What?"

"Nothing put it on then," said Jill. "I'll just check on the chicken before it starts."

"And then are you filling the glasses?" asked David.

"Do you seriously want me to answer that?"

"Tell you what, you check on the chicken and I'll refresh the drinks, ok?"

Jill did not bother to answer as she was already in the kitchen with her oven gloves on about to open the oven door, her head to one side to avoid the release of steam she opened the door, waited a few seconds then reached in and lifted out the chicken. It was cooked so she basted it with the juices and left it out for the meat to relax and returned to the living room just as the film started. She lay next to David again with her head on his chest and pulled his arm over her shoulder to rest on her breast.

"The chicken is ready I'll put it out at the first advert break," said Jill.

Jill was true to her word; as soon as the first adverts began she jumped out of David's arms startling him in the process as she ran to the kitchen. She cut up the chicken distributed on three plates along with the salad and some French bread, placed two of the plates onto trays and re-joined David in the living room with their supper.

"This chicken is gorgeous, Bianca will be sorry she missed it," said David.

"I've put a plate out for Bianca if she's hungry when she comes home."

"You spoil that girl," said David.

"And you don't?"

They finished their supper and sat back to enjoy the film. Bianca returned home at 10.15pm, forced some chicken down and retired to her room and the internet. The film finished at 10.30pm and David and Jill decided to call it a night. They were both tired as they had both kept late evenings on their holiday although David's were not as late as Jill's.

Jill was in the bedroom first and went straight into their ensuite bathroom to clean her teeth whilst David was locking the back door. She wanted to be in bed and safe when David noticed what she had done to him all those hours ago. She finished cleaning her teeth and switched the bathroom light off before stripping her clothes off and discarding them into the laundry basket. She jumped into bed as she heard David's footsteps on the stairs. She pulled the covers over her covering her head just leaving her eyes in the open so she could hide her giggles. David was in the room walking over to the bathroom, he smiled at his wife as he walked past, he switched the bathroom light on.

"JILL!!!" he screamed.

Jill was in fits of laughter as his response was so much better than she had anticipated.

"What the hell have you done to me?!"

Jill was now in uncontrollable hysterics as David wittered away to himself, Jill could hear the hot water tap running, and more wittering from David. Jill's eyes were streaming with tears as David walked into the room with two smudged red circles on his cheeks and incomprehension on his face.

"How the hell am I supposed to take this off and what the hell is it?"

"Oh come over here my little toy soldier," said Jill and set about a laughing fit again.

David just stood there in the middle of the room with his hands on his hips as he listened to his wife's hysteria, she moved out of bed over to her dressing table and took a cotton wool ball and squeezed some liquid onto it. She made her way over to David still laughing; David's morose expression had not changed which increased her laughter. She placed her left hand on top of David's shirt on his chest as she wiped the lipstick from David's face with the cotton wool ball, he grabbed hold of her bare bottom and squeezed. Jill gave out a playful yelp as she turned her husband around and sent him back into the bathroom.

Jill jumped back into bed pulling the covers up to her breasts leaving them exposed seductively, well she could still have fun while she was executing phase one.

The light to the bathroom went off as David entered the bedroom and began undressing. He looked directly at Jill whilst smiling and shaking his head in mock repudiation. Once naked he pulled the bedcovers down and slipped into bed alongside his expectant wife. He turned to her and kissed her gently at first moving his right hand to fondle her warm breasts. He moved Jill onto her side so he could hold her buttocks in his hand; he caressed her now bald area between her legs taking his time to take in the smoothness of her body. He clearly liked her shaving as he became aroused quickly moving himself on top of her so she could feel him as he moved up her legs towards her…..

"AAARRRGGGHHH!!!"

"What's the matter, what's up?" asked Jill concerned as to what had suddenly happened.

"My leg, I have cramp, oh my God!"

"Here, here give me your leg," said Jill.

Jill threw all the covers off the bed and taking the offending leg she straitened it and bent his big toe back. Slowly the pain eased but Jill kept his big toe bent back. Bianca shouted from the landing at what the noise was all about and as Jill explained she was less than sympathetic as she said, "Is that all."

Chapter 13   Sunday

Jill rose early Sunday morning, well early for Jill, 8am and began unpacking their suitcases. She arranged the clothes into various heaps, those that would go into their washing machine and those that would need dry cleaning such as her blue dress. She then arranged the heap for washing into varying heaps that would go into the washing machine together, all the while she was accompanied by her sleeping husband whom she was happy to leave as he was back in work tomorrow morning.

She piled her first load together and carried them down the stairs into the kitchen wearing just her trusty old tennis skirt and a loose T-shirt. She loaded the washing machine and with a slight hesitation turned it on, if the noise from it woke her husband then so be it she thought. She then filled the kettle and switched it on as she was gagging for a decent cup of tea.

The noise from the washing machine seemed excessive as she began to pour boiling water from the kettle over her teabag in her minion's mug, a gift from Bianca. Jill took her mug of tea into the living room and settled onto the sofa placing her mug onto the coffee table and picked up the TV guide to see if there was anything on worth watching. There was nothing of particular interest as usual the majority of viewing was repeats so she turned to the beginning of the guide and began to read through it as she sipped on her mug of tea.

Finishing her perusal of the TV guide and her tea she lifted her legs onto the sofa and began thinking of what she needed to do over the next few days. Of course Tuesday she was meeting up with Michelle and Julie in the evening, she should ring them she thought and arrange times and location, that left her Monday and the rest of the week for her two priorities. The first priority was to find herself a job which would provide her with enough income for independence should David go wandering again. Her second priority was to find who David had gone wandering with. Jill decided to make an in depth plan for each and write down each phase with notes on her progress which she would start first thing Monday once David was at work.

She heard the faint murmurs of movement upstairs but not from their room it was Bianca moving about. Jill suddenly felt happier about herself as she felt she was moving on and although still with David at present moving in a new and exciting direction that would give her more focus on her life rather than just thinking about David and Bianca. She actually nodded to herself and jumped up to reward herself with another mug of tea.

As Jill placed her fresh mug of tea on the coffee table in the living room Bianca burst into the room fully dressed with her jacket on and laptop bag slung over her shoulder, "I'm off to Nicole's again, expect me when you see me, ok?"

"Will you be back for lunch?" asked Jill.

"Mum! I don't even know if I'll be back for dinner."

With that she turned and was out the door and before Jill could ask her not to slam the front door she had done just that. Within a few minutes Jill heard David starting the shower, she had hoped for a little longer by herself in peace and quiet so she could have time just to think. As Jill finished her second mug of tea of the day David appeared dressed but with his hair still damp, he smiled at his wife and apologised for his cramp the previous evening kissing her on her cheek before making his way into the kitchen to brew himself a cup of tea. He brought his cup of tea back into the living room balanced on top of a saucer; it amused Jill that he always used a cup and saucer for his tea even at home.

He turned to his wife asking, "What do you want to do today?"

"Err washing; can you not hear the machine?" Jill answered with a degree of sarcasm.

"Well yes ok but I thought we could go out somewhere for lunch, save you cooking and washing up, then later we could order a carry out, what do you think?"

"Hey I'm all for no cooking and washing up, where were you thinking?"

"We could go to The Lords if you fancy carvery or Gino's if you want Italian, don't fancy going too far as I thought we could ring for a taxi then we could both have a drink?"

"Ok, The Lords it is, carvery would be fine."

At which point the washing machine ended its cycle so Jill darted upstairs and brought down another load of clothes for the washing machine. She began emptying the machine as she heard the TV switch on, she twitched with displeasure but ignored it, she reloaded the machine and switched it on. She opened a door in her cabinet and took out a box of clothes pegs along with a rag which she dampened under the tap. She took the wet clothes outside in her large plastic hold all with the clothes pegs and damp cloth. She took the cloth and grabbed hold of the washing line with it and walked the length dragging the cloth over it thus cleaning it.

Then began the laborious process of pegging out clothes, this part of housework she detested although she knew some of her friends loved it. Bend down pick up an item of clothing and peg onto line, bend down pick up an item of clothing and peg onto line, bend down pick up an item of clothing and peg onto line, bend down pick up an item of clothing and peg onto line.

Just how on earth can anyone enjoy this she thought? Finishing she picked up her plastic hold all and damp cloth but left the clothes pegs outside for her next load. Returning inside she shut the door behind herself and threw the hold all onto the floor next to the washing machine and walked through the living room past her prone husband watching TV and up the stairs to their bedroom and stripped off making her way into their bathroom and turned on the shower.

Jill was sat at her dressing table blow drying her hair with the hairdryer her Mum had bought her for her twenty first birthday when her mobile phone rang, turning off the dryer and placing it down so she could pick up her phone whilst still brushing her hair. She could see from the caller id that it was Julie calling, "Hi Julie, I'm just blow drying my hair, can I call you back in five, thanks."

Jill did not give Julie the option to say no as she ended the call and continued to dry her hair. With Julie's call memories of their holiday came flooding back in no particular order but by far the worst of them was the encounter with Charles in Fernando's office. With that thought came another; did she leave her DNA behind in his office along with fingerprints? Of course she did. Michelle, did she do the same? Of course she did. So if the police did indeed think Fernando's death suspicious would they find their prints and DNA and want to investigate further. Another thought immediately sprang to mind, if they did indeed find their DNA would it include sexual secretions? Of course it would. Yet another thought now sprang into her mind, if they did find sexual secretions would they also find sexual secretions from Charles and therefore his DNA? Of course they would.

This was becoming more of a nightmare than she had first thought. She began to think about going onto the internet to see what she could discover about the investigations but then became paranoid. Could the Spanish police find out who was checking up on their investigations? She dismissed the idea as ridiculous. She then determined to go on the internet tomorrow when David was at work. Then she thought, ring Julie back.

"Hi Julie, I was about to ring you when you called, I thought we could meet at The Blob Shop around the corner from the gay village at 8pm, is that ok with you?"

"Yes should be fine, are we going to the gay village?"

"I thought we could yes, why?"

"Oh nothing it's fine. Anyway, I've had a thought about the holiday; I think we need to discuss it."

"So have I but not on the phone, we will have to wait until Tuesday not before, understand?"

"It's important!"

"Ok but it'll have to wait."

"Alright, do you want me to call Michelle and let her know where and when?"

"That would be great and see you Tuesday, bye!"

Putting her mobile phone down next to her handbag on the dressing table Jill began to apply a light coating of makeup. She had decided to wear jeans and a loose fitting sky blue blouse with a pair of midsized heeled shoes, Jimmy Choo of course. Satisfied with the effect she grabbed a short denim jacket picked up her mobile phone and handbag and made her way downstairs. She found David had not moved, he was still glued to the TV screen, watching some cookery programme. She would not mind but David did not cook, he just suggested ideas to Jill for her to come up with a recipe.

"Are you going to change so we can leave?" asked Jill rather impatiently.

"I'm going like this."

"You didn't listen did you?" intoned Jill.

"What do you mean?"

"Change!" demanded Jill.

David tramped down the stairs sullenly having changed into a clean pair of jeans and a moderate blue open necked shirt which he left out of his jeans. He found Jill waiting by the front door which she opened before David made the bottom of the stairs. She now waited impatiently by their Audi whilst David set about searching for his car keys. He flicked the fob to allow Jill into the car whilst he locked their front door.

The day was pleasant with late summer sun and a decent temperature of 16 degrees. As David jumped in the driver's door he picked up his Ray Bans from the centre console, although David did not suffer from hay fever strong sunlight could produce a sneezing fit hence he always had a pair of sunglasses in the car. David reversed the car out of their driveway and Jill unwound her window to say good morning to George Armstrong as he walked Custer along their road.

Traffic was light as they drove along the A635 bypass threading through Ashton past the full carpark at Asda. Jill began to wonder just where David would park in the pubs carpark as part of it combined with the Driverslodge Hotel next to it.

The Driverlodge Hotel had a reputation for extra marital couples cavorting, some inside the hotel but also some in their cars in the carpark. Indeed Jill and David had been one of those couples three years previously after a night in the pub.

They had left the pub at 10.30pm and once in their car had come over all randy and after some heavy petting had made love with Jill laid back in the passenger seat with it flat and David on top of her with his trousers around his ankles. Their car had steamed up through their antics and as David scrambled back into his seat to start the car they began to wipe the steamed up windows whilst they were still only partially dressed to find eight eyes peering in at them. They had clearly been four peoples entertainment for the last 15 minutes, David quickly started the car and putting it into gear rushed out of the car park whilst Jill was still trying to find her bra. Jill had said that she half expected their audience to hold up scorecards.

Since that time they had themselves witnessed several couples' lovemaking and one foursome. It was also interesting to watch some of the couples entering the hotel as it was quite easy to establish which were not married to each other. David was clearly not in the mood to observe cavorting couples today as he parked in the pubs main carpark only just finding a space as they were always so busy on Sundays.

Once inside Jill found a table whilst David went to the overcrowded bar for drinks. This was the only trouble with going out for lunch on a Sunday, anywhere good was always overcrowded. Jill indeed found a table which was an achievement in itself, but it would be much busier soon and uncomfortably so. Making herself comfortable in her seat Jill looked around the crowded interior for anyone she knew, thankfully there were only one or two slight acquaintances that only deserved an obligatory nod.

Looking closer to her left side there was a family of six who had just succeeded at the bar, the husband was dishing out their drinks from an old beer advertising metal tray. As he passed a pint of what looked like bitter to whom Jill assumed was the grandfather of the children she noticed him reading the Sunday Express. The grandfather gratefully accepted his pint of beer and began to take a long drink from it, it was at this point Jill was reading the headlines on the pages spread out, one immediately took her attention. "Spanish police link poison to two murders on the Costa Del Sol".

The room was warm anyway with the number of people and the heat emanating from the kitchen but now Jill felt herself beginning to sweat, her nerves began to tingle as her neck and face broke out in a heat rash, which she sometimes suffered with her nerves despite David's attempt at humour telling her she was on the change.

The grandfather rolled up his newspaper and tucked it into his jacket pocket. David arrived with their drinks; Jill downed her vodka and coke in one giant gulp before excusing herself to David and making her way to the Ladies powder room. Making her way back Jill detoured to the bar where she bought herself a double vodka and coke before re-joining David at their table.

The pub management had stopped more people entering the pub until some left and the queue outside was growing by the minute. Jill remained resolutely quiet throughout their meal and when David asked what she wanted to do next she volunteered a resounding leave.

Jill's silence remained at home as she continued the chore of washing their holiday clothes and pegging them outside on the clothesline whilst David watched his adored TV adding to Jill's irritability. Jill was pleased when David announced at 10pm he was retiring to bed early as he was back in work tomorrow morning. Jill followed him an hour later as she expected to find him sound asleep.

Chapter 14 Monday

Jill woke to the sound of the shower running in their ensuite bathroom. She reluctantly opened her eyes to check the clock on her side of the bed, 6.00am. That was very near the time her, Michelle and Julie had returned to their hotel from their evenings out, her body forced her awake as it awaited David's body. David walked out of the bathroom smiling with a towel wrapped around his still wet torso. Her body was telling her to take him now. She stretched out a hand to grab him and pull him to her but missed as he turned grabbing the towel instead, unravelling it from his body leaving him naked facing away from her. She was naked with her breasts fully exposed; she pulled the sheets further down to her thighs. Her body was demanding she took him now.

"Come back to bed," Jill urged him.

"Not now honey, I need to go to work, I want an early start to try and clear my emails."

"I see, holidays over so we are back to the way we were are we?" said Jill annoyed and frustrated.

"No, that is not it, I love you so much Jill and over the next few weeks and months I am going to prove it to you, ok?"

"Just not this morning when I want you," Jill huffed and pulled the covers back over her body and dived her head deep into her pillows.

"That's not fair Jill, I'll see if I can leave early and we'll go out and have a meal and come back early, see if Bianca can stay over at Nicole's?"

Jill did not answer, as David continued to dress, with his jacket in hand he leaned over the bed and kissed his wife goodbye and received an uncharitable grunt from Jill for his efforts. He walked out of the bedroom and along the landing saying goodbye to Bianca as he passed her room before clunking down the stairs and out the backdoor through the kitchen. Jill heard his Audi start and reverse out of their driveway, it changed gear in the road and roared off up the road until Jill could no longer hear it. She pulled the covers tight up to her chin as she punched her pillow and dug her head deep into it sulking.

A few minutes later with her head still deep in her pillow Jill heard David's Audi pull up and park on the driveway. Perhaps he is feeling randy after all she thought but more likely he had not picked up his grey leather briefcase or mobile phone which he had left without several times.

She adjusted herself in bed, puffed her pillows up and ran her fingers through her hair and lay as seductively as she could with her eyes closed so that he would think he had surprised her. Not happy with her position she raised herself up again to view herself lying in her most seductive position possible, she lay back down and left her bare breasts exposed, happy she now shut her eyes again and waited to be seduced.

The kitchen door opened quietly as he crept inside, he picked up an apple from the wooden carved bowl on top of the freezer and a nine inch carving knife from the knife block, over the top for an apple he thought but whatever. He placed the apple in his left jacket pocket as he walked through the kitchen to the base of the stairs.

Silently he took to the stairs placing his feet carefully to the edge of each runner as he climbed slowly, he stopped suddenly as a stair began to creak, he raised his foot above it to the next runner which was silent, he continued slowly and quietly. He now stepped onto the landing and turned to his left towards Jill's room. He stepped slowly tight against the wall hoping to avoid any creaking floorboards. He noticed the door to Jill's room was open, perfect.

As he entered Jill's room he found her in bed with her eyes closed as his eyes fell upon her exposed naked breasts. He stood beside her for a brief second taking in her innocent beauty as he raised his right hand above his head and plunged the carving knife deep into her chest. Her eyes opened briefly in shock and pain as her last breath escaped her lifeless body.

"Mum have you seen my Ed Sheeran concert T-shirt?" shouted Bianca as she marched noisily out of her bedroom towards her mother's room.

He was now facing the bedroom door with his back to Jill's corpse, he turned to his left with his feet firmly fixed to the floor and took hold of the knifes grip with his right hand and stood motionless with the knife still firmly in Jill's chest.

He could hear Bianca's noisy footsteps as she entered the bedroom. In one sweeping motion he freed the knife and swung it through 360 degrees at arm's length, it cut through Bianca's neck rupturing her ceratoid artery on her left, blood immediately pumped from the wound, through his momentum he grabbed Bianca's back with his left hand and threw her to the floor landing at the foot of the bed, there was a sickening gargling noise emanating from Bianca as she tried to breath but choked on her own blood, he ended his 360 degree motion by replacing the knife into the open wound in Jill's chest.

Without giving his victims a second glance he nonchalantly walked out of the bedroom along the landing and down the stairs. As he closed the kitchen door behind him he rolled off the latex gloves he had been wearing and placed them in his right jacket pocket. He did not bother to look around as he jumped back into his Audi and reversed off the drive and placed the gear knob into drive and moved slowly along the road in no particular hurry.

He took the A635 bypass through Ashton towards the Snipe Car Retailers, a used car dealership that was well established and had a reputation in the area that belied its industry reputation. He pulled up and parked on the road leading up to the rear service entrance some thirty yards away.

Once out of his Audi he walked slowly towards the entrance lifting his right arm holding his key fob and flicking it to lock his car. The road was quiet with the occasional car passing; no one took any notice of him as he walked through the gates and onto the stone gravel of the carpark. It was an old site that had been built originally in the late 1960's and had been updated to a fashion over the preceding years.

He knew where he was going; he could see into the office window, it was empty, perfect. The window was a typical single glazed unit with a metal surround which opened out from the bottom and was locked internally with an L shaped lever approximately 3 inches by two inches, quite easily opened from the outside by levering a knife through and nudging the bottom of the L upwards. This he did with great care so as not to leave any scuffs or marks. He wanted two items, first the security tape from the CCTV which was a very old unit that used VCR tapes changed daily, each day had its own tape with the day marked by a Sharpie pen on its edge so seven tapes and secondly Tony's car keys which he thought would be either in his jacket or his desk.

Once the window was open he leaned in and took the video tape out of the machine checking it was todays tape he then replaced it with yesterdays and switched the machine off so anyone checking would just think someone had forgotten to change tapes. Tony's car keys he found in his casual winter waterproof jacket that was draped over his seat. Now he closed the window again with a piece of string left around the L shaped fastener, pulling on both sided of the string pulled the L closed locking the window then all he had to do was pull one side of the string pulling it free of the window, he rolled it up and put it in his left jacket pocket that was now free of the apple. Turning he flicked the keys fob for a black Vauxhall Insignia SRI to flash its indicators in response. He drove out of the dealership without having seen a single person, perfect.

Making his way to his destination took less than 5 minutes as it was only a mile away. He drove into the long straight car park of the school and took a space at the far end and switched off the engine and sat back to wait. Whilst waiting he unrolled a section of the tape that had been recording that morning and broke it off putting it in his left jacket pocket and throwing the VCR tape under the passenger seat.

He did not have to wait long before Michelle drove in and parked where she normally did by the entrance, he started the Insignia's engine. Michelle was out of her car and turned back and bent in and over to the passenger seat to pick up a number of books and her handbag. When she flicked her fob to lock her car as the indicator lights flashed so he moved the Insignia forward slowly at first. Michelle was walking towards the schools staff entrance she was approaching halfway across the carpark when he put his foot hard down on the accelerator, the tyres squealed as Michelle looked to her left in utter disbelief and shock that was all too late. The Insignia hit her at nearly 50mph she flew into the air over the bonnet with books and handbag flying with her; she was spinning through the air as she reached 15 feet in the air she began to fall towards the ground still spinning. Her legs hit the ground first but the spinning momentum threw her head crashing into the ground, it exploded on impact sending blood, brains and bones out in every direction for a radius of ten feet or more. She died instantly.

The Insignia SRI was already out of the carpark and back on the main road on its way back to the car dealership. Once back at the dealership he returned the car to the same parking spot he had found it although the front and bonnet was badly damaged and reversed what he had done previously, he returned the car keys to the correct pocket in the winter jacket and returned the VCR tape to the pile waiting for its correct day. He returned to his own car the Audi taking off his latex gloves rolling them up and placing them in his jacket pocket and made his way along Oldham Road turning onto Newmarket road that would take him past Daisy Nook. Passing Daisy Nook and now on Lumb Lane he turned left onto Back Lane which was pretty much a dirt track and mostly unused and parked his Audi.

Charles climbed out and opened the boot to take out a Philips screwdriver from his cars toolbox. He then unscrewed the rear number plate revealing his number plate under the one he had made of David's cars number plate. He replaced his number plates to front and back and walked the ten yards or so to Lumb Lane and finding the nearest iron drainage grid slid the two false number plates through the slots, if they were found later so be it, whoever found them would not think anything of them anyway. He now climbed back into his Audi and resumed his journey through Littlemoss and then Droylsden into Manchester and then the M56 and M6. Eventually he would take the train through the Eurotunnel.

Chapter 15   12 hours earlier

Charles parked his Audi on a side street that was almost opposite to the entrance to the property that interested him. It lay across the main road he had just turned off between Stalybridge and Glossop. It was surrounded by a five foot high dry stone wall, the type you would see surrounding open farm fields, it was clearly old and had been repaired quite inappropriately by someone unaccustomed to dry stone walling, the tell-tale sign being the crude cement pointing. Immediately behind the dry stone wall was privet bushes some 8 or 9 feet tall which guaranteed the properties privacy. There was one entrance in and out that was governed by a large white painted wooden gate that opened inwards manually into the property.

The house could be seen from the gate, a large five bedroom house built in the late sixties from light sand coloured brick. It looked original from the front but if you walked around to the back you would be greeted by a large glass conservatory that run three quarters of the length of the building. The conservatory and remainder of the length of building lead onto an expansive old stone slabbed area that was in part carrying a number of tables for entertaining and to the right away from the conservatory an extraordinary large purpose built barbeque and pizza oven. Beyond and around was nearly half an acre of garden which was fully matured and tendered lovingly with a multitude of plants and shrubs. The base of the garden led onto a small stream and tucked away in the far bottom right corner a largish garden shed which housed a multitude of garden equipment including an up to date motorised mower.

As Charles jumped over the gate and made his way directly along the tarmacked driveway towards the house he glanced at his watch, 6.32pm. He walked briskly observing the windows as he approached which remained vacant. He was planning on entering via either the front door which he thought might be locked or the side entrance to the left of the building, if the side entrance was locked also he would be onto plan B, pick the lock.

Walking closer to the house he became aware of the noises circulating the air, leaves on the branches of the trees were gently rustling in a tranquil warm breeze, he heard Steve call from the back of the house to his wife to bring him a glass of wine and there was music playing in one of the bedrooms upstairs, it sounded like Ed Sheeran….it could have been Tiny Tim for what he knew of music.

He took a pair of latex gloves from his pocket and put them on. The front door was indeed locked so now he made his way over to the left of the building as quietly as he could now aware of the way sound travelled in the warm early evening air. There was the faint sound of traffic from the main road but it appeared to be farther away than it actually was. He carried with him a shoulder bag, a man bag, he detested the term, it was slung over his left shoulder but rested on his right thigh high up. The music from the bedroom had stopped but had been transferred to the outside; he could hear one of the sons he could not tell if it was Trevor or Daniel talking to his father.

The side door was open, it never ceased to amaze him how insensitive to crime people could be. Charles accepted the open invitation opening the door he found that he was in a utility room housing a couple of washing machines, two freezers, corner units which encompassed a sink, three bicycles, various Wellington boots and a cornucopia of discarded items. It was quite a dark room with just a small window above the sink. He listened intently at the door for some ten minutes before he tried turning the doors handle, he assumed it led into the kitchen where he may come face to face with a family member which was the last thing he wanted.

He had turned the circular aluminium handle and with his ear to the door, trained his hearing for any slight sounds he may pick up. After a further four minutes of holding the handle and listening intensely he slowly opened the door towards him, it shuddered slightly as the base scrapped the red tiled floor. The sound echoed throughout the room and seemed louder than what it actually was in the deafly quiet of the utility room. He stood still with the door slightly ajar and listened again picking up only the sound of music drifting in from the outside with the occasional voices mumbling in the distance, the smell of burning charcoal hit his nostrils. A further three minutes of intense listening and he opened the door fully to reveal an empty kitchen. He walked quietly forward closing the utility room door behind him.

The kitchen lay before him, on the left was a large American type fridge, then worktops that led to a cooker then more worktops until at the end was a large double sink, Georgian windows were above the work surfaces. In the centre of the kitchen sat an island workstation approximately six feet long and 3 feet wide, along the left was a set of French doors that were open leading to a patio area and then to the right of that a barbeque cooking area which was where the charcoal smell emanated from. He could make out wafts of smoking charcoal being blown across from right to left. His right hand dug into his bag searching for the clear plastic bottle of liquid he had brought with him from Spain as he walked slowly towards the island workstation. He observed from his now crouched position the two sons, Trevor and Daniel sat opposite each other at a larger wooden picnic table. Steve was tending to the barbeque nudging at the not quite glowing charcoal; Julie leaned into him with her arm tucked around his middle.

Charles' attention was now drawn to the items on the island workstation. There were two opened bottles of red wine, no doubt left to breathe, a bowl of freshly prepared salad, a bowl of recently boiled jersey new potatoes and what must have been 5 kilos of raw cut chicken ready for the barbeque along with two sticks of French bread and a bowl of garlic dip and one of salad dressing.

He took the plastic bottle of liquid and placed it on the workstation surface whilst he unscrewed the top revealing an elongated narrow top from which the liquid could be squirted. He began with the wine squirting some liquid into the top of each bottle and then gently shaking each bottle in turn. He then moved onto the salad squirting the liquid over the top and manipulating the leaves to allow the liquid to circulate, he then rubbed some over various pieces of chicken. It was at this point he noticed he was being observed, at his feet was sitting an old sandy coloured Labrador with its tail wagging pitifully, he leaned down and patted its head. Taking a final look outside he put the plastic bottle back in his bag and made his way through the kitchen to the lounge. He found the stairs at the far end and climbing them he entered a room that would give him a view of the family's barbeque. He could see the smoke rising from the window and vaguely hear any chatter that was all he needed. He sat himself in a chair to the side of the door and waited.

Whilst sat he checked his bag again to make sure he had everything he needed. The clear plastic bottle with his homemade liquid, spare latex gloves, camp gas stove, mixing pan, mixing spoon and small sharp knife, spare plastic bottle containing his liquid. The liquid was of his own making, he had grown Amanita Phalloides otherwise known as death cap mushrooms and wild hemlock with one or two other items in the wooden hut in the garden of his villa in Fuengirola. He had then mixed them and cooked them in the mixing pan he had brought with him.

The smell of charcoal had changed; Charles rose and took a careful look out of the bedroom window to see Steve placing the cut chicken pieces onto the grill of the barbeque. Charles expression did not alter as he sat back down and closed his eyes. He set his internal clock for half an hour and fell asleep. He had trained himself over many years and varying situations to fall asleep quickly and now managed to set an internal clock to virtually any prior thought of time. He did not wake to the second but now it was usually within a minute or two at most.

Charles eyes opened like an automaton no other part of his anatomy moved, he looked quite eerie for the ten seconds he remained still. He stood up and walked over to the now familiar window. Little smoke now rose from the barbeque but the heat could be seen as it distorted the air above it. He heard the faint whimpering of a dog. He looked upon the four lifeless bodies sat around the wooden table and then noticed one still appeared to be convulsing and choking on his own vomit, it was Steve. He must have eaten last he thought. Charles turned and looked about the room checking he had left nothing and had disturbed nothing, satisfied he left the bedroom and made his way downstairs. He walked through the lounge into the kitchen and out onto the barbeque area watched solely by the grieving Labrador.

As he arrived alongside Steve his spasms had ceased and his eyes stared blankly ahead. Charles opened his bag and took out his clear plastic bottle of liquid he had used earlier and placed it on the table. He now took Steve's limp right hand in his and with it picked up the plastic bottle, he then brought Steve's left hand up to the bottle and squeezing it in his to open the bottle he spilt a little onto Steve's shoes. Satisfied he placed the bottle in Steve's right trouser pocket and let his hand fall to his side. All the time the Labrador watched him and continued to whimper quietly as if expecting an explanation from Charles.

Charles now walked off in the direction of the garden shed located at the bottom of the garden. Once there he opened the door and seeing there was a clear work surface on the right as he entered he placed the camping gas stove down on it and put the mixing pot next to it and put the spoon into it whilst leaving the small knife on the work surface as if discarded. Happy with how they looked he left closing the sheds door behind him. He walked back to the barbeque area and turned the music down slightly on an old portable Sony music system. The Labrador turned its head towards him; Charles walked across to the table and threw it a piece of chicken off the table. He now marched towards the entrance taking off his latex gloves and putting them in his bag.

Chapter 16   New Recruits

The three friends Barbara, Debbie and Angela walked hand in hand down Le Boulevard Place de Cigaro towards the Café de Blanche bitching to each other as they walked in the slightly subdued sunshine of this early October morning. They had been promised two glorious weeks in Saint-Tropez by their ever so loving husbands and instead here they were in Plage De Gigaro. It was some ten kilometres from Saint-Tropez as the crow flies.

They stormed into the café and sat at one of the outside tables Barbara putting her hand in the air to summon a waiter before she had even sat down. It was 11am and the women ordered a bottle of red wine, house red wine at that as the waiter walked off showing his distain to a local couple sat by the entrance. The waiter returned with the wine and poured it into three glasses and walked back inside muttering something inaudible under his breath.

Barbara continued, "Well we will just have to hire our own car for the fortnight as I'm certainly not staying put here."

"I can't believe they have brought us here while they live it up playing golf at the Golf Club Saint-Tropez, there's nothing here for Christ's sake!" Angela said.

"What are we supposed to do for night life here?" added Debbie.

"What did your husband say Debbie? You can jump on a bus into Saint-Tropez, on a bus! I've not been on a bus since I was fifteen years old!" stormed Barbara.

"I'm not even sure there is anywhere to hire a car here," said Debbie.

"That's not a problem we can hire one from Saint-Tropez and they'll bring it to us, it's not that we need to sort, where we are going to go and what we can do at night because you can guarantee we won't see our husbands till late, you know what they were like in Barbados last year!" said Angela.

They had not noticed the man at the next table reading Le Figaro who now took off his sunglasses and folded his newspaper placing them both on the table in front of him. He turned to the three women and smiling politely said, "I couldn't help overhearing ladies, my name is Charles and I may have a solution for you."

Printed in Great Britain
by Amazon